Around Curiosity's Edge

1

Hidden Meridians

J.P. HOSTETLER

Black Rose Writing | Texas

Second printing

ISBN: 978-1-68433-695-1
PUBLISHED BY BLACK ROSE WRITING
www.blackrosewriting.com

Printed in the United States of America
Suggested Retail Price (SRP) $21.95

Around Curiosity's Edge is printed in Garamond

*As a planet-friendly publisher, Black Rose Writing does its best to eliminate unnecessary waste to reduce paper usage and energy costs, while never compromising the reading experience. As a result, the final word count vs. page count may not meet common expectations.

Cover design and illustrations by: Jeff Brown Graphics
Edited by: Ben Davidoff

For my Grandparents

Around Curiosity's Edge

1

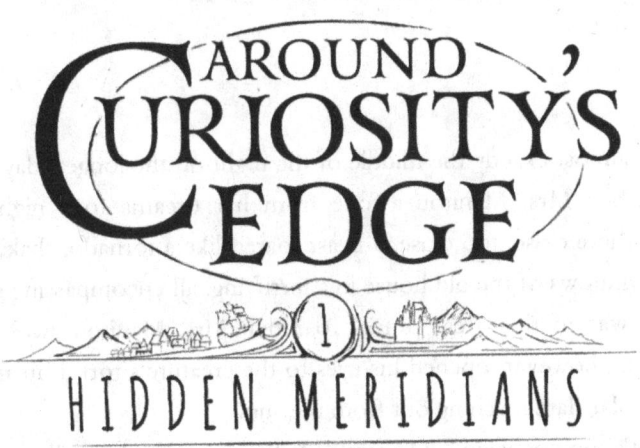

Hidden Meridians

PROLOGUE

It was almost exactly the middle of the night on the longest day of the year when Mrs. Manitou awoke from her dreams to a nightmare. Somewhere close, too close, a beast roared like a tornado, shaking the glass windows of the old house in a terrifying, all-encompassing noise.

It was to this great primal roar that Mrs. Manitou awoke. Her husband, however, opened his eyes to the creature's torrid breath, hot like a solar flare reaching out from the sun.

"It's too hot again," he grumbled. "We've got to keep the windows open." His wife, however, already stood by the window, speechless and wide-eyed as if to attend the debut of a silent film. "Rose, didn't you hear me?" Mr. Manitou swung his legs over the side of the bed, feeling his old knees *pop!* It was unusually bright in the room for the middle of the night, and as he turned to ask his wife again, he froze.

"Is that…?" Mr. Manitou stopped short, pulling his eyes closed and then opening them wide.

"Julie's place," his wife finished for him without breaking her gaze on the fire. Then she turned, a look of helpless pity covering her tired face. "How could this happen?" She choked back tears.

Mr. Manitou shook his head and pushed himself up in a hurry. He slipped into pants and an old flannel shirt, grabbing a winter scarf for a face covering.

"Where are you going?" The fear in Mrs. Manitou's voice was as scorching as the fire outside their window. Mr. Manitou was already grunting his way down the stairs.

"Someone's got to help!" he called up. "Stay here. Call the police!"

"No, Wayne!" Mrs. Manitou pleaded. "Your condition!"

But even as the words left her mouth, she knew it was too late. She listened as the front door opened and then slammed shut.

• • •

Wayne Manitou could not see well out of his right eye. It was a handicap he had gained many years earlier, when the world was a younger place and he, a younger man. Now, despite his failing vision and body that clanged with each jolted step, he moved as fast as he could through the short expanse of trees that separated the Manitou's house from the Swan's. The July air sagged with humidity, and the blazing flames churned it into an unbearable furnace.

The Manitous had known the Swans for years. After the father had passed, Wayne promised himself he would keep an eye on them. His working eye, Rose always joked. Apparently, it had not been enough. He swore under his breath, felt himself wheeze with effort, and raked the back of his palm across his already dripping forehead. His mind jumped to wondering how such a big fire could have started. And to grow so big with neither Julie nor her boy, Salem, noticing.

None of that mattered now. At the rate it was going, the fire would soon consume the house. But as Mr. Manitou lumbered not at all gracefully forward, he saw across the yard something he could not believe.

Facing the burning structure stood a group of maybe three or four people. He held his hand over his right eye, as had become his habit. The people remained.

"Help! Help me!" he shouted through his scarf.

Not one figure moved. Could they be—no? He shook his head in disbelief—wearing suits? Wayne Manitou refused to accept that such a thing could be possible. Yet as the shadows danced against the revolving firelight, so too did the figures remain, stoic statues that watched but did not move. Wayne grunted and refocused on the house in front of him, deciding that neither his mind nor his eyes were what they used to be.

The heat grew in magnitudes of intensity with each step he took. Even with the scarf over his nose and mouth, he struggled to breathe through the thick smoke that encased him. Sirens wailed in the distance. The sound gave him hope, but it was short-lived as he watched one of the house's corners collapse in a plume of orange embers. Wayne Manitou turned to look back at his own house. Through the trees and smoke and heat he could barely make out the mint-colored shutters and white carnation flower boxes his wife loved so much. He thought about her. How she had shown him the world. Taught him about love, and truth, and that people perhaps don't find him as grumpy as he found himself. A single tear rolled down Wayne's withered cheek as he plunged through the smoldering backdoor into the inferno.

• • •

The boy choked on a thick mass of hot black air. He had woken from sleep to a reality that seemed too frightening to be real. He found his way through the dark to the stairs, desperate to reach his mother's room on the first floor. He stepped and like a portal the floor gave way, sending him into a pile of debris that crushed and burned him. He tried to scream, but no noise came out. Time was meaningless in that space. The fire sought only air and room to grow. As it crackled and inhaled it opened more portals, while closing the doors and windows of his life. He knew no father was coming to save him, though there was a mother, and she needed help. He fought from the core of his being, but the smoke was too dark and debris too heavy. Then strong but gentle hands grasped him by the shoulders and pulled. Half-carried, half-dragged, he watched the house through blurry vision get farther and farther away. He tried to tell his rescuer about his mother, still trapped inside, but his throat was a desert, barren of water, and no words came out.

"Stay here," the boy heard a gruff and familiar voice say as the hands released him to the ground, and he thought he saw the outlined silhouette of his old neighbor above him. He watched the figure move back toward of the flames. All around him, the world burned. On his skin, beneath his mind, within his heart. Then, like a curtain finishing an act on stage, a dark wave swept over him, and all was still.

PART I | EASTERLY

CHAPTER 1 | WANDERWAY TAVERN

Water swirled in aqua-green spirals under the curved body of an enormous ship as it cruised toward the shore. Behind its white sails the sun climbed through the sky, casting a morning glow onto the coast and town where the ship would dock.

On the deck, leaning out over the side railing, Captain Tierney Fern adjusted the sleeves of his coat as a voice came from behind him.

"Easterly looks the same."

The captain did not need to turn to identify the voice's owner. The airy tone, as if spoken by someone about to tell a funny story, gave it away. Fern turned to his oldest friend.

"It does, Ulysses. Good thing, too. The rest of the world's changing fast enough. And not for the better. I'm happy this place is different."

Ulysses' short stubble followed his mouth up in a grin, "Come on, you know things don't change for the better on their own. It takes a little hard work. A little… belief."

Fern looked into the man's dark-blue eyes and smiled. The serene calm that graced Ulysses had always impressed him. He had hoped that their many years of friendship had seen some of it rub off on him, but as the town drifted closer, he did not feel serene or calm, only uneasy.

The captain took a few steps toward the ship's bow, folding his hands behind his back. Other, more modern looking boats, passed them, and he nodded to the sailors on board. The sailors nodded back. They were mostly fisherman or lobsterman making their way to work. Even though Fern, Ulysses, and the crew took on a very different kind of work than typical sailors, they were known in the town, and, in the early morning hours, any sailor appreciated a friendly nod.

Fern turned back to Ulysses. "Maybe you're right. Maybe the world isn't such a dismal place. I just worry we put too much faith in people."

Ulysses sighed. "Don't really have a choice. If we don't believe in each other, then what's the point?"

Ulysses nodded out toward the shore and the town. "You know it's quaint. Easterly. I never really looked at it till now, you know, studied it like it deserves, but it is. A quaint little Rhode Island town."

"Quaint how?" Fern had to ask.

"You know, weird. Like us. Trying to exist in a world that doesn't seem to notice or care."

A salty chill scurried down the captain's spine. "The Regulat cares."

"Yeah, but they don't count." Ulysses smiled. "Crazies don't count."

It was Fern's turn to shake his head and smile. "The crazy ones count for double."

"Maybe." Ulysses shrugged. "But we can't worry ourselves with secret organizations or the notions of the insane. There's a world a 'wonder out there to protect. People are forgetting about the Fringe, and it's up to us to help them remember."

"Now you're sounding like me," said Fern. "And we can't have that."

The two men, similar in height and build, looked at each other and grinned. Then, his voice somber again, Ulysses asked, "So you still think this is a good idea?"

Fern exhaled, and watched his breath float out on the cool September air. The town was closer now, close enough that they could see rain falling on the townspeople as they walked along the sidewalks with their umbrellas and sidestepped out of the way as the passing cars sprayed water onto their path.

"This is what we signed up for," said Fern. "If we don't help, they won't make it. And I don't know about you, but I've witnessed enough loss. I need to show Juniper that there's hope for others like her."

Ulysses nodded. "So, when's the meeting?"

"This afternoon."

"I'll go with you."

The rain had reached them now and fell over their faces and eyes. "I'll go alone," Fern said, and then, grinning through the rain, added, "besides, you need to be here to welcome your nephew."

• • •

It was late afternoon by the time the ship had docked, and Fern wound his way through Easterly's streets. The rain had ceased, and the air warmed with the sun whose light streamed in scattered sunbeams through a blanket of opaque clouds. Ulysses was right, he thought. Somewhere between the windy streets and buildings that looked plucked out of a Grimm's fairytale, the town possessed charm. Like a piece out of the old-world puzzle that did not fit into the current paradigm. A place suspended in time.

A small group of locals passed on the street. "Captain. Nice to see you again." Fern did not like socializing, and despised small talk, but he recognized some faces, and so he nodded and smiled back. This happened a few more times in a mannerly mixture of "Captain, been a long time," and "Captain Fern, nice to see you back in Easterly," until, with a palpable sense of relief, Fern saw the familiar sight of the Wanderway come into view.

Built of the gray stone like many of the buildings of Easterly, the archaic wooden sign that hung just above its door identified the tavern. Fern stopped before entering. He had always liked the picture of the letter 'W' which, instead of the typical straight lines, wound and curved its way up the gnarled wood of the board. A line underneath the tavern name read:

IT MATTERS NOT HOW NEAR OR FAR ONE WANDERS,
ONLY THAT ONE FINDS THE WANDERWAY.

Fern tasted the familiar mixture of seawater and beer as he stepped inside. The tavern's tiny rectangular windows allowed only silvery strips of outside light to fall across the mismatched sets of antique tables and chairs, while starving candles burned away their waxy bodies, one per table.

Fern grinned. The place was almost empty, though he expected it would not stay so for long. He knew the sea made sailors hungry and, even more, thirsty. They liked to drink, and he knew from firsthand experience that drink tasted best as soon as the ropes hit the docks.

A man behind the bar wore a raggedy white T-shirt which contrasted his messy mane of black hair. He wiped a hand across his chest, back and forth, leaving a wet smear.

"There're bets going that they got you. Maybe even killed you."

Fern took a seat at the bar. "Is that all?"

"Or that you deserted." The barkeep shrugged.

"You know me." Fern gave the man a warm smile. "I won't run."

"I do." The barkeeper flipped a glass up into the air. "And that's why I win all the money. Because I know you best."

The glass the barkeeper flipped had not come back down. It had vanished. Fern looked at his watch and then pointed at the long line of taps that ran the length of the bar. "Still have that ale on tap?"

"Dragon's Tale?"

"That's the one."

The barkeeper placed a fresh glass of amber-colored liquid on the bar. Fern took it, raised it to the man in a silent toast, and drank. He set the empty glass down with a soft thud.

"Good to see you, Tierney," the barkeeper said.

"You too, Eryk," said Fern.

Fern watched Eryk shift his eyes toward a doorway at the back of the bar. "Your guest is waiting back there. Just keep in mind that customers will come in soon. I'll do my best to keep them out."

• • •

A moment later Fern pushed aside the heavy canvas curtain which led into a back area known as the living room. It was smaller and cozier than the primary dining area, and a fire burned in the fireplace. He took a deep breath in and felt drowsy. Except for the light of the fire, the room was dark, its edges shrouded in shadowy quiet. Above the fire's stone mantle, spread out to fill the entire back wall, was a map of the world drawn on a vast piece of fabric that was frayed and torn around the edges. Fern knew the map well. It always amazed him to see how it maintained its vivid colors: the deep blues of the oceans and rivers, the golden brown of the landmasses, and several varying pigments in between for the many creatures and places it showed. His eyes dropped from the map to a person concealed under a black jacket with the hood pulled up over the head.

"That's a very special map," said Fern. "Made by Amerigo Vespucci's little brother, Alexi." The other person said nothing. "Sorry to keep you waiting," he tried again.

"You are Captain Fern, of the *Curiosity*?" The voice was soft, clandestine, more than a whisper but still hard to hear.

"I am," he answered.

"Thank you for coming."

"I'm sorry," said the captain. "But the message we received was basic. I'm afraid I don't even know your name."

"Does it matter?"

Fern caught the traces of an accent. Just what kind of accent, he could not say. The words were clean but short. Then, as if to approach a sleeping animal, he joined the stranger in front of the fireplace. The person was smaller than the captain by some inches, but Fern could not see beyond the jacket's hood.

"I know these are scary times," he said, "but you are safe here."

"Nowhere in the world has been safe for things like me for a long time."

"That's what we're trying to change."

The person turned and two hands brought down the hood to reveal a woman unlike any Fern had ever seen. Her eyes were bigger than the average person, and the dark gray-and-white color of clouds just before a storm. They drew him in, and he drifted toward her, stopping inches before her face. In the irises he saw strands of yellow, crisscrossed and messy, like threads of destiny.

"Aurora," she said. "That is my name." Tangles of brown hair fell across Aurora's eyes and fair face. She pushed some away with a hand and Fern saw that like her face, her hands were as pale as papier mâché.

"What do those mean?" He pointed at the dotted patterns tattooed across her hands.

"Endeavors," she said. "Undertakings, quests."

"Stories?" Fern tried.

She shrugged and nodded. "It's all stories." She looked young though her body, while athletic under the gray sweater and black jeans, appeared malnourished and fragile. Fern may have guessed she was only a little older than his own teenage daughter, but something about her demeanor, the way she held her chin high and her shoulders back, told him she could not be as young as she looked.

"Your message said you are in grave danger," he continued. "Can you tell me more?"

Aurora looked from side to side, as if she expected that danger to emerge from the shadows of the room at any moment. "What do you need to know? Do you want to know about last summer when they came into our villages? How many of us died? Do you want to hear how we hide in the caves of our ancestors and starve? Or maybe you need to hear about what they do. With their black suits and killing spears."

"Black suits?"

The pale woman nodded. It is them, Fern thought but did not say, not wanting to upset Aurora, who looked anxious enough.

"I just want it to stop," she said.

"They won't stop," said Fern. "I'm sure of it."

Aurora's gray eyes turned watery. Fern noticed for the first time the tiny perforations like freckles spread across her forehead. In that pattern they looked like a natural tiara. "Your boat, it's legendary," she said. "I don't know if it can do all the things I've heard, but if it can, it's our best chance."

"There is no *ship*," said Fern, "like *Curiosity*."

Aurora's face changed. "So, it's true?" Renewed energy entered her face. "You can take us to that place where we'll be safe?"

Fern was about to answer but stopped. He sensed movement in the shadows of the room. Aurora must have felt it too because before the captain realized what had happened, he saw a blur of motion and heard the thud of metal sinking into wood. Aurora strode with nimble steps into the darkest part of the room and returned a moment later with a long hunting knife in her hand, a white blade with an icy-blue handle.

"Sorry," she said, "I thought I heard something." Then, as if to tell a secret, she whispered, "I'm scared. And I am tired of being scared."

"This place you talk about," Fern continued, "is difficult to get to. The journey alone will take some time and can be dangerous."

"Nothing can be worse than how we live."

Fern nodded. They could hear muffled sounds on the other side of the living room curtain as new arrivals to the Wanderway took their seats. "I must arrange some things here in town. Could you be ready in three days?"

Aurora nodded.

"Good. Then in three days you will come to our ship. Bring the others. One hour before midnight. Post Thirty-Seven at the docks. You'll know it when you see it."

"Captain Fern." Aurora's voice trailed off. "They are not here."

Fern stopped. "What do you mean?"

Aurora turned back to the map above the mantle and pointed to a spot close to the top. "They are there."

Fern felt a jolt of understanding. "That explains the cryptic message."

"Please. I was afraid you may not come if you knew."

"The journey you're proposing will take weeks."

"If your crew is the one I've heard about, we will make it. Otherwise my people die."

If we don't do this, Fern thought to himself, we are all lost. He looked back into Aurora's pleading eyes. "Okay."

She smiled for the first time, revealing teeth that looked more befitting of a carnivorous animal than a person. She is beautiful, the captain thought, in the way wild things are beautiful.

"Three days," she said. She pulled her hood back up over her head. "I will be there."

Fern only nodded.

Aurora was halfway out of the room before she stopped and turned. "Captain?" she asked. "Why do you do it? You're human. Why help things like me?"

Fern did not look at Aurora directly. He was watching the embers of the fireplace flicker like the lights of a tiny city. "Things like you," he said, not taking his eyes off the tiny, glowing city. "Those I love most are things like you."

Fern stayed for a minute longer after Aurora had left the room. The crew might mutiny, he thought. Many of them felt the situation was already too dangerous. Then again, this was what they signed up for. The captain's fingers drummed once across the stone mantelpiece. Then he glanced up at the giant map adorning the wall and left. Fern acknowledged the familiar faces who had since taken up their usual spots as he passed through the dining room of the Wanderway.

• • •

Neither captain nor stranger had noticed the slight flickering of movement in the far corner. Neither heard the almost silent breathing as they spoke. They came close, thought Roach, considering how sharp the mythos' blade had been and how close it had come to his chest. He was sweating in a mixture of adrenaline and warmth, for the room held the heat from the fire like an oven and he finally had information his associates would want to hear.

CHAPTER 2 | POST THIRTY-SEVEN

The following morning, some thirty miles south of Easterly, a train rumbled up northbound tracks. Inside Car Four, somewhere between the front and middle, Salem Swan sat in a booth, wishing he were somewhere, or at least someone, else.

To say he was angry would be like proclaiming the sun is mildly warm; to say he was sad, like declaring that ice is a just little bit cold. He had grown up without a father, but that is not what bothered him. Despite his missing parent, his mother had played the part of two, making it effortless in a way Salem imagined only she could. She had raised him, alone. She had schooled him, alone. Salem was not stupid. He had visited with other friends and seen their families. He had seen how those families struggled to accomplish with two parents what his mom had done by herself. No, it was not his absent father which instigated his anger or sadness. It was the gaping hole in his life, still smoldering around the edges, where his mom used to be.

He kicked his backpack hard in frustration and a withered journal slid out onto the floor from the bag's open mouth. He leaned down and picked it up.

Its jacket was wrinkled leather with two gold letters inscribed on its cover:

RS

Salem knew what the initials stood for. Rigel Swan, a man he had barely heard about and never met. Still, for reasons Salem did not understand, he had held on to his father's journal, thumbing through it over the many years of his childhood. Its pages he had seen many times, flipping through them often from start to finish. He knew the old book held a vast reservoir of knowledge on a subject his mother called nonsense, mythology. Illustrations, descriptions, and stories filled the pages about a vast number of mythical creatures, their habits, habitats, even guessing at their potential whereabouts. Salem had loved imagining it all as a boy: the wyverns, giants, dragons, and trolls, the animals who could talk to people and the people who could talk back; but as time had gone on, whether because of his mom or the nature of growing older, he had realized that stories were all they were. He had loved to imagine his father was an adventurer scientist who would travel the world and uncover hidden beasts. The study of make believe, his mother always called it. She had never spoken to Salem about his father, and, after trying many times, Salem had given up asking her about his dad, deciding that the man was nothing more than the mythologies in his journal.

Salem pushed his thumb over the golden letters, feeling oddly infuriated that the journal, a remnant of his runaway father, remained, while his mother did not. He resisted the urge to hurl the old book out of the train car's partially open window and shoved it back inside his bag instead.

"You know, Salem," said the man sitting across from him, "we can talk about what happened. We should, in fact." The portly relocation manager known as Mr. Gingam checked his watch and brushed the bagel crumbs from his cream-colored shirt. Salem was almost sure Mr. Gingam had no girlfriend and possibly no friends, but somehow still found himself pleasantly accustomed to the man's voice that sounded strained but happy, as if he were being hugged too hard around the waist.

"That's okay, Mr. Gingam." Salem looked back to see his reflection in the train's window. He was tall for fifteen. Not freakishly tall, but tall enough that he could convince people he was older in the right light. His eyes were blue like his mother's and he guessed the rest of his features, including his high cheekbones and his dirty-blond hair, came from his father. He was not scrawny but also not muscular or sporty, though lately he had grown fond of running outside. He found that the constant movement and change of scenery gave him less time to dwell on what had happened. Running past the past, he would tell himself.

Yet despite his best efforts to keep the past behind him, Salem's reflection made him remember. A memory, many years earlier, came to him. He was sitting in a train car with his mother, at the age of only six or seven. He could not remember where they were going or why, just the way her arms wrapped around his waist as they stared out of the train's large windows.

"See that," she had said, pointing to his reflection in the glass. "That's another you coming to say hello."

"Another me?" six-year-old Salem asked her. "But I'm here, Mom."

"Sure, *this you* is," his mother told him, "but that you isn't." Then she tickled his ribcage with her fingers, as was their ritual when one of them said something funny.

Back in the present, Salem shook his head, letting the memory fade as the train car he sat in banked around a turn.

From across the booth, Mr. Gingam raised an eyebrow, looking genuinely concerned for Salem's sanity.

"Losing a parent," the relocation manager began, "is a gruesome ordeal. But it's important for you to know that you're not alone."

Salem rolled his eyes without intending to. He was not ungrateful toward Mr. Gingam but hearing once again about his new life as an orphan felt stale. What more could he possibly learn from learning about how "not alone" he was?

The next few minutes passed the way they had been going in the recent days. They passed like a river of slow-flowing time, the consistency of syrup instead of water. Within that river of syrupy days turned into weeks since the accident, Salem's mind had emptied, leaving him unable to cope with the complex and powerful emotions churning inside of him.

"And naturally that will be your decision once you turn eighteen." Mr. Gingam raised a small paper coffee cup to his mouth and gulped loudly. "Needs more sugar," he said, tearing open a strip of artificial white crystals labeled Crosstracks's Choice and tipping it down into the brown liquid.

"What is my choice?" asked Salem.

Mr. Gingam cleared his throat. "Like we talked about before. You're fifteen, which means you have almost three years till you are legally an adult. It's the state's duty to find you a guardian. And as your paternal situation is…" Mr. Gingam lingered here, as if there was not a word in existence which could adequately describe his thought, and then continued, "unclear, the next, and coincidentally *only*, viable option has turned out to be your uncle, Ulysses Warminster." Mr. Gingam sipped his coffee. "Better," he whispered happily to his cup before looking back up at Salem. "So, you will live with him for at least the next few months until your upcoming birthday. Then we can reassess and see if any adjustments are necessary."

"Adjustments?" asked Salem.

"We want to make sure you're comfortable. You may request a relocation. It is your life."

A gravity clung to Mr. Gingam's words as he finished. Salem found it funny that Mr. Gingam, along with everyone else, seemed to be under the illusion that he had any actual choice in anything. It is your life, was a phrase he heard on repeat. If it were true Salem would still have a mother and a father and his current situation would not exist. He would still have a house and at least attempt to go to school, instead of his social anxiety dictating him stuck in homeschooling with his mom for the past three years. It's not my life, he thought, I'm just the one it's happening to.

Salem knew he could get off the train if he wanted to. Exit at the next stop and go back to Pennsylvania to enter some foster program. But something kept him firmly rooted in his seat. It could have been the thought of a foster home or the thought of going back to the place full of memories and loss. It could have even been Mr. Gingam that kept him sitting in the train car, strange as it was for Salem to admit it. Mostly, he guessed it was all these things and, as the train rolled along the tracks, he thought, what more do I have to lose?

• • •

Twenty-two minutes later, the rusted chrome Crosstracks Regional Rail liner squealed to a stop. Salem imagined the conductor wearing a water-filled fishbowl over his head as the muffled voice gurgled through the speakers.

"Easter-Cen-ral! Las-top, exit right!"

A large gold sign adorned with ruby-colored lettering hung in the main lobby and read:

WELCOME TO EASTERLY CENTRAL STATION, CONNECTING RHODE ISLAND'S FAVORITE OCEAN TOWN TO THE MAINLAND US OF A SINCE 1929.

The lobby was a wide-open space with a black-and-white-diamond tile floor and mosaic ceiling portraying a marinescape of aquatic life. A mermaid and merman swam together at the far end of the ceiling under which a small stand, aptly named "Easterly Wind Treasures," sold candy and keychains.

Mr. Gingam pulled a crumpled piece of paper from his coat pocket. "Looks like we're headed toward the wharf. Post Thirty-Seven, Cabin

Two." The relocation manager squinted as if trying to see more on the tiny piece of paper. "Odd address," he mumbled.

"Mr. Gingam?" Salem halted in the middle of the station as other travelers moved past him in all directions. "I don't know if I can do this. I don't know anything about my uncle. My mom didn't like him and now I'm expected to live with him?"

A soft expression came over Mr. Gingam's plump face as he set down his briefcase on the tile floor. "It is acceptable and understandable that you're feeling this way, Salem. Truth be told, you will go through a period of change. However,"—now a hint of sternness crept into the normally teddy-bear-like relocation manager's voice—"you're lucky you have a family member to go to. We've been over the alternatives." Salem nodded. "All will be well," said Mr. Gingam, who, slightly shorter than Salem, had to reach his arm up to place a comforting hand on Salem's shoulder.

Salem had to give Mr. Gingam some credit. No grandparents, no father, no siblings, Salem could still hear the police officer reading through the list. He never imagined a list of everything he did not have could be so long. Still, after all the police, firefighters, and doctors had gone home, there was Mr. Gingam. Unspectacular in all except in his ability to be there when all others were not. An ability Salem was learning not to underestimate. Salem took a deep breath in as Mr. Gingam picked up his briefcase, and then followed the relocation manager toward the doors.

• • •

The terrain descended slightly from the station into the town, which spread outward toward the ocean like the fin of a great shark.

"So, where you fellas in from?" asked their elderly taxi driver through thick sunglasses as the town of Easterly grew around them. The driver's tone implied that it was obvious Salem and Mr. Gingam were not local, and as Salem looked around, he could guess why. He and Mr. Gingam stared like tourists at the different shapes of the houses and shops. Some were skinny with pointed roofs, while others were pointy with skinny roofs. Salem imagined them like something from colonial America but exaggerated, stretched out, comical and yet somehow serious.

Everything was the whitewashed color of sand, except for some wind-burnt rooftops and walls that were a dark shade of green, which reminded Salem of overgrown algae on a fish tank. Hand-painted signs hung above shop doors displaying the craft of the artisans associated or the products sold inside.

"Pennsylvania," answered Mr. Gingam. "We're coming from Pennsylvania. Just dropping the boy off here with his uncle." The driver looked at Salem in the rearview mirror. At least Salem thought he did, though it was impossible to tell.

"Penn's woods," the driver answered. "Had a cousin down there somewhere. He was a Quaker. Calvin, I think's the place."

Salem only nodded and smiled. He had never heard of Calvin.

"Penn's woods," echoed Mr. Gingam and then, pointing out the window, added, "Easterly seems like a lovely little town."

The driver looked at Mr. Gingam, allowing one of his thick eyebrows to rise above the frame of his glasses and then, sighing in the way only very old men can, he said, "I'll tell you a local secret. Easterly's a spiritual place—a sacred burial place of the Algonquin tribes for generations. There's an energy here as old as the ocean."

"Sorry," said Mr. Gingam. "Not sure I follow what you mean."

The driver picked a thick hand up off the steering wheel to emphasize the next words. "Like the ocean," he repeated. "Always changing. Never changing."

The car ride was silent then until they turned onto an avenue that opened to an array of docks and the ocean where dozens of boats bobbed and rocked like pistons in a gummy engine. They pulled up to a small wooden gate next to the road and the old man pointed. "Thirty-seven should be about a hundred feet that way."

"Good man," said Mr. Gingam. He pulled out a small leather pouch which looked more like a miniature purse than a man's wallet. "Would I be able to have you wait here?" Wordless, the driver looked down at the purse, back up at Mr. Gingam, and nodded.

• • •

The air was wet and cool. Wind blew saltiness in their faces as Salem walked with Mr. Gingam along the floating forest of boats.

"Fishy," said Mr. Gingam. He opened and closed his mouth like a baby discovering its tongue for the first time. "Can you read the post numbers, Salem? I can't find my glasses."

"There," said Salem. He pointed to the small white signs which hung on the wooden posts in front of each boat and then asked, "Mr. Gingam?"

Mr. Gingam only grunted while his hand dug distractedly inside his coat.

"We're going to meet my uncle on a boat?"

"Seems so. Not your typical minor sign-off, I'll tell you that."

The dock was an intricate system of wet concrete and wood that spanned out like a spider's web into the water.

"Here." Salem stopped. "Thirty-seven."

"Good show." Mr. Gingam finally adjusted his small circular lenses onto his face and looked up. "Oh my, that is a boat."

The ship at Post Thirty-Seven had three big masts. White sails slept in curled up slumber under horizontal beams of dark wood. Even though the ship looked old, old enough to be in some maritime museum, Salem thought its body looked sleek, almost new, as it floated on the waterline. Salem's eyes went from the top of the masts, down to the body and the front, where a very lifelike figurehead looked steadfastly forward. It was humanlike, although there were bizarre differences. Besides its two arms, it had wings like an eagle and a long tail and tailfin like a dolphin. In one of its arms was a book, and in the other an arrow. The figurehead held the book close to its chest and the arrow tip pointed forward, extended out into the world ahead.

"Yes, well," said Mr. Gingam, also studying the figurehead. "Shall we?"

As they stepped on to the floating dock tied to the ship, Salem read the name inscribed in big, looping letters along its side. Curiosity.

CHAPTER 3 | CURIOSITY

Rows of barrels stood like soldiers at attention along the dock. A small group of men and women, whom Salem assumed were sailors, worked them onto the boat. They looked a little like Salem imagined sailors may look: partially wet clothes, wind-burned skin, gruff dispositions; but there were also elements he found odd. Their proportions looked miscalculated, as if God or whoever had created them had given little thought as to arm placement and leg thickness, or finger length and nose shape.

The sailors did not seem to even acknowledge Salem and Mr. Gingam as they stood behind them like two guests who had walked into the wrong party.

"Pardon us," said Mr. Gingam. Nothing. He looked at Salem as if to muster all the courage a man of his polite nature could muster. "Excuse me!"

One sailor, a tall man with large, sunken eyes, stopped. To Salem's surprise, the barrel-pushing behind the man did not. The others readjusted, continuing as if nothing had happened.

The man approached them, and as he did Salem noticed the veins that protruded like small rivers along his unusually long neck. He also saw the chord necklace that hung down off the man's chest. At the end of the chord looked to be a piece of wood or bark and, as Salem looked closer, he saw what he thought were scratches or tiny engraved markings like runes on the wood's surface. Mr. Gingam, unable to accept the bizarre appearance of the man, only opened his mouth and promptly closed it.

After a long moment, Salem finally said, "We're looking for Ulysses Warminster."

The tall man blinked slowly. Salem wondered if he had understood. Mr. Gingam, apparently having similar thoughts, began repeating Ulysses' name in a loud voice, as if to a toddler. "Ulysses. YOO-LISS-SE—"

The man raised a long bony arm like an enormous bird who no longer had feathers. Mr. Gingam, cut off mid-vowel, fell silent.

"Wait," the man said. He turned and retreated with long strides up the gangway. Salem noted that the other sailors observed them now too, apparently deciding the visitors were indeed interesting enough.

"Oi!" A woman with bright red hair appeared over the side of the ship's deck. "Up to the weather then."

Salem and Mr. Gingam obeyed, following the bony-armed man, while behind them followed not at all shyly the strange sailors who had since forgotten their barrel-pushing.

The weather deck was wide. At its center, the mainmast reached into the sky like the trunk of an ancient tree. It rose and rose into folded sails with overlapping ropes crisscrossing in a messy loom. Voices shouted across the decks, speaking words that Salem heard but did not understand.

The woman who stood before them had high cheekbones that gave her freckled face an air of distinction both intense and endearing. Her fiery red head of hair was even more striking up close, and Salem saw she wore it in a tight braid that ran down to the small of her back. Salem saw she wore a similar necklace to that of the man who had showed them to the deck. In fact, looking around he saw that most of the sailors, independent from their other more normal clothes, wore similar necklaces.

"Hello," said Mr. Gingam. He stepped over the gangway and extended his hand. "My name is Peter Gingam, and this is Salem Swan."

"A Swan?" She turned to Salem. "How deeply interesting." Her voice was soft and reedy, like a freshly tuned clarinet. It carried in it the crisp impatience of someone used to being in command. She shook hands with Salem, holding on even after Salem tried letting go. "I'm Dorianna Bellavaro. Quartermaster." Dorianna's intelligent brown eyes studied Salem the way an art critic might study a piece of art. "What can we do for you?"

"We were hoping to find this boy's uncle," said Mr. Gingam. "A Mr. Ulysses Warminster."

A murmur shot through the ring of bodies that had formed around them. The yells and shouts that had been flying around the decks died down. Salem's skin prickled.

"You don't say," said Dorianna, the hint of a smile appearing at the farthest corners of her mouth. "I wasn't aware Ulysses had a nephew."

• • •

In another part of the deck, hidden out of sight in a side room few people knew about or even visited, Ulysses Warminster sat in silence. He often visited this spot to think, finding it one of the few peaceful places on the ship. Never mind that he had not seen his nephew in well over a decade or that he had, much to his dismay, only learned about the untimely death of his sister after his return from sea.

Ulysses buried his face in his hands. He was not the man to take on this responsibility. Sure, he could get their crew out of a pinch under dire circumstances or somehow always find the right way to lighten a mood. But taking responsibility for anyone but himself had always been, and continued to be, a major issue. How was he expected to become a father figure when he often did not properly watch out for his own safety?

A soft knock came at the door. Ulysses looked up to see the flushed face of the quartermaster Dorianna.

"Hey Lyss," said Dorianna, sounding relieved to find him. She placed her hand gently on his shoulder "I think you need to get top deck. Sounds like you have a family member up there."

Ulysses looked into her eyes. "I'm not ready," he told her.

Dorianna's expression was normally a somewhat severe degree of determined, as if nothing and no one could stand in the way of her and her eventual goals. It was one aspect Ulysses liked most about her, and it did not fail now.

"Ulysses," she said. Dorianna could have been talking to Ulysses at a dinner party or in the middle of a raging storm. Her voice did not change. "We're given what we can handle. You can handle more than most."

With that, Dorianna vanished, while her words lingered in the air around Ulysses' head like a flock of singing birds.

She was right; he thought. He would need to put on a strong face for Salem. There was much they would need to discuss. Ulysses stood. Everything would happen as it should, he tried to tell himself. "I just hope we get along," he said out loud to no one as he made his way to the top deck.

• • •

Back on the main deck of the ship, Salem and Mr. Gingam waited, rather awkwardly, while the quartermaster Dorianna retrieved Salem's uncle. The interest of the crew members seemed to grow with each passing moment, and with each unfamiliar look Salem felt more and more aware of how small the boat became.

Finally, and much to Salem's relief, he saw the bright red hair of Dorianna Bellavaro bobbing through the throng of sailors. All eyes, including Salem's, fell on the man behind her as they stepped forward.

He was slightly taller and broader than Salem, with a round face that looked as though it never fully transitioned from youth to adult. Tears formed at the sides of his eyes as he looked at Salem. The strands of gray hair nestled in throughout his stubble folded upward as he broke into a smile that seemed to Salem to be both sad and happy.

Salem noticed right away that Ulysses was his mother's brother. His eyes were the same shape and color hers had been.

"Salem?" Ulysses' voice was incredulous. "But you're huge. Last time I saw you, you were"—Ulysses stuck his hand out over the ground as if to measure an invisible dwarf—"and now you're…" Ulysses raised his hand to almost his own height. A moment later, he crossed the expanse between them and engulfed Salem in a hug. It was a tight hug, the kind that is silent and loud at the same time.

Salem had had no shortage of hugs in the past weeks, though this was different. It was not the pity of people grateful not to be him, but the understanding embrace of someone who knew the pain and shared it. Something inside Salem crumbled, something hard and sad, got smaller, less powerful than it had been, and, fighting through the awkwardness, Salem raised his arms, and hugged his uncle back.

"Yes, well." Mr. Gingam looked uneasily around at the growing group of spectators. "Mr. Warminster."

"Ulysses, please." Ulysses broke his hug with Salem and wiped his eyes. For a long moment, Salem and his uncle stared at each other. The group of bodies viewing the spectacle had grown to occupy a large part of the deck. A low murmur swelled around them. Salem caught only single words.

"Uncle?"

"Nephew?"

"Did you know?"

The origin of the words was untraceable, though they tore through the air like arrows, nonetheless. Salem imagined this was what it felt like to be the newest animal at the zoo.

Mr. Gingam cleared his throat. "Perhaps we can continue this somewhere more private?"

"Use my quarters." The voice was fresh and came from a man as he stepped onto the deck. His face was kind and angular, with blue eyes that matched the curtain of sky above. Salem could not have guessed the man's age. He may have said somewhere between thirty and fifty. He looked a little theatrical, Salem thought, wearing a dark green watch coat with large silver buttons. Then again, nothing about anything since arriving in Easterly seemed normal.

"I'm Tierney Fern," the man said. "Captain. Forgive us for… gathering." The captain looked around at the crew. A quick rush of whispers ricocheted through the group and the bodies dissipated. "If you'll follow me."

They followed the captain a short way before walking up two flights of stairs. Salem studied his uncle as he walked and wondered what kind of man Ulysses was. Having grown up an only child, Salem had always been curious about the relationship his mother would have had with her brother. It had seemed strange to him at first that they never spoke about him, or Salem's father. Though as time had gone on Salem had grown more and more accustomed to the lack of Ulysses Warminster in his life. Now, as he followed the swinging arms and broad back of the man, he asked himself not only about his uncle's character but also about what kind of relationship they would have, if any.

They reached a separate section of the deck, smaller and more intimate, with decorative railings adorning the sides. The captain strode to a pair of intricately designed doors and unlatched something Salem could not see.

"Gentlemen." Captain Fern stepped aside and let them pass into the dark.

Salem entered last into the captain's quarters. Shafts of light fell diagonally across the floor, illuminating towers of books and journals piled high throughout the room, some high enough to brush against the superstructure of the ceiling. Papers and maps covered all other surfaces, and a lone telescope, half in and half out, stood by the closest window. Three legs, crafted to look like claws, were so realistic that Salem was sure they literally dug into the floor.

"Here you are," said the captain, back stepping to the door they had just entered through. "Take as much time as you need." With that he returned to the deck, closing the doors behind him.

"Just right here," said Ulysses then, making his way to the back of the room where a massive wooden desk, shaped like the shell of a giant sea snail, was carved directly out of the hull. Salem and Mr. Gingam followed and sat on two matching chairs that faced Ulysses and the desk.

Gingam released a small gasp and Salem followed his eyes up to see something crawling across hanging pieces of fishnet. It was lanky and its white fur wrought with rings of black and brown like mismatched pieces of an overgrown forest.

"Is that…" Gingam paused, "a sloth?" The sloth turned its head at sloth speed and grinned down at them.

"Don't mind Atlas," said Ulysses. "You'll have enough time to move if he attacks."

"He attacks?"

Salem tried not to laugh as he watched Mr. Gingam recoil. He looked at the sloth's upside-down face. Its eyes were two brown marbles. Gingam shook his head in disbelief. Ulysses, obviously no stranger to the sloth, reached up and scratched its hairy chin.

"You are calm. I am calm." Salem heard his uncle whisper under his breath, as though he were speaking an incantation to the sloth.

"So," began Gingam. He glanced up at Atlas nervously, finding the existence of such a creature on this ship, in this room, inconceivable. The relocation manager extracted a thin folder from his briefcase. "Mr. Ulysses Warminster, you will now become the legal guardian of the minor, Salem Swan." Gingam opened the folder and picked out a piece of paper which he extended toward Ulysses. "There is one point," said Gingam. "I need to ensure that Salem will have a proper living space before I sign off on his release. Do you have accommodations somewhere in town? Because I'm not sure if it's best..." Gingam hesitated and then looked up at the sloth, "here."

"Mr. Gingam." Ulysses leaned across the desk and clapped the smaller man on the shoulder as if they were old friends. "I can assure you I have terrestrial habitations and that they will be suitable for my nephew."

Mr. Gingam made a noise that sounded unconvinced of Ulysses' claim. "There is also the question of schooling."

"That will be no problem. We'll get him schooled."

"Enrolled, you mean," said Mr. Gingam.

"Yeah, enrolled and schooled," said Ulysses. Salem watched Ulysses smile almost comically, though Mr. Gingam did not seem to notice. "We'll have him schooling better than a fish."

Mr. Gingam crinkled his face and said, "I suppose as long as he passes the state examinations that will be acceptable." Mr. Gingam turned to Salem. "Salem, are you okay with this?"

Salem felt hot magma gurgle under his cheeks, and he was sure they were red. He could not bring himself to look more than a second at either Mr. Gingam or Ulysses.

"Salem?" Mr. Gingam placed his hand on Salem's shoulder.

Salem made a gesture between a nod and shrug. I know the alternative, he thought, looping in his mind back to the same outcomes of foster home and uncertainty. He looked between the two men who watched him expectantly. "Yeah, I mean, I guess," he said.

Mr. Gingam seemed to calculate something in his head. "Very well. Ulysses, please provide an address here." Mr. Gingam pointed a finger to the lines on the page.

Ulysses completed the form providing an address for an apartment he claimed was visible from just outside on the dock. Salem watched as they signed him over to his new guardian. It was strange to think of himself as something one could sign for, as if he was a package successfully delivered.

"Well, then." Gingam closed his folder and inserted it neatly back into his briefcase. "That should do it."

"Excellent," said Ulysses. "Then let me show you back out to the deck."

Salem lingered for a moment as the men made their way into the open air. He felt as though he were in a dream, discombobulated and floating through a void he could witness but not control. He needed a moment to process his changing life. In the room's still, he heard only the creaking of the ship and the voices that sounded small from outside. It all seemed distant in the same way he, the Salem of today, seemed different from the Salem of only a few weeks prior. Like a reflection of himself in a mirror which had now passed by.

Salem realized he was staring into the eyes of Atlas hanging just above him. The sloth grinned at him, crookedly. At least it looked like a grin. Then it ever so slowly raised a long arm toward the next piece of net. Salem took a deep breath and walked back out into the light of the day.

Back on the deck, Mr. Gingam extended his hand to Salem. "Okay then, Salem. It looks like our journey together ends here, at least for now. I'll be back in a few months to check in on you. You have my information in case you need to contact me."

Mr. Gingam stood on the side of the deck closest to the gangplank which would lead back down to the dock and the town, while Ulysses, Salem, and the rest of the crew stood on the main deck of the ship. While the positioning may have been a minor detail of consequence, to Salem in that moment it signified the changing of a phase in his life. He was now on the ship and part of a strange unknown world he was not ready to embrace. In front of him was Mr. Gingam, who represented his old life and all he was leaving behind. Before stepping onto the gangplank, Mr. Gingam nodded to Ulysses, who nodded back with what Salem guessed was his attempt at a reassuring gesture.

"Thank you for everything," Salem said to Mr. Gingam and, shocking himself, found tears in his eyes. Then he hugged the relocation manager in an act which surprised them both.

"My pleasure, Salem," said Mr. Gingam from awkwardly inside the hug. "Stay well. See you soon."

Mr. Gingam turned and trotted down the gangway of the ship toward the spot where the taxi waited. Salem watched until he was out of sight and, as he turned back, felt exceedingly small and alone on the strange boat and in front of the even stranger people waiting for him.

CHAPTER 4 | THINGS HAVE GONE TOO FAR

The courtyard was quiet as Roach braked under the main gate, patting down his short brown hair in a last try at presentability. No matter how he patted, it always stuck up anyway. He had never been one to care much about his outer appearance, but somehow it was something which always gave him trouble. He was just a guy who consistently looked out of sorts. Whatever out of sorts meant. Roach had always believed it was because of his nature that this was true. He was sneaking around and slipping in and out of tight spaces. These were activities that had a wrinkly nature.

Even though the old abbey sat well outside the boundaries of Easterly, from its vantage point atop a nearby hill the entire town and ocean beyond was visible, sprawled below like a painting.

Around the courtyard Roach noticed that small pieces of stone—broken-off parts from the crumbling wall—littered the ground between thick weeds, and just beyond the series of buildings, sloped down at sharp angles, was the bank of a fast-flowing river which had been there for as long as anyone could remember. It presented a beautiful but melancholic setting: the deteriorating abbey and winding river set against the backdrop of Easterly and the ocean. However, Roach knew the derelict appearance was inauthentic. If he looked closely enough, it was a manufactured disrepair. Convincing enough to ward off most, except for those who appreciated what real neglect looked like. Roach pressed the button on the intercom and heard the resounding buzz from somewhere beyond the walls.

"Name," came the voice over static.

"Roach."

There was a brief pause as the voice clicked off and then from somewhere inside the gate mechanically unlatched.

Roach rolled his motorcycle up to the edge of the parking lot overgrown with weeds next to a blue pickup truck with poles, cages, and many nets sitting in its bed. The gate closed with a slam and Roach jumped, swearing under his breath. He already felt on edge and he would need to control himself.

The abbey was a complex of buildings and Roach made for the central and biggest of them, the old church. He walked through the doors of the nave. The inside was musty and cavernous, with a domed ceiling that moved upward to a central point in a basilica style, like the old cathedrals of Europe. Long stained-glass windows depicting saints and children sprinkled multi-colored light, and oiled scenes covered the walls like dried and peeling skin.

At the front, in the place once known as the sacristy, a dozen people in black suits mingled. Some held drinks and others small bite-size hors d'oeuvres. Roach stood in the back, masked by the surrounding sounds. On either side of the nave, in the place where pews once stood, were rows upon rows of machines. They were rectangular, unmanned, and connected to one another by long strips of parchment threaded through slits from one to the next like a great flat snake. The parchment moved in a symphonic exchange of clicks and whirs.

"Ah," said one person, a man with thick glasses and thin blond hair. The voice carried and reverberated. "You've returned, Roach," he said, "… and with news we hope."

Roach meandered up the center aisle. The machines whirred around him and the paper slid through in steady clicks. At twenty feet from the suited ensemble, he stopped. He felt underdressed and silly in his worn sweater and jeans. The people watched him with tight expressions of amusement that told him they were eager for him to say what he came to say, but equally eager for him to leave. Roach saw faces he recognized, though many others he did not.

"Where is Mr. White?" he asked.

"Mr. White is unavailable," said the man with glasses who had spoken first. Roach identified the man as Mr. Centralia. "But we will deliver your message." Mr. Centralia motioned him closer.

Roach knew better than to disobey. He cleared his throat and walked forward up the stairs into the enclosed area.

"There was a meeting," he began, "between the captain and… one of them." The other people stopped talking amongst themselves and stood still as statues. They faced him as he spoke. He licked his lips and continued. "It seems," he said, trying hard to imbue confidence into his words, "the ship will sail again."

A few of the people stirred.

"Continue," Mr. Centralia said.

"I believe this mytho comes from somewhere in the northeastern hemisphere."

A few of the people scoffed.

"The entire northern hemisphere," said a stringy woman with pasty skin and pasty hair, "is free of mythos. The Russian delegation reported it earlier this year. Best to check your facts, Mr. Roach." She sipped her drink. It left a smear in the shape of her lips on the glass. Everything about her irritated Roach. Mr. Roach. Roach was not even his actual name, but the title had taken hold and it was now his to bear. He would change that.

"Pardon," he said, eager to say what he needed to say and leave. "But could it be that they missed some?"

"Ms. Madison," said Mr. Centralia, "would you retrieve the latest records?"

A woman from the back of the group retreated into the ranks of machines.

"How rude of us," said Mr. Centralia. "Roach, can we get you something?" Mr. Centralia made a motion as if to offer the food and drink. Saliva built in Roach's mouth, and a low grumble answered from his stomach, though he knew taking too much of the food would make a bad impression. He nodded and took a small piece of cheese which sat on a cracker. He put it in his mouth and tried to chew it without moving his jaw.

The woman called Ms. Madison returned a few seconds later.

"Centralia," she said. She handed the man a piece of paper.

Mr. Centralia's eyes skimmed from side to side over the parchment. "Odd," he said. "One report has the Russians declaring their hemisphere clear, but there have been multiple mytho sightings in just the past few weeks."

Roach saw the pasty-skinned woman's eyes widen. It was satisfying. He resisted the urge to stare into her face and watch the words sink in. But as he looked around, he noticed the shock was not on her face alone, but on all faces in the church. Even Mr. Centralia could not hide his surprise behind his thick lenses.

"Thank you, Ms. Madison." Mr. Centralia pulled down his sleeves toward his wrists in what Roach assumed was an attempt to regain some of his prior composure.

It was warm and quiet in the church. A line of sweat had formed across Roach's brow. The first droplet descended upon his face. It rolled into the corner of his eye and he wiped it away.

"This is ridiculous," said another of the men.

"Relax, Mr. Monkton," said Mr. Centralia.

"We're too lenient, Centralia."

"You need to relax, Mr. Monkton."

"White is allowing this whole place to go to hell. Everything we worked for we might as well throw away."

"Monkton," Mr. Centralia's voice increased in volume.

"Don't, Centrali—" Monkton yelled but stopped short.

Something had flown past Roach's ear. It was long and black and stuck out of Mr. Monkton's chest like a small plant that had just broken through the earth. Roach spun his head around to see a beaming man with white teeth that seemed to sparkle almost as much as his shiny skin. Roach had known Mr. White for as long as he could remember. The charismatic leader was infamous and his name synonymous with the Regulat. No one knew where Mr. White had come from, only that he had brought an enormous influx of financial wealth to the organization many years earlier when still a young man, and had since domineered his way to the top as its leader.

Mr. White was not a tall man, and it seemed almost too planned that his teeth were white enough to make anything else dull by comparison. He looked old enough, with thin wrinkles across his face and forehead, to give him an air of experience, and young enough, with a lean body and energetic walk, that no one could have said where he fell on the spectrum of age. Lost in his age, Roach had to guess, or a man free from the concept, driven by something bigger. He had a chiseled face and eyes that were beautiful and abruptly kind. Eyes that swept across faces and spaces, engulfing them into his scope and changing them forever.

Mr. Monkton wavered where he stood. He looked like he was about to speak, his pointer finger twitching a little at his side, and then he fell forward onto his knees, followed by his belly with a thud.

"Funny," said Mr. White, "people rarely die like that. That was so… theatrical."

Everything in the church, save for the industrious machines, was silent.

"Mr. White," said Mr. Centralia, "we weren't expecting you back so soon."

"Looks as though I've returned at just the right time." Mr. White strode forward, his wavy brown hair bouncing as he stepped over the motionless body of Mr. Monkton and the pool of blood growing underneath. He walked straight to the table of food where he assembled what seemed to Roach to be a neurotically specific assortment of hors d'oeuvres. He picked them up and studied each one, as though he could taste them through the tips of his fingers. The ones that tasted good he kept, the ones that did not he returned to the platter, rejected. Mr. White then turned his gaze onto Roach, casting him under an aura of attention that made Roach want to melt into the floor.

"There was a time, Roach," said Mr. White, "when people would drive for hours to this place." He popped one of the small foodstuffs into his mouth before continuing. "Now, this wasn't because of any preacher or because of the windows or the choir or the Sunday school teachers. Can you guess what it was, Roach?"

Roach could have guessed. He said nothing.

"Belief," said Mr. White. He cleared his throat and relinquished the rest of the hors d'oeuvres from his hand back into the dish, as if he had never intended to eat them in the first place. Two of the women eyed the deposited pieces with looks of hunger beyond mere appetite. "They believed in God, Roach. Believed in a super being that controlled their destinies and answered their prayers. They took their own power, Roach. Don't you see. Took their power and gave it to something else. A fiction." Mr. White was looking up at a sculpture of a crucifix where the plexiglass body of a mangled man hung limp. "They were wrong. We are our own creators. We are our own gods."

Mr. White looked down into the face of the dead Mr. Monkton the way one might look at roadkill.

"You have done well, Roach, to become part of Curiosity's crew and earn their trust. And while Mr. Monkton, may he rest in peace, was rash with his words, he was not incorrect. We—" Mr. White paused. "I have allowed too much. This playing around has gone on too long."

"Ms. Madison," said Mr. Centralia, "please repeat for Mr. White what you have just told us here."

Ms. Madison looked at the body of Mr. Monkton on the floor, and the returned her gaze to the group with an expression that said she would like to do anything but retell the news. Hastily, she recounted the message delivered moments earlier. Mr. White listened with an eerie, unrelenting lack of emotion.

"Roach says the ship will sail again. This time to the northern hemisphere," said Mr. Centralia after Ms. Madison had finished.

"I see. I will speak to the Russians. A mistake by one of us is a mistake by all of us," said Mr. White. "Even if we need to clean up after each other," he added under his breath. "Roach." Roach shuddered under his clothes as Mr. White turned his brown eyes on him. "You will continue your role for the time being. We will see to taking care of things upon your return. Do this," Mr. White added, "and you will find yourself in a favorable light with us once again."

Roach nodded. He could accept a cue for exit when it arrived. Happy to make his way to the back, he turned where the doors of the nave and the outside world were waiting.

CHAPTER 5 | TO THE GUIDE WITHIN

Salem walked with Ulysses along the ship's bow. The sails blossomed in the afternoon wind, making a noise that sounded like the world's largest sheet being thrown over the world's largest bed.

"The ship's breathing," explained Ulysses, following Salem's gaze. "At least that's what old sailors say." The sky above was a clear expanse of blue stretching in all directions. Ulysses took time to explain to Salem the names and terms for the many things around them. There was the portside, the starboard, the stern, and the hull, the bulwark, the loof, the poopdeck, and the galley. To Salem, it was a foreign language, and he felt like a tourist in a new country, a new country where ropes hung from masts and doors and hatches led to cabins and passages that seemed mysterious and foreboding. Salem swore the crew did not look or seem like normal people. Everyone was a little too attentive and listened a little too closely when he spoke to them.

"Is everyone here always so…."

"Interested?" said Ulysses and shrugged. "We're a curious bunch."

"Are these lifeboats?" Salem pointed to one of the six boats that hung along the ship's side.

"Longboats," said Ulysses. "Actually, they were chase boats back when this was going to be a whaling ship. Nowadays we use them to get to shore when there's no dock."

"So, this used to be a whaling ship, but now…?" Salem was eager to circle back to the question, finding it hard to imagine why such a ship was still in use.

"I'm happy you're here," Ulysses said, not answering the question but producing an awkward smile as he and Salem walked. "I have little experience with this whole parent thing. But I'm not sure a parent is what you need or want, is it?" Salem did not know how to respond and to his disbelief missed Mr. Gingam. At least the persistent optimism of the relocation manager was predictable. This uncharted territory with Ulysses was, by comparison, uncomfortable. "Anyway," continued Ulysses, "this is probably a lot for you to take in. I know it is for me." Salem sensed the man was in a place outside of his own comfort zone, and found that thought oddly comforting.

"We can be friends to start," said Salem. He hoped it sounded less dumb out loud than it had in his head.

"Friends, yes." Ulysses' face relaxed. "Well, marvelous. Then, as your friend, Salem, allow me to show you around."

They made their way from front to back along the widest part of the upper deck. A few more steps brought them to an open hatch where wooden stairs descended into darkness.

"Here," said Ulysses. He stepped down the stairs one by one. "Watch your step." He ducked under the low beams. Salem crouched.

"There are twenty-nine full-timers on board," said Ulysses. "Thirty with you."

"Full-timers?" Salem asked.

"Right. Those who live on the ship," Ulysses grunted as he stepped from the last step down onto the corridor.

"And the ship—all you—full-timers," said Salem, trying again at the question. "What do you do? I mean, now we have cars and planes and trains and well, faster, better boats. What do you need this one for?"

Ulysses stopped in a way that made Salem think he had been expecting the question. He watched his uncle motion toward the coast and town.

"If anyone ever asks you that question, you tell them we are in old-world tourism. Reenactments from back in the day, sailing before steam, pirate nights on Halloween, the works."

"When you say anyone, do you mean everyone?" As Salem asked, it occurred to him that Ulysses, as opposed to most crewmembers on the ship, was not wearing one of the chord necklaces.

"I mean anyone not on this ship," Ulysses answered.

"Okay, so if you are some tourist attraction to them," Salem said, looking toward the coastline, "then what are you, really?"

A wide grin spread across Ulysses' face, and for a moment Salem saw the boy from the old photographs with his mother.

"No need to overwhelm you on your first day. We'll get you some proper instruction soon enough."

Proper instruction? Salem did not understand what his uncle meant.

"Instruction like school?" he asked.

"Much better than school," said Ulysses. "Instruction like life—authentic life."

"Watery, watery Warminster and his new baby Swan," came a dramatic voice behind them in the corridor. Salem had heard no one approach but turned with Ulysses to find a short but husky man leaning against the wall in the shadows. "Yet another orphan on board; oh, that'll never do."

"Dover," said Ulysses. "Don't you have somewhere to be?"

The man stepped into the dim light of the corridor. He wore a billowy white shirt that was dirty and had his hands in his pockets so that only his very narrow face and very curly hair were visible. Salem thought he looked much like an upside-down pear—large at the top and shrinking in size down toward his feet.

"I have right here to be," Dover said. He smiled and turned his attention to Salem. "And you must be Salem." Dover took his hand out of his pocket and extended it to Salem, who hesitated but shook it. In contrast with Dover's outer appearance, his hand was smooth. "Dead parents, isn't it?" Dover added. "Mine too. If you ever need anything, I'm all ears." Dover raised a hand and cupped it around his unusually pointed ear.

"Thanks," said Salem, and was not sure if he meant it. Dover's light-brown eyes flickered rapidly, as if they were taking in more than what was there. They seemed to say words of their own.

"Thank you, Dover," said Ulysses, sliding in between them.

"Dover!" cracked a voice from the deck above. Dover winced, and his eyes left Salem and followed the sound in an anxious flutter. "Dover!"

Dover sighed. "Alas." He waived his arms theatrically. "I am summoned." Dover looked intently at Salem. "Something tells me we have more in common than you realize, Salem Swan."

A commotion began from up above, and Dorianna appeared halfway down the staircase. "Hello, Warminster-Swan," she said. She panted as if she had just run across the deck. She looked at Dover. "When I give you a task, Dover"—Dorianna's words were icy, stripped of cordiality— "I expect it done immediately and completely to the end." Dover looked back apathetically into Dorianna's eyes. Slowly his lips parted to speak, but no words came out. He bowed his head ever so slightly to Salem and Ulysses and hurried up behind Dorianna, who had already turned up the stairs.

"Gnomes," said Ulysses. "They're always doing that."

Gnomes, Salem thought. Had he heard that right?

"But don't worry about that for now," said Ulysses. "Every ship has its Dover."

Dover was strange, surely. Salem had noticed that immediately. Though that did not make him wrong about what he said. Salem was an orphan, an orphan stuck on a boat with people, odd people he hardly knew. Ulysses looked at Salem knowingly, as though he could read his face.

"Your mom loved you, Salem. You know that. I haven't been…" Ulysses trailed off.

Salem nodded. He knew what Ulysses wanted to say, and he knew his mother had loved him. Still, the words had left Dover's mouth, crossed the space, and fixed themselves somewhere in Salem's mind like a stain he could not wash away. Ulysses put his arm around him.

"But you're here now. Come on, I'm sure you're ready to put down your things." Salem followed Ulysses through a short doorway into a cabin the size of a closet.

"This will be your bunk," said Ulysses, motioning to a bare wooden rectangle and moving to one side so Salem could stand across from him.

Salem looked around the cramped space. To call it simple would have been an understatement. A dresser sat at the back wall of the cabin against the rib of the ship. To each side was a bed. Salem noticed the crinkled sheets on the bed opposite his own.

"Someone else is in this room, too?" he asked, but Ulysses was already halfway out of the door.

"Make yourself at home," said Ulysses. "I'll come and get you later. You must meet your instructor for the next few days."

"Instructor?" asked Salem.

Ulysses winked. "You didn't think you'd get room and board here just for doing your schoolwork, did you? We're going to teach you some actual skills, too, starting with cooking."

The cabin door closed, and for the first time since leaving Pennsylvania behind, Salem was alone. As he stared at the closed door, he turned over in his mind all that had transpired over the day so far. The strange town, the strange ship, and the people on it. So many new experiences tumbled through his thoughts. It surprised him he was dealing with it as well as he was, considering he usually had trouble dealing with new people and situations. That thought alone made him panic at the overwhelming nature of it all.

He turned away from the door, hoping that if he began unpacking, he would stay calm and keep the newness of it all from overwhelming him. He pulled open the drawers of the dresser and found the two on the right already occupied. The clothes looked normal enough. A few shirts, a few pants, some socks. The shine of something underneath a shirt sleeve caught his eye, and he stopped. Hoping no one would enter the room, he delicately pushed away the shirt to reveal a golden picture frame. The picture inside was of a family. Two handsome, dark-skinned parents stood together as a line of children, all varying in height and age, stood in a line in front. The faces of the family looked somber, set into a resigned melancholy that seemed to look back into Salem, investigating him through the photograph.

Well, all the faces but one. The littlest child at the end of the line beamed. It was a big, infectious smile, and Salem grinned while he looked at it. What a crazy child that must have been. He replaced the picture, careful to fold up the shirt the way he had found it.

He opened the remaining two drawers. They were vacant save for a dead spider whose legs had curled up underneath itself. "Why do they always do that?" he asked out loud. He took out the dead spider, promising silently to give it a proper send-off once back on deck. He added the few clothes he had to the dresser and slid shut the drawers.

He laid his things to the side, and unpacked a pillow and a blanket he had brought from home, caring little about the current emptiness on his side of the cabin or the alien bunk that creaked as he laid down. New faces and questions swam around in his head like sharks, each fighting the others for space in his mind.

He reached down and from his backpack pulled up the worn journal. It was something he often did when he felt uncomfortable. He flipped it open to a random page in the middle. It showed a series of scribbled paragraphs of which Salem could only read bits and pieces. One short sentence read: *castles carved into mountains.* To the right of the paragraphs was a scribbled illustration like those found throughout the journal. This one was of mountains that seemed to possess many doorways and windows. Salem did not know what "castles carved into mountains" could mean, or what the strange-looking creatures sketched next to the words represented, but he enjoyed trying to visualize it all and hold it in his mind. He imagined he could see it in three dimensions, doorways and tunnels winding through the mountains, which would lead him to unknown adventures.

Whether it was these swimming thoughts, the fatigue of travel, or the salty still air of the cabin, he could not tell. Sleep was searching for him, and he wanted to be found.

• • •

Not far away, in the captain's quarters of the ship, Fern sat with Ulysses.

"I don't know what I'm doing." Ulysses was rocking back and forth in his chair.

"Give it time, Ulysses. He's only just arrived."

"I can tell he's bitter. I can tell he doesn't like me."

"You're being too hard on yourself," Fern reassured him. "Salem's just lost his mother and his home. Just be yourself, be there for him, and I think the rest will come."

"Right, because that's worked out so well for you and Juniper so far." Ulysses raised his eyes to meet Fern's. "I'm sorry," he said. "That was unfair."

Fern paused and looked out of the opaque glass windows at the back of the room. The last of the day was sneaking through, illuminating the cabin in a dusk light which he thought never lasted long enough. "You're right. My relationship with Juniper is not what I'd like it to be. She resents me for what I did to her mother and I resent myself for the same, plus so much more."

"Leave all that for now," said Ulysses. "Let's talk about something else. Tell me about the meeting."

Fern nodded his head, happy to change the subject. "Her name is Aurora."

"Her? You met one only?"

"Her," confirmed Fern. "And not just any woman. It was strange. She seemed so terrified. Even there in the tavern where I told her she was safe."

"Of course, she was terrified," said Ulysses. "Have you seen the hygiene at the Wanderway? Eryk has been wearing the same shirt for a decade. Frankly, it's disgusting. But anyway—" Ulysses waved his hand as if to symbolize that the cleanliness of the tavern was far out of his control. "What did she say?"

"She spoke of the Regulat. What they'd done to her and her people."

"This we knew from the message," said Ulysses. "What I want to know is what she is and how many of her there are that we'll be taking."

"Frost giant," said Fern.

Ulysses spit up some wine. "Giants! Are you insane? The last time we took giants they nearly sank the ship."

"You have the gift of saying what others only think, Ulysses, but you know we can't discriminate. Besides, those were mountain giants, creatures of the land, scared of water. These are frost giants. Maybe they won't be so… averse."

"Maybe," said Ulysses flatly and folded his arms. "So how many?"

"That's the thing."

"What's the thing?"

"We have to get them first."

"Going to giants where the giants live sounds like one of the worst plans we've ever had."

"Says the man who almost got his arm ripped off by a yeti, his skin melted off by angry infernis, his head bitten off by those wolpertingers, and my favorite, almost having his and all of our fingers nibbled off one by one by that—"

"Okay, okay," said Ulysses, raising a hand in submission, "so we've gotten ourselves into a few situations."

"You've gotten us into a few situations. This one hardly sounds like our worst."

"What can I say? Life's more fun that way."

"Life is definitely shorter that way," said Fern.

"And that enfield would not nibble them off one by one. She promised to do each hand together, five at a time."

"So you say," answered Fern.

Ulysses was peering down into his cup. "Do you ever see shapes in your wine, Tierney? Like the same way you can see shapes in the clouds."

"This is serious," said Fern. "If giants are being hunted that means the Regulat is stronger and more present than we realize." Fern paused, chewing on the thought like he was chewing on a tender piece of steak. "One of us needs to go back to Crawford. Make sure it's as ruined as we left it." Fern watched Ulysses consider the proposal. "If you're not up to it…"

"I'll stop by," said Ulysses, "but I'll need a day to do it."

"A day you have, but not more. We leave the day after tomorrow."

"Wait," said Ulysses. "What about Salem? I can't just leave him now. He'll think I've abandoned him."

"He'll be okay." Fern tried to sound as reassuring as he could. "It's only a day and you're the only one besides me I trust to do this. I'm sure Artichoke will keep him busy enough."

"I'm almost afraid to leave him alone with Art."

"Don't be," said Fern. "He won't be alone."

"I suppose you're right."

"Trust me," said Fern. "He'll be fine."

"Trust," Ulysses repeated. "I trust you, Tierney. That's why I put up with your antics."

"As if you have no antics of your own," answered Fern.

"I'll admit that being perfect isn't easy," said Ulysses. "No matter how easy I make it look."

Fern only shook his head. "Are you sure it hasn't been me putting up with you for all these years?"

"If it has, then it's been a lucky time for you, hasn't it?" Ulysses raised his glass for a toast. "To those who guide us."

Fern raised his own. "To the guide within."

CHAPTER 6 | GREEN, ARTICHOKE'S GOURMET GRUB, AND A BIT OF SASS

He is somewhere deep underground. The space is dark with no perceptible boundaries. Out in front of him, shrouded in a golden light, is an enormous tree, curved and twisted like a giant snake. Other people stand beside him, though he cannot see their faces. There is only the tree and a sound like a hummed song, reverberating all around.

He walks toward the trunk alone while the others around stand still. Droplets of water like tiny crystals hang suspended as if attached to strings in the ceiling. He breathes one in and chokes, falling to the ground as he convulses in fear and pain, searching for air. He is facedown then, attempting to draw a last breath when hands, strong but soft, turn him over onto his back.

The face that looks at him is foreign yet familiar. Not of him, but of his world. It is old in a way not of his time, but another time altogether. A time of monsters.

His vision is fading now with loss of air. He tries to scream, but nothing comes out. It paralyzes him. All he can do is look into the creature's eyes, one black, one cloudy like old milk, before everything goes dark.

• • •

"Whoa," said the blurry shape of the face. "Bad dream?"

Salem sat up in the bed, gasping for breath. He felt something wet on the side of his cheek and raised his hand to the spot. Embarrassed, he wiped away the drool.

"Yeah," he said. His head still in a fog. The face looking down at him was handsome with eyes so green they looked as though tiny jungles filled with leaves and sunlight lived inside. The boy could not be much older than Salem, though he was an inch or two taller.

"What time is it?"

"Almost nine," said the boy.

"In the morning?"

The boy must have recognized Salem's discomfort because he leaned back to sit on the opposing bunk. "I'm Adzee. Call me Zee."

Salem sat up on his elbows. Zee smiled back at him and revealed a gap in between his front teeth. Salem felt the ping of recognition. He had seen the face and that smile before. It took him a moment to recall the photograph from the drawer, the littlest child, now grown up into adolescent form.

"You must be Salem," he finally said.

Salem nodded, realizing he had not yet introduced himself.

"Sorry about your mother," Zee added, though Salem did not recall saying anything about that to Zee. "News travels fast on a ship."

"Oh," said Salem. Well, thanks."

"Welcome to the room," said Zee. "That's the dresser and the mirror." Zee stretched his arms out wide in presentation. He had the build of a giant tree frog with muscular legs that were long and extended far out into the middle of the room, even as he sat on the bed. He wore a long-sleeved tan shirt with ripped cargo pants that had holes and exposed his dark skin underneath. He stared at Salem unabridged, as if staring intensely at someone was fashionable. Salem stood up, trying to shake away the last of the sleep-fog still drifting through him.

"You'll be doing instructions with us I heard! That's great. I was afraid it would be just me and Juniper. Can you believe we're leaving again tomorrow already?"

"Yeah, instructions, my uncle mentioned that and—wait," Salem stopped short. "Did you say leaving?"

"That's just what I heard," said Zee. "Seems like we're at sea these days more than we're not."

"Where are we going?"

"Don't know yet. Captain hasn't said. Don't worry. We'll have fun."

Salem's worry must have been visible on his face. What is he going to do at sea? The thought of being out in the middle of something so vast made him woozy. "Have you seen Ulysses?" he asked. "I think he wanted to come get me. Something about going to the kitchens to get an artichoke?"

"I'll take you there," said Zee. "I have to go that way, anyway."

• • •

Salem followed Zee through a maze of tight corridors. The ship's underbelly had no perceptible pattern, and Salem wondered how and if he would find his way back later.

"If it looks like a maze down here, that's because it is."

"How long have you been here?" Salem asked. "On the ship, I mean."

"Pretty much my entire life."

"Your entire life?"

Zee slowed, allowing Salem to catch up and walk beside him. "Yeah," he said, looking thoughtful, "I grew up here."

"Really?" Salem tried to sound casual. "I can't imagine growing up in a place like this."

Zee laughed.

"Why is that funny?" asked Salem.

"Because," said Zee, "I can't imagine not growing up in a place like this."

Salem thought about what Zee had said as they walked. To think someone, roughly his own age, could find life aboard a boat so normal seemed amazing.

All around them strange pictures hung off the walls of what looked like epic scenes of faraway landscapes and times. Between those pictures hung the occasional portrait of what Salem guessed were crew members or previous captains. To think any of this was normal or a part of everyday life felt bizarre, and as the corridors of the ship tightened into even more labyrinth-like passages, Salem had the distinct sense that the anatomy and layout of the boat was not at all what he expected. It was much more twisty and turny than he would have ever imagined a ship to be. It was around the point that he thought they must have walked at least twice the length of the ship that, from around an approaching corner, Ulysses appeared.

"Salem!" Ulysses' expression was a mixture of happiness and worry. "I came earlier, but you were asleep, and I didn't want to wake you, so I left and now here you are with Zee."

"No problem," said Salem. "We were just going to the kitchens."

"I'll leave you now," said Zee, clearly wanting to give Salem and Ulysses time alone. "See you later, Salem."

"See you later, Zee," said Salem, somehow sad to see Zee go.

"I've spoken with Captain Fern," said Ulysses, steering Salem down the corridor of the ship. "And we think it's best if you come with us on our next voyage."

"Zee mentioned that," said Salem. "Ulysses, I know nothing about any of this. Sailing or the ocean or anything. I guess I didn't think I'd be going. Well, with school and everything."

"We said we'd get you enrolled, and we will. The school can understand if you take a family leave for a few months. As for the other stuff. You'll learn that too." Despite the doubt he felt in himself and in his grasp of the entire situation ahead of him, Salem found that he was imitating Ulysses' grin. He had never sailed or been out to sea, whatever that meant. Still, he had been pushing the thought of starting over at a new school as far to the back of his head as possible. He rarely talked about his social anxiety, or that it had led to his homeschooling in the first place, but he would take the awkwardness of one uncle over that of hundreds of kids he did not know. Yeah, Salem thought to himself, I can do this. It might not be so bad.

"Ulysses?" A thought burst into Salem's mind. "Are you pirates?"

Ulysses laughed out loud. "Goodness, Salem. No, we aren't pirates."

Salem exhaled. He was relieved but also somewhat disappointed with the answer as they stopped under a doorway over which a homemade sign made of driftwood read Artichoke's Gourmet Grub. The word "gourmet" had been scribbled in what looked like marinara sauce.

Then under the doorway the silhouette of a massive person appeared.

"And there is Warminster, and there's his Swan." The man's meaty body was the shape of a monster-truck tire. He held the largest cooking pot Salem had ever seen.

"Salem," said Ulysses. "This is Artichoke."

"Artorius Sebastian Link," said the man in his nasally voice, setting down the massive pot with a thud on the floor and wiping a greasy hand on his apron. He extended it toward Salem. "Head chef and magician aboard this floating wonderland. Call me Art, Arty, Artichoke, whatever tickles your fancy. Long as I don't have to tickle it."

"Salem Swan," said Salem as he took the chef's hand, realizing that it was as greasy as it looked.

"Parents were alliterates, huh?" Artichoke chortled to himself.

"Art's our happiness regulator here on board," said Ulysses.

"Good food, good mood," said Artichoke. "Bad food, well, you get the idea."

"You'll start your instructions with Art," said Ulysses.

Salem had no desire to spend time with Artichoke, who was without a doubt one of the weirder crewmembers he had met. Not to mention, Artichoke smelled like a mixture of all the foods Salem did not like to eat, including garlic and cucumbers. But Salem was in a place foreign to him, and he direly needed to understand more of whatever place it was. He nodded his head.

The mess deck or galley was the biggest area in the belowdecks that Salem had seen, containing a few rows of long tables and benches. They followed the waddling Artichoke past the rows and into two large back quarters that were the kitchens. Salem and Ulysses listened intently while the cook worked his way through the exhaustive list of kitchen protocols and equipment, careful to scrutinize each piece as he showed it to them.

"Alright, Art," Ulysses said after it became apparent the cook had no intention of stopping. "I think that's enough for the moment. You'll have plenty of time tomorrow."

Artichoke made a face, followed by a noise of genuine sadness. "I was just getting to the cutlery. Fine." He turned to Salem. "Salm—"

"It's Salem," Ulysses corrected him.

"That's what I said, Salm."

Ulysses shook his head and said nothing more. The cook turned back to Salem.

"Tomorrow after breakfast. You, me, and the other two get started."

Salem and Ulysses left Artichoke talking to himself in the kitchen and made their way back toward the top deck. Salem was about to follow Ulysses around a corner when a foot appeared from an adjacent corridor.

"So, you're the new guy." A body followed the foot. She had an olive tint to her skin that looked light compared to her black hair. Her brown eyes studied Salem so intensely he had to look away. "How old are you?" She crossed her arms and did not try at all to mask her unapproving tone. "Twelve?"

"Fifteen," answered Salem, feeling the heat rise in his cheeks.

"Well, you look like your twelve."

"Salem, this is Juniper," said Ulysses. "Juniper Fern."

The girl now turned to Ulysses. "What are you thinking, Lyss? There's no way he should come with us, even if he is your family. How do you know we can trust him?"

"I would think the captain's daughter would have a little more understanding for the meaning of family on board," said Ulysses, nudging Juniper with his shoulder.

"That's different," she said, pulling away.

"Is it?"

"I had no choice."

"Neither did Salem."

Juniper's eyes moved from Ulysses to Salem before returning to Ulysses.

"Whatever." She looked back to Salem now. "Probably best for you to keep a low profile. You know, the less you say, the less you do, the better. Don't expect me to make up for you in instructions either." She turned and disappeared up the hallway.

"Fern has a daughter?"

"The infamous Juniper Fern. You will not find a more temperamental creature on land or sea. But relax," said Ulysses, noticing Salem's thoughtful face, "you didn't expect everyone here to be sweethearts right away, did you?"

"Guess not," said Salem.

"Juniper's the girl that'll make you earn the right to stand within fifteen feet of her. But don't worry, she'll come around if you make the effort."

"Do I want her to come around?"

Ulysses only smiled and shook his head, leading Salem away in the opposite direction.

"These instructions I keep hearing about. Will we have classes or something?"

"Yes," said Ulysses. "You, Juniper, and Zee. You're all fifteen and aboard this ship that means instructions."

Salem waited, unable to respond out of the sheer fact that he was trying to comprehend how he would manage additional instructions on top of everything else. Ulysses sighed. "I'm sure this is a lot. Give yourself some time and it'll all be alright."

"Oh, I'm fine," Salem lied.

"I have to go into town and run an errand tomorrow," Ulysses added. "You'll be able to find your way back here okay?" Salem nodded that he could, though he became less sure of it as they made a right turn followed by an immediate left. "If you get lost, remember, it's a ship, so eventually you'll either find somebody or you can just climb up on deck and reorient yourself."

"Okay," said Salem. "You sure I can't help you with whatever you have to do in town?"

"Oh no," said Ulysses, "best I go alone."

CHAPTER 7 | CRAWFORD HEIGHTS

Crawford Heights had a large central courtyard in the shape of a horseshoe. It led up to the principal building, fashioned in the style of those that would have adorned eighteenth-century Paris. It oozed an assumed elitism that made it hard for Ulysses to appreciate it, even in its decay.

He took small steps as he walked across the courtyard. He moved slower than usual, knowing what had happened there and why it looked the way it did. The memories had not faded as he hoped they would.

He scoffed to himself under his breath. Here was a place where rich parents used to drop off their spoiled kids. He should know; he had been one. He walked forward, staring at the now mute fountain at its center. It was cracked and old, and its marble had turned yellow and brown with age in many spots. Stagnant pools of green water filled its basins. At the fountain's lowest level, carved out through the marble, was a forest. A diversity of trees weaved from trunk to trunk through vines, ferns, and flowers, each more intricate than the next (except for where it was chipped). The second basin atop the forest sculpture was smaller. Here the essence carved was that of fauna. Boars, horses, tortoises, a black bear, two elephants, a falcon, whales, fish, and an assortment of other animal life on Earth, even insects, sprawled in immaculate detail. The sculpted center led up to the final and smallest basin, upon which a single pair of figures leaned into each other. The bodies of a man and woman stood arm in arm. Ulysses smiled. If not for the illusion the fountain tried to sell, then for the sheer irony that the man's head of the statue had at some point, most likely during the battle, blown clear off.

A few steps beyond the fountain, Ulysses came to a flight of stairs. They led up from the courtyard to Crawford's front doors. They were big and imposing doors made of wood that looked impenetrable to rot. Ulysses ascended the stairs slowly, listening between steps. He heard nothing but a faint buzzing somewhere behind the old structure's walls.

Though run-down the building still looked to be in decent shape—but that did not mean he trusted it. In their line of work, Ulysses and the rest of the crew had learned that old things broke, all the time, without warning. It was literally a hazard of the job. Old packs, old buildings, old promises, it all broke eventually. The question thereafter was always twofold: could it be fixed, and what would it take to fix it?

At less than an arm's length from the doors, he noticed a broken padlock sprawled out on the stone in front of him. Strange, he thought, but the image was out of his head before it materialized. The buzzing on the other side was louder. Taking a deep breath in for good luck and better judgment, he reached out and gripped the doorknob in his hand. It squealed a little as it turned but took less force than expected. He stepped inside, closing the door slowly and quietly behind him as if to enter a crowded library full of irritated people.

It was the first time returning to the place since the battle that changed all their lives years earlier. He remembered the day they discovered that the Regulat was using the old school as a headquarters, a training ground, a prison. Ulysses shook his head at the memories. Back then, no one knew how bad things were. How many countless lives disappeared because people could not think for themselves? Even if he had been one of them, Ulysses did eventually find the light. That stand, he thought to himself, cost us a lot. He thought about the friends lost during the battle. It took him to many places in his mind but eventually back to Rigel, and from there, Salem. How was he going to tell Salem about his father?

Ulysses willed himself back to the present, choosing instead to focus on the growing sound of the buzz. Looking around, he noticed that the interior, compared to the outside, looked cleaned up and in the late stages of renovation. Someone has been here, he thought, but once again he could not hold it in his mind more than a second before it faded.

Dust clouds drifted around the space in swirling vortexes of amber as Ulysses made his way to the back of the entrance foyer to another set of doors which led into the school's former great hall. This space also looked cleaned up, modernized—even better than it had looked decades ago when Ulysses had been a student and Crawford had still been a school. "Odd," he said out loud.

The humming grew louder, and Ulysses realized it came from somewhere across the space of the great hall. He was not sure but as he walked, it sounded like the hum was consistent. It was not only consistent, he realized; it was melodic. This was the part where his gut told him to turn, stroll away, and inquire no further. He paused. The melody had changed, and this one was familiar. It was a song. It was a nursery rhyme. Ulysses knew it well, and that bothered him immensely.

Still frozen in place, he decided. To turn was not an option. He walked with feigned confidence, and real dread, toward the sound.

The great hall broke apart into antechambers at its back: small rooms where the faculty of the school used to meet during mealtimes to talk about the students they liked and, more importantly, the students they did not. Ulysses sensed the eerie twinge of recognition scurry up and down his spine. He was one of those students they would have talked about, and not one they had particularly liked.

It was now, in front of these chambers, that Ulysses tracked with his eyes what his ears picked up as the source of the humming. "There you are," he said, trying hard to ignore the impulses to leave that stung him like a swarm of invisible wasps. Of the six antechamber doors, he had picked the second to the left. He took a breath in and began counting to ten in his head. One, two, three… and a memory materialized in his mind.

He was standing in the garden of his house as a boy, in front of the big oak tree which always seemed to him to have been growing there since the beginning of time itself.

"Come on!" yelled his older sister, reaching her hand down from the branch. "You can do it Lyss, don't be scared."

"It's too high," Ulysses called back.

"Do what I do," his sister said. "If you must do something that scares you, start counting to ten. Before you get to ten, you need to start doing whatever it is you're scared of."

"What if I don't?"

"Just count!"

Ulysses closed his eyes. "One, two…"—he bent his knees preparing to jump— "three, four, five…"

"Jump, Lyss, go for it!"

Ulysses jumped up as hard as he could, extending his hand upward and forgetting all about counting. A moment in eternity, the biggest small thing in the universe, and his hand grasped together with his big sister's.

"There," she said, smiling and pulling him up. "Didn't I tell you?"

Four, five…

Ulysses turned the doorknob and walked forward into the humming room.

It was illuminated by light pouring in from skylights above; themselves laden with dirt and debris from the many seasons run rampant over them. The result was a fragmented assortment of weak bands of light illuminating sections of the room. A long wooden table accompanied by disheveled but matching chairs sat idly in the middle. The room's wallpaper, a netlike pattern of squares and circles, was peeling off in multiple places, exposing chunks of wall underneath. The space was otherwise empty, filled only with perfect stillness. The humming had ceased so completely that Ulysses questioned whether it had ever existed at all. "It's dangerous, Lyss," he said to himself, "questioning your sanity already at this age."

"Sanity is boring. Who wants boring?" The voice was light, almost comical, and had a boppity-bop motion to it.

An eerie chill, beginning at the back of his neck, snaked its way down toward his toes. Ulysses did not turn immediately. It was like he had somehow known the voice would come and was careful not to scare whatever it was away. Slowly, he rotated his neck, followed by the torso, and finally the legs and feet.

In the doorway stood a man. He had dark skin that looked like it had seen many days of sun and a soft wrinkle of middle age, which was both handsome and sad at the same time. He held a posture which was the sort of easy lean of a man who has accepted that the world cares little about his own personal saga. He had very round and very dark eyes. Eyes that seemed to Ulysses to be looking as much through him as at him.

"I'm sorry," said Ulysses, not sure why he was apologizing, "I didn't realize there was anyone here."

"No need for sorries," said the man with an almost cheerful waggle of his head. "Gandha cleans and Gandha listens and Gandha sings and Gandha doesn't need sorries."

Gandha wore a white-and-blue robe that stopped just short of his ankles. His hair was a dark gray. He was shorter than Ulysses with a build resembling a marathon runner. He pushed a small bucket on wheels in front of him and held a mop awkwardly in his hand, as if it might come alive at any moment and bite him.

"What is it the sir needs?" Gandha asked with a tone of genuine fascination.

"Oh," said Ulysses. He had been so sure that the place would be vacant that he had not even thought to prepare an answer to the question. "Actually, I'm a little lost," he quickly half-lied. "Was trying to get back to the main road." Gandha cocked his head in a way that suggested he wanted to believe Ulysses, but something would not let him.

"Gandha can show you how you must go." The small man raised his arms and began a detailed narration of directions, careful to gesticulate each part of the journey Ulysses would take to the main road.

Ulysses' mind raced. He asked himself how this could happen, that someone like this man was here. Yet each time he tried to pin down an exact question, it seemed to float away again, just out of his reach.

"Wha—" Ulysses struggled to even remember the words he wanted to say. The song, the nursery rhyme, was back. It was like someone had jammed the signals in his brain. "What did you say you were doing here?" he managed with great effort.

"Gandha cleans for the new school they will build."

New school, Ulysses thought to himself, but that made little sense. Crawford had been closed for decades, and after what had happened, he doubted anyone would send their children there again. "Why…" Ulysses asked, but the thought vanished as quickly as it had come. It was as if the synapses in his brain were on strike.

"Come, come," said Gandha kindly, taking Ulysses' arm with a bony hand. The smaller man's grip was surprisingly tight. "Let Gandha show you where you go."

Ulysses felt something inside himself trying to rebel. It entreated him to stop and inquire further, but before it could materialize, something else swooped in. A foreign feeling of calm that reassured him all would be okay. He did not know where the feeling came from, only that he was powerless, or at least felt powerless to it. Reluctantly, he allowed Gandha to usher him out of the antechamber and back into the great hall which to his surprise looked as dilapidated as the last day he had seen it. No longer was there any sign of renovation or construction.

"That's weird," he said. Broken pieces of metal and wire, links from chains, and other debris were strewn across the floors, as if some suicidal junkyard robot had dismantled itself in a rage, tearing pieces of its metallic body apart and throwing them in every direction.

"What is weird, sir?" Gandha asked politely.

"Well, the..." Ulysses motioned around to the debris, but the thought was out of his head before he could say anything.

Ulysses found that as he walked, he recalled less and less of what had taken place at Crawford. He also found that it did not bother him in the least.

Gandha and Ulysses approached the door through which Ulysses had moments before entered.

"Gandha has brought you here," Gandha said happily, "you must now go home, wherever that might be. Gandha wishes you well on your journey."

Ulysses looked dumbly at the smaller person.

"Thank you," was all he could think to say. He turned, descended the steps, and passed the fountain with the headless man, across the looping driveway and growing shadow of Crawford Heights, without looking back.

• • •

Gandha stood nervously for a few long seconds behind the enormous doors of Crawford Heights. He knew he had been late to catch the man, but he had erased the knowledge. All would be well, he reassured himself. He sighed and picked up his mop and bucket of props. He started humming his favorite nursery rhyme. It was all he could do to keep himself calm while he waited for the black-suited people he knew must come.

CHAPTER 8 | THE STORY OF KANE O'MALLEY

"Instructions!" barked Artichoke as Salem, Zee, and Juniper stood before him. The cook wore the same cream-colored apron Salem saw him in on the first day. Ladle in hand, Artichoke looked like a great grumpy bear, with a patchy beard and short and thinning dirty-blond hair, who had just woken up from hibernation. "You're lucky enough to begin your instructions with me. Now listen close. People out there"—Artichoke pointed a thick finger at the wall closest to the mainland—"they're getting dumber and it's my job to make sure you don't go getting dumb yourselves."

Salem turned his head, first to Zee, and then to Juniper, both of whom had bemused looks on their faces.

"Humph," said Artichoke in response to himself. "Now first things first, you need to know that no matter what you are, human or otherwise, we all have the same needs. We all need shelter, food, and love. We are all the same particles and dust. But we'll get to all that big stuff later."

"Sorry, Artichoke." Salem regretted speaking once the cook had set his tiny, sharp eyes on him.

"You can call me Art, boy."

"Um, Art," stumbled Salem. "You said 'human or otherwise'?"

"That's right. Whatever form of creature you take. That clear enough for you, Salm?"

Salem nodded his head, as the eyes of Zee and Juniper turned on him. The cook must mean animals, he guessed.

The three received varying tasks then, around different areas of the kitchen. Salem scrubbed pots and pans, cut vegetables, sharpened knives, and repeated. Artichoke rotated them so that even when Salem wanted to talk to Zee (because he did not have the same desire to talk to Juniper), it was impossible other than in short bursts of whispers.

This continued for the first two days of Salem's existence on the ship. The kitchen, according to Artichoke, was sacred. "This place," Artichoke said over and over, "it has secrets only discoverable through intense and prolonged study." It did not take long for Salem to see what the man meant, as the chef was fond of taste-testing. Even during the steps when Salem did not think taste-testing was necessary.

When the chef was not hypothesizing on the correlation between simple food recipes and the recipe for life itself, the self-proclaimed head magician on board educated his students on everything from nutrition at sea, to the dietary needs of the different crew mates, to German versus Japanese cutlery, and a few of the other choice topics Artichoke never tired of, including, but not limited to: why music (in general) hit its peak in the '70s (and never recovered); the differences between people with brains and people without brains; Artichoke's two nieces, Becky and Samantha; and the last worthwhile cartoon out there, a rhinoceros called Rigby.

"I heard we leave day after tomorrow," whispered Zee later that night as they lay in their cabin beds. Salem laid on his back, looking up at the dark ceiling.

"Any idea where?"

"Not yet," said Zee. "But it might be cold. I saw lots of cold weather stuff being loaded."

• • •

On day three, Artichoke called to Salem from the back of the kitchen. "Salm!" Salem theorized that the cook's great horizontal length must create an impressive lung capacity.

"What's up, Artichoke?" Salem called from across the kitchen.

"Scales and fire boy, call me Art."

"Sorry," said Salem.

"And stop apologizing! I need a bag of salt. You remember where they are?"

Salem did, or at least he thought he did. The cook had taken them on a brief tour of the storage room the day before.

"I do, Art," he answered, emphasizing the name.

"Hurry, too. We need to get all this stuff cooking now to be ready for dinner tonight. We'll have everyone."

Salem nodded, knowing it was best to end the conversation there. The crew would return in the evening to prepare for departure in the morning. A pit of nervous energy swirled in his stomach as he walked over to the hatch leading down to storage.

The hold was a long cavernous hollow so low that Salem's hair brushed against the ceiling. The space was dark and held rations of food, fresh water, and equipment of all kinds grouped together so that only tight passages snaked in between it all, big enough for a single person to walk down at a time. Salem stopped, unsure whether he remembered where the salt bags were. It could have been in the bags and the barrels by the wall, or in the crates stacked like the leaning tower of Pisa in the middle. Then, as his eyes followed the tower of crates down to the spot where a pile of metal rods and wooden boxes cascaded into an unkempt pile of stuff, something caught his eye. At this intersection, resembling an immature dandelion, was a small orb of yellow-white light.

It pulsed in waves of excited luminance as he looked at it. A trick of the light maybe, but there was so little light there, far too little to produce such a bright thing. It was not a ghost, at least not a ghost in the way Salem imagined ghosts to be. Spirit, he thought. Then again, he had never seen a spirit.

As he crouched, it pulsed in eager heartbeats until Salem's own heart speeded up, beat for beat, and their paces matched. He wanted to communicate with it, to tell it how pretty and lost it looked. He reached out, compelled to make contact for a reason he could not in that moment articulate or understand.

The tiny thing wavered like a mirage on a desert horizon and then, all at once, vanished.

Salem stopped, confused and sad. He moved away two of the wooden crates and pushed aside with his foot the metal pile of rods. A small walkway, hidden by the supplies, weaved in front of him. He stepped into the walkway and around the corner saw the orb again, floating as if it had been there all along. Its glow intensified when he saw it. He walked toward it faster this time, hopeful it would not get away. When he was within a foot, it vanished again. This happened three more times until Salem found himself at the back of the cargo hold, staring at the tired-looking pile of sacks labeled *SALT*.

• • •

"Art?" said Salem, as he emerged from the hold. "Are there any spirits on the ship?" The cook did not turn around but kept cutting the potatoes with the dexterity of a man of a much smaller build.

"Sprits? Of course, but I don't let the crew drink 'em till after dinner."

Salem did not know how to respond. "No," he said. "I saw something below just now. A trail of lights. They showed me where the salt was."

"Those aren't sprits boy, those are wisps."

"The what?"

"Will-o'-the-wisps, you know, the friar's lantern, hinkypunk, ghost lights?" Salem stared at the cook. "Troll toes, boy, what are they teaching in school these days?"

"What are they?"

"We picked those little guys up years ago and now they come and go as they please. Must enjoy it here on the ship, I reckon, seeing how safe it is and all. They're misunderstood, as is most everything nowadays. People think they want to lead you astray or into something bad. Truth is, they either like you or they don't and, if they like you, they'll help you; if they don't, well..." Artichoke flicked a slice of raw potato from the tip of his knife. It landed with a resounding *plop* into the water of the gargantuan cooking pot. "Harmless, though, I'd say. Must be something about you they like." The slightest twinge of a grin scooted across the big man's face as he turned and took the bag of salt from Salem.

It took the better part of the afternoon into evening for Artichoke, Salem, Juniper, and Zee to prepare dinner. Salem's mind was so caught up in what he had seen that his work became slow, a fact not missed by the cook.

"This would go faster," explained Artichoke, "if I didn't need to explain everything every time." The cook's tone was not mean, but there was a slight strain of irritation. Salem found this funny considering that Artichoke took immense pleasure in explaining just about anything he could imagine.

Night had fallen by the time the crew began entering the mess hall. Salem knew some faces from around the ship. Many he did not. Zee whispered names next to him. "That's Ena, and Nut, and Geb, and Dover, and Raiju, and of course you know Dorianna."

Salem smiled and nodded as Dorianna entered with the tall man who had first spoken to Salem and Mr. Gingam the first day. "That's Typhon," whispered Zee, waving to the long-necked man. Dorianna smiled back. Typhon tried, but the result was more of a grimace.

As the crew assembled onto the mess deck, Salem saw them for the first time in their entirety. They were a varied assortment of big, small, long, short, older, much older, and unknown. Some had large black eyes and others small eyes in which the irises were indistinguishable from the white. Some wore outdated-looking clothes and others of a fashion normal to the day. Some faces seemed kind, others frustrated; some seemed angry, while others just content. Yet despite the contrast of the crew, each looked at Salem with the same stare of intrigue.

Salem ignored the stares as best he could as he wiped the last of the tables. Instead, he concentrated on the smell of the food. It was, as Artichoke had predicted, putting the crew into a good mood. There was laughing and joke-telling and a great number of remarks that Salem did not understand but of which he could interpret the general meaning.

Next came Ulysses, followed by Fern. Salem had not seen Ulysses since his uncle had left for his errand in town. Unexpected relief washed over him as he saw him now, but as Ulysses smiled at him, Salem thought his uncle looked distracted, even uneasy. Captain Fern raised his arms, and the room grew quiet.

"My friends," said the captain, smiling. "I hope you've enjoyed the short days off the waves." A soft murmur accompanied by a few giggles rippled through the room. "Tomorrow we set sail again. Thanks for dinner to Artichoke and our novices. You know Zee and Juniper and we are happy to include our newest member, Salem Swan." Salem watched the eyes of the room turn on him, Juniper, and Zee as the crowd proceeded with a painfully slow clap. He waved with a goofy grin, a decision he instantly regretted as he looked out at the faces. The clapping died away as Fern once again raised his arms. "But first," Fern scanned the room, "let's look back before looking forward." There came then an energy, almost a pulse, vibrating through the room as the captain spoke. "So," said the captain with an air of conclusion, "I think it is prime time for a story." The crew broke now into true applause.

"Kane O'Malley," said the captain. He motioned to an old man sitting close to the front. "I believe it's your birthday today. Would you do us the honor?"

Kane reminded Salem of an oversized garden gnome as he moved from his spot on the bench. His age gave his skin a rusted color, and his face a chiseled look much the way a sculptor might try to portray early humans. A beard, long and pointed, hung off the bottom of the man's mouth and chin. Along it, small emerald pendants the shape of shamrocks stuck out here and there, weaved into the fabric of the hair.

Kane stood, moving the way an ancient tree might whose seed had waited a thousand years to sprout. Salem was close enough to hear the old man creak and crack and gasped when the tiny man did not stop once standing but proceeded with his hand on the shoulder of the man next to him, to climb atop the bench itself and from there up onto the table.

Salem and the crew watched as Kane O'Malley pulled a long pipe from a pouch hanging at his side. He lit the pipe, pulled, and smoked.

Kane reached a hand into the pocket of his trousers and pulled out a fistful of something no one could see. Slower than Salem could bear, he watched Kane reach his arm and close his hand out over the table, and then open his palm, releasing a fine golden powder that resembled miniature snowfall. There the flakes lay, reflecting off the gas lamplight of the mess deck, as Kane took another long draw in of his pipe.

"'Twas a dark and stormy night, ya know," said Kane in accented English, "when we saw the ship slip 'round the cape and into the brackish waters of the bayish moor." Salem liked the way Kane spoke.

Kane pulled back on his pipe and tilted his head toward the gold dust on the table. He exhaled out, allowing the smoke to stream into the powder. The smoke settled over the gold dust below the tiny man's face, held by the unblinking stare of his wrinkled eyes. Salem watched as the smoke moved and picked up the golden flakes, pinwheeling on itself, animating in the air and forming small shapes of gold and black. It circled a few times and settled into the shape of a flat disc. It was as if someone had taken the cross-section of the earth, allowing the rounded north and south poles to fall away.

Kane took another long pull of his pipe and blew smoke over the plane. The golden powder, first a shapeless cloud, spun into itself, and transformed into a small ship. It breached the golden cloud of smoke and settled on top of it. And there it anchored, bobbing to amaze the captivated spectators.

"'Twas bad times in Éire then for folk like me it was," Kane continued. "We'd gathered what little we had and who little we trusted, hiding out where little we could."

The shapes transformed again now, adding a tiny running band of sun-colored figurines alongside a gold and gray landmass which had appeared next to the bobbing miniature boat.

"Still they hunted us. Most of me own family'd already been taken care of, by meaning that care was taken there'd be no trouble from the likes of the Green sons and daughters no more."

The mess deck was silent as Kane spoke. Only the waves outside dared make any noise. New figures of gold appeared now, and they hunted the smaller, grabbing and stabbing them amidst much struggle.

"We were there, in a land to which we'd given much. A land we'd thrived on and made rich with life. No longer welcome but cornered in like vermin on the run. Cornered by people who couldn't tell ya the difference 'tween a rainbow and a rain cloud. 'Twas fear of the unknown that did it, ya know. You can't hope to reason with a person who's only believin' that what their eyes tell 'em. Humph," the small man snorted. "What d'ya expect? If there's one thing life has taught me it's that as greed grows, imagination dies."

The figures collected into a single colossus, holding a smaller figure upside down from the feet. The bigger smoke figure shook the smaller and Salem watched as hundreds of tiny golden flakes the shape of coins fell toward the floor.

Alongside the coins fell something else, smaller, rounder, softer things. Salem looked closer. It took a long moment for him to see the tiny tears as they rolled the wrong way up the face.

"You can believe they chased us up till the end. The people wanted us bad, they did. Wanted our luck, wanted our gold. They got neither. Came close to the heart strands of our spirit, but salvation is a curious thing."

Kane chuckled. The group of tiny figures disappeared into the miniature ship of particles. "With what remained of us, we flung out onto this boat. Steal to her we did like the thieves we were—stealing toward a freedom almost lost. Barely made it but make it we did. The ship gave us our lives and I give back to it, on this, me hundred and thirty-third birthday."

The miniature ship now turned on itself toward the open window. Its small golden sails filled, and it floated up and out of the opening into the chilly night air.

A full second of silence filled the deck before the cheers and whistles erupted. Kane smiled and bowed, cracking back into his seat.

• • •

Aurora looked up at the ship bathed in moonlight. She had taken great care to arrive at the docks unbeknownst to anyone. Fern's directions had been precise, although she had expected a more modern ship based on the stories. Voices and laughter vibrated up from the glowing orange portholes along the boat's sides as she ascended the gangway.

"Good evening," said Captain Fern, stepping out from the shadows just as she set foot onto the deck.

"Good evening," she said back.

CHAPTER 9 | BEHIND THE CURTAIN

Salty morning air filled the captain's lungs as he made his way up onto the ship's quarterdeck. He stood first at the wheel and then, stepping around it, he moved to his right to stand in front of the curved body of a bell. A frayed piece of rope swayed under the bell's open mouth. The captain knew three hard casts of his wrist would send the bell's song reverberating out over the decks. The bell meant movement. It was a command signifying that a voyage was about to begin. It would not be a surprise to the crew but a call to action.

Fern hesitated, thinking to himself as he always did before taking the plunge, if endangering the lives of his crew was worth the reward of what they might accomplish. It was then that his daughter appeared below him on the deck. The sunlight reflecting off her hair reminded him so much of her mother. Even the way she moved, the way she lifted her hand up to her brow to fend off the brightness, bore an uncanny resemblance to Aegle. What future would he leave for her and her kind if he did not do what was right today? What would be the price of inaction? These questions gave him clarity, and he could sense his uncertainty fading. Decisions, he learned along ago, were only hard until the right question came along.

We are naturalists, he thought, protectors. Smiling, he let the bell sing.

As he did, the captain met the eyes of the newest member aboard his crew. He needs to know, Fern thought, waving, and taking the stairs down toward Salem.

• • •

"Salem!"

Salem had watched the captain's eyes meet his and had somehow known Fern wanted to speak. He had come to the deck with Artichoke who, grumbling the entire way, agreed with the bell. It was time to get back out to sea. "I'm sorry we haven't spoken," Captain Fern said, dismissing Artichoke and extending his arm out to Salem. "Will you walk with me?"

Salem followed Fern along the main deck. That bell must mean a lot more than just time to set sail, he thought, as all around him the crew moved with newfound purpose and energy, like a beehive emerging from the depths of winter.

"So, what do you think?" the captain asked. "Ready to go to sea?"

The question caught Salem off guard. Of course not, he thought, and wondered if doctors ever felt ready to perform their first real surgery or if astronauts were ever truly ready to fly off into space. Not that he was comparing himself to doctors or astronauts, but the ocean in front of them was truly intimidating. "I think it's too late to turn back now," he told the captain, looking around the ship at the scurrying crew. "I don't know," he added nervously, "it's all fast."

"That I can understand," said Fern, nodding his head in agreement. "But too much time to think about something can be more dangerous than too little. I can't imagine all the things I wouldn't have done if I'd had more time to think about them."

They had come to the quarterdeck, a small area separating the main deck from the stern. Directly in front of them stood the familiar doors that led into the captain's quarters. "I'm nervous," said Salem, relieved to tell someone.

"Perfectly normal," said Fern, as if Salem's divulgence was a well-known fact. "I'd be concerned if you weren't a little nervous. Here." The captain opened the door and invited Salem inside. "There are some things you should know." They crossed the threshold into the familiar book towers and organized chaos that was the captain's quarters. Salem felt slightly calmer as the captain closed the door, cutting off the yells and noise of the crew prepping the ship for departure.

"I know what it feels like to be thrown into the darkness with no torch and no map. To be alone with only memories is a prison all its own." The captain sat down across the desk opposite Salem. "I know it is incomparable to how you feel, but we will all miss Julie. She was a wonderful person."

At the mention of his mother, Salem's stomach knotted. "You knew my mother?"

"I know this may come as a shock to you," said Fern. "Your mother did everything she could to keep you away from us after the accident." Fern released a long sigh, as if he were about to begin a long story. "Rigel, your dad, was a good friend of everyone on this ship. He was especially close with Ulysses and me. It was, in fact"—the captain grinned—"through Ulysses that your father met your mother. Did she ever mention that?"

With each passing word the captain spoke, Salem found himself equal parts captivated and terrified, wanting to know everything and, at the same time, nothing at all. He was literally leaning forward, hanging on everything Fern said. He could feel his chest tightening and the beginning of tears welling in his eyes. To think these people he thought were complete strangers had known his mother brought him a profound sense of comfort, and yet, to know that his mother had hidden such an immense piece of information from him felt like betrayal. Salem opened his mouth to answer the captain, but no words came out. Instead, the questions fired through his mind in rapid succession. Accident? Who? How?

"I can see this is a lot for you," said the captain.

Salem shook his head. "Tell me more, please."

"Very well," said Fern. "You have the right to know." The captain pointed across the desk toward Salem's lap. "I think you have something in your pocket which will help. A journal, maybe?"

Salem was not sure how the captain knew that his father's journal was folded into his back pocket. In that moment, he did not care. He pulled it out and placed it on the desk. The captain picked it up, running his hand over the cover as he did. "Mythology. We look for intelligent life all across the stars, while all the while it's right here with us. Tell me, what do you know about your dad, Salem?"

Salem shook his head, thinking about the void in his life which represented his father. "Nothing, really. I knew that my father loved books, and that he must have spent a lot of time with them studying fairytales and the worlds of made up things and..." Salem hesitated, "that he left us when I was young."

At the mention of this last part, Fern's eyes met Salem's. "Rigel did not leave you like you think he did, Salem. He was killed."

Salem felt sick. Somewhere inside he had always harbored the hope that his dad was out there and that, maybe, one day they would reunite. Still, the sadness he felt hearing the truth about his father differed from that of losing his mom and, in a way, it relieved him to have closure from the idea. "I just don't understand," he said. "Why would my mom lie to me?"

"To understand that," said Fern, "you have to know that she did it out of love and that there are people out there who sadly do not understand such love but choose instead to let fear into their hearts—and when you let fear into your heart, Salem, you make room for hate." Fern flipped open the front cover of the journal. "Your father was unique because he only had room for love in his heart. He was not capable of hate. This is something Ulysses and I still can't quite understand. Your dad could look at any being and see it for what it was at its essence—a heart, a mind, a life—a creature just like you and me, wanting to love, and learn, and find community and happiness. This made him a great naturalist." The captain shook his head as if he could not believe his own words. A glazed-over look had come into his eyes, as if in recounting the past to Salem he now found himself partially immersed in the vivid memories.

"Sir?" asked Salem, almost feeling bad to interrupt him. "Are you trying to say that the things my dad studied are real?" Salem knew the answer before the captain said anything. Somehow, he had known for a long time, but since coming to a ship, he felt as though the truth was an arrow speeding toward him, and it had now finally struck. Captain Fern's eyes returned to the present moment, and he looked up at Salem and smiled.

"Yes." Fern held up one page from Rigel's journal, on which the picture of what looked like a giant griffin was drawn. "They are as real as you and me."

"But then, where are they?" asked Salem. "Why don't we see them?"

"It's not so simple," said Fern. "The world today does not handle myth like the old world did. People used to respect ancient creatures, write stories about them, and sing songs in their honor. There was even a mutual respect between the Commons and the Fringe."

"The Commons and Fringe, Captain?" asked Salem, feeling as though he was in a class at school.

The captain nodded and turned the journal around so that Salem could more clearly see. Flipping through the pages slowly, the captain continued explaining. "These legendary creatures you see and read about did not come out of people's imaginations. Many inhabited the earth long before humans ever came along. But with time people came to fear them. Many are beasts after all and cannot learn a language like English. When people cannot understand other creatures' intentions, we become scared. So, humans pushed them away, either to extinction or to the Fringe. Your father believed that the two worlds can be united again—even coexist and thrive. I'm not so sure anymore…" the captain's voice trailed off.

"But where is the Fringe?" Salem asked eagerly, wondering how such a place could remain hidden. The captain opened his mouth to answer, but as he did a loud rapping came at the door.

"Yes?" answered Fern.

Juniper Fern burst into the room, a look of surprise spreading across her face upon seeing Salem.

"Oh," she said, "I didn't realize…"

"It's alright, Juniper. What's the matter?"

The captain's tone, his entire demeanor in fact, had changed. He was not the confident sea captain anymore, but a softer, maybe even nervous, man. Salem realized he was seeing not Fern the captain, but Fern the father.

Juniper also acted differently. She spoke differently than how she had upon meeting Salem with Ulysses. She was less confident and more distant. Both father and daughter seemed unsure of something…

"There's a fight on the deck," she said.

Fern looked at Salem, to Juniper, and finally back to Salem.

"Excuse me, Salem, we will continue after I've dealt with this issue."

With that, the captain hurried out of the room.

Juniper looked again at Salem. It was a look whose meaning is crystal clear for the sender and an utter riddle for the receiver. She followed her father out of the room and Salem followed her.

They emerged together on deck to find a circle of bodies. Salem continued after Juniper, who followed the captain as he pushed his way through to the center where two people were squared up against a single person standing opposite them. Through the morning sun, Salem squinted. The two standing closest to him faced in the opposite direction, but he was sure he had seen them already on the ship. He recalled Zee telling him they were the brother and sister known as Geb and Nut.

"They're a unique pair," Zee had told Salem after the dinner and Kane O'Malley's story. "The same in so many ways, but also different. You'll find Geb very down to earth and Nut, well, let's just say she's got her head in the clouds."

Now Salem saw the aspects that Zee had described. Geb looked earthy in his brown canvas trousers and muddied white shirt. Small pieces of green and twig stuck up and around a full but messy head of dark hair. Geb's features were in stark contrast to Nut's sky-blue dress that looked as though it was made of nothing but spare bits of wind and cloud. Oddly, Salem thought, though they were no doubt different, something about them made them one of the most fitting pair of siblings he could imagine.

The other person, however, Salem had never seen. She had brown hair and pale skin so fair as to render it almost translucent in the sunlight. Her icy-gray eyes stuck out against her dark clothes and tall boots that looked better suited for crossing mountains than oceans.

"Enough!" Fern's voice boomed when he wanted it to. He strode out into the middle. "Nut. Geb. Care to explain?"

"She insulted us," said Geb.

"I'm sure it's a misunderstanding," said Fern, looking between them and the woman.

"I merely asked," began the stranger in a thick accent, "who was the boy and who was the girl."

"That's not true," said Nut, "she called us ugly."

A few of the crew members laughed, and the siblings turned red.

"Enough," said Fern. The captain turned to the woman but spoke loudly enough for everyone to hear. "Everyone, this is Aurora Draxxon. Her people need our help. You will all"—Fern turned now to Geb and Nut—"treat her with respect." He turned back to Aurora. "Just as she will treat every one of you with respect." Geb nodded grudgingly, as did Aurora.

"I'm sorry if I offended you," she told them.

"Just a misunderstanding," said Nut, who now seemed more than happy to put the entire situation behind them.

"Now," said Fern, adopting a tone of ironic humor in his voice, "I assume that if we have time for this then we've completed all the other tasks required on a vessel such as ours?"

The crew members standing around shuffled awkwardly from side to side.

"Interesting," said Fern. Dorianna appeared at the captain's side, a look of exasperation covering her face.

"You heard the captain," she said, her reedy tone temporarily elevated to a stiff brass. "No time for this, move it."

"You must excuse me, Salem," said Fern, turning back to Salem, "but I think there are a few things I should attend to before we can properly finish our discussion. Zee will get you up to speed on prep for sailing." As if from nowhere, Zee appeared next to the captain.

"Absolutely, I will," said Zee, in a tone which sounded as if he had been there and listening the entire time. "Come on, Salem, we hoist."

Salem watched the captain depart, but his mind was still on their discussion. Three days earlier he had arrived on a train and everything had at least halfway made sense. Since that time, things had spiraled deep into the unknown.

"So, I just had a strange talk," he told Zee.

"That's good," said Zee, "those are the best kind."

"I guess," said Salem. "It's not really saying much since everything here seems strange."

"What do you mean?"

"What do I mean?" Salem tried to sum up the conversation he had just had with the captain, but each time he tried to start, he stopped again. "Sorry," he told Zee. "Sometimes I struggle to say what I'm thinking." Zee nodded, letting Salem know that he did not need to say anything more.

"Here," Zee said calmly, handing Salem a piece of rope, "pull this like this and lean back and hold it taut." Salem did so without thinking, and as he looked into Zee's eyes and face he saw no judgment there. It was the face of someone who cared beyond himself. It was the face of a friend.

• • •

The house of Wayne and Rose Manitou had two floors. Technically, there was a basement, though Rose rarely visited it. The stairs were too steep and the air too cool and damp. However, now she found herself deeper in the damp and further into the cool than she had been in a very long time, digging through boxes she had not seen in many years.

The days since her husband's untimely death had been the lowest of her life. Already an older woman, she knew that death would come eventually, but never had she expected for it to take her husband like it had so abruptly. She wanted some phone number she could call or an address she could go to. She would speak to the specter of death herself and request another go-around.

Out in front of her, like a series of sprawling islands, were scrapbooks full of pictures she had collected over their years together. Dinners, picnics, vacations, birthdays, a lifetime full of moments. She felt her chest collapsing in on itself as it had been doing sporadically over the past days. Slumping into the corner, she held one picture in particular close to her chest. It was of Wayne, shortly after they had bought their house. He was standing in front of their tiny, almost sad, garden. Rose remembered how thrilled she had been to simply have a garden with her husband. She had not cared whether it yielded ten baskets of vegetables or a single piece, because it had been theirs.

I need to get out of this basement soon, she thought, knowing that each day she spent wallowing in memories she grew more powerless to face the world outside. There was only one way she knew to deal with her pain. She would need to return to the place where Wayne died. She would need to see it with her own eyes and find closure. Though it was only a few hundred feet from where she sat, Rose knew the journey getting there was going to require all the strength she had.

CHAPTER 10 | GO

"You're sure that is all you saw?"

Ulysses nodded his head. Fern was not convinced. Crawford Heights had, at its best times, been a premier institution for young scholars. At the edge of the Easterly borders it was, at its worst, headquarters for one of the darkest organizations on the planet.

"There was no activity at the school? You're sure? You know what it could mean otherwise."

"Nothing," repeated Ulysses.

Fern considered the dark ocean before them. It was nighttime on the first day at sea. The crescent moon was high in the sky and cast a white light down onto the water. They had reached a section of the Atlantic known as the Sohm Plain. It was an area of flat ocean floor and varying depths that stretched out over that part of the world for hundreds of thousands of square miles, so that every direction looked like an endless frame.

"Then why do I feel that there's more?" continued Fern.

"Did you eat Artichoke's potatoes? I always tell you to avoid those." Ulysses smiled, but seeing the look of distress on Fern's face, turned serious again. "Look, Tierney, we know they're still out there, but I don't think they would go back to Crawford."

"Maybe," said Fern, though his voice sounded far less than sure.

"How is Salem doing?" asked Ulysses, changing the subject.

"He's curious, as he should be. I talked with him, but we were interrupted."

"Should I talk to him… about, well, you know, everything?"

"Leave all that to me," said Fern. "I told him the truth about Rigel."

"How did he take it?" asked Ulysses.

"All things considered, pretty well," said Fern. "He's the reflective type, Salem. A good mixture both his parents I'd say."

"And the Commons? And the Fringe?" added Ulysses. "Did you talk to him about all that?"

"Some of it," said Fern, "but not all. Might be for the best. The next few weeks will be a lot for him. I'm sure his journey will reveal the rest."

"That's true," said Ulysses. "Hopefully, I know him better by then."

"You will," said Fern and turned his head as a knock came at the door.

"Come in," said Fern.

"You wanted to see me," said Aurora, entering the room. She looked odd there in that moment on the ship, thought Fern, like a creature who did not belong so far out in the middle of the ocean. Then again, he looked closer; her eyes held the trace of something that he was sure was not present during their first meeting—hope. He could only describe this hope he saw in her as an icy fire, a level of determination that most would never achieve. He had seen it before and he knew, perhaps better than anyone, that it, more than anything else, would be the decisive factor if they were to win the war.

"I see something in your eyes that wasn't there before. Hope." Aurora blushed and looked down.

"For that I thank you, Captain. What do you want to discuss?"

"I believe you've met Ulysses Warminster," he told her.

"Not yet," said Ulysses, extending his hand to Aurora. She looked at it as though shaking it was the last thing she wished to do. "It's okay," said Ulysses. "I'm here to help too."

"I've heard about you," she said. "The funny-man assistant to Captain Fern. Can't take things seriously. Gets himself into trouble. Falls in love with many women."

Ulysses was speechless. "I, uh, did you say assistant?"

"Aurora," continued Fern, thoroughly enjoying the perplexed look on Ulysses' face, "can you give us an idea of how best to interact with frost giants? I'm afraid we have little experience with your kind."

"'Frost giant,'" scoffed Aurora. "That is what you call us to make us sound scary. We are the oldest of Nordic creatures. Keepers of the mountains. We are the Jotun of Jotunheim, not frost giants."

"Frost giants are cool," said Ulysses, trying to regain some lost composure. "And, as far as I know, they're usually…" Ulysses raised his arms as high over his head as he could.

"I'm only half Jotun," answered Aurora. "My father was human."

Aurora looked between the men and then, her face exasperated but determined, explained what they would do.

• • •

Above their heads, in a crevice of the ship known only to him, Roach barely breathed. He had received his name for two reasons. First, despite the multiple conflicts of which he had been a part, he always made it out alive. He was, in his unstable and turbulent way, so far unable to be killed. Second, he had an ability to squeeze into places and situations other people could never do, or more aptly, would never do.

He made use of the latter now as he tucked his foot up under his waist. He had discovered the crawl space above Fern's quarters some days before while, well, scouring the ship for just those types of places.

Listening between long, silent breaths, he tried to dampen the beating of his own heart. It was from the dark and quiet that he could best witness the world and do his work.

Some few feet below him he could hear the frost giant, or Jotun as it had explained, describing the arcane ways of her people. Only, nothing she described was as scary or disgusting or monstrous as Roach had thought. He knew what the Regulat was capable of and had done even more terrible and unthinkable things. How could it be that this mytho, this grotesque creature of common lore, seemed so civil? Something below caught his attention as confused and contradictory thoughts ran through his head.

"There was an unexpected bit of good news before I left," said the mytho below, a lightness entering her voice. "A child was born. First one in over twenty years."

"Twenty years," echoed Ulysses. "So, no other kids to play with, I guess then, huh? No brothers or sisters or cousins?"

Aurora's face was flat and unamused as she looked at Ulysses.

"That's very exciting," said Fern.

"It was," she continued. "Also, this child is old blood."

"Which means?" Fern asked.

"It means she has pure Jotun blood and can one day become matriarch."

"And that means?" asked Ulysses, his tone building off Fern's.

"And that means," said Aurora, "there is hope for our kind to continue. Like you said, Captain"—she looked at Fern — "there is even more reason to hope."

Roach's mind raced as he listened. The Regulat would want to hear this.

But wait. Why should he only bring this back? What if there was a way to act on this? Like a chess master plotting his inevitable victory, a plan formed in the man's folded-up mind.

• • •

It was late in the evening as Salem sat in the almost empty galley of the ship. Much to his disbelief, they had been at sea for ten days. With each sunrise and sunset, he grew more and more comfortable looking out and seeing nothing but water. He even found the sight reassuring, remembering back to what the taxi driver had said when they had first driven into Easterly: The ocean is always changing, and never changing. I kind of get it, he thought.

Also contributing to his newfound attitude was the fact that the ship was not nearly as small as it had first appeared. Much to Salem's relief, the countless waves that passed under Curiosity's hull could hardly be felt, and to top it all off, he was even starting to somewhat understand its bizarre inner layout, getting lost less and less each time he tried to make his way from one place to another. He had the strange sense that sometimes the passages of the ship changed, but such a ridiculous idea he kept to himself to avoid embarrassment.

But while such realizations were good and well, Salem still struggled to connect with many of the crew members. He spent a considerable amount of time alone. When not at instructions or working on various tasks necessary for life on the ship, he read his father's journal, which now had new meaning thanks to his talk with Captain Fern. Though Salem could not say why, he felt as though the farther out to sea they sailed, the further connected he became with the observations and pictures in the book. It was as though his father had already lived what he now was going through. Many times, Salem wished he could ask a question or share an observation with the man he had never known. He wanted to share his thoughts with Ulysses, though had not yet found the right moment.

When not studying the journal, he spent time with Zee. He had kept his distance from Juniper since their first interaction, choosing instead to spend most of his free time with a person who seemed equally happy to have found a new friend in him. There was something, Salem admitted this only in the privacy of his own mind, that still drew him to Juniper in a way he could not explain.

Even though she had made her feelings about him clear, he felt the slightest twinge of excitement every time she came around. No, he did not have any feelings for her. He could not, or at least should not, he told himself. She was the captain's daughter and besides; she did not even want him there. Salem decided it must be her disagreeable nature he enjoyed. To watch someone who so openly went against the grain of what everyone expected was so much different from himself that it was funny.

It was this combination of days filled with bewildering instructions, along with his long talks with Zee, that kept Salem open to the massive changes now occurring in his life. Now, sitting in the galley, Salem, fighting against his feelings of social awkwardness that swirled around inside, was attempting to do something he was not historically good at: make friends.

"The game is Go," the Japanese man called Raiju explained to them, gesturing down at the bicolored pieces spread alongside the bamboo board. "It's easy. Just circles and lines."

"It doesn't look so easy," said Juniper. She turned to Salem and Zee, who could only give back looks of genuine confusion themselves.

"It is, trust me," said Raiju, in a soft, near whisper of a voice. "Here, look, it's just line and circle, black and white stone, and wood, combined with simple rules."

Salem had been watching and still was not grasping what a good—or bad—move was. Raiju was nice enough and patient enough to keep explaining the game and its rules to them.

"Why there?" Zee asked once again.

"To win territory," said Raiju.

"Why not there?" Zee asked, pointing to another section of squares on the board.

"That is ill advised," said Raiju.

"Says who?" asked Zee.

"The gods of Go," said Raiju, raising a hand up toward the ceiling so that the sleeve of his shirt fell to his forearm, revealing the tattoos underneath. They were long and blue, forming a neon body of something that snaked its way up Raiju's forearm, and then back under the sleeve where they hid once again. Raiju was not a large person, but his presence, Salem realized, seemed large. He wore a single cloth tunic and looked hairless except for a section of black hair that began at the back of his skull and fell to just between his shoulders.

"Do you get it?" Juniper asked, looking at Salem. Salem only shook his head.

"So, if I move here," said Juniper, "that's good, right?" Raiju nodded that it was. "And then if I moved there and there"—Juniper motioned with a slender finger— "I would take this piece?" She took one of Raiju's black pieces from the tabletop. Raiju nodded again, grinning.

"You're getting it," said Raiju as he took a stone from his dish and clicked it twice against the wooden edge of the board. Salem, whose finger had been resting against the board, felt an electric jolt course through his hand and into his arm. It was as if all the shocks he had ever received in his life had regrouped to come together to attack him at the same time. He recoiled.

"You alright?" asked Zee.

"Yeah," said Salem, rubbing his arm. "Just a little shock," he said, looking at Raiju, whose face remained impassive.

The game of Go, at least to Salem, seemed to be more of an ongoing test of intelligence than a game of moving black and white pieces around. He had always been a fan of board games but was more used to the ones where the number of moves were less than the grains of sand on a beach (Raiju was fond of reminding them of this last fact). Salem wondered how anybody could get good at such a game.

"Raiju?" said Juniper, as if her thoughts had been riding the same wavelength. "How long have you been playing this game?"

Raiju looked wryly at the captain's daughter. "'Since before you were born' wouldn't begin to do justice," he said. "Still, compared to some masters of the game, I am still very much a student. Learning is not a straight line, but a circle." Raiju held up one of his circular Go pieces.

"Raiju," said Salem, letting the moment take hold of him. "If I practice and beat you, will you tell us how old you are?" Raiju's expression was almost pitiful as he looked at Salem. But, slowly, he bowed his head that he would.

Salem allowed a mischievous grin to work its way across his mouth, and he nudged Juniper the tiniest of amounts. He saw her grin out of the corner of his eye. It was the smallest action, but the elation made Salem's heart fall into his stomach.

Salem was enjoying the game and the company, but the questions raised from his talk with Captain Fern gnawed at him like termites in wood. While at first, he had needed time to even process what he had been told, he now wanted answers. How else could he be a part of this new life?

"So, Captain Fern, erm…" he stumbled over his words, fighting through the awkwardness and looking at Juniper, "your dad. Remember when we were talking, and you came in a few days ago? He was telling me about my dad and about, well…" Salem paused, feeling stupid for what he was about to say. "Well, you know, the mythical creatures and the 'Fringe' and stuff. To be honest, I didn't really understand a lot. It was crazy."

But as Salem finished talking, it was Juniper and Zee and Raiju who looked at him as though he was the crazy one. "I mean, what's with all the secrecy?"

"Captain isn't always obvious with the way he says things," said Zee, agreeing.

"Try never," added Juniper, laughing.

"Right," continued Zee, "but if you're patient and trust him, there's always something good there."

The words confused Salem.

"I guess. It's just hard for me to accept these…fairytale things," he said, and as he spoke, could see his mother in his mind and hear her voice in his ears. "I've seen reality," he said. "I mean, I've lived it. It's hard and full of fear. It will…burn your house down and take your family. Life is not a fairytale."

Juniper, Zee, and Raiju were all looking at Salem. Salem hated the feeling of being observed and could feel sweat gathering around his brow as he waited for someone else to say something, anything.

He was thankful when Raiju spoke. "This is a hard time in your life." Raiju's voice was calm and steady, and it did not waver in the least. "But just like a ship which must sail through rough seas, you will get through it."

"I just don't see how that's possible," was all Salem could bring himself to say. "Not with everything that's happened." He could feel that he was on the verge of a nervous breakdown, the kind his mother used to help him control. The absolutely last thing he wanted to do was to become upset in front of Zee or Juniper, or anyone. Raiju placed a hand on Salem's shoulder, and Salem felt the slight buzz of an electrical current at the tips of the older man's fingers. It did not hurt but sent a series of vibrating ripples through his body which made him feel, in a word, alive. Salem was seeing the context of his situation with a clarity he had never known, without the veil of fear which so often hung around him.

"Many things seem impossible before you consider their possibility," said Raiju, and then with his other hand moved one of his Go pieces without looking at it. Raiju released his hand from Salem's shoulder and the vibrating ripples dissipated. The world once again felt heavy, though a hint of the tingling lingered, allowing Salem to move beyond the impending panic.

Then two figures entered the mess deck. Obscured by the shadows in that part of the room, it was impossible for Salem to make out which members of the crew they were.

"Mind if we sit down?"

Salem knew the voice. It was slimy and smug. Dover, accompanied by another man, stood grinning over the table.

"How've you been keeping, my orphan brother?"

Salem did not dislike Dover—he had no reason to—but he did not like Dover either. "Fine," was all he answered.

"I must say I agree with you, Salem Swan; all these riddles and secrets make one a little"—Dover looked at Salem the way the devil might at God if God offered him the keys to heaven—"crazy."

The two newcomers sat down, Dover beside Juniper and the other man next to Salem. "Oh, how rude of me," said Dover, making a noise that was something between a giggle and a sneeze. "Salem, this is Karl. He's almost as new as you are." Karl extended his hand and Salem shook it. It was warm and moist, as if Karl had just come out of the sauna.

"Pleasure," said Karl, sounding almost nervous.

"Nice to meet you," said Salem, doing his best to smile. Karl looked scared and excited at the same time. He was scrawny but tall, with skinny arms and a skinny neck that looked like he had been a part of some immense game of tug-of-war where he got to play the part of the rope. Salem guessed Karl was about the same age as Dover, caught somewhere between thirty and forty; then again, it was hard for Salem to guess the ages of anyone on board. Each member had a funny way of looking so unique that the concept of age, at least the way Salem knew it, was not easily deduced. For Salem, it was clear that he was a teenager, just like it was clear that Juniper and Zee were teenagers. The same was true for the older crewmembers, like Kane, who were very obviously old. Though all the rest, those caught in the middle—Karl, Ulysses, Ena, Dorianna, even Captain Fern—were much harder to place, much more, ageless.

"So," said Dover, acting almost giddy to have stumbled upon the other crewmen, "what ever are we up to here?" No one answered. Dover smiled, and Salem realized Dover had expected it. The pasty man was playing his own game. "Well," said Dover, sliding over into Juniper, who recoiled into herself as if Dover was contagious. "This does look just absolutely, horrifyingly, complicated. All those black and white pebbles scattered around, my my…" Lightning clapped from somewhere outside, making them all jump—everyone except Raiju who, Salem noticed, had not moved but only sat transfixed on Dover with his hands flexed into fists on the table in front of him.

"It's called Go," said Salem, feeling as though someone should say something to diffuse Dover's antics. It took less than a second for Dover's eyes to switch back over to Salem, and Salem felt his stomach flop. He had offered himself up, stepping voluntarily into Dover's playground.

"Go, you say," said Dover. "But where does one 'go' when one plays?"

"You can go that way," said Juniper, motioning out the door to Dover. Dover laughed, turning his attention to the captain's daughter.

"So, Salem," said Karl in his nervous sort of way, taking advantage of Dover's distraction and turning only to Salem. "Guess we're both newbies, huh?"

"Yeah," said Salem. "I'm definitely not whatever the opposite of a newbie is."

Karl smiled. He had crooked teeth and sad eyes with a tuft of brown hair like a bird's nest. Though something about him was approachable, almost likeable. "Well, don't let it get you down," he said, and Salem could tell he spoke from experience.

"Trying not to," answered Salem.

"Because there are always other things you could do if you didn't like it here."

"Sure," said Salem, "but I want to give this a chance. Kind of feel like I owe it to my uncle."

"I understand," said Karl. "Loyalty to family is important. Just make sure they are as loyal to you."

Salem wanted to ask what he meant, but Karl had already turned his attention back to Dover and the others. Salem tried to rejoin and find the enjoyment but for some reason it had gone, and his thoughts wandered elsewhere. He had the feeling that he was watching himself from somewhere else, floating above the scene as his body sat around the table with the others. He was not sure how he had gotten to this point on this mysterious ship, with strangers in a storm, headed into a nameless voyage. He let the moment engulf him, trying to recall the utter awareness he had felt just moments before when touched by Raiju.

Outside the lightning clapped again and was this time answered by the drum of thunder.

INTERLUDE 1 | THE LEGEND OF CHINAU

14 years before Salem's arrival on the Curiosity

The sun dipped so low that it seemed to almost sit on top of the village. It was the time of the day when the parents would begin telling their children that if they did not finish their chores, there would be no supper and, worse, no story after supper. This was the worst punishment the children could imagine. Everyone did their chores.

Okagbue Ekwefi ran along behind her brothers and sisters to fetch the sticks they would use to clean out the houses. After using the sticks to sweep out dirt and other debris, the families would toss them in as fuel for the fire, which would become heat for cooking the food and light for seeing the storyteller's face.

The story to be told was one of Okagbue's favorites. It was the story of Chinua, the foolish hero who climbed the clouds to speak with the Mountain King. The story would be told by the storyteller, named Imgabwe, though he was rarely called by this name. The children and most of the village called him Bofunu, a word meaning dead tree. This was because sitting in front of the fire, one could mistake the ancient storyteller for the stump of a dead tree.

Okagbue had asked Bofunu one day how he had learned to tell such magnificent stories, to which Bofunu only replied, "I do not tell stories."

This made Okagbue confused, and when she questioned the old man again, he said, "I do not tell stories, little one, they tell me."

Okagbue did not care about Bofunu's confused notions of stories. He still told them best, and that was what she cared about.

So, it was during a cool Ghanaian evening in late summer that Okagbue's tribe, including her parents and siblings, sat around the rising flames of the central fire pit.

Rooted in his usual spot, Bofunu sat cross-legged and waited for his people to congregate. Okagbue, already seated for fifteen minutes, scanned the crowd as they assembled. She always thought faces looked most beautiful before the light and shadow of fire in the night. The dancing flames would stress the deep lines on the men's jawbones and their intense eyes staring ahead. The shadows, known to her people as "sisters of the flame," would caress the soft edges of the women's bodies, revealing only enough as to keep the Moon from becoming jealous as she looked down from above.

"It is a story of forbidden love," began Bofunu once the assembly was complete and quiet. Bofunu's voice rose with the smoke of the fire, spreading its message among the eager faces. "It began when Chinau journeyed to the mountain to hunt."

Okagbue sighed as Bofunu continued talking. She knew what was coming next. Chinau would stumble across a beautiful girl while on the mountain. She would wash herself in the mountain's stream when he would see her. Chinau would not know the beautiful girl. He would not realize it was the daughter of the Mountain King. Chinau would be so captivated by the woman's beauty that he would drop his spear without a word, unable to consider anything else but the immediate choice to approach.

It was here, at this scene, that Okagbue waited. This was her favorite part. She leaned in as she always did, hoping a closer proximity to the words would bring her closer to the feelings they elicited. At least this was what her mother would say afterwards, as always. For now, Okagbue's mother looked at her, putting her larger arm around her daughter. Okagbue smiled while she listened.

"And Chinau stepped forward," Bofunu said. "Though he no longer worried about false steps or half measures. He saw only the woman before him. She was his present, consuming his horizon. She was his past, filling the void between the fading memories. Most importantly," Bofunu said, smiling now and showing the gaps between his whittled-down teeth, "she was Chinau's future, standing before him so he would go beyond all conceivable measures to reach her."

Goosebumps rose on Okagbue's arms as Bofunu paused for a breath. It always happened when he described Chinau's love. Okagbue prayed that someone would look at her and say such words someday. If that is love, then it must be the most wonderful feeling in the world, she decided. She sat back and into her mother. Love would find her someday. Maybe it was best not to rush it. For now, she decided, she was content to hear the rest of the story. Chinau may have fallen in love with the Mountain King's daughter, but the storyteller had yet to get to the part where Chinau ascended the mountain to talk to the Mountain King.

It was then that the men arrived. Swift and hard under cloaks and hoods that hid their bodies and faces. Okagbue had not realized what was happening until it was too late. She heard the screams and felt the hands of her mother tighten around her shoulders, leading her away from the fire.

Great whooshing sounds filled the air as nets like giant spider webs floated down onto the fleeing villagers. Those not yet caught ran in zigzagging lines of confusion. Many had already taken to the air, hoping to escape. They beat their wings in frantic thumps, but fared little better than those remaining on the ground.

Okagbue ran with her mother and her father on the ground as she had not yet learned how to fly. It was the first time in her life that she met fear. It was a dirty, nasty, and mean thing that laughed all around her. She hated it. Still, it scared her and, more than only being scared for herself, she was scared for her family, for her mother and father, brothers and sisters. The big ones were brave, she knew that. But what about the little ones? Her little sister and brothers and the new baby? It all ran through her head. Right until the moment the nets closed around her.

• • •

In the distance, Captain Fern stood in silence. Above their heads fireflies were ascending upward and outward. Their lights twinkled against the backdrop of stars, so it was hard to tell them apart.

"Captain, look."

The captain did, though he did not see what he was looking at. The canvas of sky was pure, untouched by industrialization or pollution. This he saw, but this could not be what they meant. Then the first one went dark. It had risen with the others, but then vanished. Odd, he had expected to be seeing hundreds by now. The Adze loved stories, and even more than stories, they loved flying.

Then came the screams. They were high-pitched and laced with fear. The captain tensed as the skin between his shoulders tightened. The worst had happened, and he had not foreseen it.

"Did any others survive?" another of the crew asked.

The captain did not have the strength to answer with words, only bowing his head in defeat. He reached over and took the baby from the crewmate. He looked into the infant's startling green eyes. "You will stay with us," he told the tiny child.

PART II | JOTUNHEIM

CHAPTER 11 | CHITRA'S SONG

A small man in a blue-and-white tunic hung over an altar while a woman in a suit stood underneath. She had dark skin and hair, both darker than that of the hanging man.

"You didn't do what we agreed on," she said, her tone cold and impassive.

"I did!" pleaded the man. "He knows nothing. He saw nothing but the ruins."

"You're lying," said the woman.

"Please! Nothing has changed. Your secret remains."

"You know, Gandha, you may have a musical ear but you're an ugly crier." The woman turned toward two men standing behind her in identical black suits. "Bring out the girl."

"No, please." Gandha held back sobs. The men retreated to a place Gandha could not see. They returned only seconds later with a small girl. A rag tied through her mouth kept her from speaking and her eyes were red, as if she had been crying.

"Chitra," said the woman. "Your…daughter."

Gandha struggled and wriggled hard, shaking the chains like a captured bird. "No, leave her. She has nothing to do with any of this."

The woman spoke again. "In failing your task, you brought her into this."

Gandha pushed his words through sobs. "Please, ma'am, why are you doing this?"

"You will call me Regulator, Gandharva."

"Regulator," said Gandha, trying to imbue a tone of respect that his mind and body did not believe, "please, why are you doing this? What do you want from us?"

"Why does anyone do anything?" The regulator scoffed at her own question. "I am doing what is best for my kind. Longevity, Gandha, it's the only thing that matters. Being around long enough to make an impact. Isn't that the name of the game? There is only room for so many of us on this floating rock. Do you know, Gandha, why we call ourselves the Regulat?"

Gandha did not answer.

"Regulat comes from the English word 'regulate,' which comes from the Latin regulatus. Do you know what regulatus means, Gandha?" Gandha knew the regulator was not waiting for his response and that the question had been rhetorical. "It means," said the regulator, "to watch, or monitor. Now our founding members were not as simpleminded as many of their descendants today. They were people of vision. Able to see the danger brought on in allowing too many species to evolve at one time. Imagine if we had just as many Gandharvas running around as we do humans? It would be a catastrophe." The regulator cleared her throat. "Yes. Things are better this way. Things are better regulated."

She turned and motioned to the suited men. "Bring her to me."

"We've done nothing to humans. We are innocent."

"You've not done anything to humans yet," said the regulator, "but see, that is what has made us Species Alpha on Earth: we don't let it get to that point."

The regulator walked over to the girl. She was young, not even a teenager, but stood with the assurance of someone older. "Hello, dear," she said, in a voice that almost seemed to contain emotion. "Chitra, is that right?"

The girl nodded.

"Are you scared, Chitra?" The girl shook her head that she was not. "Very good, very good. Your daddy's scared enough for both of you."

"He's not scared," said the girl, unwavering, "he's sad."

"Is that so? How perceptive you are. Can you show me what else you can do? Maybe weave one of your little melodies for my friend, here? Something to make him happy?" The regulator raised her hand, bending her fingers forward twice, so that one of the suited men approached.

"But he's not my friend," said the girl named Chitra.

"Oh, Mr. Sir is a friend to all, aren't you, Mr. Sir." The man nodded. "Weave a song for Mr. Sir, dear. Make him laugh. It's hard to make him laugh."

The small girl looked up at the man, then back down at her feet. She tapped something that vaguely resembled a foot twice against the floor. It made a sound like a horse hoof. She looked at her father for an answer of what to do. Gandha could only look into his daughter's eyes and nod to her that all would be okay. "Come along, Chitra," said the regulator, "sing."

The girl lifted her chin, opened her mouth, and sang.

At first nothing happened, followed by the soft crescendo of sound. Then, as if it had always been there, it filled the space completely. It was a sound made up of layers beyond just a voice. What started as a single note vibrated and twisted, floating its way up the scale and back. Another note soon joined. It too went up and down but in the opposite direction, meeting its predecessor in harmony at the center. Then came more notes, all taking alternative routes through the musical scale until the point where they came together into a singular melody that could be described no other way than as pure. The sound was the clearest the regulator had ever heard. She knew the blessed music was a facade, a beautiful trick developed by this animal, and yet, she had to fight back the gripping urge to enjoy the music spreading through the room.

Chitra's song could be heard by all in the room, though it was the chosen Mr. Sir who heard it most. Chitra had locked eyes on the man whose stern face was melting away. Mr. Sir was grinning and, as Chitra sang, his grin became a smile. It did not take long for Mr. Sir to giggle, and soon that became full-bodied laughter.

"Keep singing, my dear," said the woman regulator, "though I should tell you that this man hurt your daddy."

Chitra sang on but flinched at the woman's words. The small girl's brow furrowed in concentration.

"This man," said the regulator, pointing a finger at the laughing Mr. Sir, "caused your daddy to hurt. A terrible hurt."

Chitra scrunched her forehead and eyebrows in effort as the tone of her song shifted. It was no longer the enchanting melody but one that was heavier, more like a screech than a song. If anger had a voice it was present there. Mr. Sir stopped laughing and his face contorted instead into shapes of a man afraid. The song quickened, the melody going staccato, with sharp auditory spikes that sounded like hot knives being plunged into cold water. Mr. Sir cried, holding his hands over his ears, and shaking his head as though a demon inside was trapped and trying to claw its way out through his skull.

The regulator raised her hand and Chitra allowed her song to die away. Mr. Sir slowed his maniacal dance. He stood there with his mouth hanging open while his eyes chased some invisible fly around the room.

"Thank you, dear Chitra," said the regulator. She turned to the other man in the suit. "Mr. Sir, take Chitra to see the lab. Afterward you can take your comrade to the infirmary."

The other man known also as Mr. Sir collected Chitra and led her away and out of the room.

"Gandha," said the regulator. "Even your young daughter has the power to drive a man mad."

"She did not want to." Gandha's face spread in desperation. "She would never…"

"Ah, ah," said the regulator, wagging a finger. "Whether or not she wanted to is beside the point, isn't it? The fact remains that she can manipulate the minds of humans and that we do not like. That is why you are not innocent. You are a ticking time bomb."

"We only weave dark music when we must, when we feel we need to defend ourselves. Gandharvas, Asparas, Chitras, we only want to bring beautiful music into the world. You of all people would understand. You are after all…"

"Enough," said the woman, a newfound rage in her eyes. "That is a convenient thing to say while strung up, but I do not understand."

Gandha could only let his head drop.

"You will not slip up again, Gandha."

Gandha shook his head, thinking about Chitra. "I will not."

• • •

The regulator walked down a long corridor, leaving the sobbing Gandha behind to be taken down by more Mr. Sirs and Ms. Ma'ams in suits. The corridor was a passageway that had once connected the church to the priest's house. It was a house that now acted as a temporary home for the leader of the organization.

The regulator pushed open the old door. Lamps with incandescent light bulbs, ones where the stringy filament curled around itself like a strand of DNA, bathed the place in an orange light. She walked through the foyer and then into a main sitting room where a few people sat talking with one another.

The regulator came to stand by a man smoking a cigar. "Constance," she said. The old man took the cigar out of his mouth. The others had stopped talking. He turned to look up at the regulator, smiling with very white teeth.

"Vera," he said in a smoky voice that sounded more like it should come from the cigar than the human. "I trust you being here means you've…looked into things."

"The Gandharva gave them nothing and I've taken measures to ensure his obedience."

"Did you bring his daughter in like I suggested?"

"I did."

"And did she sing?"

"She did."

"And?"

The regulator sighed. "And one suit may have lost his sanity."

The old man coughed a few times, waving his cigar through the air as he did. Vera could not tell if he was having a fit or just laughing. "The Sir with the—" The old man made a motion around his face.

"No," said Vera. "That one with the—" she motioned with her pointer finger toward the ceiling.

"Ah," said the man, "yes, the one with that voice. Well, we should rethink the concept of naming all non-regulators Mr. Sir and Ms. Ma'am. It gets confusing."

"Whatever you think, Constance," was Vera's reply.

The older man chuckled, and as he did the other people sitting around began to laugh as if finally allowed to enjoy the joke themselves.

Vera turned to leave the room.

"Oh, and Vera," said Mr. White. Vera stopped. "Leave the girl for now. I want to deal with her myself."

The regulator nodded, leaving the old man and others behind in their cigar smoke and laughter. Before she exited the room, she heard Constance's cigar smoke voice again.

"I am in a delightful mood," he said to the others. "I think it's high time we induct our newest member, don't you?"

CHAPTER 12 | ENA BOTO

"We weren't kidding about you learning a thing or two," Ulysses said as he walked with Salem in the morning air.

It was a chilly morning, as was every morning of late as they made their way farther and farther into the North Atlantic. Three weeks now separated Salem with his first steps on board the ship. Since his night with Raiju and the game of Go, Salem had found it easier to control his panic when it set it. He recalled the awareness the old man's spark had given him and often used the ocean to ground himself and listen to his breath. A series of routines also added to Salem's calm. Routines that helped make his life that dangerous word "normal," as Captain Fern was fond of saying.

Ulysses would come in the morning and he, Salem, and Zee would walk to the kitchens together where, often to their displeasure, Salem, Zee, and Juniper would begin their instructions. This morning broke the trend, however. Ulysses had come as usual but had requested to talk to Salem alone. They had not taken the usual route down to the kitchens but had instead stopped along the midsection on the main deck of the ship. "And not just from Artichoke," said Ulysses, stopping to finish his thought on what he was calling Salem's new education, "though he without a doubt has a lot of knowledge to pass along."

Salem only rolled his eyes, to which Ulysses grinned. He was glad to be spending time with his uncle again. But he still felt like a large part of the man's identity remained hidden to him. "Ulysses," he asked, "did something happen in town before we left?"

"Oh yes, many things." Salem heard the sarcastic humor in Ulysses' voice, but there was also the slight tone of unease. It gave Salem the sense that to pry further was unwise. As he looked around at the miles and miles of water, however, he remembered where he was and how little he had to lose by asking.

"Anything happen to you?"

"Nothing you need to worry about, Salem." Ulysses was quiet for a long second. "Do you know why I love sailing so much?"

Salem shook his head.

"Out here there is only this. There is nothing else. I can forget about it all."

As Ulysses talked, Salem could not help but wonder if he was referring to many things of his past. Salem had the urge to ask if he or his mother had been part of the 'all' which Ulysses could forget. He had the urge to ask Ulysses if he knew anything about his father.

"Well, lucky for you," continued Ulysses, ending the discussion on the topic. "There are plenty of other things you should know about life beyond food. And even luckier for you, plenty of us are here to teach them to you."

"Well, I have done nothing for actual school," said Salem as they continued walking. "I guess I could use some time for that." It was true; since arriving, Salem had forgotten about school, even if it had been homeschooling. The thought of riding a bus and walking, backpack slung over his shoulder, into a classroom had seemed impossible for him before. Now, as he looked at Ulysses standing in front of him on Curiosity's mid-deck, it was almost comical.

"Ah." Ulysses waved a hand in front of his face as if to swat the world's slowest gnat. "You can get to that later. The thing about schools these days is that they're the same as schools when I was going through. They still haven't figured it out."

"Figured, what out?"

Like a vexed philosopher Ulysses stopped, lifting one leg up onto the wooden runner which spanned the length of the ship's frame.

"Don't get me wrong, school's good for some things. Maybe you discover social constructs and the art of making, or in my case, not-making friends. Maybe you figure out what it means to follow, or in my case, not-follow rules. Maybe you find a good book or two"—Ulysses put his hand alongside his mouth — "or a good girl or two in my case. If you're very lucky, you'll have a teacher who wakes you up more than just puts you to sleep. All these things can happen, but they are not the solution."

"The solution to what?" Salem asked.

"The world does not work like a school, Salem. The world doesn't work like anything because the world doesn't work. The world just happens. All around us, every second. There are no rules or curricula or blackboards, or anything. We've gotten ourselves so damned transfixed on institutions and constructs that we've forgotten how to live." Ulysses paused for a moment, taking a deep breath that he blew back out like dragon smoke in the morning air. "Maybe I'm out of touch. Like I said, it's not all bad. There's some good in everything, I guess, if you look for it. I've just always thought of learning as an interaction. A give and take. I mean, you can tell kids about rain. About water that falls from the sky and evaporates back up. But you can't teach them the sound a drizzle makes on a field after you've returned from a long journey at sea. What it means to reflect on your actions, listen to that soft pattering of raindrops that washes away all the bad you may have done, and then brings you back fresh again."

"You can teach them about hormones. How they're released when we see someone we find attractive. But you can't put in to words the first time you kiss someone who wants to kiss you back. The moment your brain stops working and you forget how to breathe; when you're thankful your heart can beat on its own because you wouldn't be able to keep up with it if you tried."

"You can tell them to be brave. Climb high into trees and jump toward the highest branches—the ones they never thought they could reach. But the love of a sibling, of a sister to tell you can go further when you think you can't… that you must live."

Salem saw that tears now streamed down Ulysses' face, and he felt them gather in his own eyes.

"You can tell a kid that hollow bones are better for flight and that gills and air sacs allow wondrous creatures to live underwater. But you cannot relay what it means to climb a mountain and watch a griffin soaring around you. You can't translate the first time you witness a water dragon dive or sit in a garden on a warm summer night and watch lightning bugs dance. Yeah…" said Ulysses, trailing off. "I never really understood learning about the world from behind a desk."

Salem was quiet as he and Ulysses looked out into the water. He felt closer to his uncle in that moment than he had since arriving on the ship. Still, despite all the questions he wished to ask his uncle, he somehow knew to just sit there for a moment in silence was best.

Some moments later Ulysses put his arm around Salem's shoulder.

"Enough of my rambling," he said. "Let's go meet another one of your instructors."

• • •

Ena Boto moved about the ship as the water flowed under it—with no apparent effort at all. His skin was the color of mahogany wood and he had long, wavy black hair that reminded Salem of a charcoal seaweed—a charcoal seaweed that might grow somewhere on the Moon if the Moon had an ocean. The black strands ran halfway down Ena's back, where his glistening skin looked perpetually wet, as if he had just stepped out of a pool.

Salem felt good after having spent the morning speaking with Ulysses. He felt as though, little by little, he was getting to know his uncle more, and it gave him the confidence that he might be on his way to becoming one of the crew. He sat along with Juniper and Zee, all together facing Ena near the front of the ship which Salem now knew as the bowsprit. The wind blew in powerful gusts that filled the ship's white sails and sprayed ocean mist across the decks.

"Fighting," Ena said in his shortened words, "is not why you're here."

Salem thought this seemed like an odd way to start an instruction.

"You're here to learn the opposite of fighting. You're here to learn non-fighting, and I'm going to teach you by teaching you how to fight. First things first." Ena took the rolled-up blanket that had been resting at his side and threw it open. "Tools."

Ena had with him an assortment of weaponry that Salem thought could have been stolen out of a museum. Archaic but sleek knives, spears, bows, axes, and even a sword presented themselves in front of them. Salem also noticed a bag of arrows and a target.

"Wait, wait, wait," said Salem. "You're going to teach us how not to fight? But you brought weapons?"

"Finally." Juniper released an appeased sigh while looking at the blades. "Something useful."

"While these tools are effective, nothing is better than these." Ena held up his hands. "Learn to use what you've been given and everything in your life will become easier."

Juniper smiled. "I think we know how to use our hands, Ena." She reached for a knife at the edge of the blanket. No sooner had she moved than Ena had cut across the space, picked up the knife, and thrown it in a single motion. Salem's eyes could only just follow the blur. He only caught up when he saw the knife come to rest at the heart of the target a few feet away.

"Whoa," said Zee, in the way he always said it. "That was cool."

Ena rolled up the blanket. "These are where we'll get to. Maybe we can even get you specialized with a weapon you choose."

Salem could not believe what he was hearing. "But when will we need to use any of those?" he asked.

"Let's hope never," said Ena, smiling up at him, "but if you ever do need them, you'll be happy I've instructed you."

"But they're so… old." Salem did not mean to sound rude as he said it, but the look on Ena's face was unmistakable. "I just mean," he tried to save himself, "that we have more modern weapons now."

Salem could not be sure, but he thought he saw a look of question, almost pity, come into Ena's eyes. As if he, Salem, the boy who had never been out to sea, the boy who knew nothing of this strange world, could not possibly understand what he was saying.

"Old is relative," Ena said. "With old beings, things that have been around a long, long time, there is a certain way they do things. A way things have always been done."

Salem had nothing to say. Cooking he could understand, but this, fighting with outdated weapons… "But who are we fighting?" he had to ask.

"It doesn't matter," said Ena. "What matters is that there may come times in your life when you may need what I am to teach you."

Salem was quiet then, as were Juniper and Zee.

"So," continued Ena, "follow me if you can."

Ena stood and began a series of movements with his hands and arms, no weapons included. Simple enough, thought Salem, as they all copied in what looked like a silent dance. Ena's movements did not stay simple. It took only a minute before his arms twisted and bent in tandem with his knees and legs. He was spinning then, staying in the same three-foot radius but filling the space with his rotations. Whereas at first Salem wanted to laugh, now he felt his arms and legs burning. Sweat formed along his brow and, sneaking a glance at Juniper and Zee, noticed the same was true for them by their concentrated expressions.

Ena slowed down. "That's enough for now. Work on those basic movements and we can build to the more complex."

With that, Ena sat, took out a small rectangle of wood and a pocketknife, and began to run the knife over the block of wood. Salem looked between Juniper and Zee, who only shrugged. As if agreeing without saying it out loud, they all took seats around their silent instructor.

"You know," Ena said after a long moment, "where I come from in Brazil the water touches the forest, the forest touches the sky, and the stars sometimes get so close that you can reach out and pluck them, like fruit."

Ena pushed his knife along the edges of the wood in his hand. As he did, Salem saw that a shape, long and slender, was taking form.

"The outside of something does not determine its value. When we look at things, let us look not at what they are, but at what they want to become. Like the water around us, everything is in motion. All the time, without end. You are in motion. See this when you make your motions. See yourself as the art you are. Use your tools. Define your process. That is where true strength begins."

Ena wiggled his knife a few times and Salem watched more shavings fall away. As he raised his hand, palm open, a tiny, exquisite, dolphin was looking up at them.

CHAPTER 13 | LANDFALL

The jagged tips of a spiny ridge of mountains jutted into the air like the vertebrae of a sea monster as the Curiosity rose and fell on the breathing ocean's back. Four weeks and a day now separated the crew from land. Thousands of miles of endless ocean had passed under Curiosity's hull. Near the front of the boat, two crewmembers stood side by side. Kane leaned over into Ulysses close enough that Ulysses could see the old one's chapped lips and feel the stream of warm smoke-breath as he spoke.

"They say the first sight a'land reveals to each a truth."

"What kind of truth?" Ulysses asked, grinning. "And why is it the Irish always sound like they're trying to trick you when they say things?"

"It's in our blood, I suppose. Same way Americans always sound so clueless."

Ulysses laughed. "Ignorance really can be bliss, you know."

"True," said Kane and then, in his best impression of an American southern accent, "though it don't last forever."

"Doesn't it?" asked Ulysses. "Does it have to end?"

"Nothing lasts, boyo," said Kane, dropping the accent.

"You do a good job, Mr. One Hundred Thirty-Three Years Old." Ulysses nudged Kane with his shoulder.

"One hundred thirty-three. Might as well be a baby. One hundred thirty-three, pffh. Me granda was well into his four-hundreds when he passed his pot of gold. Count yourself lucky, Ulysses"—Kane nodded his head downward—"that humans live as short as they do. You're never around long enough to really see the results of your actions on the world. For better or worse."

"You have regrets, Kane?"

"A few hundred years ago I'da told ya they aren't worth havin'," said the leprechaun. "Turns out I was wrong."

"How do you figure?"

"Well, context."

"Context?"

"Yeah, context."

"I don't see it."

"Well, I'll make it real simple for ya. Screwin' up, makin' mistakes, it's good for ya. A necessary evil."

"I've had a lot of necessary evil."

"Not such a bad thing," said Kane.

"Isn't it?" asked Ulysses.

"A person who hasn't had a healthy dose of necessary evil isn't much of a person, if you ask me."

"Yeah?" answered Ulysses. "I'm not so sure. I think I'd have a good chance to tip the scale against the evil with one hundred thirty-three years."

Kane only shook his head and chuckled. "Mistakes give us strength to be brave, Ulysses. It isn't about the number of years you spend livin'. The quality of a life is not measured in its quantity."

"Though it helps to have more time," said Ulysses. "Give you more time to right the wrongs."

Kane shook his head. "You're keeping score. That does nothing for anyone. Living short or living long means nothing if you don't live well."

• • •

Captain Fern rose earlier than usual that morning. Well before the first light had crept over the horizon. It always happened on the days they made landfall. Even on days such as this when they arrived earlier than expected. The captain's own stubborn intuition refused to let him down. He stood at the helm, his hand resting on the wood, taking in the stretch of gray beach before them. It was a barren landscape. He saw the small shapes of a few houses huddled close together: the outline of a small village.

A movement to the right caught the captain's eye. He remained with his eyes forward as Aurora came to stand beside him.

"Look familiar?" he asked.

She nodded, her hair waving in the wind.

"Any people in the village?"

She shook her head. "A long time ago. We would even trade a few times a year."

Fern looked closer at the village. Its simple four-walled houses made of mismatched rocks looked, just as Aurora had said, like they had not been inhabited for a long time. All around the decaying bodies of what looked like once-upon-a-time fishing vessels littered the fields, now as integrated into the scene as the tundra trees or the bushes.

"Quiet now," he said.

"I guess that would depend on your definition of quiet."

Fern tilted the helm a few degrees to the right, calculating in his head the angle and speed needed to avoid a bus-sized island of rock off the portside bow. "You're a hard person to get a read on, you know that?"

Aurora did not look at him. "What does it mean? How can you get a read on someone?"

Fern thought about the question. "It means it's difficult to know what you're feeling, what you're thinking."

"That's my business. Why should I show it to you?"

"I just mean it's hard to help someone when they keep themselves so closed."

"You're not easy to get a 'read on' yourself, Captain Fern. Maybe others would open themselves more if you did it first?"

Fern was silent for a while.

"So," he finally said, "will we be expecting a warm welcome then?"

A rare smile emerged on Aurora's face. "I guess that would depend on your definition of warm."

• • •

On another part of the deck, Salem stood shivering next to Zee as the ship cruised toward the coastline. Though they wore thick jackets, the cold was still somehow slipping through. It felt strange to Salem to see land after so many days spent looking out at a world void of terrain. Growing up in a place without an ocean had felt so normal, and now, he could appreciate just how much of the planet was covered in water, and how little was covered in land.

It was clear Zee did not appreciate the cold. He shook so violently that Salem worried he might begin having a fit.

"You alright?" Salem asked, probably for the fifth time that morning.

Zee nodded through chattering teeth. "I just need to acc-c-c-climate."

A few hundred yards from the rocky coast the boat slowed, allowing the anchor to descend one clink at a time into the icy water. It was clear that the town had at one time been livelier, though whatever business, whatever life had been there, looked as though it was long gone. It sat desolate, an air of somber surrender presiding as the last lone resident.

Mist drifted between the deteriorating houses, which looked to Salem as though they could sit alongside Stonehenge. They were designed with only pragmatism in mind, as if aesthetics had no place or purpose. They took the long boats off their racks, packed them with supplies, and lowered them into the water.

By early afternoon, the crew set up came on the outskirts of the village. They left the houses and other buildings to be, constructing their own tents.

"Best not to be moving into those." Salem heard Artichoke say. "Don't know what kind of energies live there."

"Alright," said the captain as the crew gathered around him. An icy vapor had settled over the beach, and Salem felt as though his arms and legs were nothing but numb pegs as he huddled in close to the others. "Looks like we've landed in a no-man's-land. Since we don't know which country this place belongs to, I recommend exercising caution." A few muffled sounds of irony rustled through the crew.

"Where are we? It's freezing," someone whispered.

"Somewhere between Scandinavia, Russia, and the North Pole," Dorianna answered.

"As you all have already noticed," the captain continued, "this is not our typical pickup rescue." More ironic sounds from the cold crew. "Regardless," said the captain, the air of authority rising into his voice, "you all know what's at stake."

The captain looked at Aurora, who looked back at him. She nodded ever so slightly. "So," said the captain with a tone of finality. "I have discussed with Aurora and it seems taking the entire crew to the location is ill advised because of some…complications. Therefore, Ulysses and Ena, you will come with me and we will go with Aurora. The rest of you, under the command of Dorianna, will set up camp and wait for our return." The captain looked at his quartermaster, whose cheeks and nose were almost as red as her hair in the frigid air. "You're in charge," he told her. Dorianna nodded. "We should not be more than a day."

Salem saw the slight flicker in Aurora's eyes as Fern said this. He wondered if anyone else had noticed. If anyone had, they stayed quiet.

Fern turned with Ulysses and Ena to follow Aurora away from the beach, leaving Salem and the others in the camp.

"Now," said Artichoke, turning to Salem, Zee, and Juniper after Aurora had led the three men off the beach. "You all are the youngest and so receive the special task of finding us whatever this slice of cold rock has to offer as far as food."

Juniper released an exasperated breath. "I think that's something these two can do on their own."

Artichoke harrumphed, causing his great mass of torso to rise and fall. He was the only one of the crew who did not seem cold and with a reddened face fixed his beady eyes on the captain's daughter. She stared back at him, showing she had no intention of backing down. Salem shot a side glance at Zee. Clearly, this type of confrontation had happened before and neither Salem nor Zee had any wish to get involved.

"You think you're better than this?" Artichoke's voice carried a threatening tone.

Juniper glared at the cook, making the cold beaches somehow colder.

Salem was not sure what made him do it, but in a split second he did in fact lose control of his body. At least his mouth.

"It's fine," he said, stepping forward and drawing the attention of Juniper and Artichoke onto himself. Zee shot Salem a glance that brothers might before one leaves for war—a look that says you're brave, but crazy.

Salem could physically sense the intense stares of Juniper and Artichoke bearing down on him.

"It's fine," he repeated, taking special care to hold his stare with Juniper. "She'll go with us. We'll find food."

Salem thought for a moment that he saw a hint of the faintest smile flicker across Artichoke's disproportionate face. The same was not true for Juniper, whose fine features and brown eyes remained neutral.

CHAPTER 14 | STEALING FROM LEMMINGS

Aurora moved so fast through the mountainous terrain that Fern and the others had to jog more than walk as they followed her up the steep slopes of black and gray rock. Outcrops of boulders the size of small houses loomed like silent denizens. Their fractured bodies, layer upon layer of stone skin, showed secrets of a past conflicted.

"We have many stories about the battles that took place here long ago," said Aurora from the front. "A battle with the Igee."

Fern and the others were breathing as if just having run a great distance, struggling against the increased altitude. Aurora did not share the men's struggle. In fact, the higher they climbed the more she gained energy. Fern noticed that her meek body looked invigorated, adapted to the climate.

"These mountains and this land are the canvas of that struggle. They are remnants to remind us that forces greater than ourselves are at work."

"What are Igee?" Fern asked between deep inhales.

"Igee are everything, and everything are Igee."

"That clears it right up." Ulysses grinned at Aurora and she shot him an icy look.

"Igee are the spirits all around us that shape the universe," she said. "They are in constant struggle with one another but also come from the same family."

"They are gods," said Fern. "Like the Greek pantheon."

Aurora shook her head. "They are not gods the way you mean. We do not pray to the Igee for favor or good health. The Igee did not create us in their image, nor do they send prophets to write books about what we should do and how we should live. The struggle of the Igee is one of balance."

They walked for a long time. More than once Fern noticed he had lost his sense of orientation. He and the crew had been to many countries and places over the course of their travels. The world was filled to the brim, as Captain Fern recalled an old friend saying once. This place though, this land tucked between countries, bore a timelessness. If not for Aurora and the others, he could wander off into any direction completely unaware. It was a feeling he had not had in a long time, and he found it both uncomfortable and, strangely, appealing. Memories wheeled through his mind like flower petals twirling in the wind. Back to times when he was a different person altogether. Before he was captain, when he was just a father, and before he was a father, when he was just a lover. Even earlier, when he was nothing but a weird boy playing in his family's backyard, digging up insects and collecting leaves. Building cities from nothing with his bare hands. He was still that boy, only taller, with less hair on his head and more responsibility. It made him angry at himself in a way for letting responsibility do that to him and he wondered if it was the fate of all people to hate responsibility, that thing which also gave them purpose.

"We are close," Aurora said. "They'll know we are coming before we see them. I suggest you all stay close to me for the next few minutes."

"Don't they know we are here to help them?" Ulysses asked.

"We are short on trust these days, with your people. If they had known about me seeking you out, well..." Aurora turned on the path, ducking without looking under a branch that had swung out toward her head. "Watch yourselves," she called back. "The trees smell the stranger on you."

They made their way up the mountains where the dark grays and blacks of the stones mixed with snow, which Fern guessed never left. It was a landscape of frozen giants leaning against one another, caught in shades of color between black and white. They stopped little and when they did, only to let the men rest. At some point, Aurora put her hand up.

"We are here," she said.

They had reached a plateau on the mountainside. It was a white field in a small clearing. It looked empty and at its summit side was a vertical wall of rock, hundreds of feet high. Aurora walked toward the rock face, leaving the men standing at the edge of the snowy field. She sauntered, more than before, to the wall until her face was touching it.

"Should we follow?" Ena asked the others as they stood watching Aurora.

Fern shook his head. Intuition told him to wait. "We're out of our element," he said.

The men watched Aurora stand in front of the rock wall and study it, looking up and down. They watched her step to the side and place her hand on it, and then they watched her disappear.

• • •

The ground crunched as Salem and Zee followed Juniper Fern up the slope. The area beyond the beach was less barren. Shrubs and small trees wore a deeper shade of brown emblematic of their courage to take root. Salem squinted against the biting gusts of wind, nipping like frosty sheepdogs at his face.

"It's so quiet," said Zee. "Reminds me of nighttime at sea."

"Reminds me of a library," said Juniper.

"Reminds me of a graveyard," said Salem.

Juniper and Zee both looked at him, confused. Salem did not know why he had said it, but after a minute of thinking about it, he spoke again.

"When my mom died," he said, unsure why he was sharing the information, "a few days later we had the funeral. It was a closed casket. I remember standing in front of her tombstone after everyone had left. That was strange—being in the graveyard alone. I remember how quiet it had seemed."

"Seemed?" asked Zee.

"Yeah." Salem spoke without thinking. The words flowed out of him and he spoke with an openness he was not used to hearing from himself. "When you stand in one long enough, you realize it's not that quiet at all. Loud." Salem reached for his father's journal in his backpack but realized he had left it on the ship. He had wanted to reach for it because he had remembered a line in it which seemed to fit his current thoughts. "I remembered that graveyard feeling like a secret place which didn't want to be secret. Like it was waiting to be found and heard. This place feels like that."

The three had since stopped walking along the path. Juniper and Zee watched Salem.

"Wow," said Zee. "That's nice, and also creepy."

Then the three of them all looked between each other for a long moment before breaking out in laughter. None of them knew why they were laughing, and Salem, surprising himself, was okay with that. He knew it was not any laughter at him but a collective acceptance of where they were and what they were doing. Even Juniper was laughing, and Salem felt happy in a way he had not felt since his mom died. Happy to have shared those thoughts with others.

"What was it Art said?" asked Zee. "We can gather what we find but shouldn't need to hunt?"

"Like we could anyway," said Salem, happy that Zee had taken the conversation in a different direction.

"I don't know about you two, but I can," said Juniper.

"You can?" asked Salem.

"Yes. Come on. I'll show you."

They walked for a while longer in the quiet landscape. Salem thought he could feel the rocks watching them. He wondered if other things watched them too, but each time he looked, he saw only rocks and more rocks and off in the far distance, mountains. Pulled back to the ground on which they walked were different shades of gray and black melted into one another. Above their heads were glacial mountains of white and cascading snow. Then Zee halted.

They listened, and as they did, they realized that there was something in the air besides the whistling wind. It was another whistling sound, but softer, more like the song of a bird.

"Up here," said Juniper climbing up a nearby embankment. Salem and Zee followed.

They emerged out into a small clearing. The large, flat plain was void of any heavy snow; all around, large holes exposed dark soil. There were dozens of them, big enough that a person might fit inside, scattered every few feet throughout the frosted terrain of tundra.

"Looks like the biggest game of whack-a-mole ever," said Salem.

"What's whack-a-mole?" asked Zee.

"Never mind," said Juniper, "look!"

A hole toward the middle of the clearing was moving, or something was moving from inside the hole. Salem saw the ears first, followed by the top of the head, and the large black eyes. The strange-looking face appeared and stared at them.

"What is that?"

"Strangest-looking rabbit I've ever seen," said Zee.

It had ears like a rabbit, thought Salem, which was true. Though its face looked more like a weasel or small dog and its snout was long and tubular, like an elephant's trunk.

"They're funny looking," said Salem.

"I think they're called lemmings," said Juniper, though her tone sounded less than sure. She looked back and forth between Salem and Zee.

"What's a lemming?" asked Salem. "And how do you know that?"

"That," said Zee. "Juniper loves plants and animals, didn't you know? Don't let her meanness fool you. She's a softie."

"Ha-ha," said Juniper, making a face at Zee's comment. "Are you guys thinking what I'm thinking?"

Salem and Zee looked at her with faces that said no.

"Oh, come on," said Juniper. "Look closer at what they're doing."

They did, and as they did saw the heads of more lemmings bobbing up and down across the field.

"They're collecting berries," said Juniper.

"You want to steal their food?" asked Zee.

"Oh, they'll find more. Look at them, they're better at collecting and gathering than we'll ever be."

"Okay," said Salem, "but how do we get it?"

"Well, it's obvious," said Juniper. "Someone has to go down there where they live."

• • •

Moments later, Salem swam in darkness. "I'm still not sure that was fair!" He waited for a response but heard nothing. He had drawn the shortest of the strands of grass picked by none other than Juniper. I must remember to get her back for this, he thought, and crawled deeper into the lemming's domain.

He was not afraid of the dark, but also not fond of it. It makes you doubt everything, he thought. It was always amazing to him how his thoughts could run away in dark, creating fears he would have never had in the light. "I don't see anything," he yelled up, and after no response, realized he was talking to himself.

Juniper's voice came a long moment later. "Look harder. You lost, so you have to go find them."

Salem could hear the muffled voices of Juniper and Zee talking above him.

"Well, if you two hadn't screwed everything up and gone chasing after them, we might have had a chance," Juniper was saying to Zee.

"We were going for the element of surprise—right Salem?" Zee called down.

Salem grunted his response from underground.

"Whatever," said Juniper. Even underground Salem could hear the exasperation in her voice, and it made him smile.

"What do you see now, Salem?" asked Zee.

"Still nothing," said Salem. "I'm coming out, it's useless."

"Wait," said Juniper. "Zee will come down and help you."

"How's he going to do that? The hole's not big enough for me."

Salem heard the voices above him and waited, feeling like the idiot he was for being stuck in the hole.

"Just do it," he could hear Juniper saying to Zee.

"But it's so cold," Zee was saying.

"Oh, stop being like that or I'll tell the others and you'll never hear the end."

"Ugh," said Zee.

Salem heard the shuffle and then a short *crack*!. "Guys?" he said. "Hello?"

A light was coming in from behind him, though it was not sunlight or firelight or flashlight. It was bright and green. He heard a whirring, like a small engine next to his ear as a large firefly darted to hover in front of his face. The firefly was long and slender, and the green light of abdomen pulsated like a tiny sun. It bobbed there for a moment looking at Salem who, before he even asked the question, knew it was Zee.

"Does that help?" asked Juniper from above.

"What the…?" was all Salem could say.

The firefly zigzagged in the air and knocked into Salem's nose a few times. Then, it turned, and began flying down the tunnel, filling up the black space with its green light. Salem wiggled forward a little further, able to get one leg and knee in and up under himself. As the firefly, or Zee—Salem was not sure just yet what to call it, even in his own head—flew ahead, Salem could see the glowing eyes of the many lemmings staring at him.

To his surprise, the lemmings were not scared like he had assumed them to be. The whistling had stopped, and, in its place, Salem heard them growling.

"Guys, I don't think this was a good idea."

"Just grab a handful and come back up," said Juniper. "Unless…"

"Unless what?" Salem was eager for her to finish the thought.

"Well, I heard that they can be aggressive!"

"They look angry," said Salem. Then the reality of his situation occurred to him. Underground, in that freezing part of the world, attempting to steal half-frozen berries from lemmings. Lemmings! All the while using the light of a firefly that was also his bunkmate aboard an ancient ship. The story hit him like a wave, and he laughed. He could not stop laughing. It was too funny, too unbelievable to even take. He could hear the muffled voice of Juniper above him.

"Salem? What happened? Should I pull you out?" Salem inched forward a little more. A big lemming with oval eyes stood on its hind legs in front of him. Aboveground it would not stand above his knee, but there, in the tunnel, they were at eye level.

"Hi there," said Salem, "I don't want to hurt you."

The lemming bared its teeth and to Salem's dismay they were sharp.

"That's it," Salem said, trying to keep his tone level. "I'm coming out."

"Salem, what's going on?" came Juniper's voice again. "Sa—"

Juniper's voice cut off. Strange, thought Salem. He knew Juniper to always finish her sentences. The green light from Zee sent off excited ripples of brightness around him in the tunnel. "I know," whispered

Salem to Zee. "I'm trying to leave." The next time Salem looked up, the lemmings were inches from his face, teeth visible and growling, and inching closer. "I liked you better up there," said Salem, crawling back as fast as he could out of the hole.

It was too late. The big lemming at the front lunged, and Salem covered his face with his arm.

"Juniper, pull me out! Help!" he yelled, but there was no response. Then he felt hands close around his own waist—huge hands, far too large for them to be the hands of Juniper. Salem paused, frozen in place as his mind raced and heart followed. The humor he had found in the situation seconds before vanished, replaced with fear, as someone pulled him up into the light.

CHAPTER 15 | CITY OF RUIN AND POWER

The mountain opened in a lopsided grin that exhaled musky air like fiery breath. Fern craned his neck to look straight up at the vertical wall of rock. It took all his self-control to right himself before the vertigo started. As he looked down, Aurora emerged from the depths of the mountain once again and this time extended her hand toward the captain and the others.

"Follow me and say nothing." She let her gaze linger on Ulysses as she said this.

Ulysses turned to Fern and Ena, putting his hand alongside his mouth. "I like this already."

Beyond the cliff face was nothing but a void, an eerie abyss that made Fern's curiosity peak, along with his fear. As they stepped inside, there was warmth and the smell of mineral-rich earth. The ground under his feet was not cold and harsh as it had been outside, but softer, more forgiving. The captain hoped whatever or whoever they were about to meet was also as soft and forgiving. Hard to know in the Fringe, he thought, as he considered the many fringe beings they had helped over the years. Just because the crew wanted to help, did not mean help was always welcome.

Aurora raised her arm with a fist, and they stopped. There was the sound of shuffling as she moved away from them and then from somewhere close by she said something in a language foreign to Fern.

Fern heard Ulysses whispering to Ena behind him. "This is where they try to eat us."

"This is where they try to eat you." Ena said back to Ulysses

"I'm telling you I am sweeter, or I smell better, or someth—" Ulysses stopped talking as the dark outline of Aurora entered back into their line of sight. Even though he could not see her features, Fern knew that something had happened.

She was silent and they watched her. From behind her in the darkness, a fire ignited. A long row of glowing eyes. What began as fires lit in the distance soon became torches lighting the surrounding space until the entire chamber glowed. Fern released an involuntary gasp, and Ulysses and Ena echoed as they looked up at their surroundings. The inside of the mountain looked like the inside of an ice cream swirl. The earth spiraled up and into itself in layers upon layers of exposed rainbow rock. Reds, blues, purples, blacks, and whites mixed in a canvas that looked whipped skyward from bottom to top.

There, built into the vivid rock, were buildings and doorways, bridges and tunnels intertwined like a complex anthill. Fern was at once struck with two conflicting feelings about the place. The first was the sense of substantial power that lived there. The second was the inescapable observation that the breathtaking picture he saw was only the shell of what had been—a ruin, which, at one time, was something much more akin to Byzantium or Tenochtitlán in scale and vibrance.

"What is this place?" Ulysses head swiveled around like the others, trying to understand the size. It was many times bigger on the inside than it had appeared on the outside. "You could fit cities in here and even then have room."

"Welcome to Jotunheim," said Aurora.

From across the space, three figures of immense size walked toward them. Despite their very human similarities in look, they were not human. They had the same pale, moon-shaded skin as Aurora, but their faces were different, longer; along their hairlines Fern noticed bumps like ridges along with the perforations, and as his eyes adjusted, he saw they were small horns.

"This," said Aurora, greeting the visitors with a hand gesture, "is the last refuge of the Jotun. The original home which bore us." She looked at the Jotun, watching them now, her expression a mixture of pity and empathy. "They are the last of their kind."

"Frost giants." Ulysses looked between Fern and Ena. "Awesome."

"Jotun," Aurora corrected him.

"They?" asked Ena. "You talk as if you're not one of them."

"I am only half Jotun."

"Right, that's why you're..." Ulysses made a motion with his hands.

"Different from them," Aurora verbalized the signal. "Yes, that's why. But they are still part of me. And I am still a part of them. Even if they can't accept it." The last part she added under her breath so that only Fern, Ulysses, and Ena heard.

The surrounding Jotun were well toned and, Fern guessed, nearly seven feet tall. Their eyes were all an icy color of gray and must have been adapted to the low light, because they moved without hesitation through the dark caverns and passageways. They wore large white, black, and brown furs over their shoulders and around their wastes, and they covered their bodies in the same markings as those tattooed designs on Aurora's hands. Fern noticed they did not look at the men but gave only side glances as they illuminated the way forward for the visitors.

"You know," said Ulysses to Fern and Ena, "Rigel always talked about finding frost giants and their mountain castles. I always told him there was no way they could have survived so long. He was right, and I was wrong."

"As was the way with Rigel," said Ena, and Fern nodded.

They turned back to hear Aurora saying something to the Jotun in their language. As a language it sounded slow and heavy, as if they forged each word on an anvil and crafted them for a specific purpose.

Then, after what seemed like a long exchange of words, she turned back to them. "Now, they will take us to Forn Modir."

The Jotun turned and walked toward a staircase carved into the mountain wall. Fern and the others followed, breathing hard as they tried to keep up on the steps made for taller beings. Each one was more a lunge than a jump for the men. Fern was relieved when they peeled off from the staircase and entered a doorway, which pushed deeper into the mountain.

The doorway brought them to a circular chamber with a domed ceiling, small and simple in decorum. On the far wall, opposite where they had entered, an inviting rosy-colored light spilled out along with the sound of voices.

Aurora paused after the Jotun had already passed through to the other side. "Through there is the reason we're here."

"Let's do this," said Ulysses, taking a step forward into the light. "I hope frost giants are different from mountain giants because boy did things get—"

"Wait." Aurora extended her arm and hand across Ulysses' chest and stopped him. "There are a few things I should tell you before we enter."

"Are you joking?" asked Ulysses. "There are things you've not mentioned before we were standing here, only the four of us, ready to walk into an underground chamber full of giants?"

"They are not giants," said Aurora. "They are only giant to you. And we are above ground, only in a tunnel."

Ulysses crossed his arms. "Irregardless."

"That is not a word," Aurora said with a grin.

Fern and Ena both smiled.

"What should we know, Aurora?" Fern asked and gave Ulysses a look he had given his friend many times before, a look that said please behave. For though he, and Ulysses and Ena, had been in such situations many times before, he knew each time was different, just as each being was different, and that Aurora's knowledge of Jotun far exceeded their own.

"First, know that even though Jotun speak limited English, they are just as intelligent and more conscious than humans. So even if they speak a different language, they will read you from your body language. You must control it. Second, let me do the talking unless I tell you otherwise. Third…" she said, pausing and considering for a moment, "nope," she corrected, as if deciding that it was too late anyway, "that's it, let's go."

They walked together into the doorway of light.

• • •

The room they entered was dome-shaped like the room from which they had come, though larger and more lavish in its decorum, which gave it a presiding feeling of intimacy despite its vastness in size. There were blankets of fur laid out on wooden slats on the ground, cut from what looked to be the trunks of massive conifer trees. Multiple fires were lit throughout the chamber. Meat spun on sticks; soups of sticky-looking plants floated in carved out stones the size of witches' cauldrons.

The three Jotun who had accompanied Fern, and the others had integrated themselves into the larger group, which allowed the men to see for the first time the diversity among their kind. Some were shorter than others, and some had seen more years. All wore the same determined look: the look of warriors and survivors. They were a people not familiar with fear but taught how real and familiar it could become.

At the far end of the room, leaning back against a throne of blankets, looking out through one deep black eye and one milky one, was what looked to Fern like a living fossil. He could not help but stare. It was an action which did not go unnoticed by the Jotun, including Aurora.

Aurora stepped in front of him to block his vision from the ancient creature, "That is Forn Modir. You are not ready to talk to her yet. That will come later."

"Forn Modir?"

Aurora's gray eyes looked up and to the right as she thought. "In English it means ancient mother. We will need to convince her."

"So, what is it we need to do to make our point?" asked Fern, aware of the intense stares of the surrounding Jotun.

"Well," said Aurora, "we need to first show them you're willing to speak to them on their terms."

"We are here, aren't we?" said Ulysses.

"Yes, we are here," said Aurora, misunderstanding the question's rhetorical nature, "where else would we be?"

Fern shook his head before clarifying. "What we're saying is that we have come the entire way across the world. Isn't that enough to convince them we will speak to them on their terms?"

"Ah," came the response from Aurora that she understood. "No."

One of the Jotun had moved to stand in front of Ena and Ulysses, squaring up with them as though to begin a duel. The Jotun's body was the width of both men, and Fern thought he could see Ulysses and Ena trembling as they stood, side by side.

"Uh, Aurora," said Ulysses; he and Ena had moved shoulder to shoulder, as if squeezing themselves together would make them seem bigger to the seven-and-a-half-foot stranger in front of them. Aurora moved with speed. She came and stood next to Ulysses, looking up at the Jotun. She said something, motioning to the two men. The Jotun rumbled a reply in a voice that reminded Fern of the low roll of thunder. Then the giant creature looked between Aurora and the two men a few more times and nodded.

"Varr would like you to join him to eat," Aurora translated for them.

"Oh," said Ulysses, loosening up at the sound of food. "Why didn't Varr just say so." Ulysses swung his arm around and clapped the Jotun along the side of his thick forearm. Aurora froze and the other Jotun sitting around watched with wide eyes. Varr bowed his head to look at his forearm where Ulysses had slapped him, examining it as though he should see a wound.

Once certain nothing had changed and that the gesture was friendly, Varr looked back at Ulysses and grimaced in what Fern assumed was a try to mimic Ulysses' own goofy smile. Varr then raised his arm and clapped Ulysses the same way alongside his shoulder—throwing him into Ena and causing them both to roll to the ground. Throughout the chamber, Jotun laughed like little children. It was so loud that tiny flakes of rocks fell around the sides of the room. Varr said something out loud to the entire room, the way a comic might open an act for their audience.

"He says," said Aurora, "it's funny that such a weak animal dominates the world."

Ulysses rubbed his arm. "Charming."

They followed Varr to one fire, over which meat turned on a thick spit. Varr showed them the fresh cuts, ripping it off in large pieces and handing it out. They nodded and smiled, eating what they gave to them. Ena made a face as he bit into a large strip of meat. "What do you think this is? Caribou? Reindeer?"

Ulysses and Fern only responded with shrugs.

Fern found it had a texture vaguely similar to chicken, though also a toughness he had never tasted. They followed this same procedure for several of the burning fires, as if the journey to meet with the Jotun was as much a culinary experience as it was a life-saving rescue mission. They tasted everything from strips of meat to the roots of plants to a mashed-potato-like substance which tasted to Fern like a mixture of honey and almonds.

By the time they came to a fire cooking the upside-down body of a big-eyed cave frog, Fern could not move. The captain's stomach had grown so full that he thought he may be ill. This joined with the warmth of the place and softness of the furs on which they sat made him fight to stay awake. He looked over, finding himself both relieved and worried to see Ulysses and Ena wrestling with the same problems.

"I should have warned you all about first impressions here," said Aurora, who had, as it appeared to Fern, chosen to eat only pinch size amounts of food offered to her. "Different from humans, Jotun do not measure you by the quantity of food consumed but by the endurance you show in consuming it."

"What does that mean?" Ulysses asked.

"It means," said Aurora, "that you should have eaten much less of everything offered to you."

"You could have mentioned that earlier," said Ena, burping a little into his mouth. One of the Jotun women watching him grinned. He only nodded back, turning with a confused face of terror back to the others.

"They want to see your stamina. How long you can hold your own with them."

Fern grunted and stood. The Jotun watched him. "Right!" he said, looking around into their faces. He tried to imbue the same gravitas into his words that the Jotun's own language possessed. "We are thrilled to be here and thank you for your welcome."

Aurora rose with him now, a look of concern on her face. "What are you doing?" she hissed.

"Showing that, although we have stamina, our time is also important to us."

She frowned but stayed silent.

"We are here," said the captain, "because you are not safe. We understand we are in your home. The last one you have. We want to give you a new home. A new place. A safe place. One where you can't be found." The captain paused, hoping for a sign of acknowledgment. He did not know whether the tactic would bring a response, but he had not sailed his crew across the world to fail.

"Aurora." The voice was not loud but steady and clear. Aurora, Fern, and all eyes turned to the ancient Jotun sitting in her fur throne against the wall. Forn Modir raised her arm and motioned that the strangers should approach.

• • •

Forn Modir, or Ancient Mother, emitted an air of prehistoric energy so potent that Fern felt it ripple out from her, engulfing them, pulling them into a different time, a different place. He, along with Ulysses, Ena, and Aurora stood in front of her with a growing number of the Jotun gathering in a semicircle behind them, eager to see the proceedings. Aurora was saying something in Jotun to Forn. Fern could not be sure, but Aurora's tone sounded equal parts enthusiastic and apologetic. After what seemed like a long explanation or a brief speech, Aurora stopped talking.

Forn leaned forward from her fur throne. One of the younger Jotun moved forward to help her sit up, but she raised her hand and issued it back. She fixed her black eye on Aurora and spoke. Aurora's expression moved with the old Jotun's steady stream of words. Then Forn motioned Aurora forward. Aurora approached and, for a moment, bowed in front of Forn. The old Jotun placed her hands on top of Aurora's head and whispered something into the air. Aurora rose, and Fern saw that she was smiling. It was the first authentic smile Fern believed he had ever seen from her. Smile remaining, she turned back to Fern and the others.

"She will talk to you," Aurora said, relieved. "You may come closer."

Fern looked at Ulysses and Ena, who only looked back at him. They were oblivious to what had taken place. He stepped forward. Forn had turned her eye to him, while her other clouded one seemed to look out and over him, on to whatever lay beyond.

Just as Fern was about to speak there came a great commotion from the far side of the room. He froze, and all eyes and ears followed the sounds. It was heavy breathing, footsteps, and voices. Two huge Jotun came bounding out of a passage yelling something in their language. Then, with the same swiftness that brought the message, Fern, and the men along with Aurora found themselves tackled to the ground by the much larger Jotun. The captain groaned as the pain in his face, half of it smashed onto the stone floor, pulsed into his chest and lower body.

He faced Aurora and pleaded through expression for an explanation. She was also held prisoner, only able to dart her eyes so that Fern could neither read nor understand them. The Jotun hands tightened around Fern's wrists and dragged him up to his knees to face the throne.

"But we were getting along so well." He heard Ulysses a few feet away. The Jotun were now gathered in a huddle around their ancient mother, speaking amongst themselves and casting serious looks onto their guests. They dragged Aurora forward and berated her with harsh words.

Fern wanted to help her. At least say something to her or to Ulysses or Ena, but something told him silence was best. A few tense moments passed before Aurora turned back to the men, her arms still held behind her back. She had a grave look on her face, and she looked like she might cry.

"We have a problem," she said. "The baby I told you about, it's gone. Someone has taken it."

"Taken?" asked Fern.

Aurora nodded.

"They believe it was the men again," she said, "that is what they tell me…" Aurora hesitated, uncomfortable.

"What?" asked Fern. "Why are they angry at us?"

"The timing of all of this could not be worse. The moment we arrive, the first child born in twenty years disappears."

Fern saw the problem too, but he had no better idea than anyone else about what had happened. He looked at Aurora, aware that the next few moments were decisions of life and death.

"Am I able to speak to them?"

Aurora nodded that she understood and relayed the message to the Jotun. A few showed signs of aggression, angered that a stranger make such a request under such circumstances. Forn Modir silenced them, raising her old arms, and signaling that the captain should go ahead with what he had to say. The Jotun lifted Fern and walked forward.

"We cannot help you if you don't tell us what is happening," he said to Forn Modir allowing Aurora to summarize the message in their language.

The Jotun spoke amongst themselves. All but Forn Modir, who listened without taking her eyes off Fern and the others.

"They are questioning us now," Aurora translated in real time without looking at Fern and the others.

"Questioning us?" asked Fern.

Aurora nodded.

"They are wondering how one group of humans can hunt them and another be kind. They are wondering," she said, studying the faces of the talking Jotun, "how you are even different from those others. How can they trust you?"

"Us?" Ulysses interjected. Fern shot Ulysses a look, pleading for him to stop talking. Ulysses obeyed, though looks of concern and anger were visible on his face.

"If they have taken one of yours," Fern said, feeling as though he was a hostage negotiator negotiating his own release, "then we will help you get them back. We are here to help. To bring you away from danger."

Aurora delivered the captain's words back in Jotun.

Forn Modir listened, and as she did, a wicked smile crept across her face that made the deep lines of her skin wrinkle into thousands of tiny valleys. Seconds, long and heavy, passed like this before the ancient mother's face once again grew dark and serious. She focused her eye on the men standing before her.

"You." It took a full moment for Fern to realize it was English. The word had left her mouth like a machine, as if was manufactured somewhere inside her first. "Think," she continued, sending the second word out of production. "Us... fools." The ancient Jotun had leaned forward in her rock throne while talking and now leaned back into it, with labored breaths, as though the foreign language had taken a physical toll.

The men all shared the same expression of disbelief. Fern was not sure if he was more surprised at the matriarch's words or the fact that she had spoken them in their native tongue. Aurora was also unaware that Forn Modir could speak a language other than the ancient tongue of their ancestors. She stood with her eyes wide.

"Forn Modir, you understand?" Aurora said in English.

Forn made no immediate motion but lowered her head into an affirmative bow. Forn Modir looked resolved, as if the few English words she had spoken were enough to suffice the foreigners' understanding. She said something to Aurora in her native tongue. Aurora's face changed again to a level of surprise Fern had not yet seen.

"She wants you," said Aurora, "to explain the prisoners."

"Prisoners?" Fern asked, turning to the once again stunned Ulysses and Ena. "What prisoners?"

CHAPTER 16 | THE RIVER CONNECTION

Salem came to, opening his eyes just enough that the light pouring in through his retinas would not overwhelm him. The world looked wrong. It shifted very much like the Curiosity on the ocean waves. Flipped mountain ranges pointed in the wrong direction and the fields and stream too. Whimsical cirrus clouds formed the bottom of the picture like lily pads sitting on a light-blue pond.

Something was bumping up against him in slow rhythmic beats. It was wet, stank a little like worms on concrete after a rainstorm, and was furry. He turned to see what it was and recoiled when he realized it was the bodies of lemmings, dangling upside down beside him. They were all being carried; himself included.

Salem felt fear and confusion and most of all dizziness. What would be big enough to carry him so? He did not know whether it would be better to play dead or try to get the thing's attention. He considered the limp bodies bumping him and decided that playing dead was not a choice if actual death was coming for him, anyway.

"Hey!" he said, twisting his body around as far as he could. He only spun, pulled back around by his own momentum. Whatever or whoever held him did not seem to notice. Salem made a mental note to scream at Juniper for pushing them into the lemming burrows. Juniper! Zee! He craned his neck and torso around like an owl to see whatever he could. Zee's limp body came into view for the briefest of moments, also held upside down in the air. Salem rotated back around and tried a second time to turn, straining as far as he could. He saw Juniper in a similar situation, held by something else. A sense of dread flooded into him and he hoped that they were alright. It was getting harder and harder to focus. Gravity pushed the blood through his skull, creating a tremendous pressure against his eyes and temples. He tried picking his head up, but it was too heavy.

"Hey!" Salem said again, loud enough that he felt faint. He was seeing little blotches of white out in front of him.

The inverted sights rose and rotated around in a panorama, until he was staring into the electrified eyes and moon-colored face of his captor.

It was not so dissimilar to a human, but bigger, much bigger. There were two eyes, a nose, a mouth, but then also a row of small rigid horns protruding along the forehead. And the eyes: the thing's eyes were so light they were almost white except for the yellow. He realized he had seen similar eyes. It took only another second for Salem to remember where: Aurora.

They stared at each other for a few long seconds. It said something to the others like it and stopped. Water flowed somewhere around them, and the rays of sunshine from above cast a warm midday glow.

The giant lowered Salem to the ground and placed him alongside the lemmings in soft grass. There he rested for a moment, letting the blood flow back down into his body. He sat up on his elbows.

They were on the bank of a river. Salem guessed it was early afternoon as he squinted up at the sky. Despite the circumstances of being captive, he could appreciate that the landscape was breathtaking. Then, pulled back into the present, Salem's eyes returned to the three enormous creatures as they waded into the water. They were giants, he decided. They must be. And Aurora must come from these giants. But then, he thought, why was she not giant, too? Giants, Salem marveled as he rubbed his eyes and even pinched himself on the hand, running through all the possible clichéd scenarios for what he might see.

The three giants had all left whatever they carried along the riverbank. Salem crouched by Juniper and Zee but paused. The giant who had carried him watched from a few feet away but did not move to stop him. The giant, deciding it could catch Salem again if it had to, only watched and continued wading into the water with the others.

Juniper and Zee, though unconscious, were breathing. He touched their arms and hands, hoping to rouse them, but neither budged. Salem sighed in a mixture of disappointment, relief, confusion, and exhaustion. As he sat back on his ankles and looked around, he saw that they seemed in one of the few places of true green amongst the snow and gray-and-black rock formations. The air was fresh and crisp, and the water in the stream gave off a chilled mist. He watched the giants. The one who had carried him had an exposed chest and sad-looking face, while the other two, with covered torsos and slenderer bodies, portrayed an air of femininity. He watched as they stopped halfway into the current and reached down with their muscular arms to pull up long green strips of plants.

One of the slenderer giants, Salem thought was a she, because she wore a thin brown fur pelt across her chest and torso. She hovered with her back bent over the water. Salem saw the range of markings up her arms, and then watched as, in a sudden movement, she immersed them beneath the water. No sooner were they under, than she had pulled a large wriggling fish out of the stream, holding it up to show the others. They all smiled, and Salem grinned with them. The giant who had carried Salem looked back across the river, catching Salem as he stared. Salem's heart skipped a beat, and he tensed, expecting punishment for observing. To his astonishment, the giant raised its arm and motioned for him to join.

The water was frigid on Salem's feet as he stepped into it. All three of the giants watched him. Salem felt crazy for what he was doing but the water was so cold it gave him no time to think. He stepped forward.

The river's gentle current made wading possible, and the rocks at the bottom were smooth and easy to walk on. Where the water came up to below the giants' knees, it was well up above Salem's waist by the time he had made it to the middle. He cringed and exhaled sharply as it rose above his thighs, rushing through his more sensitive areas. The sun warmed his upper body and he concentrated on that feeling while everything below his waist numbed.

"Now what?"

Salem watched as it used its powerful arms to grasp a bundle of the shoots, and twist and pull. Detached plants in hand, the giant raised them to its forehead, allowing the droplets of water to fall over its face, and then raised them skyward over its head.

Salem looked down into the water. Small fishes and crawly things moved across the bottom. He reached down and took hold of the nearest patch of the thick and fibrous green shoots just as he had seen the giant do. Scrunching his face up, he twisted, but the plants did not give way. Instead, they held tight against Salem's arms and even seemed to pull back against him. Before he realized what happened, his feet had slipped from their places on the rocks and the water engulfed him.

Time slowed. He looked around at everything happening beneath the water's surface. He had always felt like underwater was different from the world above in that it formed its own dimension. The fish swimming around and the things crawling along the bottom did not seem to notice a stranger from above in their midst. It was as if the world underwater was there before all the things above the water and would be there even after the things above the water had gone.

Once again, Salem felt the hands reach around him, though this time they were gentler. He gasped for air as the giant pulled him and held him long enough that he could find his footing again on the rocks. Salem held the giant's arm and looked up to see its watery eyes look down at him. Those eyes had been wary, maybe even angry. Now they seemed less so, perhaps even curious at what a strange creature Salem must be. Salem nodded his head and the giant only stared at him, unblinking. Then, the giant repeated the motion he had shown before, reaching his hand and arm down into the water, grasping the plants, and pulling hard and upward. Holding the shoots of plants suspended in the air, he brought his arm up to his face, touching the plants against his forehead and looking skyward. The giant then motioned with a nod of its head that Salem should try again.

Salem did, careful to not grasp too much of the plants, and to pull hard and fast enough to break it away. He thought about the lessons they had taken with Ena Boto and tried to imagine not only his hands as his tools, but his entire body as a unified machine. It worked. He braced his legs against a large, flat rock, used his hips and core up through his chest, shoulders, and arms, and pulled a handful of shoots up above the water. The giant did not smile, but only nodded his approval. Salem nodded back but allowed himself a grin. The entire interaction had taken place without words and somehow, Salem realized, words had never been necessary. He waded between the giants, gathering up what shoots he could and distributing them, like they had done, along the side of the stream.

He checked on Zee and Juniper as he dropped the shoots on the bank, but neither had moved from their spots in the grass. Salem waded back out a tenth time into the stream, but the giant stopped him with a raised hand. Salem halted, confused and a little nervous. The giant put its hand to its chest, patting over the middle.

"Vinyr," it said in a slow voice. Salem nodded that he understood. Vinyr took his arm and pointed it at Salem. Salem copied the act and said his own name out loud. Then Vinyr nodded and pointed down at the water and back up at his own chest. Salem did not understand. He walked toward Vinyr, stopping before the giant's colossal frame. Salem looked into the water, seeing only the swaying plants and a few guppies swimming in circles. He looked at Vinyr for an answer. What did he want? The giant motioned with his hand to his eyes, pointing at each and then back down toward the water.

"Sinni," said Vinyr, repeating the movement.

At first Salem thought the giant was telling him the word for water but that did not seem to match the sign language. Salem looked down again into the clear current, trying to look more closely this time. He felt the air move and looked over to see that Vinyr had knelt next to him in the stream so that their heads were on the same level. The giant's head was huge next to Salem's own and on its face, broad and spanning in its own type of landscape, Salem could see the finer details of not the thing, but the being, next to him. He could see fine wrinkles that had started to crease on Vinyr's forehead, whether from the sun or from age or a combination. He could see the gentle grooves under the giant's eyes, where lack of sleep or excessive worry lived. He could see small scars on the moon-colored skin and traces of red in Vinyr's eyes. Salem felt at that moment the strangest thing. It was an indescribable yet palpable understanding for the being that stood next to him. As if all the boundaries that existed had never existed at all. Vinyr pointed with his finger to the water and Salem followed with his eyes. This time, when he looked at the water he perceived a new sense of life there, and all that was happening in that strange world was enhanced. The shoots of plants danced with the current. The rocks had become their own sort of natural painting, arranged in the only way that made sense. The guppies Salem had seen earlier were no longer just schools of tiny fish, but individual life-forms moving in unison with their scales reflecting in dozens of colors. Was this the same Earth Salem lived on? It did not seem like it. A window had opened to a place.

It was unclear how much time had passed when he looked back up. The other two giants had moved back to the shore and gathered what they had collected. Vinyr had also retreated to shore, and Salem followed.

Salem could walk next to the giants so long as he also carried what they gathered. The lemmings were not as small or as light as they had looked before, and the grasses from the stream were damp and water-laden. Juniper and Zee were still slung over the accompanying giant's backs, though now, Salem saw, in a gentler manner than before.

They had been on their way for a few minutes when a figure appeared in the distance. It was small at first, but as it grew closer, Salem could see that it was another of the giants. Salem thought he felt the ground shake as the giant slowed and trotted up to them. Breathing, it exchanged words with the others in a language that sounded like something very old and very powerful. Vinyr looked at Salem as they spoke. Salem could not tell if it was a good or bad look. He thought he had a good idea that it was not good when Vinyr picked him up again and slung him over his massive shoulder.

• • •

It was a jostled and turbulent ride. Salem had never been carried by running giants, and no part of him wanted to repeat the experience. They had covered much terrain in a short time, over hills and long stretches, so that he wanted to vomit. The mountain had been nothing but a speck back at the river, and now, as it loomed like a stoic god, they entered it.

Juniper opened her eyes.

"Wha…" Her head bobbed up and down in tandem with the giant's footsteps.

"It's alright," said Salem, relieved to no longer be alone with their captors. "They have taken us."

"You don't say, genius." Juniper's voice sounded weak, but her sarcasm came through. Salem smiled. At least she's still herself, he thought.

"Yeah, well, how would you know?" he said to her. "You've been out for hours."

"I have?"

Salem nodded.

"What about Zee?"

Salem motioned with a nod of his head to Juniper's far side where Zee was being carried.

"He's alright?"

"Yeah, just recovering, I guess."

"Where are we?"

"I have no idea. Inside a mountain?"

Juniper looked around. Her eyes widened as she realized something much larger carried her. "Oh!" she said. "What are they?"

"I don't know that either," said Salem. "But they're nice, sort of…" Salem hesitated. "Well, they were and then they weren't anymore."

Vinyr turned to look up at Salem. The giant's face was mixed, as if it could not decide whether to be friendly or mean. Vinyr put his hand over his mouth that Salem and Juniper should be quiet.

"I guess that's a universal sign," Juniper said to Salem in a whisper.

The mountain had swallowed them now. Salem's eyes adjusted to the reduced light. He tucked his head in, hoping he would not hit it on any hard ceilings. He caught glimpses of Juniper and she too seemed to hold on tight, trying not to dread too much whatever would come next.

The tunnel brightened. The rock walls were shiny and glimmering, as if hundreds of children had painted them with glitter. They emerged out into a vast space. Salem looked up and saw the walls rising in a great cone shape and at the top, a natural opening, the world's biggest skylight. Fading sunlight poured in from the sky.

Salem felt Vinyr's hands reach up and bring him down to ground level where he could stand for himself. Then he felt Vinyr's massive hand come onto his shoulder and push him down to his knees. He looked around for an explanation. To his right Juniper was in the same position and Zee, coming awake, was sitting back with his hands held behind his back by a giant. Salem looked to his left.

"Salem!"

"Ulysses?" Salem said, astonished. He made a move to get up but Vinyr's hand stayed firm on his shoulder. There was no moving from his position. Ulysses was kneeling with a giant behind him, as were Fern, Ena, and Aurora next to him.

"I guess we will need to have a little talk later?" Salem watched his uncle's familiar smile and smiled back out of sheer happiness to see familiar faces. Fern was not smiling and did not look as amused as he observed Salem, Juniper, and Zee with concern that Salem thought was severe, even for the captain.

A commotion ahead drew their attention forward. Coming toward them, supported on each arm by two Jotun aids, was an ancient-looking giant, though she was smaller, only the size of Aurora. Goosebumps rose across Salem's neck and arms as he looked at her. Her eyes were different, one black, one cloudy like spilled milk. I've seen her before, he thought.

"So," the ancient giant said in slow but clear English. "We have you."

CHAPTER 17 | FROM THE ASHES OF THE OLD WORLD

The sun was a pale circle sitting on an invisible string in the sky. It would not set over that northern world, at least not during the summer months.

Roach was in a good mood despite his current predicaments. It was so easy to sneak away from the crew after arriving he almost felt bad about it. His low profile helped. His profile was so low that he would at times go entire afternoons without being asked to take care of a single task on board. There was the gnome. The chubby fringer latched onto him as though he had never had a friend in the world. In this case it worked in Roach's favor. Once on the beach, Dover played his usual role of bothering everyone and everything, and even more lucky it was enough that Roach walked away without saying a word.

He grabbed the few meager supplies he would need and made it over on the second of the longboats. Once to the beach, it was just a matter of helping to set up the first tents and then sneaking off. Nobody ever missed him.

Getting the child had also been easy. Fern and the others distracted the mythos beautifully. Roach half smiled as he walked. He was unaccustomed to everything going so well to plan.

Sure, he struggled under the weight of the kidnapped frost giant, or Jotun, or whatever they called themselves. They were all mythos anyway. He stumbled down the slopes as he made his way to the drop point.

Yes, he deceived Fern and the others again, though he admitted, at least in the privacy of his own mind, that such deception had been easier in the beginning. Back then he overlooked the little kindnesses and the strange warmth it brought him to be accepted by others. The problem with nice people, he told himself, is that it was too easy. They will be kind no matter what the circumstances, and that just was not how the world worked. There was something wrong with such thinking. Roach always earned acceptance through hard work and hurt. He had grown to crave it. No, he was not sick for that. Is a soldier sick for serving in the army? Tough love, he heard someone once call it. That is what he needed, and it would be different if he were a crew member on the Curiosity. At least he assumed so.

"Bunch of soft-bellied…"

The child cried out from within the sack, kicking Roach in the ribs. He grunted and cursed the child.

He held up the sack with his mouth close to the fabric. "You'll go soon enough." A small ball of fist shot out, catching him in the nose. "Ow! God!… Stupid little…"

Words reeled through Roach's head as he descended, with the grace of a tumbling boulder, the slick mountainside hills. He abandoned his standard antics, allowing himself a few rare minutes of raw conspicuousness. He was stumbling through his thoughts. Thoughts of forgiveness, acceptance, and even, in his more tumultuous fantasies, praise for his thinking above and beyond what they asked. He saw the Regulat leaders in line, one behind the other, waiting to touch him on the shoulder and restore his status of Regulator, the right to take a new name, and shed the title "Roach." Regulators selected their names after the cities they helped to cleanse. His was already picked. These thoughts propelled him, as they had for many months, forward into the unknown.

A cold gust of glacial air pulled him back into the present. The child was getting heavy and squirmed hard. He poked it a few times with his finger to settle it down, but his finger only came back hurting.

It was at the summit of yet another small mountain where Roach stopped, looking around, trying to figure out where he was. It was impossible to get his bearings when everything looked so similar. Was it the ridge? He looked down at his locator, shaking the small machine. Things rattled from inside. It reminded him of an old calculator. It was standard issue for regulators, at least it when he used to be a regulator. Upgrades were surely issued since, but the Regulat had not seen it fit to provide one to him. Tough love, right? They primarily used locators only in emergencies, such as the discovery of new fringe groups, or maybe Roach started talking out loud, "when kidnapping a sacred infant from a band of angry mythos who might rip one's arm off." Yes, he reassured himself, perhaps he was right to use the locator.

The child yelled out again, and Roach opened the sack. It was only a compact bundle of silvery flesh. It looked up at Roach with amber-yellow eyes. Still bundled in the thick furs, it looked irritated. Roach knew it was important to keep it alive, if only so Mr. White and the rest back at headquarters could do as they pleased with it. He reached in and wrapped an added layer of fur around its midsection, careful to avoid its not so tiny and grasping hands.

There was a soft whirring in the air from somewhere above him. He spun at the sound, unaccustomed to being surprised. A matte black vehicle approached from below. It rolled on tank-like treads over the snow. It dropped below the mountain, moving behind a pass. The cold air whistled, and the baby squirmed in the sack. Roach could feel the goosebumps crawling over his skin as he waited. After what seemed like a considerable amount of time, he saw the outlines of figures making their way up the mountain.

• • •

"Hello, Roach." The man was the obvious leader of the band. His English was layered in a thick Russian accent and his skin around his face crinkled like very dry paper. He was flanked by three additional people, all possessing tired-looking faces. Then, the man spoke. "You recognize me?"

Roach nodded that he did and greeted the man with his title. "Mr. Chernobyl."

Mr. Chernobyl nodded. Everyone in the organization knew who he was. He discovered the mythos living in the small Russian town over a half century earlier and triggered one of the most decisive moves of the Regulat's war against nonhuman entities. Not a tall man by any means, Mr. Chernobyl made up for his lack of height with the widest, flattest shoulders Roach had ever seen. Roach imagined that anything resting on those shoulders would never slide off.

Mr. Chernobyl turned his head and spat something green brown into the snow. "Your colleagues from the American delegation reached out to me. This is a most urgent matter to the cause." Mr. Chernobyl's eyes sparkled like glass, as if having just taken a hit of a euphoric drug. "We all work together. Americans, Russians… However,"—Roach sensed for the first time the slight tone of impatience in the flat-shouldered Russian's voice — "this better be worth our visit. Because of you, I will miss the second half of the Moscow–Kazan football match."

Roach lifted the sack in front of him, opening it wide enough so that Mr. Chernobyl and the other stone-faced Russians leered in with eager eyes.

"Otva`li," Chernobyl said in Russian. "Look at you."

Roach watched the hard expression of Mr. Chernobyl's face transform into one of disbelief. The international regulator, known for his stiffness and apathetic nature, looked like a child with a toy. A toy he got to play with before all the other children. Even more, Chernobyl was the kid who wanted to play with the toy in front of all the other children just to make them feel bad about it.

Mr. Chernobyl reached his hand into the sack, and Roach pulled it away.

"I thought I would meet with at least one representative from my delegation."

Mr. Chernobyl smiled. It was a languid smile of a man who knew he possessed the power, and so too the control in the situation.

"Your delegate is on her way. However, we thought it would be best if we came right away."

Roach did not argue but nodded. He could not have waited in the cold with the child.

"Okay. Let's go."

"Nyet."

Roach did not speak Russian, but he knew what it meant.

"I do not care if you come," said Mr. Chernobyl, "but I have explicit instructions from your delegation that you are to deliver your message, in this case your package, and return to your mission."

Roach let the dread and anger and despair creep in. They were all too familiar. This was supposed to be it. His double life was supposed to finally end.

He stammered to produce a response. "I can't be expected...No, I-I can't go back."

Mr. Chernobyl raised a hand and smiled, issuing the two other regulators forward with a bend of his pointer and middle fingers. "Oh Roach, I have heard you are good at what you do. I'm sure you will find a way." Roach was no longer listening. He was too busy trying to figure out what could come next for him. There was no plan to get back to the ship, much less fool Fern and the others yet again. Roach may have maintained a low profile on board, but it was still a profile, and someone would notice at some point that he was absent. The regulators moved forward, and one put his hand around Roach's shoulder, establishing their control. The other took the sack. Roach did not let go at once, but locked eyes with the black-haired Russian regulator. She had a thin face and thick makeup over her cheeks to cover up the circles under her eyes. She tugged at the sack and Roach released it. The child inside screamed out again, and Mr. Chernobyl smiled an eerie smile at the sound.

Mr. Chernobyl took a cigarette and match out of his pocket. He lit it with the ease of someone who had done it so many times it was beyond a habit, now a simple movement necessary to sustain life, at the level of opening a door or taking a bite of food. "Come now, Roach. You realize why they want you to continue, don't you?" As the regulator spoke, the cigarette seesawed up and down in his mouth.

Roach met Mr. Chernobyl's brown eyes.

"They're taking the neeshtos to the place."

As a once active regulator, Roach knew that neeshtos was the Russian's term for mythos. If he remembered it meant "nothings." Roach had not considered it, but it was where they would go. For him to stay undercover all the way to the fabled hideout seemed unbelievable, unachievable, and yet, there was something about seeing what sort of place it was that sent a wave of excitement down Roach's spine.

"Imagine." Mr. Chernobyl showed his yellowing teeth. The man was close enough that Roach could have smoked his cigarette with him. "Imagine if you help the global Regulat uncover their sanctuary. It would be…"

"The end." Roach, finishing the Russian's sentence.

"Of them, yes," said Mr. Chernobyl, "and the true beginning of our time, of your time."

Roach trotted down off the slopes of the mountains with renewed energy. They would commend him on recovering the child, of that he was sure, and if Chernobyl was right, it may only be a matter of staying on board long enough to make it to the place, the so-called sanctuary that sat, for as long as he could remember, just outside the Regulat's reach. Rumors told that there was no place. It was even said that Fern and the crew never rescued as many as believed. The Regulat employed eyes everywhere, from the densest metropolises to the most remote islands. Roach tripped over a rock and rolled his ankle, giggling like a man possessed. Change was coming and he would arise, like a cockroach after a nuclear storm, from the ashes of the old world, and step into his rightful place in the light of the new one.

CHAPTER 18 | YGGDRASIL

The air was dense and heavy to breathe. They trudged, or at least Salem felt like it was a trudge, through passage after passage of what he was discovering to be a vast, ancient city. Along the pathways were dozens of buildings carved into the stone, all vacant, all with the same eerie energy of age and better times behind them.

The walls of glittering stones he had seen upon entering had transitioned to a solid deep purple color of a single rock that showed their distorted reflections as they moved through the mountain. He and the other prisoners walked in rows, side by side, between two groups of the silent giants, or Jotun, as Ulysses had told him moments earlier. "Call them Jotun or nothing at all," Ulysses whispered. "They're temperamental." The name was foreign to Salem, and not one he remembered ever learning or hearing. It reaffirmed for him that everything since coming to live with his uncle on board the ship had been a series of stranger and stranger events. And yet, here he was, twisting and turning through a reality of lost cities and giants! The spell of reality hit him hard and threatened to throw him into an anxiety attack. Lucky for him, Zee spoke.

"Where do you think we're going?"

Salem shrugged.

Ulysses leaned forward from behind Zee. "We're going to see the Jotun's special tree."

"Not just a tree." Aurora had extended her head next to Ulysses. "It is Yggdrasil. The sacred tree." Salem wanted to ask Aurora why she, a relative of the Jotun, was being held as a captive. He decided not to.

Ulysses smiled and shifted his body away from Aurora so she could not fully hear him. "Like I said, a veeery special tree."

"So, this tree is important to the frost giants?" Salem asked.

"They are Jotun," said Fern, looking back over his shoulder as they walked. "And I suggest we all start speaking and acting as though this is as serious for us as it is for them."

Everyone was silent then as they were led by the oldest of the Jotun, an ancient creature called Forn Modir, who limped using her gnarled staff as a walking stick, causing all behind to her walk at the pace of a trudge.

Directly in front of him, Salem could see the large back of Vinyr, the Jotun from the river. He distracted himself by studying Vinyr's many tattoos. He thought they looked a lot like a mural an artist might paint.

A few more steps and the path leveled out, easing into a flatter, wider area where the ground became soft like dust. The sound of running water came into earshot. It was comforting to Salem and gave the sense they were not as far into the earth as he had assumed, though there remained no light except for that given off by the torches held in the Jotun's hands. Even with his eyes adjusted, Salem felt like he had no real sense of where he was in relation to the cavern walls. The shadows and light reflecting in the darkness made the space seem like it was expanding and shrinking, as if the mountain itself was moving around them.

The Jotun slowed and Salem and the others had to penguin-waddle to keep from bumping into each other.

"There," said Aurora. "Yggdrasil."

"Bless you," Salem heard Ulysses whisper to Aurora, who only shook her head, irritably.

Salem did not immediately understand what he saw because he was not able to comprehend the size and scale. What he had thought was the side of the mountain or a large column of rock rising was not rock at all, but the inconceivably enormous trunk of a tree that twisted both up and down through the mountain like a spinal cord which held the mountain together. The sound of water had exploded and as the torchlight expanded through the space, waterfalls showed themselves across the walls, falling into a void of space and nothingness around the trunk. Some of the waterfalls were large and gushed while others were weaker, more like water coming off the rainspout of a house during a summer rainstorm. "We are now directly over the ever-giving spring," Aurora explained. "And that," she motioned to the tree, "is Yggdrasil."

"I can't see the bottom," said Juniper looking down, and then, looking up, added, "or its top."

Salem followed her gaze over the side of the rock into the depths where the tree's trunk descended into darkness. He also saw nothing but the water of the waterfalls disappearing beyond the light of the torches. When he looked up, he saw only the great wooden plant piercing up and into the mountain above. Though they could see the water falling around them, the only sound was the faint disturbance of air caused by the liquid dropping into the void below them. It gave Salem the eerie sense that he could now hear splashes from an almost unimaginable depth below, as though the spring said to sit at the base of the tree was deeper than he cared to imagine.

"You will never see the bottom or the top," said Aurora. "Yggdrasil was once the bridge between worlds. Though it remains here and always will, I'm afraid that bridge has been closed for a long time."

Looking upon the scene now and listening to Aurora's words, Salem realized he had seen it before. The vision of his dream returned.

—He is somewhere deep underground. The space is dark with no perceptible boundaries. Out in front of him, shrouded in a golden light, is the enormous trunk of a tree…

The Jotun herded Salem and the others to stand side by side in front of the tree. Then the Jotun joined hands and Aurora showed that they should all do the same. To his right, Salem took Juniper's hand. He found there was something unbelievably comforting about holding it. To his left was Vinyr. When he took the Jotun's extended hand, he felt like a toddler putting its hand inside its parent's. Vinyr's hands were rough and, though Salem was sure that Vinyr could probably squeeze his hand into nothing but dust, like one of those knuckle-grinding handshakes the kids used to do in school in his pre-homeschool days, Vinyr held his hand gently. It was in that moment that Salem felt a spell of dizziness disorient him. He closed his eyes and held tighter to the hands of Juniper and Vinyr for support.

He opened them a second later to see Forn Modir approaching a stone bridge which extended out to almost touch the trunk of Yggdrasil. As she did the Jotun around chanted. It was at first a low rumble, a soft, soothing ohm. However, with each step the old Jotun took toward the behemoth trunk, the humming grew an equal degree louder. Salem could feel it pulsing through Vinyr's arm and hand, shaking as the vibrations grew in intensity.

Then he felt an energy ripple through him. It came first from Vinyr's body and seemed to fill him up completely. A warmth as if his blood had transformed into a heated syrup. He guessed that Juniper and all present must have felt it too, judging by the looks of concentration on their faces.

Then Forn Modir touched the tree with her hand, completing the connection of hands to Yggdrasil, and Salem felt the warm feeling grow and bubble up into a hot wax that seemed to stir up and poke at every nerve ending in his body. It was triggering things, digging into parts of his mind and past that he had buried away. He felt a bizarre mixture of anger and joy, and confusion and acceptance swirling inside like sharks fighting over a kill. Pictures of his past materialized. He saw his old house, with its slight lean to one side and the small forest that he would explore as a boy. He remembered the many creatures he discovered in that small patch of wood and the stories he would tell himself about their lives. He found it funny that such memories could be so far away and so close at the same time, as if in his mind there was no concept of distance, only his choice to pull the memories back to him or let them float farther and farther away.

He swallowed, trying harder than he ever had to ignore it all and watch the swaying Jotun who seemed, with their moonlight skin, to be in a state of tranquility he did not share or understand.

It was then that the yellow and green veins started creeping outward, beginning on the body of Forn Modir. Salem realized as he watched that the glowing light followed the designs imbued on the Jotuns' skins, so that each tattoo looked like an illuminated landscape of neon rivers. It had a similar effect on the visitors, winding up and around them like vines over an old house.

Salem felt his pulse quicken as the green light reached him. He closed his eyes, preparing for the worst. No pain ensued. He felt only the calm release of himself. He no longer felt angry or joyful, sad, or accepting. He felt nothing but awareness.

He did not know how much time had passed when he opened his eyes. Standing in front of him, only inches from his face, was Forn Modir. Roughly his height, she stared into his eyes, and he thought about how much her face resembled a map. The wrinkles around her forehead and chin were valleys. The bags under her eyes were lowland swamps. Those eyes, one foggy like a storm and the other clear, were two oceans. Locked in each other's eyes they stood and again, he recalled his dream.

—The face that looks at him is foreign yet familiar. Not of him but of his world. It is old in a way that is not his time but another time altogether. A time of monsters.

"Not monsters," Forn Modir said to him. Her words came out slow like icebergs colliding in a frigid sea. "No, not monsters, but others. Different and the same."

Then the edges of the old creature's mouth moved, and Salem saw that she was smiling. She spoke again, but this time her voice was different. It was louder, multi-layered, and deeper. Salem realized that the chanting Jotun now spoke in unison through her.

In that big, booming voice she said, "Watch." Salem obeyed and as he did a picture materialized before him. It wasn't one from his memories, but something new. He was outside the mountain, among the fields and hills and rivers. He was gliding over the landscape. It was the world like he had never seen it. Vast forests covered the earth, and mountains rose above the clouds. Everything before him was pristine and flourished with life. He was inside Jotunheim. Not the ruined city but a metropolis teeming with life, both Jotun and otherwise. The vision sped forward, and Salem watched with horror as the great city and its inhabitants diminished and shrank away, until only a ruin like a skeleton remained.

Then, as quickly as it had come, the vision faded, and Salem only saw the face of the old matriarch once again and listened as she spoke in the collective voice.

"Many lives depend on the actions of few. You are the bridge, a connector of worlds. Without change, this place and its children will vanish forever. That change begins with the *lagr*, the little one." Salem saw the image of the newborn Jotun child flash through his mind. "She is the key to rebuilding Jotunheim," the voice continued. "We need your help. Will you bring her back to us?" Salem was quiet, unsure of how to answer given that the question felt much more like a command. Again, the voice persisted. "Will you get our child back, Salem Swan?" Salem was not prepared to hear his name. How was he supposed to fulfill such a mission? What did he have to do with the Jotun and their lost child?

"I don't understand." Salem tried to recoil but was held in place.

Then the old Jotun extended her hand. Salem put out his own hand, and she took it, turning it over to show the palm. "Salem Rigel Swan. Yggdrasil sees your heart, and it is good. Worlds long adrift now come closer. Jotunheim must survive for balance to remain. Promise us here, in front of the tree of life, that you will bring our child back."

The words reverberated inside Salem's mind. Then he looked down to see Forn Modir impressing her wide thumb into his palm. As she moved it back and forth over his bare skin, he could feel the area itch and burn and had to suppress the urge to pull his hand away.

"Salem, do you promise us this?"

Why me? Salem wanted to ask again. This must be a mistake. I am not a part of all of this, it is all new to me… But then something caught inside of him. There was no new or old here, in whatever place this was. Someone, or in this case something, needed his help.

He was not sure what made him do it, but he nodded. "Yes," he answered. "I promise."

Then, swift as it had come, the burning and itching in his hand stopped, and Forn Modir removed her thumb. Inscribed in Salem's palm in the same dark ink fashion as the tattoos adorning many of the Jotun bodies was a symbol—a circle, and inside, a tree. The tree's canopy extended up and around, wrapping at the sides to form the shape's perimeter until rejoining with the tree's roots at the bottom.

"It is finished," said Forn Modir, once again speaking in her own voice. Then she bowed her head and walked slowly back toward Yggdrasil.

• • •

In another part of the world, more suited to normal people, Mrs. Manitou waited. It had been almost four months since the sudden passing of her husband, and it was the first time she had conceived of leaving her house for the outside world. She no longer dwelled in the basement, graduating to the doorway where she now paused before taking the first step. The door and frame were a cherry red color she and Wayne had picked out together. She let her hand slide over the red frame. It felt like nothing more than dried paint on dead wood. Wayne will not walk through this door again, she thought, and had to stop herself from collapsing.

It was not the death of her husband which made her sad, but the fact that she continued to exist without him. She knew wherever he was, Wayne was at peace, though a large part of her wished that when one partner died, the other followed. Seahorses, she thought, remembering something a friend in her book club had told her. Seahorses mate for life and the death of one often brings about the rapid decline of the other. Just natural, she thought, peeling herself from the door and walking out into the yard.

She walked through the short expanse of woods which had separated their house from the Swan's. The Swan residence no longer stood, the fire had made sure of that, except as a few small piles of burned rubble the firefighters could not take away. This is where it happened, thought Mrs. Manitou. The eerie thought of Wayne's last steps and breaths crept through her. Right here, not over three hundred feet from his bed. Rose stepped over a charred piece of wood that looked like it once belonged to the staircase. Underneath it, she noticed the glint of a picture frame. She bent down and picked it up. It was, as she expected, a family portrait wherein two parents held a baby. Rose remembered the day the Swan family had lost Rigel. Even though the man was long lost in the delusions of his studies, reading books about fairytale creatures and lore, Rose remembered how loving he was toward his wife and son and how hard it had been for Julie to recover. How she had thrown herself into Salem. Though she never said it, Rose wondered if it could have been Julie's attempts to control and protect Salem's life that had made him such an awkward boy. She had never supported Julie's decision to pull him from public school and homeschool him instead. Wayne had always told Rose it was not their place to interfere in the Swan's life. Three miscarriages early in their marriage had made their chances at having children impossible, and with each passing year adoption had seemed like less and less of a choice.

Rose held the portrait to her chest, imagining how much it must hurt for a child to lose their parent. Salem must feel as though his world imploded. Like me, she thought, and then, holding the picture back out in front of her, felt the first strands of an idea pull together.

• • •

Salem showed Ulysses his palm as Curiosity came back into view. They walked with the Jotun who, since the ceremony at Yggdrasil, no longer held them as prisoners. Something about what had happened at the tree had apparently proven to the Jotun that Salem and the others were not the bad humans. Whether it had to do with Salem's interaction with Forn Modir, he did not understand.

"She made you promise?" Ulysses touched Salem's palm. "Does it hurt? I can't believe it." Then, Salem felt a hand grab hold of his arm. He turned to see Aurora.

"Yggdrasil spoke to you?" Salem nodded and watched a look of shock come over her face. "Show me." She reached down and turned over his left palm, gasping. Juniper and Zee, along with Fern, Ulysses, and several other crew members also peered over shoulders to get a glimpse of the image on Salem's palm. "This is the sign of the great tree. What else did you see?"

Salem recounted the events which took place and as he did the surrounding faces became more and more a mixture of confusion and worry.

"This is not normal," said Aurora. "Never in my lifetime has the tree chosen to answer our call." Salem did not know how to answer. His perception of normal was in such a state of flux that it no longer had a basis of normal versus abnormal.

"But wait," asked Ulysses. "What did Yiggiedrizzle do to Salem?"

Aurora's face was one of astonishment as she looked at Ulysses "You're a naturalist, really? You do this for a living?"

Ulysses smiled widely and shrugged. "Where's your funny bone?" he asked, looking around Aurora's sides. "It's just a funny word is all"

"Yggdrasil," Aurora continued, "is an ancient tree which connects the worlds. When we make the ceremony to the great tree, never does the tree talk back. There are only a few times in our history when it is said to have done so." Aurora paused before continuing, fixating Salem with a grave look that made her already light eyes look transparent. "Certain gifts come after having a conversation with the great tree, or so the legends go."

"Gifts, eh?" added Ulysses, nudging Salem. "Are they shareable?"

Aurora shook her head. "Such gifts are not materials things like you people like. They are unique to the person and can quickly become a curse if not managed." Salem was feeling his stomach drop. Why did he have to be cursed? Aurora must have seen his fear because she swiftly added, "If you are indeed to be a champion for our people, Salem, then the tree will have given you something to aid you on that journey. I only say curse because, if you do not learn how to control it, that it was it may become."

"But why me?" asked Salem, feeling once again out of control of his own life. "What could I possibly offer the Jotun? And what is this gift I have to control?"

Aurora shrugged. "It's not our place to question such things. Yggdrasil sees something in you, and that we must all respect. As for the gift, we will have to wait and see what it is."

"Try flying!" said Juniper.

"Or find something super heavy and see if you can pick it up," tried Zee.

Salem smiled at them, appreciating their attempts at humor despite the tense moment. He looked from their faces to the faces in the small group around him. Ulysses, Captain Fern, Ena, Aurora…each expressed mild disbelief, though none of them looked unsure. None of them looked as though they thought Salem was the wrong person or not good enough for whatever he was expected to do, and for that, he was grateful.

CHAPTER 19 | THE LAST PIXIE

Tristan stepped up to stand in front of the Regulat cabinet. Nervousness was not an emotion he associated with himself. He had excelled in school with praise and always with ease. There had been no need for excuses and nervousness.

Nervousness, this thing that happened to other people, was, in fact, a depressing member of the human psyche, to which Tristan assumed a definitive air of immunity.

It was therefore alarming to him that his stomach felt knotted, and his bowels wanted to move from the inside to out. He was not used to the cold perspiration that had appeared as a thin layer of film in his palms, or the slight increase in his pulse that made him wonder for the first time in his life if he had undiagnosed arrhythmia.

"Initiates." The Regulat's patriarch, known only as Mr. White, stood before them.

Tristan's pulse quickened as he and two others stiffened their stances, not unlike military men standing at attention. They stood at the front of the church in front of a maroon red curtain behind them. Below them, in a semicircle, was a grouped assortment of Regulat members.

Mr. White had a microphone taped to his cheek. Its fuzzy head hung next to his lips, like a sidekick who thought itself more important than it was. Tristan watched it bob up and down as the leader spoke. "The Regulat has seen many great initiates rise through its ranks." Mr. White's words were crisp and well-articulated. Tristan heard the top and bottom of the regulator's lips smacking together as if he were eating a lollipop. "Many of those initiates, who stood where you stand now, have done great things."

Mr. White motioned with a hand to the group of people standing behind him. Tristan recognized some, at least the most famous. Mr. Hiroshima was old like a prehistoric relic with slits for eyes and a saggy face which looked to have some gravity sickness, as though the skin could not wait to dissolve into a puddle on the floor. Ms. Centralia and Ms. Accra stood side by side, both short and stout with beady eyes and smug faces as they snickered and looked toward the attractive Ms. Orleans. Tristan had always thought of them as evil stepsister types. He just was not sure if Ms. Orleans was Cinderella or the stepmother. Mr. Manchester and Ms. Cologne stood beside them. They were one of the Regulat's favorite love stories. Two young Regulator initiates who, through the course of their duties, found love in the purification of Earth. Tristan had to grin to himself. He had imagined himself a full member of the Regulat so long that this final trial seemed almost ridiculous; and yet, here he stood, ready to be judged along with the rest.

Mr. White motioned to the boy on Tristan's right. "Edward. You are first."

The boy called Edward, a lanky youth of Filipino descent, stepped off the slab to stand at ground level in front of the half ring of people. Mr. White, followed by Mr. Okanogan and a regulator Tristan did not know, led Edward down the center aisle of the church and out of the back.

Tristan was not sure how much time had passed when Mr. White, followed by Mr. Okanogan, reentered. The other regulators, who had since retreated to sit and whisper amongst themselves in the church, looked to Mr. White, who only shook his head. Tristan felt his heart start up again. Edward had failed. It was the first time Tristan felt genuine fear that, despite coming so far, despite ascending for judgment, he could still face rejection. He expelled the thought. He refused to believe that he could fail and join the ranks of blind humanity, of the masses. His feet ached as he watched Mr. White speaking in the group. He wanted to run toward and away from those who were about to judge him.

Then Mr. White detached from the huddle. Tristan already knew what was coming as their eyes met. "Tristan. You are next."

Mr. White led Tristan down the hall of the church. Tristan synced his steps with the Regulat's special communication machines as they whirred around them. It was not only nervousness coursing through Tristan. It was an all-present awareness that each step he took brought him toward or away from where he wanted to go, and all he wanted to become.

They exited at the back of the church and turned right. Tristan knew the left would take them to the old priest's house. Their path now would take them either to another subsection of rooms or somewhere else. They walked down the long hallways, which seemed void of activity yet full of latent energy. Tristan knew where many of the doors and passages led. He had come to know the space over the years, choosing to spend his time with the Regulat rather than at his parent's home.

Mr. White halted in front of a large door. It was one of the few doors Tristan had never entered, though he had seen it many times, only ever closed. Black and made of iron, it had thin twisted bars across its face, like the root system of some unkempt garden bush. Mr. White produced a key of the same color. It was long and crooked and tied into a brown leather band that dangled down like a cat toy as he inserted the key into the door's hole.

"Do you know where this goes?" Mr. White did not turn around. He had since switched off his microphone and spoke now at a more intimate volume.

"No, sir."

Something clinked inside the door and Mr. White pushed it open. Stone stairs that looked much older than the church descended into dim light.

Mr. White stepped down onto the first step and motioned for Tristan to follow. "This is why you are here."

• • •

The catacombs possessed a certain sweet smell Tristan could not place, something caught between perfume, mothballs, and lavender. The ceilings were low and the corridors tight. Stone boxes lined the walls.

"Longevity, Tristan." Mr. White ran a hand over the grooves in the stone as they walked. "Longevity has been the greatest achievement of humankind. The creation, proliferation, and perpetuation of our species has allowed us to take control of a chaotic world. These halls attest to that story, but we can see the true success of what our kind has done in the work we do." Mr. White had slowed his pace, stopping to stare every few feet at the old stone walls of the passageway. Tristan took it as a cue to do the same. He looked at the stone boxes formed into the wall. Many bore the handiwork of stone masons, possessing crosses, or pictures of saints, or roman symbols showing years or positions. "The church had some things right," said Mr. White, noticing Tristan's survey of the engravings, "though its fatal flaw was inclusion."

"Sir?" Tristan was eager to understand the meaning of Mr. White's words.

"Protection, Tristan." Mr. White looked into Tristan's face and Tristan noticed for the first time the intensity of Mr. White's stare. "Protection of what one has and a critical strategy to maintain what one has achieved." An air of pride had entered Mr. White's voice. "Tell me, Tristan, what is the Regulat's purpose?"

Tristan knew the answer better than his own name but hesitated, double-checking in his mind to not make some critical error. "To ensure human existence." Tristan paused, knowing there was more. "And success by vigilant guidance."

"And what is vigilant guidance?"

"Vigilant guidance is the calling of our kind. It is our true purpose to bring order to the chaotic world."

"And what is order?"

"Order is the purest state of existence. Order is salvation."

Mr. White grunted to himself, satisfied with the answer. Tristan was sweating, but with each answer gained confidence.

A few hundred feet brought them to a part of the corridor which widened out in a fork like a reptilian tongue. Boxes continued to line the walls and at the center, waiting, stood a group of people all dressed in black. All but one.

"We stop here," said Mr. White. Tristan and the others obeyed. Five people dressed in black cloaks stood in the background with a single woman, dressed in bright red, swaying in the foreground. Tristan had never seen such a woman. He had never seen such a dress. He imagined it was not so different from one flamenco dancers in Spain might wear, though this dress had no frills; it was sleek and smooth. It looked cut and tailored to the measurements of the woman's body. Tristan tried not to stare, but the sheer attractiveness of it all overcame him. She had a body like an hourglass that curved out, then in, then out again. He could smell her; she was the perfume permeating throughout the catacombs. His breathing slowed, and he took a big breath in. Gathered around a stone hearth, they watched him, and waited. Even from the distance at which he stood, Tristan could feel the heat rising from the hearth's center. It rose and circulated in waves, the mouth of some small volcano, pushing itself against his face and making the air sit all around and on top of them.

"Now comes the time." Mr. White smiled a miraculous, white smile. "Now comes the time when you may prove yourself committed to our cause." Mr. White turned to Mr. Okanogan and nodded. Mr. Okanogan walked forward into the darkness behind the fiery pit, followed by two of the men in black. Tristan waited, as was his only available option. The feelings of apprehension had become less prevalent. He tried to ignore the woman in red before him. He repeated instead to himself why he was there. There was only here and now and his goal: his acceptance into the most elite group of humans on the planet. Later was nothing but an illusion. He would face this here and now, or he would not.

A scream erupted from the darkness causing Tristan, but none of the others, to jump. The scream devolved into sobs as something scraped toward them along the stone floor.

Mr. Okanogan, followed by two of the men in black, emerged from the darkness. The two men in black held in each hand the wrist of something. As they emerged into the light Tristan saw the orange-tinted skin, the two arms extended. They belonged to a small body, part flesh, part feathers and wing. It had green-brown mossy hair that trailed behind its back in a broken braid. It was crying in semi-silent heaves and twisting and writhing in ever weaker convulsions.

"The last pixie," said Mr. White. The pixie was bigger than Tristan imagined pixies would be. It had a small frame and big orb-like eyes that were tear-filled and red. It made noises like small whistles between cries as it looked up and around at the people surrounding it. The initiates had often looked at relics collected by the Regulat throughout the many laboratories and study centers. Skulls, vertebrae, skeletons, and carcasses. But seeing such a thing alive gave Tristan a far different feeling. Mr. White singled Tristan out. "You, initiate Tristan, will exterminate the last of the pixies."

Mr. White produced a syringe from the inside of somewhere across his chest. A long straight needle protruded out of its front. The pixie wailed when it saw it and squirmed away. One of the men in black smacked it across the head and together the two men held it down. Mr. White held the syringe out to Tristan. "Before you receive your mark and join the ranks, you will take this device and continue the order we seek to create. The last initiate failed to do so, and we deemed them unworthy. I believe you are different."

Tristan had known the Regulat's mission. He knew what they expected of him. The thing pinned down to the floor in front of them was subhuman; it was a disruption to the order of nature and only existed as a threat to him and to humanity. Still, when he looked into its eyes, Tristan detected that the pixie had all the same abilities of perception as he. He wondered for a split second if it could comprehend why it was there. He wondered if it had watched others endure the same fate before it. He wondered if it could love. He wondered if it could hate.

Mr. White shook the syringe at Tristan, following it up with a look that told Tristan to wait any longer would be unwise. Tristan expelled the thoughts from his head, terrified that they would somehow publish themselves and become public to the waiting faces around him. He took the syringe and turned to the pixie.

The thing had since stopped sobbing or showing any emotion at all. It now sat stone-faced, looking forward into nothing. The two men in black held it down as Tristan moved closer. He was aware of the eyes watching him. Mr. White, Mr. Okanogan, the woman in the red dress. The man in black on the right pushed one of the pixie's wings out of the way, revealing a spot behind its shoulder. He motioned that that was where Tristan should insert the needle. Tristan moved closer. He moved close enough that he could smell the distinct air coming off the pixie's leathery wings and see the faint dust they gave off. This was the source of the lavender, though he was now close enough to smell the creature's blood and sweat. He lowered his hand to insert the needle. At an inch away, the pixie turned its head toward him, looking at him with its deep eyes and stolid face. Tristan stopped for a moment, frozen in where he was and what he was about to do. The look on the creature's face was not one of self-pity but, Tristan realized, the reverse. The pixie felt sorry for him.

Willed either by his own conviction to belong or by the slight pressure he thought he felt from a hand on his shoulder, he pushed the needle into the pixie's skin. If Tristan thought it would be easy to do such a thing, he was, in that moment, proven wrong. He felt cold and hot at the same time as he forced himself to watch the pixie's eyes glaze over, its limbs and wings go limp, and its life force fade.

• • •

Mr. White looked triumphant. "Well done, Tristan." Tristan watched the two men drag the motionless body of the pixie into the darkness. "We expect that will be the first of many order-creating acts on your part."

Tristan's hand was shaking in a mixture of adrenaline and something else. If it was sadness, he would not bring himself to admit it. He had crossed over something. Some threshold of what he wanted, into becoming what he was. The years of words, reciting oaths and creeds, committing himself to the dogma of the Regulat: it had manifested itself into action. He only nodded his head and grinned to his comrades standing behind.

The woman in red approached him now, taking him in with her large black eyes and inhaling. The movement made her shoulders rise and her chest contract so that Tristan could not look away. She looked between him and the hearth. "Approach, initiate." Tristan found her voice just as curvy as her hips. "Approach and receive your mark."

Tristan placed one foot in front of the other until he was standing beside the woman and in front of the hearth. He was not sure if it was pheromones, or the heat, or a mixture of both, but a sudden feeling had overtaken him. It was emptiness and fullness at the same time. He swayed where he stood.

She spoke close to his ear. "What you feel is growth. Your cells are revitalized. Through your body pulses blood of purpose. Blood of action. It's heavy now, but over time it will become light. Over time, you will come to crave more of it."

Mr. White stepped up next to the woman. "Fire purifies. It cleanses the forest and fields when they grow over with weeds the same way it creates the heat that kills the bacteria in the water we drink."

The woman in red reached out and took Tristan's left arm. She had smooth, cold hands that felt good against Tristan's hot skin. She guided Tristan's arm toward the mouth of the hearth.

Mr. White narrated while she worked. "We wear the mark to remind us." Tristan could feel his skin starting to burn in the distorted air rising from the hearth. The woman reached into the fire with her free hand, pulling out a long metallic needle not unlike the one he used on the pixie. "With this mark you, Tristan, slayer of pixies and all things which threaten the longevity and happiness of our kind, of humankind, enter the ranks of those who would see order preserved." Tristan winced as the tip of the needle touched his forearm. He did not watch as the woman in red painted. Mr. White's voice grew louder. "Now, you will be marked, and you choose your assignment. As you know, if you succeed in clearing your region, you will claim its name as your official regulator title." Mr. White's face contorted into a shape of utter glee. "But first, Tristan, we welcome you as a rising regulator, to the Regulat."

CHAPTER 20 | MERIDIAN SLOTH

Salem felt like a seasoned sailor around the Jotun as they stumbled around the ship. They had reengineered the hull for Forn Modir and her aides to use as quarters while the rest of the Jotun used every bit of spare space available on the ship. Though not perturbed by the cold, the rocking motion of the ship was not something any of the large guests enjoyed.

Artichoke harrumphed around the deck. "Had to move around half the damn supplies." He hoisted an enormous barrel of freshwater against his gut next to Salem. "We picked up the last of the Georgian Garden faes a few months ago. I could fit all of them into my spoon drawer."

Salem smiled as he listened, wondering if there were any faes running around in the kitchen now as much of the cutlery did seem to vanish only to return with gorgeous engravings in a language he could not read.

"Salem!" came the voice of Zee from above the hull. "Come and help us."

Salem took the stairs that would lead to the top deck, leaving Artichoke grumbling behind him.

"What's going on?" he asked as he emerged onto the top deck.

"We," said Ulysses, striding up next to Zee and smiling, "are trying to convince Aurora here that she has made serious progress as a sailor."

Salem looked behind Ulysses' shoulder to see Aurora watching them. She stood with the other Jotun who, since coming aboard the ship, seemed to have adopted Aurora as the most experienced seagoer. It was true, Aurora had at that point gathered the most experience out of the Jotun. Still, Salem had to suppress a smile as he watched her put on a brave face for her people.

"We are not used to water," she said, as she stepped away from the uncomfortable Jotun to join them.

"Oh, you'll all be fine," said Ulysses. "Look how far you've come already."

Aurora looked at him as though she might hit him.

"I'm not sure you've convinced her," said Zee, looking with his bright green eyes from Ulysses to Aurora as if he expected a fight to break out.

"Sailing is like learning to walk or talk," said Ulysses.

"I don't think so," said Aurora.

"Sure it is. You don't remember learning to walk or talk but at some point, you said your first word and took your first step. Sailing is no different. The trick is to see the true face of the ocean."

"The true face?" Salem had to ask.

"Sure," said Ulysses. "You've got to look at the ocean the same way you look at people. You can't try to take it all in at once; you'll get overwhelmed. You see those?" Ulysses pointed over the starboard bow of the ship at a choppy section of water. Salem and the others nodded. "That's a school of fish. And there, you see that?" They looked to the other side and felt the gust of salty wind blow across the deck. Salem shivered while Ulysses raised his head to the wind. "There you see the clouds rolling in." Ulysses' expression changed as he studied the horizon. He turned to Salem and Zee. "What do you say we check on the captain, boys?"

• • •

The sheet of dark clouds rolled in like an angry army. Roach felt like the eyes of every cumulonimbus soldier were on him. He had gotten lucky on his return to the encampment when almost no one had questioned him on where he had been. When the fat cook did inquire into where he had been, he had made up a lie thanks to the foresight of Mr. Chernobyl who, before leaving Roach, had given him bundles of wood as an alibi in case of such a situation.

Still, the entire ordeal had been far too close. Roach was never supposed to still be in this situation. He had done what he had set out to do, finished, thank you very much; give me back my regulatorship.

Then the thought struck him. What was it that the Regulat had tasked him with anyway? At one time, it was to gather information on the ship and Fern. Find out their current plans and relay information back. Roach had been so eager to regain favor with the organization that he had not for a second questioned any of it. The realization set in that an end date, an end goal to the mission, an end to anything, had never been specified. Since that time things had kept growing, kept evolving, until now that he wondered whether he would ever find his way out.

He stood toward the back of the ship, pretending to rig a line which had, for the past ten minutes, been rigged and tightened. To say he was frozen with fear would be an inaccurate description of how he was feeling. It was not fear. Though still there, the fear had receded, overtaken by something else.

Roach was paralyzed with indecision.

The words of Mr. Chernobyl rang in his ears. It would be your time. Imagine, this thing that had started out as a chance for Roach to redeem himself what little he may, could become the single greatest development in the fight for a pure world. Crewmates approached, and he squeezed his thoughts back into their artificial forms. He knew there was more than one being on board the ship that could peak into the thoughts of others. The consideration made him wonder whether anyone on board already suspected anything. He ran through the list, feeling reassured that, if he had already been found out, Fern would not have waited to act. The logic brought him comfort. The sound of thunder broke through the clouds in front of them. Roach was going where no member of the Regulat had gone before. The man no one expected anything from would deliver everything.

• • •

"Tierney?" Ulysses called as he pushed open the door to the captain's quarters, followed by Salem and Zee.

"Here," came the voice of the captain.

They followed the sound of the voice through the room. Fern was on a step stool. It was the first time Salem had seen the captain looking discombobulated or flustered. Fern was reaching up, hand gripped tight around one of the ropes hanging down from the ceiling, coaxing an angry-looking Atlas.

"The clouds, Tierney," said Ulysses, unaffected by what he was seeing. "We're close."

"I damn well know, Ulysses," said Fern, stretching further toward Atlas, who reached a clawed forearm in the opposite direction. "Damn you, Atlas. You know what you must do."

"You know there are better ways of getting him," said Ulysses, walking toward the struggling captain.

"I refuse to fatten him up," said Fern. "We need him fit."

"Oh," said Ulysses, walking behind the captain's nautilus-shaped desk and reaching somewhere within. He pulled out an opaque jar.

"What's that?" asked Salem, suppressing an urge to laugh.

"Just a little concoction I whipped up, which remains irresistible to meridian sloths."

"It fattens them and makes them less able," said Fern through clenched teeth.

"Meridian sloths?" Salem asked. No one answered.

"It's only a little hodgepodge of things," said Ulysses. "Elderberries, yarumo leaves, crushed cricket legs, and my secret ingredient."

"Your secret ingredient?" asked Zee.

"Peanut butter," Ulysses whispered, motioning with his thumb toward Fern, "though the captain doesn't like me giving that one to you know who."

Ulysses opened the jar and Salem smelled the peanut butter. A memory flashed through his head. He and his mother used to sometimes eat peanut butter right out of the jar by the spoonful on the couch just before their favorite Sunday night show. It was a nice memory, though it did bring the sticky sensation into his mouth.

"Now," said Ulysses, who had taken a dried marble-sized pellet from the jar and begun to approach Atlas from below. The sloth, Salem saw, was already reacting, arching its pointed face and goofy grin behind itself and down to look at Ulysses. Ulysses turned to grin at Salem and Zee. "What did I tell you?"

Fern had since stopped struggling and only watched now, still perched up on the stool, as Atlas shifted his body down toward Ulysses.

"It's not real love," said the captain grudgingly.

"That's right," said Ulysses, scratching Atlas' chin, "you know who really takes care of you."

The sloth reached a three-toed arm down and Ulysses reached his five-fingered hand up, handing the pellet upward. Salem watched as Atlas opened his mouth ever so slowly, placing the treat onto his outstretched tongue.

"Meridian sloths, Salem," said Fern, stepping down from the stool, "are one of the rarest and most fantastic of Earth's creatures."

Atlas was slipping down off the ropes and onto Ulysses.

"Unfortunately," said the captain, "there are far too few left. We are not even sure how many."

"Why 'meridian'?" asked Salem.

"Ah," said the captain, smiling and moving toward one of his book towers. "Sloths haven't always had the best reputation, you know. The word 'sloth' even denotes laziness and inactivity."

"But sloths are lazy, aren't they?" Salem asked.

"Far from it," said Fern. "They're just slower. The world today rewards speed, efficiency, industriousness. Alone these things can be helpful, but together, they destroy the beauty of what the sloth brings."

"Which is?" asked Salem.

"Moving slowly is not a bad thing, Salem. On the contrary, it allows one to see things differently and take in more of an environment." The captain was flipping through a book he had picked up. "Meridian sloths like Atlas can even go a step further. Give him to me, Ulysses," ordered Fern. "And one of those treats."

Ulysses smiled and handed Atlas over to Fern.

"Atlas can slow down so much," said Ulysses, filling in where the captain left off, "that he can see things we cannot."

"See things like what?"

"You're smart, Salem," said Fern, "but slow on the pick-up like your uncle."

"But once we get it…" Ulysses tapped his pointer finger against his temple.

"Yes," said Fern, "once you get it. Whenever that ends up being." The captain walked with Atlas to a large globe that occupied one of the captain's many tables. "Things like meridians, Salem. Folds in the fabric of the world so fine and small that you and I cannot see them."

"You mean like the prime meridian?" Salem said, recalling one of those obscure things he learned in school. "Isn't that the imaginary line that cuts the Earth in half?"

"Quite right, Salem, and quite wrong. It does cut the Earth but is far from imaginary. It's one of the few meridians we ever hear about. There are countless meridians." The captain readjusted Atlas so that the sloth now rode on his back with its arms crisscrossing around his neck like some living backpack. "Some even go places."

It was happening again. Salem could feel the strange mixture of wonder and irritation mounting as he listened, as if the captain were divulging some piece of semi-trivial information that was common knowledge. Ulysses and Zee showed interest, but no surprise in what the captain was saying.

"So, these meridians… go places," Salem began, trying to navigate his way through a logic that made no sense. "And Atlas can see them because he moves that slow?"

"Quite right," said the captain. "Though our dear Atlas can do more than just see them. Can't you, you supine superhero," the captain praised as he stroked the meridian sloth's arm. "You languid lunatic. It's time to go up again." Atlas was grinning and as Salem watched him with the captain, a sudden shock rippled through the ship, jolting them all to one side. Salem grabbed on to a nearby table to keep from toppling over.

"Well then," said Fern. "What do you say? Shall we see what hidden meridians are waiting for us out there?"

Together they made their way back onto the deck where the entire crew was gathered, all transfixed on the ominous sky and turbulent waters in front of them. It relieved Salem to see that he was not the only one struggling to cope with the fear of an angry ocean. The Jotun were terrified, huddled together and begging to retreat to the hull of the ship. Salem watched as they filed past the crew and down to where Forn Modir would comfort them. It surprised Salem to see crew members looking tense. Ulysses stared at the sky with an unconvinced grin. Dorianna stood still, clinging with white knuckles to a rope attached to a mast. Artichoke was next to her and even he, for the first time since Salem had known him, looked unsure of what to say or do.

Then they reached the point where the stormy sky met the ocean and Curiosity began to move up and down over the water like it never had. Its mythical masthead which Salem had grown fond of pointed almost straight up at the layer of clouds, only to seesaw back down toward the dark mirror water. Rain fell. First in a spray like a mist, then thicker and heavier. Heavy droplets smashed against their faces and hands. Until that point, Salem had felt secure to at least know that he was at sea with experienced sailors. Those who knew the ocean and could navigate and understand it. Though in that moment, looking across the faces of the sailors he had come to know, Salem became acutely aware that while they may understand the sea, no one, not his comical uncle, the organized Dorianna, the patient Ena Boto or clever Raiju, nor the wise Captain Fern could control the vast creature which controlled them now.

Salem looked at Zee and Juniper, who stood to either side. The looks on their faces told him they shared his feeling of unease and that they too were mesmerized by what they saw.

"You okay?" said a voice from behind him. Salem turned to find Aurora. Salem could only think to nod back to her, finding no words to reply.

Captain Fern had moved up to the front of the ship. He still had Atlas, and as he moved toward the bowsprit, he reached around so the sloth could grab onto one of the thick ropes hanging down from the foremast. The sloth hoisted itself up and climbed.

The surrounding waves grew with each succession in size, causing the ship to throw itself over them in bigger and bigger fits so that Salem had to control the urge to scream.

"Aurora?" he asked after a moment, unsure why he felt the need to ask her the question right now. Aurora looked at him. "What does sinni mean?" he asked, recalling the word Vinyr had shared.

Aurora smiled. "It means," she said, grasping to the railing as the ship jerked to the side, "connected."

They were in the storm now. The mist had become a torrent of rain that beat down in angry sheets from all directions. Salem could not see his hands in front of him. Flashes of lightning illuminated the sky in still-life freeze frames. The crew were frozen and could only watch as the ocean took hold. All except for Atlas. With each streak of lightning the sloth appeared higher and higher until Atlas had reached the topmost part of the ship's largest mast. There he extended a clawed hand up into the sky as the ship bent forward into the maelstrom.

Salem saw the small fold of light break through the spot where Atlas' claw stopped. He gasped, horrified at the thought of Atlas being struck by lightning. The light did not come and go like lightning, however, and Atlas remained. It poured through the spot in the sky just above the sloth's outstretched hand, as if some divine entity were peering through with her flashlight. The shipped dipped again, sucked into the swirl of the water, and Salem felt as though his stomach had detached from his body the way it might during the initial drop of a rollercoaster. The dip was short-lived as they were pushed up in the opposite direction, causing Salem to lose his balance and yell out as he fell backward. Two hands on each shoulder grabbed him and he turned to see Zee and Juniper at his sides. Zee yelled through the rain which had grown to a roar and handed Salem a piece of rope, motioning that he should tie it to himself and hold on with them to the rails lining the ship.

Salem found himself in a moment so full of stimulus he had no immediate emotional reaction, only able to witness the spectacle and hang on. A spectacle which was evolving by the second as the distance between the ship and water grew. Salem did not realize that Curiosity was in the air until Juniper pointed it out to him and sure enough, he saw the ship, as if suspended on invisible ropes, navigating the space between the clouds and earth. Up and up the ship rose, and the small section of light opened by Atlas grew, until it enveloped everything around them.

As they entered the clouds, the roar of the rain slowed to the whisper of a drizzle, until it was replaced altogether with a silence that bordered on eerie. Salem could no longer see the water over the ship's side. There was only brightness then, and he wondered if they were about to arrive at the gates of Mount Olympus, or heaven. His thoughts were, however, discarded as the invisible ropes that kept them airborne snapped, and the ship dropped. The last thing Salem felt was a hand coming into his own. He did not know whose hand it was, but he held it back and closed his eyes.

INTERLUDE 2 | ON A SMALL GREEK ISLAND

34 Years prior to Salem's arrival on the Curiosity

Tierney Fern stood at the edge of a forest somewhere on an island in the Aegean Sea. The vegetation was dense. Huge bushes and small trees with vibrant flowers grew close together, making it difficult to imagine a way through.

"What do you think?"

Tierney had not heard the captain approach. "About what?" he asked, trying to play it cool.

"Well, this," said the captain in her no-nonsense tone. She nodded her head forward toward the island before them. Behind them, the crew of the Curiosity was already beginning to pack and prepare for the journey.

"It's nice," said Tierney, "though I'm still not sure why we are rescuing these things… I mean, from what I understand, nymphs cause more trouble than good."

The captain looked down at a nearby branch; she reached out and rolled between her fingers the bud of a small berry that would in the coming days most likely fatten and change color.

"Do you think you do more good with your actions than bad?" she asked without looking at Tierney.

"I would like to think so," he answered.

"And if I had never met you and only ever heard about you from other people or things, how would I know that?"

"I guess you wouldn't," said Tierney.

"But you would expect a fair shot to explain yourself and maybe, if you had been less than perfect, to start over or try again?"

"That sounds like it would be fair." Tierney could already guess where the captain was going. Allowing him to stumble, not always so gracefully, into his own answers was her way of helping him see.

"Can you see why the nymphs, despite their reputation, also deserve a fair shot?"

"Yes," said Tierney, "All things deserve the right to exist on their own terms."

Tierney knew he had quoted the captain. The captain nodded her head as if hearing the words for the first time.

"Good," she said, "then, you can start by finding one we haven't been able to reach yet. The family is quite worried about her and we need to be off tomorrow. I fear the Regulat is not far behind."

"Who is she?" asked Tierney.

"Her name," said the captain, "is Aegle."

• • •

Tierney stepped over a branch sticking up and out of the ground. It looked like an arm reaching up to grab him. He had walked for thirty minutes and there had been no sign of the nymph. The captain had given him no description of what to look for or what to say when and if he found her. He knew it was important that he convince her to join them and retreat to a place where she would be safe. "It is her own life she is playing with," the captain had told him before he set off. Great, he thought to himself. Just what he wanted, the responsibility of someone else's life on him. He did not even have the details of his own life under his control. He had come to the ship only months before with little clue of what his life was about or where it was going. He had had no expectations, or at least, he had thought he had had none. Still, he had never expected to discover what he did on the ship. He had never thought to suspect the vast amount of goings-on that were taking place behind the "curtain of the world," as the captain called it. He stepped over another appendage of root.

"Hey!" The voice was sweet and melodic.

Tierney turned around, but no one was there.

"Here, buffoon," said the voice.

Tierney looked up to see a young woman sitting along a scraggly branch of a tree. She swung her legs underneath herself.

"Where are you going?" she asked.

Tierney considered her for a moment, deciding how to answer.

"Oh my," she said, "I'm sorry. I didn't realize you're stupid."

"I'm not stupid," said Tierney.

"That's what a stupid person would say," said the woman. Tierney could feel himself blushing. She was exceptionally pretty, with olive-colored skin and hazel eyes.

"Aegle?" he asked, as she smirked down at him.

"Who's that?" asked the woman, smiling.

Then she tumbled off the branch into a backflip, landing on her feet with a dexterity Tierney had never seen.

Tierney had received no verbal confirmation, but the smile told him everything. It was beautiful and spread across her cheeks as they curved up into crinkles at the corners of her eyes. She had a mess of dark-blonde hair with streaks of lighter blonde intermingled like rogue rays of sunlight.

"I need to bring you with me," said Fern, finding it suddenly hard to string his thoughts together into a coherent sentence as he looked at the beautiful thing in front of him.

"I'm not sure what you're talking about," said Aegle.

Fern caught once again the tone Aegle had used and tried to give it back. "I think that you know what I mean."

Aegle looked at him, and Fern swore he saw her eyes twinkle.

"I think I need to bring you with me," she said.

"Bring me with you where?" asked Tierney.

"It's obvious from your clumsy feet and loud manner that you, not me, are the one in danger," Aegle said. "I think it's of big importance that we change that."

She was imitating him. Tierney could hear it. It was not hurtful; it was endearing.

"But you know there are others coming for you..." he tried once again to make her see reason.

"We were here before humans, weren't we, girls?" Aegle stroked the bark of a nearby tree the way one might a lover. "And we'll be here long after they're gone."

"I'm not so sure about your logic," said Tierney, "but I admire your outlook."

They walked together down the path. It was not a well-worn path like the ones Tierney had often hiked as a boy. It had a wildness to it, as though it would allow passersby to walk down it under the pretense they accept the truth that not they, but the forest, was in control.

"You walk loudly, even for a stupid person," said Aegle from in front of Tierney.

"I don't think you understand the gravity of the situation," said Tierney. "If you don't come with me you will be in danger." He had followed her, but only because he could not convince her to follow him. He figured he should at least stay with her. The captain had after all tasked him with retrieving her and bringing her back.

"I am always in danger," said Aegle, laughing in front of him and sprinting forward. She leapt with the agility of a large cat, grabbing with both arms outstretched onto the branch of a tree. She rotated a full one hundred eighty degrees before dismounting with a backflip. She landed, throwing her arms up.

"There are some… who do not have your best intentions in mind."

"Is it men?" asked Aegle. "Or satyrs?"

"Men, yes," answered Tierney.

"Men never have our best interests in mind."

"Not all men are the same," said Tierney.

"Pssht," said Aegle, smiling, "at least the satyrs are honest about their intentions."

"You cannot stay," said Tierney. He could feel his patience thinning. "Your family is coming. Will you not go for them?"

"But this is my home," pouted Aegle. "These trees are my sisters. The river is my brother. How could I leave them?"

Tierney did not see a river, but as they turned a corner, the sound of water rushed to greet his ears. Aegle approached the edge, dipping her bare toes down into it.

"How are you, dear?" she asked, and before Tierney realized what had happened, she had stripped herself of her dress, exposing the backside of her naked body and dived into the water. He had hoped for a moment that she had been calling him dear and asking him how he was. She broke the water's surface a second later with her face glistening and her hair soaked down around her head and neck. Tierney could feel himself trying to resist the urge to look at her. He attempted to look around at the surrounding forest. Nothing was even close to as interesting.

"Come in," said Aegle, "and I'll show you."

The warnings circled through Tierney's head. He had always heard to be careful around nymphs. They possessed the knack for seduction. Still, something in Aegle's eyes told Tierney that her intentions, at least in this case, were genuine. Against his better judgment, Tierney stripped down to nothing. Attempting to hide his manhood in front of the wide eyes of Aegle, he crept up to the water's edge.

"You are shy," said Aegle. "Maybe you're not as stupid as I thought."

Tierney entered the water in slow motion, inhaling further and further the deeper he got.

"Oh, it's not even cold," said Aegle, splashing him.

"Give me my time," said Tierney. "You didn't even think I'd get in."

"I had my doubts," said Aegle, "but also my hunches."

Tierney allowed her to explain to him the intricacies of the water. Why it flowed the way it did and how it did so. Then they exited the river. He had not seen Aegle dry off or get dressed, but as he turned around from picking up his clothes, she stood near him, dried and clothed.

"Come on," she said, "we have more to see." She took him further through the forest, talking about the trees and their ages and their preferences. "And what trees do you have at home?"

Tierney was surprised by the question. "Uh," he said, "there're oaks, and maples, and junipers, all kinds."

"Junipers? Don't know those. What a funny name."

"Yeah, they're beautiful trees. I think you'd like them."

"I like them all," said Aegle. "And I'd like to see one."

They came to a field full of long golden grass stalks. "Here," said Aegle. "Let's stop here."

Tierney had lost track of how much time had passed since finding her. He could not bring himself to worry about getting her back to the ship. He was not sure what had happened in the hours they spent together, but the thought of not being safe did not exist. He was there with her and nothing else mattered.

Aegle laid down in the golden grass, spreading her arms and legs out as if she were making a snow angel. Tierney laid down next to her.

"Now," she said, "I will show you something. Look up there." They laid on their backs in the grass, looking up at the few cirrus clouds smeared across the blue expanse of sky.

"What am I looking at?"

"My parents are up there," said Aegle.

"Your parents?"

"Well, my mother is. She visits sometimes."

"Oh," said Tierney, not knowing what to say. He wanted to say something. Either to tell Aegle she was foolish or that he was not. Though as he looked over at her and saw the severity of her expression, he decided against it. "Well, they did something right in making you, Aegle," was all he could come up with. It was cliché, he knew, but the words were true and that for him justified their use.

"Ugh, I dislike that name. Can't you call me something else?"

"Why?" asked Tierney. "Aegle is a nice name."

Aegle only shook her head. "If I have a daughter," she said to the sky, "I will name her... Juniper. After your trees, I have yet to see."

"That is also a nice name," said Tierney, and he meant it.

Aegle turned her head toward him. "You're still stupid," she said, and she kissed him.

• • •

"Well, of all the things I didn't expect to find," said Ulysses as he burst through the bushes on the edge of the clearing. Tierney was blushing, he could feel it, but he did not care. "What are we up to here?" said Ulysses, clapping his hands together, "and can I join?"

"Of course!" said Aegle, smiling.

"Of course not," said Tierney, getting up. Ulysses was smiling big, and Tierney knew he would hear about this again.

"We were worried about you two being gone for so long. Guess we had good reason to be," said Ulysses, winking. "Was he bothering you, ma'am?"

"Oh, on the contrary," said Aegle to Ulysses, "I believe I was bothering him." Tierney was not sure what it was. Whether it was the way she had answered the question, the tone in which she said it, or the afternoon they had just spent together. Something stirred inside him he had never felt before. He would discover soon, however, that he had stumbled on that most mysterious and terrifying of phenomena. Tierney Fern had discovered love.

PART III | VAEL

CHAPTER 21 | THE FRINGE

The water was calm as Curiosity glided over it. The only sound was the steady flapping of the sails in the warm, dry air. Salem relaxed his grip on the ropes, feeling the stiffness in his knuckles as he did.

The sky was mixed with shades of yellow and white, filled with a phosphorescent light that painted the world around them in a sharpness that enhanced all it touched. This light was new to Salem. It had a quality to it, a hue that enriched the details of things. Salem noticed for the first time things like the design of the wood on the deck, the lines of fatigue on the faces of his fellow crewmates, and the sparkles reflecting in the water like thousands of tiny galaxies in space. The air buzzed with a unique energy—rich, vivid, and alive.

"You're lucky," said Ulysses, coming to stand next to him, "to see this place so soon."

Salem's eyes fell onto the space where land met the water. A long strip of sand, looking much like the curved arm of a dancer, extended out into the glassy surface. The ship floated up alongside the arm and he heard the clicking metal of the anchor as it was dropped.

"What is this place?" he asked Ulysses.

"Welcome to the Fringe. Not always easy to get to but worth the visit every time."

"Fringe?" asked Salem, remembering what Fern had told him weeks earlier. He was also sure he had seen the word more than once in his father's journal. Salem had always thought that fringe was just a way to describe the creatures his father studied. Beasts of the outside, the periphery. Never did he think it would be a place. "Ulysses, where are we exactly?"

"To be honest," said Ulysses, "no one really knows. The Fringe exists just beyond the Commons. That is, the world you and I know best—the world dominated by people. Far as I know, back in the days when the two places were more friendly—you know, before humanity got all terrified of beasts and monsters and such—you could travel back and forth between them so that there was no Commons or Fringe at all. Just one world. But then some more powerful creatures than you or I decided they needed to protect themselves from, well, people. So here we are."

"Did magic bring us here?" Salem asked, readying himself for an answer he would not be able to believe.

Ulysses sucked air in through his teeth, making a sharp whistling noise. "Magic is a tough one. I guess you could call it that. It's more like energy brought us here, and those who know how to manipulate energy can use their 'magic' to do it. Know what I mean?" Salem shook his head and his uncle laughed.

"But how is it that no one knows about this place?" Salem had to ask.

Ulysses looked at his nephew incredulously. "What do you mean? We're here, aren't we? We clearly know about it."

"Well, yeah," said Salem, feeling exasperated, "but I wouldn't consider you and us normal." Salem realized as he spoke that he had included himself in the group.

"Very true." Ulysses rubbed his hand over his chin. "There isn't a straightforward answer to your question about why the Commons knows so little about the Fringe. It wasn't always that way, but I guess as time has gone on most people don't want to know about the bigger world. Heck, they don't even want to know about what's beyond their front yard. The wild places of the world aren't like the cities and towns of people. They're," Ulysses searched for a word, "well, they're wild. There's mystery and wonder and danger. When you're there, in those wild places, you aren't a visitor but part of it. We fool ourselves with buildings and beds and refrigerators and the lot of luxury we know. If you look deep down inside yourself, you'll see. You're wild. That's what scares people. That's why we build houses and lock our front doors and wall ourselves off in cities. Imagine all around you is the most beautiful music that ever existed, but you lack the ability to hear it. Even worse, you have the ability, but you've forgotten how to use it." Ulysses grinned at the worried expression now apparent on his nephew's face. "Don't worry. I don't mean to scare you. Let's just take it all one step at a time. Look." Salem followed Ulysses' gaze to see Curiosity's anchor sinking into the water. "We'll be ashore soon, and you'll see exactly what I mean."

• • •

The sand sounded like sugar as Salem stepped into it. It was fine and a mauve-violet color he had never seen. The tiny grains were so granular that it was more a powder than the beach sand Salem remembered shaking out of his clothes during visits to the seashore as a child. He still did not know what the place was, but the way the light painted over it made him think vaguely of heaven or a paradise. This made him think of his mother and, for a moment, he felt closer to her than he had in a long time.

"Surreal, right?" said Zee, crunching down next to him on the sugar-sand.

"It's…" Salem could not find the words to describe what he was seeing. The beach was long and stretched up and down as far as he could see. Turning his gaze inland, he saw the hilly dunes that formed a natural border between the beach and what lay beyond. Not far beyond the closest dunes stood two pillars on either side of a wide dirt road. Far off in the distance Salem could see the shapes of giant buildings the size of hills or asteroids that seemed to have landed there at some point and never moved again.

"That's Freedom Road," said Zee, following Salem's gaze and pointing toward the gate. "And this is Go'an Beach."

"It doesn't seem real," Salem finally said. "I mean"—he picked up some sand and let it fall through his fingers—"it looks real enough but like a dream world, you know?"

Zee nodded next to him. "I guess it kind of is. Come on, then." Zee put his arm around Salem's shoulders. "They'll be arriving soon. They always seem to know when we show up."

"They?" asked Salem.

"Things that get displaced," said Captain Fern, walking past them, "same as anything else: need a place to go."

Minutes later, the crew had all disembarked and stood gathered on the beach. Curiosity rested silently behind them in the water. A humid vapor had drifted in, obscuring the beach and everything behind it so it was just shifting shadows. Still, through the misty fog, Salem could make out shapes moving toward them. There were big shapes, much bigger than a man, and smaller ones. There were round ones and ones that looked like they slithered or crawled. There were some that floated, and some that flew and some that hopped; many traveled in large clumps or in groups of threes and fours, or just as lone forms.

"Wha—" was all Salem could say.

"Fringers," said Zee happily.

Some were animals, or at least Salem thought they were. Some were humanoid in form, but not in appearance. Others were things the likes of which Salem had never seen. As he watched the group approach, he witnessed at the same time the changing of many of the crew members. "What are they doing?" he asked Ulysses, pointing to the crewmembers removing their necklaces of wood inscribed with runes.

"Taking their true forms," Ulysses said, smiling. "The pendant of the ship protects their identities in the Commons because it's necessary, but here, here they can be as they are."

They watched as Geb transformed into something like a cross between a rhinoceros and a giant shrew, while his sister Nut expanded into what Salem could only describe as a bird made purely of cloud.

Dorianna's already highly distinguishable features enhanced to reveal long elegant ears, and her skin had turned a charming combination of gray and green.

Artichoke had grown even larger than Salem had ever seen him, with huge hands and feet and skin that looked hardened and taut; he also looked the happiest he had ever been in Salem's recollection.

Kane trotted forward, beaming as a band of tiny leprechauns, all yelling rapidly in their old-world Irish accents, enveloped him. Typhon, the quiet member of the crew that had first showed Salem and Mr. Gingam up the ship all the weeks prior, became a four-legged serpentine creature with many heads.

Salem felt the strangest sensation as he watched the many beings reunite with one another. It was at first a soft sound inside his head and, as more and more creatures came together, it grew to a much louder noise of voices, calls, shouts, and whispers. It was as though he could hear the thoughts of everyone around him but could not control the way it all ricocheted around in his head. At the same time his palm, specifically the marking the tree made by Forn Modir, burned so he had to grasp it with his other hand.

"You alright?" Ulysses asked, hearing Salem gasp and looking at his nephew with a worried expression. Salem nodded and looked toward Typhon.

"What is he?" he asked, trying to mask his discomfort for sheer shock. He did not know what kept him from telling Ulysses, but he kept the pain in his palm and the raging voices of the surrounding others to himself.

"Hydra," Ulysses told Salem, following his gaze to Typhon. Obviously, Ulysses had bought Salem's act, not suspecting anything more than his shock at witnessing the reunion of the fringers.

"Ulysses," asked Salem, as another new thought entered his mind. He took a step back, letting the noise inside his head subside briefly, "are you?"

Ulysses chuckled and shook his head, to Salem's relief. "No necklace on me, Salem. I am only a human who believes in diversity. But we are welcome here too."

• • •

Tristan stood on the periphery of the room while Mr. White sat with other regulators in the fading light of the day.

"Now," said Mr. White, "it's come to my attention that Roach"—Mr. White grinned in disbelief as he spoke—"Roach, yes, Roach, has gone with the crew to the beyond." Rising murmurs and sounds of shock vibrated through the room. "I know, I know," said Mr. White, raising a hand so he could continue, "regardless of how unfathomable it is, we must nonetheless see this as an opportunity."

"Roach is unreliable," said a bunched-up man with an Australian accent from around the table.

"I understand, Mr. Perth," said Mr. White, "but have you done what he has?"

Mr. Perth was silent. "I didn't think so," said Mr. White.

"How do you know he made it?" another regulator asked.

"I went to the Eastern Hemisphere delegation myself." Vera said, stepping out from the shadows behind Mr. White. Tristan had not heard or seen her enter. "Mr. Chernobyl himself," she continued, "assured me that Roach departed with the crew again."

"And what of the rest?" asked Mr. White now, prompting Vera to complete what she wanted to say.

Vera cleared her throat. "Roach also took something."

Silence dominated the room as each person, Tristan included, waited. "The creatures in the north are known as Jotun, more commonly 'frost giants.' They were on the verge of extinction with no hope of survival until recently when the first Jotun in over two decades was born. Now, you may think," continued Vera, "that this doesn't sound like groundbreaking news. What's a single mytho after all?"

"It's hope," said Mr. White. "Hope which we cannot allow."

"That's right," said Vera. A cart was wheeled into the meeting room. Something sat upon it, wrapped up in a thick blanket so that no one could see what was underneath. Everyone was silent as the blanket was pulled away to reveal the child. A few gasps drew through the room. Vera waited for effect and nodded. "Yes, you know what this means. We now hold the key to their future, their hope."

"Why is it still alive?" asked another one of the regulators. Tristan, and everyone else, knew by the accent who it was before turning. Mr. Odessa was a thick man from Texas who was notorious for his love of meat and lack of control over anything and everything leaving his mouth. Mr. White dropped his head and sighed. "How some of you ever became regulators is a mystery to me."

Odessa stared with a blank expression, not understanding the stupidity of his question.

"We do not want to kill anything yet, Odessa." Mr. White said, staring intensely into the man's face. Tristan saw as the fear crept into Mr. Odessa's eyes. "This child could become the most pivotal, most influential, most divisive move we as an organization make since our founders deliberated a pure world many centuries ago."

The regulators sitting around sat quietly. They knew Mr. White was not finished, and they knew that he would clarify for them what he meant. They were counting on it.

"We now have the future of yet another species in our hands. What is it we want?" Mr. White asked rhetorically. The leader of the Regulat stood now, doing it slowly and meaningfully.

"To ensure human existence and success by vigilant guidance." Mr. White looked directly at Tristan. "And what do we need," Mr. White continued, scanning the awaiting eyes of the seated regulators, "to do that?"

"More regulators," said Odessa with fervor.

"Mr. Odessa, after today's meeting you and I shall take a walk. The true key in moving forward, you see, is not increasing power but eliminating roadblocks. What we more desperately need is to rid ourselves of those who would oppose us. We have reached a critical tipping point. We are not the same as we were all those years ago at Crawford." Mr. White was smiling his infamous smile. "Here is what we're going to do."

• • •

Night crawled over the sky as Salem sat on a beach dune with Zee on one side and Juniper on the other.

"I just can't really believe all of this exists," Salem admitted. Something was making its way in front of them, throwing up small clouds of sand as it burrowed. It had a head like a lion with whiskers, the body of a caterpillar (with tiny rows of digging feet), and a tail that looked like the fan of a Japanese geisha.

"Amazing," said Zee as he reached down and let it crawl into his hand, "how blind we are to all the forms life takes." Salem and Juniper both looked at Zee, who only shrugged. "What?"

"Sometimes you say smart things," said Juniper in a tone that Salem thought may have even bordered on kindness.

"I will take that as a compliment," said Zee.

"Guess we should go down," Juniper said. "Everyone will head into Vael."

"Vael?" asked Salem.

"Oh yeah," said Zee, "Vael is the biggest city in the Fringe. It's great. It's got a market, amazing food, and even an academy!"

"I would have believed you about the city and the food… but an academy? Like a school? Come on Zee, can't you just be honest with me?"

"Salem?" said Juniper, looking serious. "You saw Zee turn into a firefly. You've helped rescue the last of an almost extinct species of frost giant, you've passed through a disrupted meridian into a variable half-world"—Juniper was running out of breath and her voice was rising—"all that and you're having trouble believing they have a school? That's it, I don't get it. Boys are morons." Juniper turned and walked away with this final decree. Salem turned to Zee, and they shrugged at each other.

"Why didn't you tell me?" Salem asked Zee.

"Tell you what?"

"You know," said Salem, "about you."

"What about me?"

"That you're a fringer!"

"Oh," said Zee, smiling. "You never asked!"

"Seriously," said Salem. "So, are you a shapeshifter? Can you turn into other things, too?"

Zee shook his head. "Nope, just that. I'm not a shapeshifter. I'm an Adze."

"What's an Adze?"

Salem discovered a whole new level of respect as he listened to Zee's story about the Adze, about how they were persecuted and pushed out of Ghana over many centuries.

"That was all before my time," added Zee, "but the choices of the people that come before us can impact us very much."

"It's alright if you don't want to talk about it," said Salem. "I get that retelling some histories is difficult. I had no idea that you lost your parents so young. I'm so sorry."

"It's okay," said Zee, "It was a long time ago, and I wanted you to know. You've heard everyone talking about the Regulat, right?"

"Kind of," said Salem, "but only in bits and pieces. What do they want?"

"They're a bunch of crazies," said Zee. "They think that by killing off every species that could challenge humanity, they can create a better world."

The thought seemed bizarre to Salem as he looked around the loving and gentle groups of diverse beings. As far as he could tell there was absolutely no threat to anyone around.

"What does that even mean?" he asked. "How would getting rid of all this make the world better? I think it would only make it more boring."

"Like I said"—Zee let the little sand creature circle around his wrist and back into the sand—"they're crazy."

"And your family," asked Salem, remembering the photograph, "are they all…?"

"I was the only one who survived the night the Regulat destroyed my village."

"Zee, I…"

"It's alright, Salem," said Zee. "Again, a long time ago."

"Doesn't matter how long ago it was," said Salem. "Pain doesn't die."

"No," Zee agreed, "it doesn't. But it need not control us either."

"Hey!" Salem and Zee turned to see Juniper walking toward them again.

"Think she's going to tell us how dumb we are?" asked Salem.

"I'd say the chances are better than bad."

"Get up," she said in a friendlier tone—at least for Juniper—that suggested she was no longer annoyed. "My father wants to see us."

CHAPTER 22 | THE CODE OF BEINGS

Salem walked with many others in a grand procession along Freedom Road, leaving Go'an Beach and the silhouette of the ship to shrink behind them. For most of the crew, coming to the Fringe was an all too joyous reunion with loved ones and friends.

"Welcome to Vael," said Ulysses as they walked, leaning into Salem and tracing with his finger the sprawling skyline taking shape.

Vael did not look like any city Salem had ever seen in the Commons. There were no tall buildings or skyscrapers, and he did not hear car horns or the sirens of emergency vehicles. Instead, he heard a sonorous roar of voices and movement, of cries and squawks—like a soundtrack of Earth if all the voices of all the animals and people were to be mashed together.

Again, Salem was having difficulty distinguishing between the noises happening outside or inside of his head. At one point it all got so loud that he reached out to hold Zee's arm.

"Salem, you alright?"

Salem nodded, managing a weak smile.

"I'm worried about you," said Ulysses from Salem's other side. "Since Yiggiedrizzle and the giants, you've seemed preoccupied."

"I'm fine." Salem shrugged Ulysses off in the most normal voice he could manage, still unsure of why he did not want to talk about what was happening to him. He felt like he was back trying to force himself to go to public school and experiencing the same sensory overload. He could not deal with it then, and now, with the addition of the strange headaches, it was all feeling like too much. He motioned forward toward Vael, fighting through his feelings of worry. "I'm excited to see the city!"

"Me too!" said Zee, though Salem could see that neither Ulysses nor Zee or Juniper looked convinced that he was fine.

Whereas structures in the Commons were designed with function in mind, with sliding doors for easy entry, sharp building corners matching city blocks, and angled roofs made for rain and snow to run off, the buildings in the Fringe were less inclined to adhere to the conforming nature of humans. It was as if the buildings themselves could get up and walk around at any moment. They were less domesticated, less designed with definitive purpose and more free-spirited. In a word, they were wilder. Their edges were a little more curved and their doorways and windows formed into shapes that were not just the rectangles or archways Salem was used to seeing, but oblong shapes or very short and wide shapes built not just for humans, but for many kinds of beings.

Salem looked at Ulysses, urging him for further explanation.

"When the first crews arrived at the Fringe bringing the first fringers," said Ulysses, "they had little of anything. No one knew what they were passing into. Hidden meridians were a mystery, still are, and when they stumbled onto this place, just outside the reach of the humans who wanted to hurt them, well, they built Vael."

"It's a lot to take in," said Salem.

"It's overwhelming," affirmed Ulysses. "And yet they dared to go further. No one knew what to expect. No one knew if the next step was the end or the beginning. But they dared." Ulysses paused for a moment, and Salem knew his uncle was about to enter one of his philosophical moments. "It's something unique to living things," said Ulysses. "We don't care about the odds. We don't care about should or shouldn't. There is only the will to get to tomorrow and the hope that it will be better than today. This place was their tomorrow."

• • •

Not far away, Aurora watched her people struggle with the realization of everything that had transpired over the previous days. She was having, as she had had in the past few days, moments of doubt. She wondered if she had made the right choice to seek Fern and his ship. Where were they, after all? This place did not feel or resemble home. Had they left behind their past and their roots for a future which didn't exist?

She felt a presence approaching and turned to see Forn Modir coming up the path, albeit with her wooden staff. Forn did not have her aides with her, and Aurora wondered how the ancient mother had left behind all her scared Jotun children without them realizing.

Forn came to stand next to her but said nothing. He was small for a Jotun and shrinking with age, but still stood almost at eye level with Aurora. They looked out together at the expanse of water.

"What troubles you?" asked Forn in the Jotun language.

"I worry I have made a mistake, Mother," answered Aurora.

"There are no mistakes," said Forn. "There are only actions and reactions. You did what you thought was right for us."

"I made a choice against your wishes," said Aurora. It was true. She had attempted to persuade Forn, along with the other Jotun, to seek the help of the ship and had been unsuccessful.

Forn shook her head. "A guiding light is hard to see when one is blind."

"What if we cannot cope here?" asked Aurora, her tone almost pleading. "Already I feel that the air is far too hot."

"Calm down, child," said Forn. "Our people would have never survived this long if we were not adaptable. If we cannot learn to adapt, then perhaps we deserve to perish to the times."

It was an old saying among the Jotun, and Aurora nodded.

"The captain said we should meet them in the town hall."

"Oh," said Forn. "Is that so? What is a town hall?"

"I think it's where they wish to welcome us."

Forn nodded.

"Old Mother?" asked Aurora, addressing Forn with the matriarchal title representative of her status. "Did you know I would go?"

Forn was quiet for a few minutes, and Aurora waited.

"I find I know less and less these days," said Forn, "though something about your eyes told me you would not be dissuaded. And, as time went on, I believed to myself that we could not stay in our home."

"You did?" asked Aurora, shocked. "But you were so against it all."

"It was necessary," said Forn. "I needed the others to see strength."

"But wouldn't it have just been easier to agree with me?"

Forn shook her head. "A leader must consider perception. If our people believed that I was ready to allow us to just give up our home right away, they would not have the strength to begin here anew. We will need the strength to one day return. Or is that just something the sea captain says?"

"I believe in him," said Aurora, thinking of all Fern and the others had done for them, "even if I do not always believe in myself."

"Then we should have hope that you were right to seek him out."

Aurora felt glad to have Forn Modir behind her. She smiled and asked, "should we go down for introductions?"

Forn Modir smiled her ancient smile at Aurora. It made Aurora feel a sense of comfort she needed in that moment. "Everyone has always doubted you, child. Your mixed parentage did you no favors, and yet still you fought to be a part of both a human and Jotun world. You were rebellious, obstinate, and thick-headed." Forn smiled again, and this time placed her hand around the back of Aurora's neck. "Though I think you may be the one to save us."

• • •

"Jiminy!" exclaimed Fern as he and Ulysses entered the city hall of Vael.

"Captain Tierney Fern," exclaimed a booming voice from the opposite end of the large chamber. "We weren't expecting you yet, but happy to see you I am. I hope you come with good news."

The captain smiled at hearing Jiminy's familiar way of "backwards" talking. He strode forward into a town hall already filled with residents. Visits from Curiosity and its crew were no small deal in Vael, and such arrivals always drew large numbers. Maybe we call them 'fringers' on the other side, Fern reminded himself, but here they're just beings like me, trying to have a life.

Even though he was no stranger there, Fern was always in awe of the place. To him the city hall of Vael was one of the most impressive structures in any city he had seen whether in the Commons or in the Fringe. He found it resembled the hull of a massive upside-down ship, with walls that bent up and around like a ribcage. It was built of fringewood, like most everything in the Fringe, because of its far superior properties to anything that existed in the Commons. Fringewood did not burn, yet it was a powerful conductor of energy, and it was flexible enough to bend and strong enough to withstand even the most extreme of pressures. Designs and engravings had been made into all fringewood surfaces of the hall, telling the stories of how the fringers escaped the world of the Commons and came to Vael. Many of the stories found on the hall's walls were continuations of legends and folklores of peoples across the world of the Commons. Fern knew that most every person who called the Commons home considered the fantastic beings in front of him just that, characters in stories from long ago. Fern looked out at the living embodiment of the legends and could not help but feel somehow sorry that legends were all that they were. Someday, he thought. Someday humanity will be ready to live again in diversity. Someday people will remember all the stories they have forgotten.

Fern walked down the long chamber, nodding with a smile to the familiar faces who stood to greet him. This was not only as a sign of respect, but because he—and this was true for the entire crew—knew much of the Fringe as a second home. Many of the residents would invite him for dinner in the coming nights to exchange stories, life updates, and memories. They would want to know about Juniper and about the status of her mother.

He came to a stop after traversing the length of the great room. Ulysses stopped with him. They had reached a half circle of chairs where a special group of the creatures, leaders by the look of their posture, waited. There was a humanoid with fins as ears that tilted its head back and forth as it looked at the captain. There was a man and a woman, both dressed in a single piece of material that seemed to be made from the skin of some waxy prehistoric rain-forest leaf. There was also a snake woman with rows of small wings, a tiny dragon which sat on the shoulder of what could only be described as a troll dressed in the latest fashion of England in the 1880s, and then, at the center of the semicircle, there was a cricket. Sporting an ornate sash of gold, it looked around with giant green compound eyes and felt the air with its antennae.

"Jiminy!" said Fern, smiling and extending both his hands forward with the palms showing.

"Tierney," said the deep voice of the cricket. Jiminy hopped down from his place to stand in front of Fern so they were the same height. The ground vibrated as he landed, and the cricket lowered his antennae and rubbed them into Fern's palms. They were covered, Fern knew, with tiny sensory hairs far superior to any of the captain's own abilities of touch.

"Jiminy!" echoed Ulysses in mock imitation of Fern's own salutation. The cricket turned to Ulysses. Ulysses extended his palms out like Fern and Jiminy repeated the procedure but, before retracting his antennae back, flicked one upward and caught Ulysses in the nose.

"You still bring this one with you, huh?" said Jiminy to Fern as Ulysses rubbed his nose and frowned.

"I'm still lucky enough to have him around," said Fern.

"Humph," said the cricket. "Well, come in and make yourself comfortable. We have things to discuss."

Long fringewood tables were pulled out with benches that lined the city hall from front to back. Fern always made note that no resident of the Fringe held any special office over any other resident. It was the simple mantra of the Fringe that each member should contribute to the society in the way they could. Even Jiminy, who no doubt held special rank among the residents as speaker, carried two benches, one under each set of two arms, as he hop-walked on powerful hind legs. Once assembled, the residents sat, or laid, or stood on the benches in whatever way worked for them best. Then, as was customary in the Fringe, the society of witches would lay their enchanted candles at the bottom of each of the engraved murals that ran the length of city hall. Reciting an incantation together, the light from the candles would jump from the wick into the crevices of the engravings, flowing up through them like water down a river, so that within a matter of seconds the walls of the building glowed with hieroglyphs, with stories.

Then the doors at the far end of the hall opened and Aurora, along with Forn Modir, stood with the rest of the Jotun behind them.

Fern was not surprised to see all the Jotun enter together. He had seen it before with displaced families and groups. It was natural and good to seek safety and comfort as one. He thought about Juniper. He thought about Aegle.

The Jotun made a powerful impression, not only because of their physical size but by their energy. They walked together like a giant beating heart that pulsed vital blood into the air with each step. Aurora walked with Forn at the front and as Fern watched her, he noticed a difference in her manner. She stood tall and wore a look as if to tell the world that she was ready to face whatever was coming. The other Jotun by comparison did not look as confident, though Fern had to admit that their stoic nature gave little away. They walked up the middle and, as was customary in the Fringe, the many residents who had come out to welcome the new arrivals smiled and began cheering and shouting greetings in their many tongues. They arrived to face Jiminy and Fern, and the others gathered at the front.

"Greetings, travelers," said Jiminy. The words Jiminy chose, travelers in this case, were on purpose. All the creatures of the Fringe had been proud in their previous lives, and it was a pride which did not die. Calling new residents travelers implied a sense of journey, that maybe this was just a stop along the way, and not a last escape from a life they were sad to leave behind.

"We welcome you to this place of refuge." Jiminy spoke in a slow, booming English and Aurora translated back to Forn and the others behind her, and the words were then translated through the ranks.

"Thank you," said Forn.

"Excellent," said Jiminy. He jumped, half fluttering with outstretched wings down the shallow flight of stairs to the Jotun.

"Now," he said, arched upward to see their faces. "There are a few observations we should discuss before you get yourselves set up. We understand you are tired. Soon we will eat and rest. This will not take long, but it is necessary."

Forn nodded.

Jiminy's antennae circled around each other. "I like you all a lot already." The giant cricket hopped back to where he had been before and extracted, with a grunt, a book the size of a small child, throwing it open without looking at the page. "The Code of Beings," he read for everyone present and then shifted his eyes back to the Jotun. "As was set down by the earliest residents of the Fringe. This is the code we live by. Should it be broken, you will face banishment from Vael and be forced back to the Commons or on to the great beyond. First," he read without looking, "this is a place of safety. We expect therefore that each resident act in a manner that puts the safety of us all first. We all know how it feels to be hunted, pushed out, and unwanted. This is a feeling that we do not want to bring on anyone else and are expected to take care of one another. So look out for your fellow fringers and embrace the home we have here."

"Second, you are free to seek a spot here in the Fringe where you would like to make your home. However, in doing so you may not inhibit in any way the dwellings or lives of others. There is plenty of space. If this should become an issue, take it up with the Vael high council and myself. We have translators and interpreters to settle disputes and I pride myself on over a decade of peace between fringers." Applause came from the hall and Jiminy raised the top two of his six arms to quiet the assembly. "Finally, each resident has their own past; respect it and they will respect yours. We look toward the future here."

All the Jotun nodded in a synchronized up and down movement, as though they as a collective understood what Jiminy's words had meant.

"Excellent," Jiminy said again, motioning that the Jotun should sit at a long set of tables prepared just for them. Jiminy took his own place next to Fern but before sitting, turned again to the congregation gathered in the hall. "Welcome to new friends and residents," he said, holding up his cup. "May you find comfort, warm beds, full stomachs, and, most of all, peaceful minds."

"Pulse!" came the cries of the many residents sitting inside the great hall.

"Pulse?" Fern heard Salem ask Juniper a few seats away.

"It's how you say 'cheers' here," she whispered back. "As in, we are still here, and our hearts still beat."

Fern smiled to himself as he listened to his daughter's explanation, allowing himself a small moment of private pride.

"Pulse," Jiminy echoed and, leaning into the captain whispered, "I'm eager to hear of the other side. Tell me, what has changed in that wild world of ours?"

• • •

Sometime later Fern stood on the balcony of the room, always given to him during their visits to Vael. The balcony was a wooden half circle with an intricate railing that reminded him of Curiosity. Though Curiosity was not built entirely of fringewood, it had received upgrades over the years, whereby fringewood had improved its quality and aesthetic. Fern placed his hands upon the railing, much the way he would do on the ship. The streets below were emptying, the day-goers heading indoors as the night-goers took their place.

Down in the street Fern saw a small being the size of a child and covered in puffy black fur with only a brown cloak as a covering. In its hands it carried a long pole, much longer than its own short body, with a tiny square on the end. Over its shoulders and back were strung many satchels. It bobbed up to the first of the streetlights which were only skinny pillars in the ground with small square platforms at their tops. Then, resting its tool against the platform, the furry black creature chirped. Fern waited and watched as a tiny glowing body emerged from within the layers of black fur.

It looked like a small person, but with larger transparent wings on its back. Using its hands and feet, it climbed until it reached the streetlight's square top. There it stepped onto the platform and taking a moment to first yawn and stretch and rub the sleep from its eyes, it began to clap. Its claps were slow at first and then they increased in frequency until its tiny arms were no longer visible; and then, the small thing halted its clapping. It extended its arms over its head and in the space between appeared a ball of light. The small thing with black fur chirped again in approval before detaching from the illuminated light and moving onto the next where the process was repeated. Fern noted that each light differed from the one before it, so that the streets of Vael were lit in a vast array of hues.

"I enjoy watching the fairysmith work," said Fern, without turning around.

"So, how much did you say to the kids about their instructions?" asked Ulysses.

"Enough," said Fern.

"I'm concerned," said Ulysses. "A lot happened to them in the north. That's all still fresh."

"Eagles," was all Fern said.

"Eagles?"

"Eagles," repeated Fern, "will traumatize their young in a series of falls while they're in fledge."

"Sounds horrible," said Ulysses.

"But necessary," retorted Fern.

"So, you are trying to traumatize these kids?"

"I am trying to give them the push they need to become the minds the world needs."

Ulysses stayed quiet for a while. Fern did not mind.

"We've known each other for a long time," he said to Fern, "and rarely do I question your ideas, but lately you've seemed a little off."

Fern looked on. Ulysses continued talking.

"Could these decisions, uncharacteristically rash, have anything to do with her?"

Fern's head jerked hard toward Ulysses, who noticed that he had struck an uncomfortable chord.

"I don't know who or what you're talking about," said Fern.

"I've been there for you before and will continue to be there for you like you were for me. If you don't want to talk about this now, that's fine."

Fern did not answer. Both men looked out at the glassy surface that was the endless ocean of the Fringe.

"I'm not so good at this parenting thing." Fern looked down in guilty admission. "It was always me. Then it was the crew. Lastly was her, and I'm terrified more than ever of it."

Ulysses smiled. "You think I wasn't scared when I got the call about Salem. I fought them on the phone the first time. Tried to tell them he would be better off in foster care. Who does that?"

Fern laughed. "You're lucky they didn't listen to you. There's something special about that boy. I can feel it."

"He's got his father in him," added Ulysses.

"I'd say between him, Zee, and Juniper we have our hands full."

"Seems so," said Ulysses. "I may not be his biological father, but Salem must have some of me and Julie in him, the way he acts."

"If I remember correctly," said Fern, "you and Rigel were similar."

"We were, and I miss him," said Ulysses.

"I do too," said Fern.

CHAPTER 23 | UNEXPECTED KINDNESS

Roach had expected a run-down place if he had expected anything at all. The Regulat often perpetuated the belief that this so-called sanctuary, this place where the ship would escape to, was nothing more than a wasteland zoo where already-dying things went to die. Some back-alley, chaotic, destitute sort of place. Then again, Roach was the first one to see it; how would they have the slightest clue what to expect? It was the way they always talked about mythos. How could it be possible that these subhuman entities coexist? The thought of them ever living anywhere like the place Roach was now and doing it with peace and governance was beyond anything he had imagined.

Roach had seen the light and watched the sloth guide the ship through the meridian. He had stood at the edge, watching the world drop away beneath him. The entire event had brought him to a place of such disbelief that he had felt ill. So unreal was his predicament of late that he was even beginning to find such occurrences humorous.

He had stood on the beach with a stupid grin, watching all manner of mythos come to together to greet the crew. He witnessed how the members of the crew dropped their human guises once arriving here, glad to meet the things that looked more like them.

"What do you say, soothsayer? Are you coming?"

The gnome called Dover, the only crew member who had grown even the tiniest bit close to Roach since he had made his way onto the ship, had invited Roach to meet his so-called family. Roach knew that Dover was an orphan. Dover made that very clear very often. Still, Dover had insisted that gnomes, unlike other things, did not associate themselves with immediate family groups. They were, they liked to say, the world's largest family. Inclusivity, despite what any legends or stories of gnomes were told, was the mode of operation. So, not wanting to raise any further suspicions, Roach walked with Dover off the beach and toward the rising skyline of Vael.

If only Roach could have somehow transmitted a video to the Regulat to show them what he was seeing. He wondered whether they would believe him.

"So, all your kind are gone?" Dover's face was one of genuine curiosity.

"That's right," said Roach, "snuffed out by the Regulat; I am the last."

"'Tis a cruel world we must fight through, I know," said Dover with his usual theatricality.

They passed through the town and came to the edge of the forest. They had disturbed no one, and no one cared to disturb them. It took them the better part of an hour, and Roach found himself lost in thoughts and observations.

"Now," said Dover, turning to Roach before entering the dense foliage. "Before we go in, know that gnomes are the loveliest of bunches, but we take just a little while to warm up to a person. Do try to make a good impression for me, would you? I rarely bring friends."

The word had left Dover's mouth like an arrow and buried itself somewhere deep into Roach's chest. Friends. He had used Dover to fend off questions aboard the ship, often using the camaraderie as a guise. Never had he considered the gnome a friend. Yet, as they entered the forest and the first of the other "Dovers" whooped and yelled,

Roach wondered if he had done more during his time on board than he knew.

"Dover, Dover, oh Dover!" a child swung down from the trees and landed with a thud before them. "Look, everyone! Dover brought a starving man!"

"Hello, Biloboy," said Dover, patting the young boy on his head of messy hair, "you seem to be just as transparently tumultuous as ever."

"I don't go by that name anymore," said the boy, standing with chest out. You may call me by my proper name."

"Well then, Willian," said Dover, straightening his own stance and nodding in mock salute, "I shall do just that."

The boy nodded in approval. Other people were swinging down from the trees now and appearing from pathways that Roach had not seen. They were Dover's size, with similar shape and build. Short by human standards but stocky and healthy looking. Roach had always thought Dover was large for a gnome but saw now that he had been mistaken how big gnomes could be.

"Well, look at that," said a man dressed in rags with long unkempt hair and a beard that gave the impression he had never seen a mirror, much less knew they existed. "Never thought we see loner Dover bringing anyone home to meet the pack."

"Don't discredit yourselves, Tori," said Dover. "I need to socialize you lot somehow. This is more for you than for him."

"What's your business then?" said the messy person.

"Does one need to declare business to visit their family?"

"Oh alright, alright," said Tori, pulling Dover in for a hug, "you must at least help us cook."

"Hello, sir," said the boy, poking Roach below the ribcage, "you look like you'd enjoy supper."

Roach had been witnessing everything happening around him and had somehow forgotten that he was visible. He swallowed.

"Nice to meet you too," he said to the boy.

The messy-looking adult approached. "Oh, he talks! Thank goodness! What's your name then?"

Roach provided the alias used since arriving onboard Curiosity.

"Well," said the person, exaggerating the name and making it sound long and ridiculous. "You shall join us for dinner, and we expect to hear all about you and your secrets."

Roach froze. They knew. Somehow Dover had discovered his identity. The gnome laughed and slapped Roach on the shoulder with a thick hand.

"Did I say secrets? I meant egrets. You keep birds, don't you? Any man worth a mashed potato keeps birds."

A large group of somewhat dirty but beaming people had assembled around them now, and Dover and Roach followed them deeper into the forest. A group of children surrounded Roach, all pestering him with questions about what was going on in the world beyond the Fringe. Roach despised anyone within a child's age range, and this experience was doing little to improve that perspective.

They came to a place where a group of trees with trunks a few feet apart from one another had grown inward in the form of an archway like lovers entering a lifelong embrace. Or, Roach thought, enemies locked in an eternal struggle. Between the trees hung a curtain of ivy. Two gnomes hung on branches on either side and pulled the ivy curtain apart as they entered.

"Everyone always thinks gnomes like to live underground," said Dover to Roach as the surrounding bodies thickened, "and that may have been true back on the other side where stupid humans would force us to look after their gardens." Dover had a look of disgust, which vanished as he looked around at the forest community. "But here we live wild. We live free. Welcome to the glen!"

The glen was an extension of the forest. Branches like hundreds of interlocking fingers formed dwellings amongst a canopy of vine bridges and hidden passageways. Ladders and zip lines allowed the inhabitants to move from canopy to the forest floor and back again.

The group of children and other people who had walked with them disbanded, finding other more interesting things to do. The smell of cooking and herbs wafted through the air, and Roach realized for the first time since arriving how hungry he was. A magnificent smell rose from the stoves and he could feel the saliva gather in his mouth.

"So," said a large and very plump gnome looking not unlike Dover, as he came over and took a seat by Roach. A smaller but just as corpulent woman was with him. She smiled as though it was the only expression she knew how to make. Roach was not in the mood for conversation, but the prospect of food was appealing enough. And he was a guest. He wondered what the Regulat would think of what he was doing. There was no protocol or plan for what to do once he had made it to this place. This was, as had been much of Roach's life, the definition of adapting to the present moment. Then came the question Roach dreaded most. The more obtuse version of Dover asked, "What's your story?"

If there is one thing Roach was less than interested in digging into, it was his past, be it fiction or fact.

"Nothing of much interest," he answered, hoping the gnome would take the hint and drop it. The gnome looked at him and then at the woman who, still smiling, only giggled.

"Come on. Dover tells us you are a soothsayer. The last of your kind. Now that is a pity if ever there were one. Still, to be the last of anything means there must be a hell of a story underneath that thin frame and surly attitude."

Roach looked into the gnome man's eyes. There was no malice. They were goofy and a bit off-putting, but kind, utterly, ostentatiously kind. A flower was resting on the gnome's shoulder, and as Roach looked closer, he wondered if it was not growing there.

"Yes, well," said Roach, starting to sweat. "I suppose I have had to accept my fate."

"As you should," said the man.

Roach was quiet for a minute. No one seemed to mind.

"I had a job," said Roach, "and I failed."

"This happens," said the gnome man, taking a large swig from a wooden mug in his hand. "Though I hardly think this should be the reason for such melancholia, my friend."

There it was again, that word. Roach could almost feel himself recoil when he heard it.

"This job was not like other jobs. It was a matter of life and death." Of course, the gnome did not know exactly what Roach was talking about, but it did not matter. The core of the story was the same, no matter what Roach was talking about. He had been tasked with something and had failed. It was that simple.

"Well, have you made amends and tried to live your life better since that day?" asked the gnome, resting his wooden mug on his knee. The thigh was so wide that the gnome did not need to hold the mug. It sat there by itself, without the slightest wobble.

The question was an interesting one for Roach. Had he made amends and tried to be better since that day? He was sitting where he was and had achieved that which no other person in Regulat history had. That must count as better, but is that what the gnome had meant?

After dinner, Roach excused himself from the festivities. The food had been as good as it looked. He was not sure what kind of food he had eaten, or what the ale-like liquid was that was now sloshing around in his stomach. He did not care. He felt lighter, more adjusted to his light frame, than he had in a long time. He walked for a while under the canopy of the tree houses until he came to a small clearing. There was a group of gnomes gathered around a fire at one edge, playing music. A wooden flute, y-shaped stringed instrument, and circular drum were in a melodic conversation with one another. The group paid Roach no mind. The clearing was otherwise vacant. Roach went to the empty side and sat down on the ground. He leaned back and against a log that had once been the body of a tree. He looked around, wondering to himself why his life had taken the turns it had to bring him to his current situation.

A rustling noise to his left forced his head to turn. Something the size of a house cat jumped out of the bushes.

"You scared me," he said, unsure what the thing was or why he was talking to it. "Back at the Regulat we would have you dissected and stuffed in no time." The small animal only cocked its head. It was part rabbit but had antlers like a deer. It had big eyes which took in the light from everything around. "Jackalope," said Roach, remembering something he had learned about them years earlier. "We thought you were all gone." Roach wondered how many other fringers the Regulat did not know about. "You don't seem like you could do much, though, to hurt people." Saying it made him remember his mission, whatever it was, and he pulled out the locator from his pocket.

He pressed a few buttons, but nothing happened. He smacked it against the log but only received a flicker across the screen. "Figures," Roach said to himself, "useless piece of junk." He looked at the jackalope. It was sniffing around in the air. It turned its attention back to Roach and hopped over and sniffed at the locater. "Here," said Roach, sticking it out like candy, "think you can get this to work? Not sure if it would be in your best interest if you did."

The jackalope inspected the locator and then reached out with its gnarled paws like hands and took it. "Fine," said Roach, "as long as I get it ba—" The jackalope took the locator in its mouth and bit clear through the screen, causing a firework of sparks and crackles to erupt. "Hey!" said Roach, "that's exactly what you shouldn't have done. Maybe you are better exterminated." He grabbed the broken locater back and tried turning it on. It only sputtered for a moment before screaming out a final dying whir. "Excellent," said Roach, but the jackalope had moved closer to him and yawned. Before Roach knew what was happening, it had dipped its head down into his lap. "Well, uh, that's not right, uh..." Roach stuttered, but it was too late. The cool night air sent a chill down his spine but the jackalope was warm, and emanated heat through him as it slept on his lap. Roach looked up at the sky and, for the first time in as long as he could remember, took notice of what was there.

CHAPTER 24 | REYNARD AND IRIS

"So, what was it they said we had to do?" Salem asked as he, Zee, and Juniper passed the last boundaries of Vael into the world of the Fringe beyond.

"My father said we head toward the mountains until we get to Reynard and Iris," said Juniper.

"And they are?" asked Salem.

"Dunno," said Juniper, looking at Zee, who only shrugged.

"Well, do we at least know how to get where we're going?" asked Salem, shrugging toward the towering mountain range that loomed in front of them.

"My father said we just need to stay on Freedom Road," said Juniper.

"You mean to tell me all the times you've been here, you've never gone beyond the city?"

"We haven't been here that often," admitted Zee, "and when we were, we weren't allowed to leave the city. Until now. They're strict with us on the ship if you haven't already noticed."

"I'm sure we can figure it out," said Juniper, an uncharacteristic tone of optimism entering her voice. "My father's a worrier and I know he wouldn't send us out unless he was sure we'd 'make it.'"

The morning light was bright and brought with it the crisp sharpness Salem remembered from first arriving. Sounds came from places off the path as they walked, sounds of bongs and squeals and buzzes and many other noises that would have been strange to hear at home in the Commons but did not seem so strange in the Fringe.

"The first thing we come to should be the dancing forest," said Juniper, pointing out ahead of them to the line of foliage.

"The dancing forest?" repeated Salem.

Juniper's words came true a few minutes later when they came to the edge of a vast expanse of trees and other plants. The plants looked like plants, somewhat, but they seemed to Salem to be restless, less rooted than the plants back home. He could swear that despite the lack of wind, the bushes, trees, and vines were swaying where they stood.

The forest was alive with the sounds of night by the time the three saw the light cutting through the darkness.

"Fire is fire no matter which side one's on," said a voice from somewhere ahead of them.

"What?" Salem asked, though he could see no one.

"I didn't say anything," said Zee. Salem saw the outline of Juniper shake her head.

He smelled the smoke in the air as the light in front of them grew. Around another tree, the light showed itself to come from a small fire. A silhouette, thin with pointy ears and no larger than a child, was outlined against the flames.

"There they are," said the same voice. It did not sound mean or nice, or like any emotion, only calm. "Come and sit. You must all be weary."

Salem looked at Zee, who looked at Juniper. Juniper shrugged and walked forward, pushing through the foliage to find a child-sized fox tending to the flames.

"Come," said the fox, as it jumped down off its log seat to greet them. "Don't be shy. Have a seat."

Salem sat on a stone close to the fire. The air had grown cooler in the night, and he found he was glad for the fire's warmth.

"Now where has Iris gone?" the fox asked.

There was a rustling sound in the trees above and something swooped down, catching like a falling star off the light of the fire, and landing on a low-hanging tree branch a few inches to the left of the fox's head.

"Ah," he said, "there she is."

Salem knew the word beautiful. He knew the word elegant. He even knew the word divine. He did not use them but knew them. He had always thought such words would come to his mind when the time was right. Yet, as he looked upon the bird creature called Iris, he knew, somehow, that neither beautiful, nor elegant, nor divine, nor a combination of them all could do justice in describing her. She emitted something beyond what he could see; it was something he could only feel; it trailed behind her and surrounded her like a sweet perfume. He felt as though he could breathe it in and inhaled.

She perched on the branch, fluffing her feathers up a few times and stroking them back down with her beak.

"She's…" Juniper said but did not finish. No one said anything for a moment. The only sound was the crackling of the fire.

"When you're blind," said the fox, "you learn that there are two types of beauty. The kind that you see with your eyes and the kind you see with your heart. I am Reynard, the guide and your instructor, and this is Iris, daughter of the sun."

Iris looked up. She had a deep blue plumage on her back and around her sides. It extended all the way down into her long tail feathers that hung like a regal cape behind her. Her wings were laced with feathers of yellow and orange that reflected off the dancing firelight so that it looked almost as though the wings were gold, heated and smoldering, waiting to be hammered into form. Streaks in the same color ran like rivers up her chest through her neck, culminating at her head, which was speckled with what looked like thousands of tiny white stars.

"Where have you all come from?" asked Reynard. "Wait, wait, let me guess. I love guessing."

Salem could not imagine how the blind fox named Reynard could know, considering that Salem himself would not have been able to give an answer if asked.

"It was cold there," said the fox. "You smell like pelts"—Reynard shuddered as he said this—"and like cave water and..." Reynard hesitated. "Memories."

"That's amazing," said Zee. The fox bowed.

"Now, I think it's right you all introduce yourselves," said Reynard.

"I'm Juniper," Juniper offered, "and they are Salem and Zee."

Reynard turned his head to each of them, looking at them with what Salem was sure was the fox's own version of sight.

"So," said Reynard, "you're the young ones on the ship?"

They nodded, and the fox jumped down from the log on which he stood. He walked over to Juniper. "You're Fern and Aegle's daughter," he said. "I'm sure the forest appreciates having you here."

He walked over to Zee. "I like your color, adopted son." Salem could not be sure in the low light, but he thought he saw Zee blush at this.

Finally, Reynard walked over to Salem and paused, sniffing the air. "You're a Swan," he said. "And a mythlinguist, I feel!" Reynard perked up at this. "Rare these days."

"A what?" asked Salem.

"You can communicate with creatures of myth," said Reynard. "The ones that don't speak your common tongue like me. When they want to, they can talk to you, and you to them."

Salem was dumbstruck. How could it be? In the same moment, his hand was burning again, and he felt a different, sweeter voice than Reynard's in his head.

Hello, it said, *I'm Iris.*

"That explains it!" Zee was saying next to Salem. "Back in Jotunheim, the tree. It must have given you that ability to help save the lost giant!"

"Right," said Juniper. "Salem, what am I thinking?"

Reynard shook his head. "That is not how it works. It is not telepathy. You will need to learn to control this, Salem Swan, and soon. I can sense it's already a burden for you."

A vortex swirled inside of Salem's mind, making it impossible for him to even ask a question. Patient? Was the fox joking? Did he understand what kind of mental turmoil he had just created? Reynard nodded to Salem with a look that seemed to imply he understood and in the same moment, reached down into his leather bag at his side, producing a black bracelet in his paw. Then, holding the bracelet close to his canine mouth, Reynard whispered into it. Though they could not tell what the fox was saying, what was being spoken was old, very old.

Reynard stopped speaking a second later. "Hold out your left arm," he told Salem, and Salem obeyed. "This obsidian band should help shield your mind from invasive thoughts. It is not a permanent solution, but it will help you until you're able to control your gift."

As Reynard placed the bracelet on Salem's arm, Salem felt an immediate sense of relief as if a vast amount of pressure were being drained out of his head. "Thank you," he told Reynard, and meant the words with his full being.

"You all have big shoes to fill," he said, addressing them all. "I hope you're up to the task."

"Who said anything about filling shoes?" asked Juniper. The fox gave her a knowing look.

"Is that how you all ended up here?" asked Salem, thinking about what the fox had meant. "You were saved by the crew and the ship?"

"Not all at once, but over time, yes," said Reynard. "Though there are other ways to get here."

"I'm sorry," said Salem, unsure of why he was apologizing. Maybe it was the way the fox spoke, but it seemed clear, even in this extraordinary place, that these extraordinary beings were not at home.

"Don't be," said Reynard. "We are safer here. You think we had wonderful situations back on the other side?"

"I don't know," said Salem.

Reynard sighed. "I do not expect you to understand this yet, but it's different for us. First, they love you, maybe even worship you and then over time want to control you and worse, hate you. Every single time." Iris cooed. Reynard shook his head. "Not all of us wanted to leave. Iris had a good thing going. She was doing fine in her jungles for a long time. She loved it there and would have stayed had it not been for us convincing her to go."

"But why convince her to go?"

"Isn't it obvious?" said Reynard.

Salem shrugged. "Why not stay and fight?"

"Is it better to fight for a dying hope, or flee for the chance at a new future? We knew it was going to get worse for us the longer we waited. It's what humans do."

"So, this place," said Salem, "this Fringe. It's like a hideaway?"

"Hideaway, sanctuary, alternative"—Reynard shrugged—"call it what you want. I like to think of it as a good night's sleep. You know how many of those I had back on the other side?"

Everyone was silent.

"Well," said Reynard after a moment, "better get some rest. You should all be fit for tomorrow."

"But we have to get back," said Juniper.

Reynard shook his head. "Not tonight." There are some blankets laid out already. It shouldn't get too cold."

"But—" said Juniper, to which Reynard raised a paw.

"I'll take you back," the fox interjected, "just not yet." Juniper made a face like she would speak, opening her mouth and holding it. "You're in the right place, Miss Fern," said Reynard. "Instruction is not meant to be obvious. Trust me."

Salem looked at Juniper and Zee, both of whom seemed to share his lack of understanding of most of what the fox said.

"I'll bet this is what my father planned all along," said Juniper. "Making us come out here for more instructions without telling us."

Reynard only chuckled. "We'll leave early; get some rest."

Night stretched itself over the sky. Salem was on his back in the grass, his hands behind his head, using a sweater as a pillow. Juniper was on one side of him, Zee on the other. Reynard had long since dozed off. The fox was curled up around the fire, now only embers, in a brownish-red ball of fur.

"I still can't believe all this," said Salem, feeling relieved to be wearing the obsidian bracelet. "At least not fully."

"Why is it so hard to believe?" Juniper asked and turned her head toward him. He turned his head back to hers, their faces inches apart.

"You have no issue accepting all of this?"

"Why would I have an issue? It is what it is. I don't understand why you have an issue."

"I don't know either," he said.

"It'll take a little time," said Zee from Salem's other side. "But that's normal for someone who's only just arrived."

"I hope so," said Salem.

"I wonder where we're going tomorrow," said Zee, yawning.

"Me too," said Juniper.

Salem was awake after both Zee and Juniper had fallen asleep. He had watched as Juniper closed her eyes and folded her hands under her head. He was not sure how long he had watched her before he realized what he was doing. He was glad she had not noticed and turned his attention away.

On his back, he looked up at the sky. The edges of the surrounding trees framed it in a circuit of twisted shadows. He scratched at his left palm without thinking and then lifted it to his face to find the emblem of Yggdrasil a bright blood-red color. It burned, as it had before, like a sunburn, though this time it was visible, almost glowing, even in the darkness. Salem was glad to have the obsidian bracelet to help stay calm. Still, he knew that the glowing emblem on his palm was a reminder of the promise he had made.

CHAPTER 25 | REVELATIONS

"Lift!" Ulysses yelled across to Fern.

"I am!" came the reply. "Are you?"

"Of course!"

Fern grunted under the weight of the beam and hefted. He felt the countereffort come from Ulysses on the other side, and together they hoisted the beam up onto the pile of the others. Jotun around them lifted beams by themselves with little more than heavy breathing for effort.

The Jotun had made their temporary home in the northern part of Vael, on a elevated hill that overlooked much of the city. Aurora had joked, which was unlike Aurora, that it gave them the sense of a mountain, albeit a tiny mountain.

"You need to get back in the gym," said Ulysses, teasing Fern.

"Is that right?"

"I'm just saying that we have a few more of those to go and you look ready for tea."

"Or wine," Fern offered.

"Or wine," Ulysses echoed.

"This won't work," said Aurora, breaking away from two arguing Jotun to come and talk to the men.

"What do you mean?" asked Ulysses. "Sure, it's temporary, but this will be a fine start to a home for you all."

"I don't mean the building," said Aurora. "I mean all of this. How do I convince them they will be happy here?"

"You don't. They will need to discover it for themselves."

"The only thing keeping them going now is the prospect of returning home."

"Good," said Fern, "then use that for now. Get them to make the best of their present situation."

"I am trying." Aurora's expression told Fern there was more. He saw that Ulysses felt it too.

"What is it?" Ulysses asked, putting down his end of a beam and placing a hand on Aurora's arm. Fern caught the trace of affection in Ulysses' action.

"Is there a hope of going back?" she asked, half pleading. Neither Fern nor Ulysses spoke.

"Is there a hope of going back?" she repeated. Emotion welled in her voice and it needed to stay subdued. The last thing they needed was a band of worked-up Jotun.

"Yes. But you will be here for the foreseeable future," Fern said, keeping his voice level and having no intention to lie.

Tears formed in Aurora's eyes. She had known already. Still, Fern thought, she would need some time to process it.

"The Fringe is a fine place," said Ulysses. "And I promise you it is our mission to end what is happening and bring you all back to the world you once knew."

Aurora nodded her head that she understood. Still, her eyes held back tears.

"The best thing," said Fern, "is to focus on building a life here. Literally one step in front of the other. You know"—Fern looked out across the Jotun— "the focus on new things, even the smallest things, can be a wonderful distraction against homesickness."

"I want in," said Aurora.

"I'm sorry?" said Fern. "What do you mean?"

"I mean, I want to join you as one of the crew. I cannot just stay here and watch."

"But you're needed, Aurora; you have responsibilities to your people."

"Let me talk to Forn, at least," said Aurora. "Please don't deny me this, Captain Fern."

Fern knew better than anyone where she was coming from with her argument. He looked at Ulysses and saw the same expression on his friend's face. He nodded his head in agreement.

• • •

Roach was by himself again. He could not spend one more minute with the gnomes. They were far too nice. They gave him things, be it hugs, drinks, or advice. It was, in its own way, sickening. Yet what disturbed Roach far more was the small tickle of a feeling that was starting to appear during those times. He was, terrifying as it was to admit, enjoying the kindness.

Roach had nothing against kindness. He would be kind to people he liked and expected it in return. The issue was that he was experiencing an absurd level of kindness from fringers, things he had always believed to be incapable of such deep and exclusively human emotions. He felt confused and somehow angered by it. He almost hoped this was all some dream and that, soon, he would stumble onto the real fringers: those things of legend which would rip apart men for no apparent reason at all, suck out the blood and organs and souls, and end humanity at all costs. He had so far seen no such behavior.

The country around Vael was as varied as the creatures who called it home. Wilderness, thought Roach. It is for good reason that people do not inhabit such places. He walked on a sand flat somewhere between the city and the forest. It looked like the dried riverbed of some prehistoric lake, with large cracks running through the floor. He was watching his feet as he walked. His shoes were worn but comfortable. He sidestepped, avoiding a crack in the ground. It reminded him of the saying that if you step on a crack (in those days meaning a suburban sidewalk) you would break your mother's back. Roach snickered. If it were his mother-in-law, he would have stepped on all the cracks in the entire plateau. The thought reminded him of what he had lost.

Michael had been the epitome of a beautiful man, and it had perplexed Roach every day and night that he had been so lucky to end up with him.

Their three years together were the happiest of Roach's life. Michael was an artist. He was loving, thoughtful, and a beam of light in Roach's otherwise bleak existence. So deep was their love, that Michael had often tried to convince Roach to leave the Regulat and find safer work. Roach shuddered to himself as the memory snaked through his mind. He had been so stubborn, so insistent that he could have both. Besides Michael, the Regulat was his life. How could he have chosen? Was it wrong to want to have both?

Roach hopped over another crack. He recalled the day Michael had come to Crawford Heights. Other regulators would tell him later that Michael had not heeded their warnings and had entered areas better left alone. That he told them he only wanted to look at the things in the cages. Perhaps to see what kept Roach from committing to him. Roach had told him so many times they were not nice things and that the Regulat was doing a service to humanity. Michael could not understand, or he would not; that was all Roach knew.

"Damn artists," Roach said out loud to himself. He had always hated and loved most of Michael's romantic notions.

From what Roach heard after the incident, it had happened so fast that it would have been impossible to prevent. A newly collected mytho, those unfamiliar with the cage, were always the worst. Michael had not screamed, they said. He had only stood there with a peaceful intrigue on his face as the thing reached out and took him, thus ending the life of the only man Roach had ever dared to openly love.

• • •

An assembly was underway in the great hall. Many of the elders or leaders from each group of the Fringe were eager to speak with Fern and the members of the Curiosity.

"What are you saying, Tierney?"

Fern did not answer Jimminy right away. He had hurried back with Ulysses after helping the Jotun, though was now unsure if it was a good idea with the way the discussion was turning.

Jiminy was not human, but it was easy enough to read his face and hear his tone of voice. Sentient creatures are not so different from one another, Fern knew from his own life experiences.

"Things are not stable," Fern said, trying to look and sound calm, knowing how emotional the topic was for the many beings of the Fringe.

The talk continued back and forth for some minutes. A few of the others in the hall gave opinions. Someone argued that the residents had not only a right but a duty to defend their homes and themselves. Jiminy listened to each of their concerns. It was his ability to listen and listen well that had made him speaker of the residents. Fern had to give him credit. The cricket endured all the residents' thoughts and concerns and had to reconcile them with his own. All this Jiminy did most of the time with extreme grace, though there were times like the present when Fern had to accept the reality of how difficult things were.

Talk of returning to the Commons to fight for what they had lost was not a new discussion in the Fringe. It was the longest-standing question and reoccurring conflict among the residents.

"Yes, yes," Jiminy told them, turning back to Fern. Fern knew Jiminy was only relaying the thoughts of the greater group and yet, the captain sensed the passion hidden inside Jiminy's tone. "Why is it you get to be out there fighting a war that concerns us all?"

The question was direct and justified. Fern cleared his throat. "The enemy is well equipped and merciless," he said, focusing hard on the evenness of his tone. "My goal, as it has always been, is to reduce the number of casualties. Keep the life and the lives that you all still have."

"If we continue on this current path, nothing will be left to go back to," said Jiminy. Any of the other residents who could understand English nodded their heads in agreement.

"May I ask," said Ena, stepping up beside Fern, "why you are so eager to get back? The world as you know it is disappearing and the one you inhabit serves all your needs. What is the rush?"

It was not Jiminy who spoke now, but another of the residents.

A wolf the size of a small horse lumbered forward, fixing its arctic eyes on Jimminy and the captain.

"Fenrir wishes to speak," someone whispered.

"A home is a very special thing," the wolf said in a voice of paternal soothing and raw power. "And while it's true that we survive here in this place, we long for our true home."

The wolf's words stopped and a howl, either from another wolf or something else, erupted from behind it. Within seconds, primordial howling filled the hall.

"We will need to wait," said Jiminy to Fern, flicking his antennae from side to side irritably.

The howling continued for a while, subsiding first into a low growl before fading out. The wolf called Fenrir was quiet and next to it now stood a large thing composed of clay. Tiny pieces fell off it as it took a step forward.

"Prometheans do not want to live outside our home any more than we wish to live outside our own skins." Its voice was a gurgle like a sludge. "Your mind remains intact and much of who you are, but there is a center, a piece of your heart, which is missing. We are thankful for what this place gives us but don't intend to give up the world we left behind."

Fern bowed to each resident who spoke. They were, after all, legends in their own right. "We do not expect this," he told them. "We only wish to make it a better place for you to return to."

CHAPTER 26 | MR. CANCUN

The last rays of the Mexican sun beat down on the beach. Tristan imagined he could feel his skin sizzling under its relentless assault so that he had to smile as he watched the orange orb drop below the horizon, as he trudged up a mound of sand alongside three of his fellow regulators.

"Join Bramble as a first test," Mr. White had told Tristan. "It will prepare you well for the much bigger plans we have for you."

Bramble, thought Tristan, what a goofy name for a regulator already as goofy as they come. Bramble was shaky in every sense of the word. The way he talked caused his words to shake; the way he walked caused his body to shake—even the way he stood and looked at something or someone made his eyes look like they were shaking. Tristan did not like it and yet, he had to admit that there was a tenacity, a vibrant positivity that lived across Bramble's short stature and boyish face which was, well, inspiring.

Bramble held up a wavering hand, letting Tristan and the other two know they should stop. There they crouched down behind the dune full of beach grasses to wait.

"They'll be here soon," said Bramble. "It's almost dusk." Tristan could hear the nervousness in Bramble's voice and understood why it was there. What Bramble was attempting was the biggest endeavor a regulator could undertake. The goal and mission of any regulator was to locate creatures of myth and legend, conscious and intelligent beings, and study them. Regulators were like scientists in that way, always working to understand the intimate habits of other creatures. They targeted mythical life because it was mythical beings above all others that posed the biggest threat to humanity. Then, once a regulator felt they knew their target well enough, it was time to regulate. Just as Mr. Hiroshima had coordinated with America to wipe out an entire city of vampires, and Ms. Cologne staged an attack on a church in Germany to eliminate the largest family of kobolds ever found, so too had Bramble spent many months studying the Cueyatl and had now devised a plan.

"Remember," said Bramble, looking at Tristan and the other two regulators. "Cueyatl are aggressive and, even though their poison is only mildly toxic, too much could be bad."

"Now, Tristan." Bramble turned to Tristan with reliable tremble. "I'm supposed to give you some guidance about how I planned this."

The last thing Tristan wanted in that moment was to listen to Bramble, but he wasn't about to defy Mr. White, and knew that a successful review from Bramble would help his already glowing reputation within the Regulat organization.

"I had to speak to quite a few locals," Bramble continued, "to learn about Cueyatl sightings and had to spend a considerable amount of time here myself in observation. Most of the common people don't know about the Cueyatl."

"Right," added Tristan. "Just like most common people don't know about mythos at all."

"Correct, Tristan. But some old commoners have not forgotten. If you talk to them. They remember." Bramble produced a giddy smile. "And these mythos are sneaky and smart. They knew I was watching them. They dig holes, but once I found their tunnels, they would leave and dig them somewhere else until I could finally track them here. They're old creatures, from back during the Aztec times even, and they know this land better than anyone." Bramble raised a quivering finger to his nose like a student who had just figured out the toughest math problem in class. "Better than anyone except me."

"Are they easy to spot?" Tristan felt the slightest twinge of interest for the first time. "I thought most mythos remain out of sight of humans."

"Most do," confirmed Bramble, "but these Cueyatl have developed quite the habit for piña coladas."

"You've got to be kidding me," said Tristan. "Little poisonous alcoholic frogs, huh?"

"That's right," said Bramble.

The sun had disappeared over the horizon, leaving the world around them painted in a mixed veil of orange that was being overtaken with the purple of night. The moon was out, sitting right in the sky in front of them, and Tristan was getting uncomfortable laying on the dune.

The nature of their work forced him and the other three regulators on the mission to wait until the commoners had left. Commoners being anyone who did not know about mythos or mythological life. Pretty much everyone, Tristan thought to himself and grinned. The Regulat had for a long time been a secret organization because, even though what it did was for the good of every person, that did not mean people always understood. It was easier to stay "unannounced," as Tristan had often heard Mr. White explain, though staying hidden often meant hiding and, in situations like laying on a beach dune for two hours, meant being uncomfortable. Tristan was happy when the last of the commoners left the beach for their hotels and Bramble leaned up onto his elbows, licking his lips and looking like a kid about to open a birthday present.

"You all have your costumes?"

Tristan and the others spread out in a line to the left of Bramble and nodded their heads they did, and they were ready. Disguised as hotel sanitation workers cleaning the beach, they would have a story in case any commoner was to come asking questions. Then the head of the first Cueyatl popped up above the sand.

"That's the slime I was talking about, see," Bramble hissed into Tristan's ear as he and the others peered over the dune at the frog's head glistening in the fresh moonlight.

The Cueyatl rose further out of the ground and Tristan saw that the legendary amphibian was on its hind legs, thick and muscular. It stood as tall as a small child and surveyed the beach landscape around it. Once it was reassured that all was clear it croaked down into the hole. A similar croak answered it, and all over the beach similar holes in the sand emerged. Tristan watched Bramble grin.

"I am so good," Bramble whispered.

"What will they do now?" Tristan asked.

"Watch," was all Bramble answered.

There were at least ten Cueyatl on the beach then. They spread out across the sand, picking up all the trash and other things left over by the hotel guests. One stumbled onto the remains of a romantic dinner, left abandoned by a careless couple. On a blanket sat a half-empty bottle of wine and some slices of assorted cheese. Kicking the cheese so it spiraled out into the waves, the Cueyatl picked up the wine bottle and held it up to the sky against the moon to see how much was left. Satisfied with the amount, it croaked and took a large swig. The other frogs leapt over in great hops, all bunching around the wine and taking swigs at the mouth so it was not long before the bottle dropped with the hollow thud of empty glass back on the ground.

"Just wait until they find what I planted," whispered Bramble back across to the others.

"Planted?" asked Tristan.

"They have a soft spot for tequila," Bramble hissed.

A croak erupted from close to the water as another of the frog warriors picked up, just as Bramble had foretold, an almost full bottle of tequila. In a joyous cacophony, the child-sized frogs croaked and hopped their way over to the hero who was already passing the bottle around in a circle. Tristan was astonished at the speed as he witnessed the bottle's contents disappear.

"That was amazing," he said as less than two minutes later an empty tequila bottle was dropped into the sand.

"I know," said Bramble, "too bad they aren't paying customers or else I'd open a stand right on the beach."

The Cueyatl then started doing something strange. They started dancing, joyously, in a circle, jumping up and down and croaking in low guttural tones to one another. In the dim light of the night and with the hotel so far away it could have been seagulls, or anything, making such movements, but from where Tristan sat he could see the smiles and hear the croaked laughter of the frogs as they frolicked.

"You know what you need to do?" Bramble asked, readjusting himself as though he was ready to strike.

"I need to grab at least three of them for study," said Tristan, who, for a split second, felt a little ashamed about ambushing the happy-looking amphibians.

"Right," said Bramble, extracting the long standard issue instrument, nicknamed "the sub," which was short for "subduer." It was the standard tool of the Regulat when interacting with mythos. Tristan held his sub tight, wondering just how he was to capture three of the Cueyatl alive. It was also standard procedure that a few mythos be, if possible, taken alive for further study. We are also scientists, Tristan thought to himself, as he gripped the rod that was his subduer.

"Are you ready?" Bramble asked Tristan and the others. They all nodded that they were. Bramble turned back to the dancing Cueyatl in front of him. "Now is the time," Tristan heard him whisper unevenly under his breath, as though Bramble alone was experiencing a minor earthquake. "I finally get to earn my name."

With a movement much quicker than Tristan thought him capable, Bramble scurried up the dune and was gone over the side. It took Tristan and the others a second to catch up, but soon they too were over the dune and sprinting toward the beach.

The Cueyatl would have seen them much earlier when sober. Tristan would learn later just how genius that part of Bramble's plan had been. Bramble had almost reached the first of the dancing frogs before they realized anything was amiss. The first turned and tried to croak in that guttural sound only frogs can make to warn the others, but Bramble was ready. He thrust the long rod-shaped weapon through the frog's chest and pulled it out again as fast. Many of the frogs were still jumping around and only a few had caught on to what was happening, but by the time they had, it was too late. Tristan and the others had already caught up with them.

Tristan grabbed one frog from its back, careful to use his gloved hand and leave his sub on stun to only shock and not kill it. It was ironic, he thought while he was still fighting, that the Regulat's weapon of choice should be called a subduer when it was much more often used to kill.

The frogs regrouped and more emerged from beneath the sand.

"Don't worry!" Bramble shouted from somewhere in front of Tristan, though Tristan could not see him. "They can't hurt you if you don't touch them! Keep going!"

The slimy body of a Cueyatl slammed into Tristan's face and he could taste the sourness of the slime and the sweet bitterness of the tequila mixed with something salty and gooey that he assumed was blood. The Cueyatl were nicknamed "warrior frogs" for a reason. Tristan remembered reading that in the archives. He now knew why. They were ferocious. Since ancient times, Cueyatl had been associated with gods and other deities. He felt a hard kick to the back that made him yell out as another came around and caught him across the head. He saw stars and his face met the sand. At ground level he saw the body of one of the other regulators lying motionless and felt once again a fear that things may not go to plan.

Tristan willed himself up through the pain and further assault of the frogs and switched his subduer off stun. He had taken over three and now he felt angry. He lashed out with a fury, batting as if to beat a piñata at all the greenish-brown bodies flying around him until everything in front of him became a blur, and he wondered if he might faint. The surrounding beach twisted and swirled, and he felt exhausted with eyelids that weighed a thousand pounds. The last thing he saw was the ferocious greenish image of an amphibian leaping toward his face.

• • •

Tristan opened his eyes to find the distinct face of Bramble smiling his not so attractive smile down at him.

"I told you not to come in direct contact with them, rising regulator," said Bramble, reaching down and pulling Tristan up. Tristan felt sick.

"What about the others?" he asked.

"Tallahassee is in critical condition. Too much frog slime and a kick to the throat. They'll take him in for an examination. Castello is beat up, but fine. You?"

"Fine," said Tristan, ignoring the pain pulsating through this body. "And the Cueyatl?" asked Tristan. "Did we get them?"

Bramble beamed, and Tristan knew he'd been waiting for someone to ask him the question.

"Did we ever!" he exclaimed. "They're gone, man. And you stunned four! White will be ecstatic."

Tristan was relieved. He did not care so much about whether Bramble had a successful mission, though he wondered if, in the spirit of being a team player, he should. He cared that he had completed the first proper task that had been given to him. Sure, he had done the pixie, but that, he knew, had been only a minor test.

Dawn was approaching and Bramble bumbled across the beach.

"The cleanup crew should be here soon," he said with a cheerfulness he struggled to maintain. "The real cleanup crew."

Less than ten minutes later, two black pickup trucks pulled onto the sand. Four men got out of each. They were not regulators, Tristan knew, but hired hands, contracted to work, and ask no questions. First, they loaded the body of the wounded regulator, then they dragged the bodies of the Cueyatl away in the sand and threw them into the back of the trucks. It was close to sunrise when they threw the last bodies in. One man then brought a large sack to Bramble. Tristan stood not far away, still lost in his thoughts, when he saw Bramble motion that the man should talk to him.

"You can put the live ones in here," he said, giving Tristan the bag. "And take these." He handed Tristan a thick pair of gloves.

Gingerly, having no desire to increase the sickly feeling coursing through him, Tristan muscled the four stunned bodies of the Cueyatl into the bag and dragged it over to the man again. The man looked at him and exhaled with a small chuckle. He took the bag and slung it over his shoulder. Then the men covered the trucks with tarps and within two minutes had pulled away, leaving the remaining regulators on the beach.

Tristan once again joined Bramble, who was wiping some greenish-blue blood off his communicator. Turning it on, Bramble held it to his mouth, looking at Tristan as he did. "It is done," he said. A few seconds passed.

"Good," returned a voice from the other end. The communicators made it almost impossible to tell who it was talking, but Tristan was certain who it was. "Then," said the voice of Mr. White to Bramble, "congratulations, Mr. Cancun."

CHAPTER 27 | WATER DRAGON

Light had returned. The fire from the previous night lived once again. The smell of food drifted through the air making Salem's stomach growl as he sat up from the soft patch of ground that now held the imprint of his back.

"Oh, they're up." Reynard the blind fox was leaning over the fire. Using a curved wooden ladle, the fox stirred a small pot of mush, or at least so it looked to Salem. As he gazed inside, he saw leaves, berries, and what looked like long pieces of tofu.

"Smells good," he told Reynard, but the fox only hummed a tune to himself and nodded.

Juniper and Zee were also waking up, yawning, and looking around in half dazes so he was relieved that he was not the only one who felt out of his comfort zone.

"I dare say," Reynard continued in his antiquated and theatrical way of talking that Salem was realizing to be common with fringers, "if you sleep that long every day then I'm worried about the future of us all." Iris cooed over his shoulder. "Oh, I have to tease them," he told her. "That's what young ones are for."

"Looks good," said Zee, leaning over the pot.

"What is it?" asked Juniper, grimacing as she peered in.

"Nourishment," said Reynard, looking displeased with Juniper's tone. "But if it's not good enough for you, Ms. Fern, then please fast or find your own breakfast."

Salem and Zee both held their breath. Juniper, quiet for the briefest of moments, clicked her tongue in consideration. "Oh, it's plenty good enough, thank you, Reynard."

Reynard nodded and in a swift motion began apportioning the breakfast into small bowls. Then Reynard showed them how to use their hands to scoop the food instead of using a fork or knife as Salem was expecting. The substance Reynard had cooked could be called a porridge, though it contained flavors, mixtures of savory and sweet, along with ingredients Salem was sure he had never tasted before. There was honeysuckle and sage, and where at first he thought the bowl and the portion was too small to satisfy his hunger, only after a few bites he felt sated, as if he had had the perfect amount of food.

"We should go," said Reynard, collecting the bowls and packing them into a small backpack. As Salem and the others followed the fox's lead, packing their things into small rucksacks brought from the ship, Reynard continued speaking. "Today's instruction is about connection. You may remove your shoes and socks and stow them in your bags." Salem, Zee, and Juniper looked between each other, grinning as if to ask whether Reynard was serious. "It's okay," Reynard added, "what might seem strange to you is not strange at all. Come, come. We need to get moving."

Salem could not remember the last time he had walked barefoot. The faint memories of his old backyard came into focus, though they were filled with his mom, and he let them fade before they could become too clear. With each step he could feel the dirt in between his toes and found that as they walked, he recognized more and more the slight differences and changes in texture of the leaves and other debris as they folded beneath him.

Iris flew over their heads like a rouge ray of sunlight, encouraging them on with her soft coos while Reynard spoke from the front of the line. "Touch the leaves. Feel the solid ground under you. Listen to the hidden networks that connect you to it. Blind is a matter of perspective. Close your eyes if you can and see what I mean."

Salem closed his eyes, trying to do as Reynard said, but stubbed his toe on a rock. "Take your time," he heard Reynard say.

"Reynard, what is the difference between the Fringe and Commons?" As he walked deeper into the strange world, Salem was eager to get answers to questions he had been thinking about since first departing with the ship from Easterly.

"Long ago there was only one world where all creatures lived," said Reynard. "Beings of the sea, the mountain, the forest, the sky, the plain…humans were just one of many groups of sentient beings. We used to interact with the people, tell each other stories, and share food, water, and goods. But at some point, everything changed. I still remember seeing the first walls go up." Salem saw the back of Reynard's reddish-brown neck shudder as he spoke. "At first the people just wanted to defend themselves against other people, it had nothing to do with us, but that fear turned into a fear of anything nonhuman. Creatures like me and countless others were scapegoated. Called monsters, beasts, manipulators, child stealers, thieves… People drew pictures making us look hideous and grotesque and called it art. They changed their stories, blaming us for their problems and mistakes."

Salem and the others listened, as it became clearer and clearer that the topic was difficult for Reynard to discuss.

"The world we had known no longer welcomed us. Now run by humans, scared humans, humans obsessed with control. So," Reynard said with an air of smug finality, "we moved." Reynard sidestepped off the ground onto a flat rock, where he stood and faced them. "There are still elements of the Fringe in the Commons, you know. You call them the wilderness. Places you do not go because they are too wild, too untamed, and your hearts are too filled with fear. It was in that place that we, the outcasts, sought refuge. And as we got farther and farther out, we crossed over into a new place. A wilderness beyond the reach of people. A place we call the Fringe."

• • •

It was early afternoon by the time Reynard stopped, forcing Salem and the others to stop short behind him. The trees had become smaller in that part of the forest and as Salem traced the line with his eyes, he saw that the green of the trees became the blue of a vast lake. Reynard brought them to the shore where he relinquished his own rucksack and showed that they could do the same. Behind the lake a range of mountains loomed like giant sentinels. Salem surveyed the scene, taking in the breathtaking view like a photographer trying to capture a panorama. Then he saw something not far off break the water's surface. A shape, clear and shiny, was rising above the water and cruising toward them. Salem took a step back. It was normal to be afraid in this situation, right?

At first, he thought it was an enormous water snake but as it got closer, Salem saw that the long neck, a brilliant color of cerulean blue, belonged to a body still concealed under the water. The creature was menacing and majestic at the same time and Salem experienced a sense of awe similar to seeing Yggdrasil or the Jotun. It was a feeling that he was looking at something ancient and sacred and, oddly, something scared. Is that…?" he said out loud to himself and then stopped. "No," he answered, "it can't be."

"She's amazing," said Juniper.

"How do you know it's a she?" asked Salem.

"Don't be stupid, Salem."

"I…" Salem didn't know how to respond.

The creature reached the shore dropping large globules of cerulean from its arched neck onto their heads and shoulders. As she came to rest in front of them Salem was struck with the sense that he could hear her thoughts.

"Give her a little space," Reynard told them. They obeyed. Iris circled, swooping low and cooing at the creature in the water.

"Ichara," said Reynard. He pronounced every syllable. The name sounded powerful. It imbued something when spoken. Something Salem could feel but not understand.

"They picked her up from Scotland just last year," Juniper explained. "I wasn't there but I heard about it."

"But she's…"

"A water dragon," said Juniper, finishing his sentence.

"Nessie," said Salem, remembering blurry images he had seen in storybooks as a kid. Ichara shuddered then.

"I recommend you call her by her true name," said Reynard.

"Ichara," Salem said, unsure why he sounded so shy when he said it. Ichara turned her head and lowered it to their level. She looked at them through a jet-black eye the size of a dinner plate. Secrets lived in those eyes. Salem was sure of it. Old and fragile secrets but secrets all the same. "Ichara," he said again. She turned her head a few degrees, pinpointing her gaze on him. He could sense whatever thoughts were happening inside of her, she was holding back from him, analyzing whether she could trust him. Salem still wore the obsidian bracelet which he was sure helped to shield her thoughts from him.

She hovered still as a lifeless object. If he had not seen her move, not felt the heat coming off her glistening body, he would not have believed she was real. He watched the sides of her mouth pull back and lift to reveal teeth like pocketknives. It was not a menace but a movement, akin, he thought, to a human smile. The dreamlike state Salem had succumbed to since arriving on the Curiosity was not shrinking but growing in complexity. Looking around him he realized it had just grown again, adding an extra layer of uncertainty to everything he thought he knew.

"Well?" said Reynard. "Who will ride her first?"

Ichara clambered with her large front fins up onto the shore. Zee shook his head and turned to Juniper who, with a smile across her face, said, "I will!"

Gingerly, but without hesitation, Juniper climbed onto the great creature's back, gasping as her hands contacted Ichara's sapphire skin. "Beautiful," Salem heard her say from up above them.

Ichara responded with a buck. It was a playful gesture but hard enough to make Juniper shout in surprise and lean forward, wrapping her arms around the water dragon's thick neck. Salem laughed, finding it funny that the infamous Juniper Fern, the disagreeable know-it-all daughter of the captain, would be surprised. Juniper shot him a glance from Ichara's back and Salem saw something he had not seen before. A lingering look that made it impossible for him to take his eyes away from her and her from him. Then, as fast as the contact had happened, the strange something was gone. He felt certain that Zee or Reynard would have noticed. But if they had they did not make it known.

Then, in a silent series of underwater kicks, Ichara and Juniper were moving away from the shore. Juniper leaned low, close to Ichara's neck, her face set in a serene expression of calm. Salem wondered how she could remain so relaxed. He even admired her in that moment as he and Zee watched their shapes navigate the farthest reaches of the forest lake.

It was not too long after Ichara's silhouette grew once again in size as she returned with Juniper to the shoreline.

"Amazing," was all Juniper could manage through deep breaths of air.

"Why are you breathing so heavy?" asked Zee. "All you did was hang on."

"You try," she said between heaves. She landed on the ground with a soft thud beneath her feet and hugged Ichara. Ichara grumbled back with a low rumble.

"Oh no," said Zee.

Juniper rolled her eyes and looked at Salem. "Well, Salem," she said, looking at him. "You're up."

Salem approached Ichara. Heart beating fast, he smiled up at her. She looked down at him, and then lowered her head followed by her neck so he could see her thick and shiny skin. Her fin was outstretched, hovering like a platform in the air, inviting him, daring him. He stepped up and swung his leg over, realizing there was no saddle, no strap for his hands or holds for his feet. Looking back to the shore he saw Juniper watching him. She had her arms outstretched like she was trying to hug an invisible tree. Salem leaned forward and wrapped his arms around Ichara's neck. Her skin was wet but to his relief he could grip it. He took one last look at the shore, feeling more confident now, and nodded to the friends watching him. Then Ichara turned and with one mighty kick of her flippers sent them cruising into the water.

She moved faster with each successive kick until the things on the land were nothing but blurs. Then, bit by bit, Salem felt her open her consciousness to him. *Salem Swan*, he heard her soft but powerful feminine voice in his head.

Ichara, Salem answered with his thoughts.

You have the gift of understanding, she said. *I have never interacted with a human who could understand.* Salem felt the surge of primitive energy rush from her to him. She was an intuitive being, and he leaned when she wanted to turn or ease up on his grip when she slowed. He saw why Juniper had been so excited. He had been on pony rides before at fairs as a child, but this was different. This was not just a ride; Salem was sure of that. He imagined what it might be like to live on the water's surface as Ichara could and cruise so that land travel would seem painfully slow. I could get used to this, he thought, and for the briefest of moments let go of his hold on Ichara's neck. Arms open wide, he too could glide across the water: effortless, wild, and free.

Ichara laughed. *Could you get used to this?* she said. Then Ichara's back arched and Salem gasped, lurching forward in a mad rush for the security of his hold. Ichara's neck was bending down into the water, and to Salem's horror her body was following. Salem meant to scream, call out, but it was too late. He did what any sane person would do. He closed his eyes and held his breath.

When he opened his eyes, he was not dead. Neither was he soaked, and he could breathe. He still clung to Ichara, the great dragon of the water who, he was realizing, was being gracious enough to share her world. She encased them in what looked like a giant bubble of air. It wrapped around them beginning from Ichara's head all the way back to her tail. *You're showing me*, Salem thought to her, and felt a sudden and deep sense of gratitude. *You're welcome*, Ichara answered. The water just beyond their bubble was distorted, like images in a wavy mirror. Other creatures swam around them. Some were fish, some were fishlike, some were part people, and others were shapes and body types Salem had never seen. They slowed down to look at Salem and Ichara. Salem felt exposed, like a fish in a tank, yet also safe on Ichara's back. He thought of Vinyr and the stream, the world that had existed beneath the surface. It seemed like a lifetime ago and a world away. Maybe not a lifetime but at least a world away, Salem grinned to himself, memories of the trip to Easterly, the rescue of the Jotun from Jotunheim, the passage through the meridian, and all that had happened since coursing through him.

It seems you have a promise you must soon fulfill, Ichara told him. Salem nodded from where he clung on her back, knowing she understood. *But you have much doubt inside.* Salem nodded again and Ichara spun in a 180-degree circle that suspended them in the water so that her face was inches from his. *Know this, Salem Swan, there is much strength in you. But should you feel weak, remember, you are never alone.*

• • •

It relieved Tristan to be back at headquarters, though part of him still craved the thrill of what he had experienced with Bramble. The exhilaration he had felt was indescribable, like fulfilling a destiny.

At Mr. White's behest, he watched the craftsmen assemble the last pieces of the new project. The engineer was precise in his movements.

So precise, that it was unclear where he stopped, and where the creation began.

There was something captivating, Tristan decided, about watching an artisan work. The way the hands moved in calculated synchronization, not with the brain, but with something bigger. Something far above them, while all around them. As if the final product itself was controlling the artist, willing its own birth through the hands of another.

This must be the way of any great thing, Tristan thought as he watched. For the greatest things, the ones possessing the capacity for real impact, are not created out of randomly assorted circumstances, but out of calculated need.

Tristan wondered whether he was to be someone of such influence on the world. He smiled to himself after considering the question. To him he was, but why then did he feel so much doubt? Was it that everything had always come so easily to him? Did he feel like it was not deserved? Or maybe that it was expected by all those around him, that he would achieve so much so quickly. The thought was unnerving. To be so good as to create the expectation of delivered greatness. Tristan had never considered himself just ordinary, but did he really believe what he had been told his entire life? Did he believe himself to be extraordinary?

The engineer began welding two pieces of chrome together, sending golden sparks up into the air like a volcanic eruption.

• • •

Above the streetlamps of Easterly the stars shone in the frosty night air. Rose Manitou stepped off the bus in the city's central bus station, wondering to herself second after second if what she was doing was right.

Having gone back and forth more times than she could count, Rose had concluded that she would meet Salem, if only to speak with him and find out how he was doing. She had learned through the Minor's Relocation Agency and a very polite man named Mr. Gingam that Salem now lived in this little town called Easterly. Mr. Gingam had disclosed Salem's guardian's name though he made mention that it was against policy. So it was that Rose Manitou, never one to enjoy getting behind the wheel of a car, had booked her first bus ticket in half a century, and embarked on a journey which would take her farther from her home than she had been in a very long time.

The town she had arrived in was small and peculiar. She had heard that New England had its own style of buildings and architecture, but she was not prepared for how different Easterly looked from towns she was used to. It was charming in its own way, she had to admit, but something about the people seemed off. As though they belonged only halfway to reality and lived the other part of their existence in a dream state.

These were the thoughts in her head as she identified the sign of the Wanderway Tavern. It was the recommendation of her bus driver that Rose start her search for Salem there. The small stone structure sat along the street as if it were asleep, tucked in against the many other buildings of Easterly.

As she stepped inside, Rose was met by the uncomfortable realization that she was the only non-local in the bar. Every face turned toward her. Even the live musicians, one guitarist and one violinist, stopped playing, leaving their amplifier to drop into an awkward tone. Trying to draw no attention to herself, Rose approached the bar. She was relieved that as she did the musicians picked up with their next song allowing the music and the conversations to continue. The barkeeper, a man in a sweaty white T-shirt was deep in conversation with two younger women across the bar. "Excuse me." Rose waited but nothing happened. "Excuse me," she tried again, this time louder. Again, her weak voice elicited no response from the barkeeper.

Frustrated, Rose turned instead to a man, around her own age with dark skin and thick sunglasses, who turned in response to survey her.

He wore a long coat with the collar pulled up so that it obscured the bottom half of his face. "Do you know where I might find a Ulysses Warminster?" she asked.

At mention of the name Ulysses the man raised a huge eyebrow. "You're looking for Ulysses?"

Rose nodded. "That's right. Warminster."

"Aren't we all," said the man. "Ulysses owes half the people here money. The ship is never in port long enough to pin him down."

"I'm sorry," interjected Rose, "ship?"

The man took a long swig of his beer before answering. "Yeah, the ship. Curiosity. Slip Thirty-Seven." With that the man slapped a twenty-dollar bill on the bar and left. This confused Rose; Mr. Gingam had not told her that Salem's uncle was a sailor. The address she had was for an apartment in the town. Reaching into her purse, she took out a pen and paper, she scribbled down Curiosity, 37. Then, reaching her breaking point, she said in her most stern voice, "Excuse me!"

At this, the barkeep, along with several patrons around the bar, turned with looks of surprise. "I need a room for the night. Am I able to get one or do I have to take my business elsewhere?"

CHAPTER 28 | PREPARATIONS IN VAEL

Almost two millennia had passed since the first crew, full of fear and hope, vanished through the disruption and discovered the Fringe. They had not known, as is often the nature of discoveries, what they found. They had not known it would change them. They had not known it would change the world. And they had not known it would save lives.

On the day of newcomings, they strung flags throughout Vael. The flags were all mirror images of one another, hung out across long strings much like the prayer flags in the Himalayas.

The flag of the many was simple in its design. It was a triangular shape with a deep blue background the color of ocean water after a storm. At its center was a small circle like a dot. From the dot three rings, each one bigger than the next, expanded out like ripples following a raindrop.

Jiminy studied the large central flag of the many from his window, watching all the smaller versions flap in the breeze. He enjoyed the Newcomer Festival. For him, it was the epitome of what the Fringe was. A legacy he continued as its speaker. Besides, it was a chance for him to speak in front of the community, and that was not something he liked to pass up.

These were the thoughts in his head as Rudolf entered.

"What's the matter, Rudolf," Jiminy asked, "you look flustered."

The clown was red in his face so it matched his red nose.

"Oh, the usual setup for the festival," said Rudolf. "You know I try to outdo myself."

"That I do," said Jiminy, straightening the decorative covers he wore over his antennae for such occasions, "and that is why you are the only one I trust to handle such an event as the Newcomer Festival."

Rudolf gave a slight bow. "You flatter me, Jiminy."

"You deserve it. But you seem frazzled beyond festival planning."

"It's true," said Rudolf. "I've heard some things I don't like."

"Things are always being said that we don't like, Rudolf," said Jiminy. "The more you ignore them, the happier you'll be."

"Right," said Rudolf, shifting in his oversized shoes. "Well, I don't know, just heard that some of the residents think you were too easy on Fern and the crew. That we, as a community, should do more to get back. I mean we don't even know what it's like on the other side anymore. All we have to go on is the word of the captain and the crew."

"A captain and a crew who bring us newcomers," said Jiminy. "Why don't we ask the Jotun what it's like on the other side and see what they have to say."

Rudolf gulped in the loud, theatrical way only true clowns can. "I understand," he said. "All I am saying is that maybe it's time we stop pretending…"

"Stop pretending what?" Jiminy was getting angry.

"That we are going to stay here forever."

"And what's wrong with staying here forever? Hasn't it given us all we needed? Hasn't it provided the refuge we sought?"

"Without a doubt, Jiminy," agreed Rudolf. Jiminy chirped. "Though," the clown said in a small voice, "you know it is not the same, and some even said…" Rudolf hesitated now.

"Said what, Rudolf?"

The clown played with a small ribbon that stuck out of his sleeve.

"Rudolf," said Jiminy, stomping one of his legs so hard on the ground that the clown jumped with a yelp.

"They say that you want to stay because you're power hungry, because you like the control your position gives you."

Jiminy paused. He remained still for a long time. The only thing that moved was the tiniest vibrations throughout his wings—for a cricket, no matter how happy, or angry, or sad, can never ever fully stop the vibration of its wings.

• • •

In another part of Vael, Aurora stood once again in front of Captain Fern.

"I want in," she said.

"I know what you want," he replied.

"Then you know what I'm willing to do for those I care about. What is the problem?"

Fern hesitated for a moment, considering how he wanted to answer Aurora's valid point. He had no argument for why she should not join them on board and for the cause. He knew he was denying her, but he did not know why.

"Do you know," he started, "what it means to be a part of the crew?"

"I believe it means being loyal."

"That is part of it," said Fern. "Anything else?"

"I can imagine," said Aurora, "that you only take those who have experienced such situations firsthand."

"Helpful," said Fern, "but not a deal breaker."

"Then what?"

"You have fight in you," said Fern. "That's good and bad."

"I can control it," said Aurora.

"I believe that—some days—but that isn't my biggest problem with the idea."

"Please," said Aurora, her tone wavering.

"The bigger picture," said Fern. "Crew members aboard the Curiosity see the bigger picture."

"I do," said Aurora without thinking.

"I'm not so sure," said Fern. "Seeing the bigger picture means holding the end goal in mind. It means deciding for the greater good, even when the immediate implications may be harmful to yourself."

"I understand," she said. "Sacrifice."

"I just don't know," said Fern.

"I deserve the chance to prove it."

"Now that," said Fern, "is something I agree with."

Aurora's features relaxed.

"I am not only being this way with you, Aurora. I respect you and what you've done for your own and know that I challenge everyone who wants to become a part of this crew. We are often doing and seeing things others do not want to do or see. It's often not fun what we do. We operate without recognition, behind the curtain." The captain paced back and forth, lost in thought. "To know you are trying to do what is right," he continued, "but to be weighed down by the sheer numbers of those who have been brainwashed into thinking they are all there is. Are you ready to operate like that?"

Aurora scrutinized the captain. "Tierney," she said, using Fern's first name for the first time. "I am already operating like that. Give me the chance to make a difference with you and the crew."

"Sometimes one can feel so…" Fern trailed off. "Invisible. One step forward is countered with five back."

"Well, Captain," she said, "Isn't it better to invisibly do something than to visibly do nothing?"

CHAPTER 29 | FAIRY LIGHTS

The streets of Vael were illuminated in the frequencies of a hundred different colors. They did not clash with one another as one may think so many different colors might. They complemented each other much the way instruments in an orchestra do, binding on spider-silk lines of energy into a single entity; transmuting from individuals to a whole, from particles to an atmosphere, from tones to a song.

Zee leaned over into Salem. "Fairy lights."

"Yeah?" said Salem, surprising himself with how he did not sound surprised and accepted not only what Zee had told him, but that he was there at all.

Zee nodded, pointing to a small furry creature with a long pole that moved from streetlamp to streetlamp. "That's the fairysmith. He watches over the fairies. Funny creatures, fairies. They say that no two fairies' lights are the same and that, only when a fairy meets its life partner, do their hues synchronize and their colors match. They say most fairies go their entire lives and never find the one with the color matching their own."

"They say," said Salem, smirking. "Who is 'they,' anyway?"

The city of Vael had transformed since Salem had first seen it. It now swelled with beings and noise and color. Tents lined the streets between the mismatched buildings and, even though Salem was a newcomer himself, everyone was in such a festive mood that, despite feeling overwhelmed, Salem felt festive.

"And what happens when a fairy finds the one with their color? And why is it you know so much about fairies?"

"I know a lot about a lot of things," said Zee, smiling to Salem. "And they say when the lights of two fairies do sync, time stops."

"Time stops? But time can't stop."

"Can't it?"

Salem said nothing and then smiled to himself. If what he was seeing around him was possible, then a brief pause in time and space would be possible too.

"I guess I don't know. Okay then, why does it stop?"

"To make room for a star," said Zee.

"A star?"

Zee nodded. "When two colors, unique in all the universe, find each other, a star of their color is born."

Salem looked up to the sky as Zee said this. The first stars were just becoming visible in the early evening darkness. Salem thought they looked like little holes poked into a canvas. He wondered what could be behind the holes to produce so many different little lights. Was it a place? Could one walk there or float? Was it a thing? Could one talk to it or look into its eyes? Was it nothing but an empty void waiting behind the thin veil they called the sky? Would the sky one day rip away and reveal the truth?

"Do you think that happens?" he asked Zee, pulling his mind back to the present moment.

"What, that a new star is born? Sure, why not; but I don't think it only happens for fairies. Look how many stars there are up there." Zee made a grand motion with both his arms to the sky. "So many. They can't all be from fairies."

"Who else then?"

"Us."

"You think we have colors too?"

"I know we do," said Zee. "Otherwise the world wouldn't make sense."

Salem liked the answer, but as they threaded their way through the crowds of diverse beings, he wondered what it meant when something made sense. What made sense to one person did not always make sense to others. He wondered if he could ever make sense out his changed life. Lost in thought, he almost did not realize the voice behind them was in fact speaking to them.

"Hi, Zee." Salem turned with Zee to face the voice. She had a round face, and kind and intelligent eyes. The epidermal opposite of Zee, she had skin so fair that it was almost tinted yellow. She had golden blonde hair and was taller than Salem and almost as tall as Zee.

"Hi, Sinziana," Zee stuttered. Salem felt the awkwardness of affection rush in like icy water. "This is Salem," Zee blurted. "Salem, this is Sinziana."

"Nice to meet you," said Salem extending his hand. Sinziana bowed but did not shake his hand. Salem could sense that it was not a rude gesture, just deliberate to her nature, as if bowing was the only option. Salem took back his hand, and bowed back, copying her. She smiled and turned her attention back to Zee.

"It's nice to see you again, Zee," she said, still smiling. "I'll be over at the concert later. Will I see you there?"

"Yeah," said Zee, with an air of impassivity in his voice that Salem had never heard. "I could be over there later, I think." Salem had to smile to himself.

"Great," said Sinziana. She smiled again at Salem and then bigger at Zee, and Salem noticed that she had straight teeth that all came to a point at the ends. She then slipped back into the crowd.

Zee exhaled in relief once she was out of sight.

"What's the matter? I think she's into you."

"No, you don't," said Zee shaking his head.

"I do," said Salem. "But what is she? You may not want her biting you."

"Oh, I'm not scared of sharp teeth, Salem," said Zee. They both laughed.

"Well you should go to the concert then!"

"Yeah, maybe I will now just to make sure we get good seats," said Zee. "You'll be okay without me?"

"I can manage," said Salem, trying to sound more confident than he felt. "I'll meet you over there in a little while." Zee nodded and Salem smiled as he watched his friend dive into the crowd.

Alone, Salem walked on into the gathering masses. Hung between the buildings around him were flags which he had learned earlier displayed a design called the "flag of the many." He like the rippled look of the design as the flags waved in the breeze. He brought his eyes back down to the street, witnessing the reality of what the flag represented. Before him was the sprawled-out city center marketplace he had learned was called Laza Plaza, named to honor a past captain of Curiosity. The marketplace had transformed from a busy hub of trade into a frenzied circus of wonder. Salem felt as though he had been thrown into a magical world where the impossible was not only real but walking and breathing, living and laughing. The streets had filled with an uncountable number of vendors so that, as he walked deeper into the festival, it was almost impossible to see Vael's unique buildings through the vivid awnings.

To his right, dwarves sold their handcrafted wares at a stand. Visitors to the stand were bartering with the dwarves with goods of their own. A large golden-brown monkey with wings was attempting to negotiate the trade of a dwarven axe for a tiny object that shimmered in his hand like a crystal. To Salem's amusement, the dwarf which the monkey was hoping to negotiate with was not interested in such a trade, and only shook his wide head on his thick neck, making his long beard shake from side to side.

To his left, Salem saw a row of what he could only describe as tree people performing something which he could only assume was a kind of education. There were long boxes of soil and on one side stood the tree people, while on the other stood an assortment of passersby who had become caught up in whatever was happening. Then, with their wooden hands, the tree people took the hands of the guests standing opposite. With both sets of hands hovering over the soil, they called seeds forth. "See," one of the tree people was telling the audience. "A garden can start with only one seed." Then the tree people handed the seeds off to the individuals so that the next set could step up.

Just beyond the dwarves and the people of the tree stood a ring of torches, all varying heights and widths, arranged in a circle. In the center it looked like a portal into another world might open in the ground at any moment and something strange and terrible might step out; but a single figure dressed very much like a ninja knelt there on a knee, holding in each hand two glistening sabers. Salem watched as the person began a series of silent and complex spins, making the sabers appear more as sparkling sticks of ice than as metallic shards. Then, in a motion fast enough to appear as magic, the sabers were swinging through the torches, collecting bits of flame along the way until their curved bodies were covered in licking shades of orange and yellow. Like boomerangs returning to the hunter, the fire dancer caught the instruments with a precision bordering on mechanical, to which the crowd surrounding clapped. Salem too clapped along with the audience. He even smiled and laughed, and then a hand touched his shoulder.

"Enjoying yourself?"

Juniper stood to Salem's right wearing a dress he had never seen before. It was dark maroon with gold sparkles and tailored as if it had been designed only for her. Her hair was pulled to one side and she had replaced her typical boots with low-top shoes. Salem realized he was seeing her bare ankles and legs for the first time.

"I, uh…" he stuttered. Juniper smiled.

"You uh?"

"You look," Salem started again and stopped. He did not know why he had stopped. He felt like he had swallowed something spicy. The captain's daughter stood in front of him, much as she had so many times before, though something was different. It was not the physical beauty, though that was very real too. It was something deeper, something she gave off that she had not before. She was letting something come off her like some natural perfume he could not smell or see but only feel. He wondered if all girls had that ability. Salem took a step closer, not saying a word.

"What is it?" Juniper asked, in a tone of voice that made him feel embarrassed and confident at the same time.

"Nothing," he mumbled, feeling they both knew it was a lie and that that was okay.

They turned and walked together. Their steps fell into a cadence and Salem tried to think of something to say. He could not think of anything. He was happy to walk beside her.

"The stage should be right over there," said Juniper. Salem followed her arm and, on the way, caught sight of something else.

"What's that?" he asked, pointing to a thin alleyway that shot off from the main street.

"Don't know," said Juniper. "Why?"

"Not sure," said Salem and began walking over toward the space.

"Where are you go—" Juniper said. "Ugh, whatever." She followed Salem.

The corridor-like space Salem stepped into was tucked in between two buildings. It was tight so that only two people could walk side by side through it. He stopped and turned halfway through, facing Juniper. "What is that smell?" he asked. Juniper's nose crinkled as she sniffed the air.

"It's—" she said and stopped. "Cinnamon?" Salem knew she was right. The spicy flavor floated in and around his nostrils before landing on his tongue. "Look," Juniper said then, pointing up to the groups of small nests lodged in between the windowsills and balconies of the strange apartments.

"What are they made of?" Salem asked, reaching up to the one closest to the ground and breaking off a small piece with his finger. As he did a head appeared over the side of the nest. He held the small piece of nest close to his face. "It is cinnamon," he said.

"Wait a minute," said Juniper, "I've heard about these. These are cinnamon birds."

"What?" asked Salem. The head that had appeared over the side of the nest did in fact belong to a bird. Its head was a round white sphere the size of a golf ball, and the beak protruding from the face was long and twirled around itself, much like a cinnamon stick, to a point at the end. The cinnamon bird chirped. It hopped up to stand on the edge of its nest and inched closer to the side with each successive sound. "I think it's angry at me," said Salem.

"Well, you are destroying its nest."

Feeling guilty, Salem handed the small fragment of cinnamon back to the bird. The small creature bobbed its head to one side before taking it in its beak.

"Feel better?" Juniper asked. Salem nodded. "You know," said Juniper, "I heard something about these birds." She had a look in her eye which Salem had not seen before.

"Oh yeah?" he said.

"Yeah," she said, "it's supposed to be good luck to kiss under them. Or something like that."

Salem could not speak. He felt his heart thud up to double speed and he hoped it would not burst out of his chest. "Really." Suddenly, he felt that Juniper was too pretty to look at and he studied the nests again with great interest.

"Yeah," she said, "really."

Salem felt as her warm fingers slipped into his cold hand. He wished that his hand were warmer. "Sorry," he said.

"For what," she said, and he realized that her face was closer to his than it had ever been.

"My hand is a little cold."

"I can feel," she said.

"This is weird," he said then.

"Sorry?" she said, sounding surprised.

"I thought you didn't like me. I mean, it seemed like you didn't."

"I didn't," she said. "At least not a first."

"So why now?" he asked.

Juniper shrugged. "I don't know. You're just more tolerable than you were before."

"Oh, well that's good," said Salem, looking away from the nests and into Juniper's eyes. He looked down at her lips. He had kissed a girl before, though that kiss had been different, something small and funny. This, whatever this was, felt much bigger.

"You're nervous," said Juniper. Salem could not tell if it was a statement or question.

"Nah," he said, lying. "So, have you kissed lots of guys under these nests?" He had meant the question as a joke but the look on Juniper's face told him that he had made a mistake.

She pulled her hand out of his and took a step back. "Of course not. You're the one who wanted to come this way."

"I didn't mean it in a bad way," Salem said, trying to recover.

"Oh, then how did you mean it?"

The damage had already been done. He could tell. "I just meant..." he said but stopped.

"It's alright," said Juniper. "It was weird anyway. Let's just go find Zee." With that she was walking away from him. Salem was not sure what had happened. For one second, he had felt like the world was changing around him. The next, he felt like it had all disappeared. "I'm such an idiot," he whispered to himself, and followed Juniper through the remaining nests and into the space beyond.

• • •

Not far away Captain Fern stood on a hill overlooking the festival. To his right stood Ulysses.

"Glad to see they're hitting it off," said Ulysses, motioning toward Juniper and Salem who had just emerged to stand close to the stage.

"It's a strange thing," said Fern, "watching a part of you grow into its own thing."

Ulysses hummed in agreement.

"Now," said Fern, turning his attention to a man who had just broken off from the crowd. The man's strides were hurried but meek. "I think it's about time we took care of our little problem."

"I was wondering," said Ulysses, "when we were going to get around to that."

CHAPTER 30 | HISTORIES AND HOPE

Mr. White drummed his fingers. First the left hand, starting with the pinky and working toward the thumb, then the thumb of the right hand rising like a wave until its pinky rose and fell with a soft pat on the table. A pause, and then off the fingers went again in the other direction. This was the only sound in the room: small repetitive thuds, like the tiny heartbeats of a sleeping monster.

Fifteen of them had come and more would arrive. He looked around at the faces, studying each one the way a collector might survey their collection. He was careful to give adequate eye time to each person at the table. He was a firm believer in what he liked to call "personalized attention-giving."

A breeze worked its way through the windows of the old house. It pulled cool air in on a draft that smelled of wet leaves. It was the kind of night Mr. White liked. It was the kind of night that felt as though all the world was greeting him and everything was on his side.

"As this table represents," he began, "we are together in this endeavor."

That only humans occupied the table and no human should be above another had become a staple of the Regulat. This was ironic, considering Mr. White sat at the same level of the others, albeit in a chair more deserving of the title throne. Each person knew it but said nothing. The unspoken truth among them was that it was better to have a leader who evoked fear and knew what he wanted than to make do with a benevolent but indecisive pleaser. Constance White was in every way the former.

They had invited Tristan to the meeting, he thought, because of his performance in assisting Mr. Cancun, formerly Bramble, in his extermination of the Cueyatl.

"Influence." Mr. White paused, letting the dying sound of his voice reverberate through the room. Dramatic silence was his favorite rhetorical device. "Influence is the chisel that carves the stone. You are here at the dawning of a new age. Throughout history, we have struggled. We have fought amongst ourselves and with other things for petty slices of land or reserves of resources. But what for?"

There was silence in the room.

"What was the goal? What were we trying to achieve beyond surviving from one day to the next? My friends, we have been ready for some time to break free of our animalistic chains and ascend to the next level of understanding. Our founders knew this"—Mr. White shook his head—"they were cursed with being ahead of their time. I know their curse. Alas, we here are on the cusp of realizing the true destiny of humanity. Allow me to take you on a journey of what will be." Mr. White rose now, and paced around the room, behind the backs of those seated. "I believe in a world free of toil and conflict. I see a place where our children can learn and grow and be safe from the threat of others. I hear beautiful human voices. I feel the energy that comes with our global rise. Diversity among species as a way forward is a myth. There is nothing to be gained in allowing the weaker forms of life to exist. Realizing humanity's mission as the purifiers of existence: now that, my friends, is the way forward and we will realize the pure world."

Tristan excused himself from the room. He did not see Vera come out after him.

"Everything alright, Tristan?"

Tristan stopped, surprised to see the right-hand lieutenant of Mr. White addressing him. He paused for a moment to compose himself.

"It's all exciting," he said, "everything that's happening."

"Oh?" Vera asked. "You think so?"

"I mean, it's happening. The pure—"

"It's still a long way away," interrupted Vera. "We've come close before and seen it all fall apart."

Tristan was not sure what to do or say. He did not know much about Vera or her past. He knew she had come from a turbulent background and had somehow risen fast through the ranks of the Regulat, gaining favor with Mr. White. One could see ambition just by looking into her dark eyes, which matched her dark skin. There were rumors that her past was mixed. Tales that she was not as pure as she led everyone to believe. Tristan decided it was best not to inquire too much.

The two walked together to the end of the hall and down a winding flight of stairs. The second floor of the old priest house, once a lounge and greeting area, now housed artifacts. Tristan had never been through the doors, closed to all except full regulators. He hesitated.

"You're my guest," she told him, opening the door and issuing him inside. The space was enormous and well lit. Tristan stopped after walking through the door.

The artifact room was a museum of sorts with raised stages like little islands. They held every manner of skeleton and obscure relic one could imagine. "That," said Vera, pointing upward to a huge skeleton standing next to them on the stage, "was the last platypus bear."

Tristan looked up at the imposing skeleton. It had been positioned so that the arms were raised, ready to strike at something. It did have the bill and tail of a platypus.

"And here," said Vera, walking toward another of the stages to a place where a glass jar the size of a barrel sat, "a siren." Tristan peered into the jar at the scaly body wrapped around itself. At the top he could make out the face. It was a soft face, neither masculine nor feminine. The siren looked like it was only sleeping.

"You don't mean the sirens, like as in the-journey-of-Odysseus sirens, do you?"

"Yes," said Vera, tapping on the glass. "I caught this one myself, in fact."

"So, there are still more?"

"For now," she said.

"Vera," said Tristan. "Are you…" He hesitated.

Vera looked at him. He was not sure if the look was a challenge or an invitation. "I wanted you to see this place, Tristan, so you know what we're up against. Many of these creatures will use their seductive beauty to play with your mind. None mean you well. Each one would seek to either control you, eat you, or destroy you. That is the sad truth, and that is why we do what we do."

"I think I'm ready."

"There is no such thing as ready, Tristan. There is only the corrupted world and the pure world and those who do what is right. Stay here a little while longer and look around. It'll be good for you." Vera walked back to the door.

"The captain and the ship," said Tristan. "How are we going to know where they are?"

"I have a feeling," said Vera, "that they will come to us."

• • •

Below the house and the meeting of the regulators were many souls held captive.

Gandha had done everything that had been asked of him since being taken in by the organization called the Regulat. He had spied for them. He had lied for them. He had watched his family suffer at their hands. So, it was in the dark and cold of the cell he cried. He had discovered that there were different ways to cry. There was the common sad cry, often appearing in brief spurts like the summer showers he had known as a boy. There was the angry cry which rolled in like a herd of cumulonimbus clouds, razing everything in its path. Then there was the helpless cry. It was, Gandha now knew, the worst kind of cry one could experience. It was the worst, not because of what it brought, but because of what it took.

"Hope," said a voice from the darkness.

Gandha paused between the semi-silent heaves, seeing nothing in the darkness. A small column of light spilled through the window of the door, but he still saw nothing but the cold floor.

"Hope," said the voice again from somewhere. It was a calm voice, and Gandha noticed that it did not increase his suffering.

"When all else feels lost, hope is the one thing that can still belong to you."

"Who are you?" Gandha asked. He heard a scratching sound from somewhere else in the room, like something being dragged. Then, in the arm of light splashed out in front of him, he saw the head of something. It was flat, and angular, and accented by big black eyes with little balls of white that caught what little light was in the room. As it moved into the light, Gandha saw that it was large and thick. It had a long neck that connected back into a massive shell. Two forefeet came forward and Gandha saw that it was so large it had to drag its body across the ground.

"I am here," it said. "And you need not cry, brother. Help will come."

"Help will not come," Gandha replied. "Help does not exist."

"You must have faith." The huge thing had dragged itself all the way over to Gandha. Its face now seemed to levitate in front of his own. "For without faith, what are we?"

"They took my faith from me when they took my family."

"No," it said, "they took your family from you. Your hope they cannot take."

"What do you want from me?" Gandha did not have the desire or energy to argue.

"I want what any fellow prisoner would want. A cellmate who chooses hope over despair."

Gandha looked up into the thing's eyes. They were black with white spindly strands poured into them like the mixing can of two contrasting colors of paint.

"What do you want me to say? I feel hideous and cannot bear to look at myself inside. I feel like I've let the people I love down."

"Maybe you have, maybe you haven't. Either way, what does it matter?"

"It matters because I could have prevented all of this!" Gandha was angry now.

"I hate to break it to you, Gandha, but you couldn't have prevented anything."

The huge reptile had taken two giant steps back and allowed its legs to drop at its side. "Whatever has happened to you until this point was always going to happen. So, it does nothing to dwell on an already written past. The past is as good a reference as any, but no place in which to be living."

"You don't understand. If you had lost your wife and daughter, you'd see it my way."

"Loss. I know loss. Loss is that thing that will keep you up at night. Loss is the hot needles that prick your skin and make your entire body hurt. Loss finds you at your highest points, latching onto you like a steel leech and dragging you down into the depths. Oh, I know loss, and he's no friend of mine."

"There is no going back," said Gandha with a tone of finality.

"No. You may not know this now, Gandha, but time only moves in one direction for a reason. With the movement of time comes gravity. With gravity comes suffering and with suffering comes love."

"What are you saying?"

"There is no love without loss."

"But what is the point of love if loss is what happens?"

"I've always found that seeking the point in something is counterproductive to understanding its nature. If you want simple physics, there is no point to anything, and that is the greatest point of all. Anger is forgiveness. Sadness is rejoicing. Fear is bravery. Losing is loving. Besides"—the thing shifted its great mass like a small mountain— "all is relative. Loss will engulf you if you let it. Hang on to one sliver of hope and anything is possible."

Shadows from outside the room were passing in front of the door. Gandha heard voices, and then he heard a voice that he knew. He scrambled to his feet as fast as he could.

"Careful. If they see you peeking, they'll punish you both."

Gandha did not care. He pressed his face against the porthole of the door. There, with a man in a suit holding one of her arms, was Chitra. Behind walked her mother in the same fashion.

"I see," said the tortoise, "hope lives in you still."

INTERLUDE 3 | THE BATTLE AT CRAWFORD HEIGHTS

12 years prior to Salem's arrival on the Curiosity

The sun shone across the road in bursts of white. Julie squinted against the glare as she pulled the car into the driveway. She looked into the rearview mirror to see Salem sleeping. You little rascal, she thought. Wait until I tell your father. The three-year-old had just thrown a tantrum in the grocery store, only to fall asleep on the way home.

She carried Salem into the house, surprised at how fast he was growing. We will not be able to carry you like this much longer, she thought, and smiled as she laid Salem down on the sofa in the living room.

The spring air felt good as she carried the rest of the groceries from the car into the house. She set them down on the island in the kitchen and listened for a moment to the steady breathing of her little boy. She began unpacking the groceries, and then she paused.

The breathing had stopped.

She closed the refrigerator door and turned around. Salem, using one hand to rub sleep from his eye, stood in front of her. In his other hand, he held out a small brown rectangle.

"Hey, I thought you were asleep."

Salem shook his head and handed her the journal.

"Thanks," she told him. She turned the journal over in her hand. "Strange. Your father never forgets his journal."

Salem only shrugged, turned, and walked to the living room where his toys were waiting.

Julie flipped open the cover of the book to see Rigel's familiar handwriting. She had learned, through the letters, notes, and later, vows, to read his scratchy yet elegant prose. As a professor on myths and legends, Rigel was constantly scribbling ideas for new lectures and books. It was his teaching opportunity that had brought them to Easterly, to instruct at the well-regarded Crawford Heights.

She flipped through the first few pages of Rigel's journal. Normally she would not do such a thing, but it was in her hands, and she was curious. She had read only a page before she closed the book and slid it into her purse.

"Salem, honey," she called. "We're going out again."

She buckled Salem into his car seat in a hurry. Her mind raced between what she should or should not do. What she had read in Rigel's journal should not have scared her like it did, and yet, there she was, rushing to find him. Her husband was a kind man and intelligent in the book-smart sort of way—though Julie had learned that his book smarts did not translate well to world smarts. She knew about the people who did not appreciate Rigel's work. The ones who thought what her husband did was wrong, and how they threatened him for it. What she did not know was how far such threats had gone.

• • •

The campus of Crawford Heights was quiet as she pulled up to it only a few minutes later. The students and most of the faculty were gone, but Rigel had stayed late as usual.

As she walked through the main courtyard, past the fountain, she heard shouts. They were coming from behind the school. She looked back to the shady spot in the parking lot where Salem waited in the car. Through the rolled-down window she could see his sleeping face and the small plush griffin he held in his arms. Any car ride longer than ten minutes was bound to put him to sleep. Confident he was okay, she turned back toward the noise and hurried around the side of the building.

Crawford's gardens and sports fields were a series of spaces so intricate that faculty and students alike often got lost. Julie held Rigel's journal close to her chest as she walked down one path and then another. It had all been a trick, she realized, reading Rigel's written words back over to herself in her head. His assignment and placement at the school only happened so they could target him. They. Those people who sent him letters and left strange encrypted voicemail messages that he should stop his research into mythology and the quest to find those so-called legendary beings.

She passed through the line of trees separating the first garden from the next and froze. Rigel stood there alone, his back turned to her, confronting a horde of what looked like angry bankers.

"Rigel," she said, in a shrill tone that startled even her. He turned to her, and as he did, one of those people standing opposite him released a projectile into the air. He only had time to open his mouth to respond to Julie before the object, the long piece of black, embedded itself deep into his chest.

Julie's heart felt like it was being ripped out of her. Rigel, her husband, Salem's father, was crumbling to the ground. All he ever wanted was to discover, to connect with those things of legend in which no one else could believe. Julie included. If she had only known how far he had come, how much he had done for building an understanding of the so called "fringe beings" with the public. She was moving toward him then, in slow motion. She willed herself to move faster, but the scene felt like a nightmare that she could only watch and was powerless to control.

Then something, a hand, grabbed her arm and held her in place. She turned to find none other than her brother, Ulysses. Ulysses' face was grave, and he was not alone. All around him stood other people she had never seen. People who looked determined and angry as they faced the suited people across the garden.

"Leave now," he said. "It's not safe. Take Salem and leave."

"I can't leave him," she answered, motioning to Rigel's body on the ground.

"We will help him. Go."

Against everything inside herself telling her not to, Julie ran. Salem was awake and crying in the car.

"It's okay, my love," she said to him, feeling as though her entire world had ended right there in the courtyard of Crawford Heights.

She did not look back as she drove away. She swore to herself she would not introduce their child to that kind of life. He would be normal. No one would hunt him. She would shield him from that danger, even if it meant not telling him about his father. They would leave Easterly, and she was determined her son would not be back.

PART IV | EASTERLY

CHAPTER 31 | THE FLAVOR OF LIFE

Fern sat behind the massive desk in his study, knowing that, in a few seconds, the door to his quarters would open. Though it had not happened yet, his gut told him it was coming. He smiled and turned the page in the book he was reading. A few seconds later, the doors creaked open.

Karl walked in, followed by Ulysses. They came to stand around Fern's desk, waiting.

"Thank you for coming," Fern said. He could tell that Karl was nervous; though, to be fair, that was the man's default appearance.

"You wanted to see me, Captain?"

"Yes, Karl, that's correct. How are you?"

"Fine, Captain," answered Karl. "And you?"

"Well, thank you," said Fern. "I hope you had a pleasant experience in the Fringe."

"Yes, Captain," said Karl. "I spent time with Dover and the gnomes. They were kind to me."

"Good. You should never underestimate the kindness of others. Karl, the reason I asked you here is because I want to share a short story with you."

Ulysses sat, and the captain extended his hand that Karl should do the same. Karl hesitated, calculating the reasons for such a meeting. After a moment's pause, Karl sat.

"You know Ena, don't you, Karl?"

Karl nodded that he did.

"Ena, like you, showed up one day in Easterly requesting a meeting with me. He explained to me the atrocities which had been committed against his people and expressed a desire to join the crew." Fern could see the beads of sweat lining Karl's brow, even though the air that flowed through the cabin was cool. "Dover"—the captain shook his head as if to laugh to himself—"Dover was similar. He showed up here one night drunk, scared, and angry. He wanted to right wrongs and since that day he's been a pain, but he comes through when you need him, as you learned in the Fringe." Fern paused. "You came to us too, Karl, in such a way. A fleeing survivor of the East Coast soothsayers."

Fern watched Karl nod.

"Karl, call me naïve but I search for the light in others before the darkness."

"As is right, Captain," said Karl.

Fern hummed in agreement. "Yes, well, Karl, it's come to our attention that perhaps someone aboard this ship has proved me to be naïve." Fern saw the man straightening himself in his chair. "I will not pretend that secrets aboard this ship do not spread."

"Like wildfire," Ulysses added. Fern ignored him.

"As I'm sure you may have already heard," Fern continued, still looking at Karl, "we could rescue all the Jotun but one. A child was taken from them around the time we arrived. Now"—Fern got up and walked out from behind the desk—"I am asking all the crew members who stayed back at camp to remember if there was anyone of our crew who went missing during that time. Karl"—the captain looked in Karl's eyes—"can you recall anyone leaving camp while we were gone?"

Karl did not answer right away. He furrowed his brow and looked up to one side. "I think," he said, "Artichoke sent Zee, Salem, and your daughter, Captain. To… look for food around that time."

"This we already know," said Ulysses.

Fern nodded. "Yes, they were captured by Jotun and brought to us. I will speak to them. Anyone else?"

"I was out gathering wood, but I didn't see anyone else."

"Very good," said Fern. "Thank you, Karl, for your loyalty and honesty."

"Captain," said Karl. He and Ulysses rose together. Ulysses smiled and nodded at Karl. They both approached the door to leave.

"Ulysses," said Fern. "Would you mind sticking around for a minute?"

Karl left the captain's quarters, closing the doors behind him. Fern and Ulysses were silent for a few seconds.

"Well, that took an unexpected turn," Ulysses said. "I thought you wanted to make a statement."

"I did, just not in the way I thought I would." Fern sighed. "I think he'll be more valuable to us this way."

"What way?" asked Ulysses. "As a spy walking free?"

"I would expect he knows we know," Fern said.

"How can you be sure?"

"Intuition, how else?"

"Well," said Ulysses, prodding the claw-footed telescope with his foot, "as long as this doesn't come back to bite us."

"Oh, I think there's a sliver of good inside everyone," said Fern. "I have the feeling that Karl's wants to show itself."

"There is also a sliver of bad in everyone." Ulysses' voice had dropped, and Fern could hear the embarrassment.

"Your past put you here, Ulysses. Never forget that."

"Pasts like mine don't just go getting forgotten," said Ulysses, smiling.

• • •

Back up on the top deck of the ship, Salem looked out at the water. He felt comforted to see the ocean again. It was not that he was ready to call himself a sailor, far from it, but something about the rise and fall of the ship over the waves and the salty breeze that came with it gave him peace, as if at any moment the ship could alter its course and try something new or head off on another adventure.

He took a breath in. There were the things outstanding, such as the kidnapped Jotun child and the many questions left unanswered from their time in the Fringe. He exhaled, turning the obsidian bracelet over on his wrist. Since receiving it in the Fringe, the bracelet had helped calm his nerves, along with his newfound abilities as a mythlinguist. He had tried to talk to Ulysses and Fern about his gift, but to his surprise they could not provide him with any real support.

"Hard to say," Ulysses had told him. "I've never heard of anyone who can do such a thing. Very cool. I think it'll take some getting used to."

Salem had been disappointed with the lack of knowledge from the crew regarding mythlinguistics and disappointed in himself for his inability to accept his gift: something everyone told him was something cool. He had taken to finding comfort inside his father's journal. Since arriving in Jotunheim, life had become such a whirlwind that Salem barely had time to touch the journal. Though now, in a time when he experienced difficult thoughts that others could or would not understand, he enjoyed sketching and writing about all he had seen in Vael.

He had just finished a sketch of Ichara, the water dragon, when he realized what time it was, and that he was already late for instructions with Artichoke in the galley. Unfortunately for Salem, Zee was nowhere to be found and Juniper had declined to join, having avoided him since the Newcomer Festival. Salem wondered how they could both find their way out of instructions when he was stuck having to attend.

"Always nice visiting the Fringers," said Artichoke with a guffaw as he chopped one of the thick Fringe plants in half. "But nicer cooking what they give us."

"What do you mean?" asked Salem.

"Well, just what I said. The stuff we get from there is good stuff, grown right." Artichoke motioned to the pile of plants and crops given to the crew from the Fringe. "Crops, you know, they're like children."

"Children?" Salem had said the word out loud and regretted his decision, knowing it would lead to an Artichoke-length explanation.

"Yeah, children," continued the boisterous cook. "Plants respond to the way you grow them. They need to be cared for like a kid. They need attention like a kid. But most of all they need to be appreciated like a kid."

"And that makes them taste better?"

"You bet it does," said Artichoke. "Ever taste an unappreciated child? Disgusting."

Salem only shook his head, repulsed but accustomed to the cook's humor.

"Thing is, back on this side we stopped appreciating the things we grow. We forget that what we bring into the world we do not bring in to make ourselves feel better. That is a byproduct. We grow as a gesture. Growing things, growing good things, that's how you flatter old mother."

"Old mother?"

"Nature, boy."

Salem had never heard Artichoke speak so much on a topic not related to, well, Artichoke. He stayed quiet, unsure what to do or say. To his astonishment, Art continued speaking while his knife rose and fell over the stalks.

"All the time you are releasing energy from your body, even when you don't feel it. While you're doing this, you're also takin' energies from others. Plant or animal, man or woman, common or fringe—whatever—we aren't different. Juju, vibes, energies, whatever you call it, it's flowing through all of us. When we stop appreciating, it taints the stuff flowing between us. Just as when we take notice of our influence over that which we grow, it yields the flavor of life."

In a movement faster than Salem's eyes could follow, Artichoke flicked his wrist, sending a small sliver of chopped stalk through the air. It landed in one of the cook's outstretched palms. Hand open, Art extended the piece to Salem. Salem took it and put it in his mouth. He knew before the saliva congregated that the flavor was not the external casing of a thing the way he knew flavor. It was, even in the tiny piece, the embodiment of the thing itself.

"Taste that?" Artichoke asked. "That is the energy."

Salem only nodded, feeling it coursing through his entire body.

"It's not the thing itself, which is something special. We are all just things. Collections of atoms held together. It's the way you see a thing which makes it what it is and it's the way you appreciate a thing which provides the real nourishment."

Salem swallowed. "That was amazing. How did you do that?"

"I did nothing except make you aware."

"Of the energy?"

"That you appreciate the energy. Most people don't think twice about what they eat, much less if the things they're eating should be eaten. Consumption is not bad; look at me." Artichoke patted his rotund belly. "We need to consume. Need fuel to burn to make these meaningless shells we call bodies do some much needed good."

"Like cooking?"

"Cooking's only good if you do it right. Nothing worse than bad cooking. Guess anything is like that, though."

"Artichoke, why did you become a chef?"

Artichoke paused mid-cut.

"I became nothing."

Salem shook his head. "I don't understand."

"We don't become things, Salm. You were complete the day you were born, hatched, or sent your first root down and your first leaf up. Take you, for example. That tree gave you a gift, right?" Salem nodded, rubbing his obsidian bracelet as he did. "Way I see it," said Artichoke, "you were always a mythlinguist. That was all just part of your journey. We don't become; we uncover. Each of these new things you're exposed to in life chips away at the person you think you are until there's nothing left but, well, you. Then it's just up to you to like who you are and maybe even embrace who you are."

"But what if we never uncover what we are supposed to be?" asked Salem.

It was Artichoke's turn to shake his head. "It's not like that. You're already complete, don't you see? Everything from here on out is choices."

But Salem didn't see. "I guess," he said to Artichoke.

"I can see you think a lot," said Artichoke.

"Is that bad?" Salem asked.

"Reckon the way you're doing it is," said the cook with a grin.

"I don't know any other way," admitted Salem.

"Here," said Artichoke, and handed him another of the chopping knives, "start cutting this like I'm doing."

Salem obeyed, and though he did not think cutting would change anything, as he let the knife fall like the waves under the ship outside, he began to feel better.

CHAPTER 32 | DEFINITIONS OF THE PAST

The crew changed in the days following the visit to the Fringe. Each looked as though they had regained something, elements of youth or energy or just contentment they had not had before.

Kane looked like he had regained fifty years of youthfulness. The tiny man sprang from table to table as he fiddled a tune on something that looked like a cross between a violin and a walking stick. The crew clapped with the beat.

"Enjoying yourself?"

Salem had not seen Nut approach. She had flowers strung through her hair and looked very pretty.

"Where's Geb?" he asked her, knowing that he never saw her far away from her earthy brother.

"Somewhere around," she said. "Where's Juniper?" She was smiling. It was a knowing smile, the kind someone makes when they have won an argument.

"What do you mean?" Salem asked.

"Oh, the denial is almost as cute as the truth."

Salem was not sure what she meant. The small upturn of her lips told him it was best to say less on the subject.

"Cheers," said Geb, emerging out onto the top deck of the ship with a drink in his hand. "Here you two go." He handed cups to Salem and Nut. "Sorry Salem, yours is the not so fun kind. Maybe in a few years we can have a drink."

Salem raised his glass like he had seen the other crew members do, and Geb smacked his own against it, taking a large gulp before continuing.

"Your uncle is down there dancing with everyone. You should go down—it's too good to miss. I think he's twirling Dorianna around now and she doesn't like it."

"Really?" asked Salem, who thought Ulysses had seemed rather serious the past few days. "I didn't know Ulysses liked to dance so much."

"This is just your uncle's kind of thing. He's legendary for getting parties started." Salem could tell Geb was enjoying his ale. "Oh yes," said Geb, "even back when Ulysses was on the dark side, he still knew how to party."

"On the dark side?" asked Salem, not understanding.

"That's right. Your uncle wasn't always the enlightened, what should we say, cat you see today. He used to work for the Regulat."

"Wait," said Salem in disbelief, "you mean the Regulat that hunts fringers?"

"That's right," said Geb, taking another loud gulp. "Ulysses was on the fast track with them."

Salem sat stunned. Geb did not seem to notice and only rocked his head back and forth in time with the music. Tiny leaves and twigs fell out as he did. "Yeah, but he smartened up before going too far. We don't hold it against him."

Salem was quiet.

"Don't worry about it," said Nut, placing her hand on Salem's shoulder. "We all have parts of our pasts we are less proud of. The important thing is that we can change."

On the outside, Salem smiled. On the inside, he was unconvinced. "I guess so."

"Well, what do you say, sis?" Geb asked Nut. "Should we go back inside?"

"Yes, let's," she answered. "You'll come in too?" she asked Salem.

"In a minute," Salem answered.

Salem watched the siblings, one of the earth and the other of the sky, walk back inside. The music in the mess hall and the sound of laughter did little to keep him in the spirit of celebration. Why should his uncle's past mean so much to him? Was not Ulysses now a man of integrity? Did not everyone have some darkness in their stories?

He was confused. In the last few days, he had hoped, and rediscovered a basis for understanding his life and, perhaps, a way to pick up the fragments of himself he had tried to forget. It had been achievable because of one thing: trust.

He had not known what to expect of his uncle since the day Mr. Gingam had left him with the strange crew aboard the strange ship. The first impression was lost among the sea of emotions that had slapped him like a proverbial hand in the face. He felt like the sting of that initial slap had never abated.

The further Salem got from his old life, the more scared he was of losing what little remnants of his past he had. Weirdly, he also felt that the farther away he got from his past, the more he saw a potential future. Salem wondered if it was always required to let go of the old to make room for the new. Why couldn't they both exist together?

The thought brought him back to Ulysses—a man who was part of his past and also his future. His uncle, with his quirkiness and humor, somehow had a way of making him feel comfortable and safe. Still, secrets remained. There was more to tell. He was sure of it.

He walked along the weather deck. It was almost empty, and night was falling fast over the world.

A small orb-shaped light appeared a few feet in front of him. It had shown itself once before to him in the cargo hold. He had forgotten about the incident but was elated to see it again. It pulsated, and Salem thought he could hear it hum. He stepped toward it and as he did, the will-o'-the-wisp vanished only to materialize a few feet further in front of him. He kept following it until he came to the front of the ship. It stopped in front of the bowsprit and vanished. It confused Salem. Why here? A moment later the light appeared from the other side of the deck, and Salem thought to follow it before noticing that someone else was.

Juniper saw him first. Her face was expressionless as she turned to lean over the rail and rested her chin on folded arms.

"Hey," Salem said.

"Hey," she said back, still looking out at the ocean. "They're funny things, the wisps." A wisp appeared in front of her face and she poked her finger at it.

"They look for you too?" Salem asked.

"I'm not sure they look for anything," Juniper sighed.

"What do you mean?"

"I think they help other things look."

"For what?"

"Whatever those things need, I guess. No one knows why they do what they do. Just that they don't follow any rules. They like you or dislike you."

Salem was happy just to be talking to her again. "That's a lot of pressure," he said, "to be liked or not liked."

"Not if they like you." Salem could hear Juniper smile. "What's bothering you?" she asked.

"It's nothing," said Salem.

"It's funny," said Juniper.

"What is?"

"I think everyone can lie when they want to."

"I'm not lying."

"Everyone can lie when they want to," Juniper repeated, "and when they don't want to lie but try anyway, they become terrible liars. It's like you're begging me to get it out of you."

"I'm not." Salem could hear the childishness in his own voice. Juniper only turned her head, looking up at him with expectant eyes.

Salem leaned against the railing so that their bodies touched each other. The contact relaxed him.

"I just heard some stuff in there that I didn't know, and it kind of bothered me."

"About what?"

"Did you know Ulysses was a part of the Regulat?"

"Of course," said Juniper, "everyone does."

Salem looked at her in disbelief. "And no one ever told me?"

"Why would I do that? It's for Ulysses to tell you. Besides, what does it change? He is who he is now, regardless of what's happened in the past."

"It changes everything," said Salem, breaking eye contact with her.

"Really? And how's that?"

"Well," said Salem, "it just...does."

"It changes the way you see him?"

"Well, yeah," said Salem.

"Yeah," said Juniper, turning to look at him with a stare which was both hot and cold. "Means nothing now, though."

"Doesn't it?"

"Only if you want it to. The past doesn't define us."

"So, what did your dad do then he deserves you being mean to him?" The words had slipped out before he could realize what he said. Juniper's expression hardened, and Salem knew he had ventured into a place where she did not want him to be. But he held her stare. The question belonged to one of the many which had been in his mind for the past few weeks and he felt he had a right to ask it.

"What Ulysses did in his past had nothing to do with you," said Juniper. "You have no right to judge him, because you weren't even a consideration."

"You said that the past does not define us. Sounds like, whatever happened, you're letting the past define how you see your dad."

"Stop, Salem."

"I'm just trying to understand."

"Maybe you should just try to understand yourself before you try to understand other people."

"I just…" Salem said.

Juniper's eyes were watery and angry. "And I thought maybe you were getting it."

"Get what?" said Salem. He wanted to protect whatever dignity he had left. "No one tells me anything. I'm expected to just figure it all out."

"There is no manual, you idiot. It's not like anyone here has a book for you on how to live here or be a part of this world."

"I didn't even ask to be here."

"Yeah, well, then it's better for you to go back to what you know."

"Probably," said Salem, not believing the conviction in his own words. Even though she was strong, he could see the hurt on Juniper's face.

"Fine," she said, standing upright and, without another word, walked away from him.

CHAPTER 33 | AEGLE'S RETURN

It was not lost on Jiminy that crickets were known for their singing. Every morning, every afternoon, every evening impromptu concerts spring up in all corners of the planet. For crickets, Jiminy knew, their ability to sing was always there. Like being able to jump great distances or fly on sheets of wind, it was part of what they were—nature's blessing. There were no questions as to how they sing. There were no questions as to why they sing. There was no need for such questions. There was only the simple acceptance that what was, was, and that was good.

Jiminy also knew that among the billions of created things, be they cricket or otherwise, there would always be those who defy their nature. In doing so, such individuals carve out a new existence, reissuing and redefining nature itself. Many do not realize that nature craves defiance, for it is only through defiance, a questioning of nature, that evolution occurs.

Jiminy had never wished to be a singer. In a family of hundreds of thousands of singers, it was not something one so admitted. He may as well have wished to no longer be a cricket. No, what Jiminy wanted, though it was not the popular choice, was to defy his nature, and in doing so, evolve.

If he had learned anything from his time as speaker of the residents of the Fringe, it was that groups may be good for some things but making unified decisions in a timely fashion was not one of them. Sure, they thought they knew what they wanted. But thinking about something and having something happen are two very different things. That was why it was concerning when Rudolf showed up at the door, panting as if he had just run a long way.

"Jiminy," Rudolf said. "I've just come from the flats."

"Slow down, Rudolf," said Jiminy, concerned to see his small friend so flustered. "What's happened?"

Rudolf caught his breath for a moment. Jiminy watched the clown's small chest rise in heaves.

"Aegle is gathering the factions."

"Aegle?" Jiminy repeated. "You mean she's out?"

"I didn't believe it either. Not after what Fern did. Then I went there. The stone is moved. She's out."

Jiminy slammed one of his huge back legs down in frustration, causing the room to shake and Rudolf to depart from the floor.

"She will want to unite them against me."

"Not against you, Jiminy. She is uniting them against Fern and the ship."

Jiminy turned to Rudolf. "An attack on Fern and the ship is an attack on me. Curiosity brought us here and they are who backed me to become speaker."

"I know this, Jiminy, and the residents do too. We can deal with Aegle," said the clown.

"How would you deal with her?"

"Address the residents," said Rudolf. "Let them know that a return home is still the plan."

Jiminy studied the decorative attire he wore as speaker of the residents. He had—though he could not admit this to anyone—thought that he did not want to leave the Fringe. That he could in fact live out his days there.

"You know, Rudolf," Jiminy began saying, "I was never much back home. I was the runt. They never believed I'd amount to anything. Now that I am here and I have amounted to something, the world I knew seems so…undesirable."

Rudolf walked over beside him, his red shoes squeaking. The little clown had been loyal to him since the beginning and Jiminy had learned to not underestimate loyalty.

"Speaking of Aegle," said Rudolf, "she is on her way here now to talk to you."

Jiminy sighed. Somehow, he knew it would come.

"If it's going to happen, it's going to happen."

• • •

Some minutes later outside of the office belonging to the speaker of the residents, Aegle stepped up to the door and adjusted her sleeve. She knocked three times.

"Come in," said the voice she knew was the speaker's.

"Hello, Jiminy," she said as she entered his chamber.

"Hello, Aegle," said Jiminy, "I heard you might stop by."

"It's been too long," the nymph said, smiling. "It seemed like the polite thing to do."

"Politeness is one way to describe what you're doing."

"What I'm doing? What I'm doing is looking out for us all. The same thing I would expect you to be doing."

Jiminy's antennae quivered in irritation. He knew what she was saying. The worst part about Aegle is that she never just came out and said anything. She would hint at it and prod at its soft spots between the lines without ever addressing it.

"You know I've always had the best interests of everyone here in mind," said Jiminy, maintaining his composure.

"Would seem that way," said Aegle, picking up a juicy-looking piece of fruit from the tray and running her hand along the tablecloth which glistened in the morning light. "Though some fringers would say you live well among us."

"I…" Jiminy didn't know how to respond. Of course, he lived well, but didn't they all? He had taken on additional responsibility in becoming speaker of the residents. Did not that deserve a little more in earnings? "I've never been secretive that I like nice things. You can fault me for that. You of all people should understand."

Aegle smirked and said, "We are only concerned that you have grown attached to this lifestyle here in the Fringe. Though it may suit you, that does not mean it suits everyone. Beyond this, you are speaker of the residents and therefore an ambassador of us all."

"We cannot always control the way things go," said Jiminy. "Maybe some of the other residents should focus more on being thankful for the Vael we've been given, than raising constant concerns for a world which chewed us up and spat us back out."

"Ah, Jiminy," said Aegle, moving closer to him. "See, that is where I believe you're wrong. I believe we can control the way things go. So much so I'm sure we can find our way back into that world sooner than we may think. You forget that it wasn't the world that chewed us up—it was humans. And as for spitting out, well, Tierney and his ship may think they are doing some greater good, but they are the ones who move between this place and home. They are not bound to one place as refugees."

"They protect us."

"That may have been so, but at the rate humans are going are we even sure we will have a world to go home to? Look at what they do to our own planet…"

Jiminy was silent. Aegle smiled. "So, you agree, I see."

Jiminy barely moved his mouth. "I didn't say that."

"You didn't need to," was all Aegle said back.

CHAPTER 34 | POINTS OF VIEW

The crew gathered on the deck of the ship. It was the first time since departing the Fringe that Salem had seen them together in their entirety. He had grown to know almost all of them as friends, or at least, he thought, more than just acquaintances.

The mood was a quiet anticipation of things to come. Not the anticipation akin to excitement. The anticipation that brings about stress for everyone involved.

Fern entered the galley and stood in front of the crew. Salem thought the captain looked tired, as if he had not slept well.

The captain's voice sounded strained as he addressed the crew. "We have some decisions to make. Easterly is only a few days away. We need to decide what to do once back."

Kane blew out a plume of white-gray smoke from his pipe in the front row. "Perhaps you could give us some context?"

"As you know," said Dorianna, filling in for the captain who seemed lost in thought, "we've run into some issues. The Jotun child is still missing."

At the mention of the child, Salem looked down at his palm. It had been burning more in the past days, and he had the strange sense that the child was in grave and imminent danger. I need to tell Zee about it, he thought.

"But we've already clarified that wasn't us," said Artichoke. "How do we know one of the Jotun didn't turn on their own? They weren't happy about the relocation."

"None of my people would ever do that," Aurora said.

"I'm just saying," said Artichoke, "no need for jumping to conclusions, but we should consider all options."

"Noted," said Dorianna. She looked now at Aurora. "It's alright, Aurora, he's not accusing anyone." Dorianna turned back to the rest of the crew. "The question at hand is what to do, or better, if to do anything. Maybe inaction is the best course of action?"

"We have to do something," said Fern, rejoining the conversation. "The Regulat will not wait to act."

"What do you mean?" Raiju asked.

"I don't have all the details," Fern admitted, "but we know they're gaining momentum again. And we know they may have the child. The questions are these," the captain continued, "as Dorianna pointed out: are we ready for them, and what are we going to do?"

"We could turn around now and go back to the Fringe?" offered Dover in the uncertain tone of a question. A few of the crew members snickered and Dorianna delivered a swift whack to the back of Dover's head. "Ow, I was just offering a suggestion."

"You know as well as anyone, Dover, that hiding in the Fringe is not an option," said Dorianna.

"I'm afraid she's right," added Fern. "Returning to Vael or any of the cities of the Fringe won't do much to stop what is coming."

"And what do you expect is coming?" asked Ena.

"I don't know," said Fern. The captain straightened his jacket. "But we should be ready." There was silence on the deck. "I know," said Fern, "that you are all scared about what could happen again. About returning to that terrible time when we thought everything we hold dear would disappear forever. It was not so long ago."

"What you're talking about sounds a lot like a return to war," said Raiju. "This ship is supposed to be a way for us to hide. A way to be sneaky about saving what few we still could."

"You're right, Raiju," said Fern. "And look at what we've done already. Hasn't it all paid off?"

"Why poke the bear?" someone else asked. "Let's stay under the radar." A few voices echoed their agreement.

At that moment, Salem was not sure what came over him. Despite a flooding anxiety urging him to run out of the room, he spoke—his first word: "Um."

He stepped forward then as everyone turned their eyes on him. "I kind of lost my home a few weeks ago. I didn't know what I was doing or where I was going. I've seen a lot of things in the last few days that I thought I'd never see. Things I never thought…" Salem paused. "It seems stupid to say when I look at all of you now, but things I never thought existed. At first it was all… too much. Maybe it doesn't seem like it to you all, but for someone like me, it's a lot." Some crew members looked at each other with small nods of understanding. "Still, every day I got it a little more. At least, I got less surprised by things. I even started to feel accepted here." Salem looked at Juniper and Zee as he said this. "I've been getting more okay with everything, if that's even possible. I have an uncle who I haven't seen since I was little. You took me on as a member of your crew. I got a new bunkmate and made new friends. I've…" He waited, searching for what he was trying to say. "Become a part of something."

Sweat was gathering under Salem's clothes and he had goosebumps. The combination was uncomfortable, but to his disbelief he kept talking. "After losing my mom, I wanted to shut everything out. Try to forget and ignore or… I don't know. It was the only thing that felt right and the only thing that felt good a lot of times. Still, you've all somehow been there for me. That is something I will never forget. It's something I cherish and something I don't want to lose." His voice was rising. He had not intended to give any kind of motivational speech, but could not stop the words from spilling out, anyway. "I don't know who the Regulat is or how dangerous they are, but if there is one thing I've learned since meeting all of you, it's that this world, even though we don't understand it, belongs to us all."

"You don't know what we've lost," said Nut. Geb nodded with his sister.

"No," said Salem, "I don't know what you've lost. But I know about loss and how much it makes you feel like nothing. Like there is nothing left for you. Like anything can't be as good as it was in the past. Then"—Salem could feel the words coming to him as if from somewhere else—"I learned something about loss I didn't know. I learned it from all of you. I learned that loss could lead to new things. Things I would not have gotten to know if I hadn't lost." Tears were in his eyes and he spoke through them. "There is no replacement for what we have lost. But losing doesn't make it over."

He took a breath. Some faces were smiling at him, some were also teary eyed, and some were expressionless. "I don't know what's right. But I'm tired of feeling helpless. They gave me a responsibility. It's a promise I have to keep, and I will keep it." He had no idea what to do next. Then Aurora stood.

She looked at him and then said, "Me too."

One by one, the crew followed her until everyone was standing.

• • •

"I'm proud of you," Ulysses told Salem a few minutes later.

"Thanks. I'm not sure what made me say those things."

"Your father would be proud. You sounded like him up there."

Salem dropped his head. He still did not know how to ask Ulysses about his past.

"You knew my dad well?" Salem asked.

"That's how I came to the ship," said Ulysses, "and yes, we were close. Your father, Tierney, and I were close friends."

"Really?" asked Salem, surprised. "Fern too?"

"Oh, the captain wasn't always so…"

"Captainy," offered Salem.

"Exactly," said Ulysses. "Captainy—wait till I call him that."

"It would be strange to think of him not captainy," said Salem to himself.

"Once you've seen someone a certain way, it's hard to imagine them as someone else," agreed Ulysses. "Guess we all carry parts of our past with us. It's just heavier for some people than others."

"Do you?" asked Salem, broaching the subject.

"Of course," said Ulysses.

"Ulysses," said Salem. "I heard something the other night. Something about your past. Is it true?"

Ulysses turned to Salem, a look of worry and intrigue transitioning across his face. "The past is full of a lot of things, Salem. What did you hear?"

"That you used to be with the Regulat. The same people doing all the terrible things I'm hearing about now."

Ulysses sighed. "Yes, there was a time when I confused what I wanted. I let myself get corrupted by certain ways of thinking."

"What happened?" asked Salem, and then, before Ulysses could answer: "Was my father with you then, too?" Salem was dreading the answer but needed to know.

"No, Salem, he was not. Your father was the reason I left the Regulat behind."

"He was?" Salem felt immense relief in knowing that his father, whoever he was, had never been a part of such a society.

"You know, the Regulat isn't made up of bad people," said Ulysses. "Well, there are bad people in it, but many of them are only confused."

"They don't seem to be good people."

"I'll give you that," said Ulysses. "But sometimes something so clear to someone can be very unclear to someone else."

Salem considered what his uncle said. "Living that one with Juniper right now."

Ulysses laughed. "Want to talk about it?"

Salem shook his head. "That's okay. I don't even know what we would talk about."

"My advice," said his uncle, "try to see things from her point of view."

"Even if her point of view makes little sense?" Salem asked.

"Especially then," said Ulysses, smiling.

CHAPTER 35 | NEXT STEPS

There were few places where Reynard felt comfortable. He preferred the forest. He preferred open spaces. Seldom did he set foot in Vael, and when he did, only with good reason. Iris flew low above his head and cooed.

"You're the one that wanted to come into town," he said back to her. She cooed again.

"I don't hate organized places. I just dislike what organization does to the mind. You've heard of 'groupthink.' All this all-for-one nonsense and us and them…it just furthers the divide."

The crowd was already gathering in Vael. It was the same square which hosted the Newcomer Festival only days before, and they could still see remnants of the party along the street.

"Must be important if Jiminy is making such a big deal as to announce it all like this."

It was true, Reynard knew. Jiminy's proclamation, whatever it was, was strange for two reasons. Proclamations, or any kind of very public speech or announcement, were uncommon in the Fringe. Beyond that, it was strange that it was happening only days after Fern and the ship had departed. Reynard had an eerie feeling in his gut that the two were linked, though he kept it to himself.

It was late morning when the noise in the crowd reached its peak. Jiminy appeared on the raised stage. The giant cricket looked composed, as he did. As speaker of the residents, Jiminy was expected to be the voice of the beings of Vael. A job criticized but one which no one wanted.

"Thank you all for being here," Jiminy began in his booming but smooth voice. "It is important that we all talk about what is going on here. I would like to make all of you aware of what is happening in the Fringe."

• • •

Across the meridian the discussion between the crewmembers of the Curiosity was in no sign of ending. Salem wondered if the crew could ever find agreement on what to do. Salem, Zee, and Juniper listened as the more senior members of the crew spoke.

"Well, we know things can't keep going the way they have been," said Ulysses. "That much we knew before this trip to the Fringe, and we confirmed it during our time there."

All members of the crew nodded in agreement.

"We need to fight back," said Aurora. "We need to take a stand before the Regulat gets any stronger."

"That is true," said Captain Fern. "But we cannot have another Crawford."

"What is Crawford?" Aurora asked.

"Crawford Heights," said Ulysses, "is a place."

"And what happened there?"

"It was a school," continued Captain Fern. "For many years it was the premier school of Easterly. Many people thought it was creating the best of the best. Future leaders of the world."

"If only they'd known," said Ulysses.

"There was no way of knowing back then," said Fern.

"There were signs," said Ulysses. "Looking back, there were always signs."

"Of what?" pushed Aurora. Salem leaned forward, also impatient to learn more.

"Corruption," continued Fern. "Signs that certain things, bad things, were being taught. Schools of thought were endorsed, rehearsed, and repeated. Schools of thought that taught children to be selfish, narrow-minded, and cruel."

"I'm confused," said Aurora. "I've always heard that Easterly is a haven for fringers…"

"True," said Fern. "Fringers have long found safety in Easterly. But that is also why the Regulat chose Easterly for its school."

"As you may or may not know," said Fern to Aurora, but also to everyone, "the Regulat is an ancient organization. Their roots run deep, and their actions are driven by beliefs that have been practiced over generations. They started Crawford, hoping to create a generation of children who would grow up believing lies."

"You know a lot about this school," said Aurora.

"I should think so," said Fern. "I was one of its students."

"You?"

"Believe it or not, yes," said Fern.

"We both were," added Ulysses, looking at Aurora. "But our pasts are not our futures. Once we saw what was happening there, we stopped."

"But when did you find out?"

Fern and Ulysses looked at each other. "I guess around the tenth grade?"

"Sounds about right to me," said Ulysses and continued, "yeah, right about the time they brought in Rigel."

"Rigel?" Aurora asked.

Ulysses looked at Salem. It gave Salem the strange feeling there was more to the story than was being told. "He was a teacher at the school. Specialized in connecting mythology and the real world. At the beginning we didn't know. But as time went on, it became clear why they brought him in. He was to be killed."

"Enough," said Fern, looking from Ulysses to Salem. "What you asked about Aurora and what we are talking about now are two different times. At such a young age, Ulysses and I could do nothing about

Crawford Heights for some time. So, we did the next best thing we could."

"We joined the opposition," said Ulysses.

"That we did," said Fern. "And some years later we found ourselves a little older and a little bolder back at Crawford Heights to right the wrongs we knew they were committing."

"It is a war," said Ulysses, his voice grimmer.

"It is a war," echoed Fern, "and that day at Crawford it was a slaughter."

"But you won?" asked Aurora.

The captain shook his head. "Nobody won. There is no winning in a situation like that, only losing. We went there with friends, with family, to fight for a world we believe in where the definitions of sentience are not limited to a certain species."

"We did everything we could," said Ulysses. "To reason with them, to spare lives, to help them see the perspectives and value in others. But there is no rationalizing with fanatics."

"In short," said Captain Fern, "we don't want to repeat what happened that day at Crawford. We know the Regulat still exist, but I for one believe we must find other ways to deal with them."

"You know, in the Amazon there is no direct combat, per se," Ena Boto chimed in from two rows back. "Why deal with the enemies face to face? Take away their means, and you take away their ability."

"What are you saying?" asked Fern.

"I'm saying that not all battles, and not all wars, need to be open-field conflicts. That's archaic stuff and we don't have the time…"

"Or the multiple lives," added Ulysses.

"Or the multiple lives," agreed Ena, "for it. There's something to be said about cunning and a little creativity." Ena looked over toward Salem, Juniper, and Zee as he said this, and winked.

• • •

In another part of the ship, Roach paced. He had left the crew meeting early. It was not that he was uninterested in what the crew was going to do, it was that it conflicted him from within. In truth, it mattered little to his immediate future what the crew would do once back. Once again, Roach had to think about what he would do. And once again, the choices he had made left him feeling more alone than ever.

Fern and Ulysses had been more than fair with him. A fact which made things even more complicated than they already were. If White had found out Roach was a double agent, he would have killed him on the spot. No hard feelings, just business. It was so much easier that way. All this, seeing the good in others that Fern always talked about, was exhausting.

Roach knew that the captain knew. Even if Fern had not come out and said it. Roach also knew that it was part of Fern's tactic to play things that way. So Roach had been given a fourth chance by another group. Or was it a fifth chance? How many chances were allowed before they stopped being chances and just became a sad excuse for an existence?

Roach pushed the thoughts out of his mind. He would need all the mental prowess he could muster if he were to survive what was coming.

CHAPTER 36 | THE CROW'S NEST

Stars blanketed the night sky over the ship and ocean as the crew carried on inside the galley.

"Have you been up there yet?" Juniper asked, turning to Salem, and motioning at the small basket-shaped stand at the top of Curiosity's mainmast. The three had left the crew inside the ship, making their way out onto the quiet main deck.

"No" said Salem, "I didn't know we were allowed."

"Juniper, we shouldn't," said Zee, his face a mixture of worry and excitement.

"Oh, come on," she said, smiling. "You two are too uptight. Everyone's in the galley. We'll be quick." With that, Juniper turned and strode with confidence toward the mainmast that rose high above their heads.

They clung to the ropes that hung down in loops big enough that they could slip their hands and feet inside. The higher they climbed, the cooler the air was, and the more exposed Salem felt. It was an exhilarating kind of exposure that made him forget everything else. He pulled himself up a few times and the only thing around was sails, whooshing air, and the sounds of the ocean below.

"Guys," he said, "is it normal that the rope shakes this much?" They were too far up ahead. They must not have heard him. Salem could feel his arms getting tired.

"Don't forget to use your legs!" he heard Zee yell from above.

It was good advice. Salem let his legs find spots in the ropes. The few seconds of letting his weight up helped. He could still feel the rope moving from bottom to top, like an enormous ligament, tensing and relaxing, tensing and relaxing, as it held the ship's structure in place.

"Keep going," he heard from above. "It's harder if you stop."

Salem clung to the ropes and closed his eyes, letting the elements wash over him.

As he swayed there, he felt the air. It had the same wetness to it but was colder than on deck. There was the wind that pushed the air. It was freer than on deck, more playful but also more daring. It came in big gusts that made everything wobble. Salem was not afraid of heights, at least he did not think he was. Still, as Juniper and Zee called down to him from above, he found it difficult to take the next step. Something wanted him to stay where he was; something wanted him to return to the deck.

The seconds passed as the wind pushed him back and forth on the rope. Keep going, he thought. Everything I have been doing, even now, is a matter of whether to stop or keep going. It was, he realized, the same question he had faced the day Mr. Gingam had showed up at his house, asking him to make the journey to Easterly. Stop or keep going? It was the same question his mother would have had to face after his father left. Stop or keep going? Stopping meant safety in a way. It meant turning around and hanging tight to what he had already achieved. Nobody would fault him for that. Then the thoughts of all those people hugging him came flooding back. All those people saying they could not imagine how hard it must be for him and that they were there if he needed anything. The pity had come, but Salem remembered how bad it had felt.

People that lose things do not want to hear sorry. They want a way forward. A few months previous Salem had imagined a future limping along, a future uncertain.

Salem had no idea what to expect as he sat all those days ago in the train car. Nothing was like he expected it to be, and as he clung to the ropes between the sky and sea, he realized that was not a bad thing.

He opened his eyes and saw Juniper and Zee above him. Keep going, he thought, and reached one hand up to the next piece of rope.

Moments later, he climbed up through a small opening into the wooden structure known as the crow's nest. It was large enough that the three of them could just stand together, shoulder to shoulder, looking out in different directions at the shifting plane of water that fell off the edges of the world around.

Sounds from below were carried up through the wind. The sides of the crow's nest were high, a safety precaution for those tasked with keeping a lookout. Salem peered over the side and down. It was higher than it looked from the deck. He brought his head back up.

"Guess you guys have been up here a lot?" Salem asked, trying not to feel too bad about how scary it was for him to climb up and even stand there now.

"Almost never," said Juniper. Zee nodded that it was true. "My father always said it was too dangerous."

In the distance, the first lights of the coast were just becoming visible through the night air. It brought into focus that which Salem had not yet faced. The entire voyage that had felt like a dream was ending. In front of them, coming closer with each second, was reality.

"Guys," he said. "I need to go get that child back." Salem caught himself off guard with how forward he sounded.

"Us?" asked Zee. "We should wait for the crew."

"They've been discussing for days." Salem could feel the pressure building inside. "I made the promise to Yggdrasil for a reason. I don't understand it yet, but something inside is telling me I have to do this."

"Okay," said Juniper. "Then we will go with you." Though Salem saw that Zee's face was less sure.

"Only problem," continued Salem, "is that I don't know where to start." As he finished speaking, he watched a wry smile come over Juniper's face.

"There's a place in Easterly that is supposed to…" she trailed off. "I heard my father talking to Ulysses one day about it. It's an old church that the Regulat uses as their base of operations. I'll bet that's where they're keeping the child."

Curiosity rocked over the waves below and they felt the almost imperceptible swaying of the crow's nest as Salem and Zee looked at each other and then back at the stern face of Juniper.

"I don't know," said Zee. "The crew is a crew for a reason. I mean, we are supposed to decide together, and us doing this by ourselves wasn't the decision."

"We're doing it for all of them down there," said Juniper. "And you both know the tree only made Salem promise. You know he needs our help, Zee. He'll never make it on his own."

"Hey," said Salem, but had to smile because he knew, just as Juniper and Zee knew, the words were true. Then Zee looked from Juniper to Salem.

"Okay," he said. "Let's do it."

CHAPTER 37 | BREAKING AND ENTERING

There was an old-fashioned streetcar that rode from Easterly's east side and docks across town to its west side. The west side of town, or inland side, rose into a set of hills that overlooked the town and the ocean beyond. The streetcar, a rustic brown in color with faded gold paint like that used at Easterly's train station, departed every thirty minutes. It would rattle along its old tracks, going just fast enough to be useful, and just slow enough that the people inside the car and those outside on the sidewalks could catch glimpses of each other.

Curiosity had been tied into the docks not yet a full day before Salem, Juniper, and Zee sneaked off the ship toward the place where Juniper claimed the Jotun child may be. They had waited throughout the morning and afternoon, working as they had been now for weeks through their instructions with Artichoke and Ena. It surprised Salem that just a few quick minutes of practice each day, be it in cooking, martial arts, or any of the areas their instructions covered, had allowed him to improve beyond anything he thought he was capable of. He could make many of the dishes from memory, be it soups, stews, puddings, or many of the simpler meals the crew liked to eat while at sea. He could move through his motions and breathing without getting winded or tired. He joked with Zee about how bad they had been at the beginning, and how far they had come now. Still, Salem wondered about more than a few things on Curiosity. Ena had yet to show them the weaponry they had seen during the first lesson or explain why it was they may need it or whom they may one day use it against.

So as the sun set and the crew gathered in the galley for dinner, the three made themselves inconspicuous, tiptoeing off the boat and up the docks. The streetcar had already pulled away as they jumped on.

Salem had to admit as they made their way across town and up the hillside of Easterly that the set of buildings coming into view gave him a lingering feeling of creepiness that he could not shake. He had always thought that structures like churches, places where gods and other things were supposed to inhabit, held a strangeness, especially at night.

They walked through an open gate into a courtyard where an assortment of different vehicles was parked. Salem guessed the place was an old churchyard or abbey, though in its current state looked more like it could be used on the set of a horror film.

"It's eerie," he said, looking up at the dark shapes of the buildings that sat like little mountains in the darkness.

"And quiet," whispered Zee.

"You should be too," hissed Juniper.

They walked up to the church, listening side by side at the big front doors. Muffled voices were coming from the inside.

"We can't go this way. It's too obvious," said Juniper.

"There," said Salem, pointing to a smaller single door further down the wall. They scurried down to it. "This is better."

They made their way inside. The hall was long and empty. Lantern-like lights hung from the ceiling every few feet. The floor was tiled and in the pattern of black and gold diamonds.

"We want to avoid the Regulat," said Zee. Salem and Juniper both nodded.

"And we need to find the child," said Salem. "Maybe it's best if we split up?"

"No," Juniper hissed again, "definitely not."

"But this place looks big," said Salem.

"Exactly," said Juniper. "What if one of us gets lost."

"If we stay together, we're never going to get anywhere in time."

Juniper and Zee were quiet. "Let's say," said Salem, "that we plan to meet back here in thirty minutes. We can all go in separate directions for fifteen minutes, and then we'll turn around and meet back here and figure out the next step?"

"I don't know," said Juniper, "something tells me we should stay together."

"I think Salem's right," said Zee. "We need to split up."

Voices were coming down the hall.

"Quick, in here." The three ducked into a small passageway that broke off from the main corridor. They huddled silently together, waiting. The voices approaching were female and sounded casual.

"He says the most ridiculous things sometimes, doesn't he?" said one.

"But does he mean it?"

"That is always the question, isn't it?"

"I just hope he had enough brains to let the thing know who was boss after that."

"Sydney was never one for brains, Ursula, you know that."

"Oh, but I do like him."

"You like everyone these days."

"I've always liked everyone."

The two women stopped before the place where the three hid. They dropped their voices into a low whisper.

"But did you hear about that initiate, Tristan?"

"The young, handsome one?"

"Yes, he was quite the showman last week in Mexico. Centralia and Cancun were even calling him the 'little bullfrog fighter.'

"Oh, it is a lovely thing to get some fresh meat into the ranks, isn't it?"

"And now I heard he's up for a big job."

"What do you mean?"

"Apparently, he's running point on the takedown of the ship. Supposed to kill the captain himself."

Salem felt Juniper shudder against him.

"White gave him that? As an initiate? He must be something special. That is an absurd job."

"Makes you wonder, doesn't it?"

"What do you mean?"

"I mean, is the boy really so talented or is White using him?"

"White can be…" the voice paused. "Rash. But I don't think he would be careless with resources, especially if this boy is performing as well as we've been hearing."

"Yes, yes," said the other. "Well, I suppose time will tell."

"Yes, I suppose that is true."

The women started walking again and speaking in normal tones.

"I have to go down and see White now. You want to join?"

"Oh no, I have to be in the lab five minutes go."

"Okay then, I will see you at the feast later? I heard they will show off the new prize that's come in from Russia."

"Oh yes, save me a seat!"

The women departed in different directions down the corridor.

"Okay," said Juniper, "I'm going to follow the one going to meet White."

"I'll follow the other one," said Zee.

"And me?" asked Salem.

"Did you see those stairs when we first came in?"

Salem remembered the stairs and nodded. "Okay, I'll take the stairs."

"Okay," said Juniper, "but we'll meet back here in half an hour?" Salem and Zee both nodded.

Salem looked back at them as he made his way down the silent corridor toward the staircase.

He took the stairs one at a time. With each step he imagined a different stage of the journey he was on which brought him to the current moment. Step one: leave the burned-down past. Step two: set sail with the estranged uncle. Step three: rescue the legendary frost giants of Jotunheim and bring them to the hidden land of the Fringe. The list in his head continued, as did the steps, as he pushed his foot down. The staircase went straight for a few steps and then turned back around on itself, continuing to move upward in the opposite direction. It opened onto the second floor.

Salem stood in a small chapel, a smaller version of the church downstairs. There were a few rows of seats and small stained-glass windows that sat without light, looking sad. There was a podium at the front. A book sat on the podium. Salem checked around the room. It looked empty. He walked up to the podium, choosing to go around the side of the seats rather than through the middle.

The book seemed to stare at him from the podium where it sat. He walked over to it. It was not a big book, but its cover looked old and worn. It read, Short Histories of the Regulat.

Salem took the cover and a few pages in his hand and turned it open to a random page.

October 1673,
A note from Sir Birmingham to Mr. Smith of America:

Dear Mr. Smith,

A new order is being established. As we expand in the world, it has become clear just how delicate all this is. We must take certain actions to ensure things stay as they are. We in the European delegate are prepared to do what is necessary. Even over the past year, we have made massive strides to eliminate many of the threats our ancestors faced. Though we are still small, we would trust and hope that you, our American family across the ocean, would see the opportunities that collaboration will bring. You no doubt house one of the world's largest collections of alternative beings, or mythos, as I believe you call them, in the colonies. Surely you, Mr. Smith, understand that the sooner they are taken care of, the sooner humanity will become safe.

I look forward to your prompt reply in this matter.

S. Birmingham

A small scribble had been made under the text printed on the page. Salem tried to discern it.

First steps toward an international Regulat.

Salem closed the book. First steps toward saving humanity and creating a new future? Salem did not understand. What had mythological creatures done to deserve such treatment?

To the right of the podium was another door, ajar. Salem entered the next room.

The place was like a museum with beautiful glass windows that let the moonlight from outside stream in. In the surrounding space were skeletons, sculptures, jars, and pictures. There were single bones, teeth, sets of arcane-looking jewelry. The space possessed a very real sense of doom and wonder.

Salem stepped around one of the raised parts of the room. On it was a laid-out gown. The gown was white and black, and a mixture of beads and necklaces were spread across it. He stared down at it. It was identical to the gowns he saw the witches wearing in the Fringe during the first city hall feast, when they had enchanted the candles to paint the walls.

"I wouldn't touch that if I were you."

Salem froze.

"It belonged to a witch. You never know what they cursed, you know."

Salem turned. A boy stood at the other side of the room. He was handsome and seemed to possess a confidence Salem was unaccustomed to seeing in such a young person. Salem guessed the boy could not be much older than he was and found himself even a twinge envious that he could not find the same confidence in himself.

"Is there something in particular you're looking for?" asked the boy.

Salem's heart beat faster as he searched his mind for a response. "I'm just looking around for now, thanks," he said, hoping his voice did not waver as much as he thought.

"That is what the artifact room is for. It's a bit of a showoff room for what the Regulat has accomplished."

"I'm not sure if I would say accomplish," said Salem.

"Oh," said the boy, taking two steps closer. Salem held his ground. "Then what would you call it?"

"The way I hear it, the Regulat has caused a lot of pain. A lot of unnecessary pain."

"The way you've heard it?" The boy said. "It would fascinate me to know what you've heard about the Regulat. Here I was thinking you were just some local kid who'd gotten a little too curious. Would have been better for you if that were the case. What is your name?"

Salem did not answer right away.

"Gingam," he said. "My name is Jim Gingam."

"Yeah," said the boy, "we're going to pretend for now, for the sake of moving this along, that that really is your name. So, Jim, tell me what you know."

"I know that this is wrong," said Salem.

"What is wrong?"

"What you do here."

"And what is that?"

"You kill things that aren't human. Things that don't even want to hurt you."

The boy picked up a large curved tooth sitting on a desk next to him. "I think you've received some false information, Jim."

Salem waited. What was this kid talking about?

"I doubt that," he said. "And what is your name, now that you know mine?"

"Oh, thank you for asking. I won't lie to you. My name is Tristan. And I should rephrase. You only received incorrect information. We eliminate what's unnecessary; however, you are wrong when you say that they don't want to hurt us."

"What do you mean?" asked Salem. Tristan had stopped moving. He and Salem stood a few feet from each other. The boy was Salem's size, but more muscular. He had thick brown hair that was messed up in a way that looked intentional, and dark eyes.

"There is the world, and then there is the world we could have, Jim. Most people accept the world because they do not understand that they could have it any other way. They go through life believing that this is it."

Salem had the odd sense that, as he listened, he had heard the words before.

"Believing in something more and trying to control life with your hands are two different things," said Salem.

"Are they?" asked Tristan. "Don't be dumb, Jim. Do you think the world will just change because you believe in something? Some grand ideas? The world changes because we make it change."

"I just don't understand how killing can be the answer," said Salem, more to himself as he looked around.

"Diversity is a myth," said Tristan. "No matter how fantastic something might seem, it does not have your best interest in mind. Unity through purity is the only way."

"But humans fight among each other all the time," said Salem.

"Of course, we do, but what I am talking about, what the Regulat seeks to achieve, is bigger than any one conflict between humans. It's a worldwide transcendence."

"You realize how that sounds," said Salem.

Tristan tilted his head.

"Brainwashed," continued Salem.

"Maybe I am," Tristan admitted. "But then, if I am, so are you."

Salem was stunned. He was not used to hearing such accusations thrown around at him. Especially ones which concerned the entire world and how people saw it. Salem felt himself growing more unsure by the second, intimidated by how convinced Tristan was as he spoke. Maybe this kid and the Regulat had a point. How could anyone who believed in something so completely be wrong?

"Since you are clearly interested," said Tristan, taking yet another step closer to Salem. Salem took a step back. "Oh, don't worry, Jim, I just wanted to show you how we identify mythos."

"Mythos?" asked Salem. "You mean fringers?"

"Mythos. Fringers. Mythological beings," said Tristan. "Yeah, the lot of them." The boy pulled out a device that looked to Salem like a hybrid between a calculator and a TV remote that had received serious upgrades. It was thick and had a curved form so that it fit nicely in the palm of his hand. "We call this a LITE," said Tristan, flipping it up into the air and catching it back. It can do some amazing things."

"Like turn on your TV?" asked Salem.

"No," said Tristan, smiling, "that's one thing it can't do. Locate, identify, track, and eliminate. This device can tell us who has mytho in them and who doesn't."

"You need a device to tell you that?"

"It's not always as easy as you may think. So many fringers take a humanoid form. Best to be certain."

"You're crazy," said Salem.

"If you mean I'm persistent, then I'll take that as a compliment."

"It wasn't," said Salem.

Then Tristan smiled and pointed the LITE at himself and pressed a button. Its small screen lit up. "Human. One hundred percent," read Tristan off the screen.

"Congratulations," said Salem.

"Thank you," said Tristan, "I never take it for granted."

Salem was wondering how long the conversation would go on. Soon Juniper and Zee would meet back downstairs. Salem saw no way to get there without taking Tristan with him, and that was not an option.

"What about you?" asked Tristan.

"What about me?" asked Salem.

Tristan turned the LITE toward Salem and before Salem could do or say anything, pushed the button.

"Interesting," said Tristan, "very interesting."

"What's interesting?" asked Salem.

"According to this, you're a mutt."

"A what?" asked Salem.

"A mix. Not human. Part something else."

"That can't be true," said Salem. Even if he believed what Tristan was saying to him, how could he be something other than human?

"I know that technology isn't always perfect," said Tristan, "but these aren't often wrong."

"But that can't be," said Salem. "I would know."

"Not necessarily," said Tristan. "Depending on what your other half is, it may only come out later in life, or not at all."

Salem was silent.

"Did you know both your parents, Jim?"

Salem did not answer.

"I'll take that as a no," said Tristan. "Well, Jim, looks like you're staying here with us for a while." Tristan reached behind his back and pulled out something larger than the LITE. Something that looked like a mix between a long pistol and baton.

"I am leaving," said Salem.

"I'm afraid you can't," said Tristan. "Not only are you trespassing, but you've just become an interesting subject for us here."

"Salem!"

Juniper and Zee burst through the door behind them, where Salem had come through minutes before.

"We were waiting for you and you weren't coming. We know where they're keeping the..." Juniper caught sight of Tristan. "What's going on?"

"Salem," said Tristan, smiling. "I knew you didn't look like a Jim. Salem, Salem, I've heard that name before. Tristan's eyes scanned the top of the room. "Ah yes, that report; you're the new boy on board the Curiosity. Is that right?"

All three said nothing.

"Your silence speaks volumes. And you two are identifiable enough. You're the captain's daughter, Jupiter."

"Juniper," Juniper said back.

"And you, with those eyes, you're the Adze," said Tristan, beholding Zee. "Oh, how funny that you should walk in here. Your sister's well, by the way, if you care to know."

"What are you talking about," said Zee. "They killed my family years ago."

"I wouldn't be so sure," said Tristan.

Salem looked at Zee and saw that his friend's eyes were wide.

"So, it would seem that we have ourselves in a bit of a predicament," said Tristan. "Easiest thing would be for you all to come with me."

"We're not coming with you," said Juniper.

"As I've already told Salem, Captain's Daughter, you have no choice in this matter. I'm not about to let three members of the Regulat's most pressing threat stroll in for a look around and stroll back out the door."

"I'll stay," said Salem. "Let them go."

"No," said Zee and Juniper together. "That's not happening."

"You told me yourself that I'm a mix," said Salem. "I'll give myself to the Regulat. Just let Juniper and Zee leave."

"An interesting proposal," said Tristan.

"I'm not listening to any more of this," said Juniper, grabbing a creature-filled jar off the table and readying herself to hurl it at Tristan.

"Easy, darling," came a different voice. A man walked in behind him. "That is one of the first specimens I collected. I would hate to have you destroy it. Throw one of the basilisk bones, if you must throw something."

Juniper held her glare but stopped and put the jar back down.

"Juniper Fern," said the man stepping forward. He was not tall, but his impeccable grooming made him seem large. He smiled, showing his teeth as though he were going to be judged on their whiteness. "Your reputation precedes you. That legendary rage—but then again, you are your father's daughter."

"You know nothing about my father."

"Oh," said the man, "I know a thing or two."

"That's enough, White."

Salem and the rest turned to see Fern walking through the doorway.

"Well, well," said the man, making his smile bigger than Salem thought possible. "Tierney Fern, as if this evening couldn't get any better."

CHAPTER 38 | THE MEANING OF HOME

Jiminy stood before a large group of citizens gathered in Vael, his wings quivering with anticipation.

"'Home' is a word which means something to us all," he began. "We each see different pictures in our mind when we think of that place. Some of us think of fields of dancing grasses, some of us think of restless seas, some of us think of the boundless skies. Still, some of us think of dark forests, filled with foliage so thick that we feel safe. Some think of open mountains, where we look from peak to peak. Some see places of cold, where the air is crisp and fresh. Or places of warmth, so cozy that we never want to leave.

"For some of us, home was a place of pain. For some of us, home was a place of joy. For many of us, home was a place of both. I believe what all of us have learned here is that home, no matter what pictures you see in your mind, is not in fact any one place, but the feelings such places provide."

The crowd was quiet as Jiminy paused. He was testing the silence. Staring it down and taking it apart to understand what kind of silence it was. Most of the time, he thought, silence acts very much like air. It floats around, minding its own business. Sometimes, though, silence does more. Much like air in a funnel cloud as it spins to form a tornado, silence doubles back again and again on itself, creating a vortex of doubt in the listener's mind. This is the fear of every orator. However, if one befriends silence, taking it on not as an adversary but an ally, it becomes the most useful of tools. For silence wielded the right way becomes an echo chamber of truth.

There were those who believed that things in the Fringe were okay. They were happy to have survived long enough to find themselves living there. Of course, as is with any society, there were also those who had different opinions. It was clear, however, that everyone missed home. Not the Fringe, but their homes across the meridians that now existed in the Commons.

Jiminy had never seen such a divide among them. In all his years as speaker of the residents, he had always been able to maintain a sense of unity. But things were changing.

"I understand," he said, facing the vast crowd. He had been giving many public announcements, and while he enjoyed them, he was coming to despise them more and more. He was learning that an ambassador for the masses is seldom anything more than a mouthpiece. He would be celebrated when times were good and spirits high, and ridiculed when things went the other way. "I understand that there are mixed feelings among many of you."

A mixture of noises, cheers, and boos came up from the crowd. Jiminy waited to continue.

"We all want to do what is in the best interest of the majority."

"Go home!" someone shouted, and the crowd cheered.

"Yes," said Jiminy, "we would all like that, and no one is counting out that we may soon return. However, we need to all be aware of the present. It has taken us many years to build this place and create this society. I, for one, will be cautious of how I throw it away to head back to a world which may not welcome us."

The crowd had grown quieter now, and Jiminy knew he had struck a chord.

"Everyone here has lost," he said. "We can repeat this a million times and the losses will still be there. That is the nature of pain. It will never, ever, fade."

Jiminy's powerful voice had grown soft, but he allowed it to build in crescendo now. "But in our loss is also growth. Look at all we have gained. Is it not a miracle that we have been able to build this society in a place which should not exist? We have been given the chance at a second life here, a chance to coexist without the worry of being hunted or pushed to the brink."

Others lifted an old resident, a small toad-like creature, above the crowd. "Jiminy," she croaked, "your words are right, but you know as well as we that this place was not meant to be forever. We want to go back to the places we are from. We are thankful, but tired."

"As is right," replied Jiminy. "We just need to be patient a little longer."

"What would you say to those who think we should go now?" asked another resident.

"I would say such ideas are ill-advised if not dangerous. And whoever is spreading them," he added, "should think about what it is they are proposing." Though Jiminy had not told her name, he knew that as the residents looked across those gathered, they were all thinking of the same face.

• • •

In another part of the Fringe, another assembly of residents gathered around a different speaker. Aegle never intended to be a leader. Someone had told her once that that was how the best leaders came to be. It was a thought that always went through her head when she stood in front of others, trying to convince them of something.

She walked through a group of scared faces, representatives from some of the largest factions of the Fringe.

"You all know why you're here," she said, "and no, it's not because I've asked you to come. You're here"—she stopped in front of a hairy resident with multiple rows of legs that looked like a giant caterpillar—

"you're here," she said, "because you believe. You're here because what I want is what you want."

She moved through the bodies, this time careful to weave between them and touch each one on the shoulder. This was never anything she had been taught. It was just something that she felt she should do.

"We may have come here with the best intentions, but that does not mean those intentions should keep us prisoner. How long has it been since the oldest of us were forced to leave the world behind? Artemis, how long?"

The ancient creature called Artemis was thought to be one of the oldest of the residents in Vael.

"One thousand one hundred and eleven years."

"One thousand one hundred and eleven years," Aegle repeated. "Billy," she said, looking at another, "how long for you?"

"Nine hundred and…" Billy grunted and counted something along its claw like appendages. "Nine hundred and something."

"Nine centuries and counting," repeated Aegle. She shook her head. "I'm sure you're as thirsty for the waters of home as I am. My friends, we need not live according to the rules of others any longer." Aegle raised her arm and looked above the crowd to the hill at their backs.

They turned, and as they did, realized that what loomed behind them was not a hill but something else. Someone was running along the top of the giant thing, cutting ropes that were holding what looked like a massive tarp lying in place. As the figure moved, the tarp fell away, revealing the ribs and body of the vessel underneath. Aegle smiled as the faction leaders gasped.

"My friends," she said. "Home may be closer than you think."

CHAPTER 39 | MAN

"Hello, Constance," said Fern. The man's smile receded for briefest of moments as Fern said his name.

"Tierney," said the man in mock genuineness. Mr. White's smile reverted to its eerie width. "This would have been so much easier if you would have let us know you were coming by."

Ulysses stepped in next to Fern.

"You know that's not our style," said Fern. He and Ulysses walked up to where Salem and the others stood, between them and the regulators.

"Yes, well," said the man called Mr. White. "To what do we owe the pleasure of your visit?"

"There are so many things I'd like to say to you right now, you piece of…" Ulysses stopped as Fern raised his hand.

"Leave it for now," Fern said, "There is no point."

"Yes, Ulysses, you indecisive, pathetic excuse for a human. Best to leave it, or you'll only get burned."

Ulysses' face was the coldest Salem had ever seen.

"It's been a long time, Tierney," said Mr. White. "How have things been?"

"I thought we made it clear the last time that your organization is not a welcome one."

"That may be, but I'll tell you something. I thought long and hard about things after our last interaction and, you know what"—Mr. White chuckled to himself— "frankly, I don't care about what you say. Our work is for something bigger than any of us. We don't have the pleasure of caring what others think about what we do."

"Funny how right you are about that and how wrong you are about your chosen work," said Fern.

"Don't bring your morals in here, Tierney. You who sends your children and their playmates snooping around in the business of others."

"You shouldn't even be here," said Fern.

"That's exactly what I was about to tell your daughter," said Mr. White. Fern took a step forward with a balled fist, but Ulysses placed a hand on his shoulder to stop him.

"Speaking of which," said Mr. White, "I want to show you someone. I think you should all already know each other." Mr. White made a motion with his hand and from behind him in the doorway a man appeared.

"Karl," Salem mouthed under his breath.

The scrawny crew member was dressed in similar attire to the regulators. Karl did not look happy or sad, or anything. He looked impassive.

Fern said nothing and Ulysses only stared hard at Karl.

"You traitor," said Juniper.

"Roach has proved himself quite useful to us," said Mr. White. "As a prior regulator stripped of his title, he has been more than eager to prove himself again and regain what was lost. I must admit that I was surprised how easily you trusted, Tierney. I mean, if I would have known anyone with a sad story and a little emotion could join the crew, I'd have used that a long time ago."

"I don't regret taking you on as part of our crew, Karl," said Fern, looking directly into the man's eyes. "I know," said Fern, "that what you experienced with us was real for you." Then there was silence, and Salem could see the thick film of sweat gathering on Karl's forehead. "Open the window, Karl," insisted Fern, politely. "It is warm in here."

"My name's not Karl," said the man weakly, though he did make his way across the room and crank open the long vertical windows that lined the wall of old house. Salem noticed the look of relief that seemed to come over everyone's faces as the cool night air rushed inside.

"Oh, oh," said Mr. White mockingly, cupping his hands together and swooning dramatically. "I know it was real for you, Karl. The time on our little boat."

Salem saw Tristan smile from behind Mr. White and felt his dislike of the other boy grow. How could anyone like the pompous attitude of the Regulat?

"Roach," said Mr. White, addressing Karl. "Why don't you show your curious crewmates our newest team member."

Roach hesitated and looked at Tristan somewhat pitifully. Mr. White rolled his eyes without turning around. "Tristan will help you."

Tristan and Roach disappeared from the room.

"It's serendipitous that you're all here," said Mr. White. "We've just finished up a little project which I think you'll find most interesting."

Roach and Tristan reentered the room. Behind them, a clinking sound, like metallic horse hooves, was audible. It grew incrementally until a robot the height of a tall human walked through the doorway. It was humanoid in appearance, though it was boxy and did not have the grace of an organic life-form. Still, Salem recognized immediately that it possessed an uncanny gleam in its eyes, as though it could listen and understand.

"I'd like to introduce you to MAN," said Mr. White. "This is only the prototype but what promise it shows." Mr. White clicked his teeth as of to admire his own words.

Salem and the others stood motionless and speechless as MAN stopped in front of them. Copper in color, MAN was imposing in the same way a bully could scare kids on the playground—big and mean.

"You see, we have reached a critical tipping point," explained Mr. White. "The earth can no longer support so many organisms and it's time we look toward our greatest gift for help."

"Robots?" asked Ulysses.

"Intelligence," said Mr. White, "incorruptible intelligence paired with the human purpose."

"You are a looney," said Ulysses. "And I really mean it, I'm not just saying it because I like the word."

"In the past," continued Mr. White, ignoring Ulysses' comment, "it was up to us, the regulators, to do the footwork, be the soldiers, and regulate this world of ours. But now"—Mr. White directed his arm toward MAN to introduce him—"now we can truly regulate what's being done. Don't you see"—Salem realized that Mr. White was no longer talking directly to them but speaking more like a preacher in a church—"we have things now we've never had before. We have a chance now that we've never had."

"What do you expect is going to happen?" Ulysses stepped forward now. "You're going to build an army of these things and then wipe out all life on Earth except for humans and then things will be utopic? You really think this idea of a pure world is what nature intended?"

"You do remember some of what we taught you here," said Mr. White to Ulysses. "You know as well as I do that the pure world is coming."

"A pure world," said Fern shaking his head. "A pure world is a world free of control. A world free to grow as it should and as it will."

"That is a world of chaos, Tierney. How can you be so blind? Order is the way, and we were put here to bring order."

"Your ideas of order wander deeply into the realm of tyranny," said Ulysses. "You would take life, control those around, and play the role of the creator and the taker."

"If that is what it takes," said Mr. White.

"No one should have that right," said Ulysses.

"Ah, but you don't understand free will, Ulysses. It's your choice to be here right now and my choice to act as I please."

"You're a plague," hissed Ulysses, "a disease on this earth that should be eradicated."

Mr. White shook his head. "It's such a shame you chose the path you did. You would have grown so well with us."

"I can't even imagine," said Ulysses. "Soon it will just be you and your robots, White; then they will turn on you and then you will understand."

"Oh"—Mr. White was smiling again—"there are so many things that could happen. For now, though"—the man's eyes were twinkling—"everyone does what I say."

Mr. White snapped his fingers and MAN buzzed to life.

"MAN." Mr. White pointed to Ulysses.

It happened before anyone could react. MAN had raised its chrome arm and shot what looked like a dart into Ulysses' chest. Ulysses gasped and Fern caught him.

"No!" said Salem, who started to run toward Mr. White.

"Stop," said Fern, and Juniper and Zee held Salem back.

"MAN," said Mr. White, "retrieve."

In three steps the robot man had walked over to Fern who, still holding Ulysses, held up his arm. MAN pushed Fern out of the way easily and wrapped Ulysses' body in a cocoon-like net in its arms, dragging him away.

Salem struggled to see through his tears, but he could see the venom in Fern's eyes.

"So avoidable," Mr. White was saying. "Though keeping his mouth shut was never Ulysses' forte."

"Shut up!" Salem yelled. "I'll kill you."

"Oh," said Mr. White. "Well, I guess that answers the question of who you are. You must be his nephew. The boy who lost his mother and got to go live with his not so magical uncle on the magical ship. I knew your father, Salem." Every word Mr. White spoke made Salem feel angry, and sad, and curious at the same time. "Oh yes," continued Mr. White. "He was a headache for me until I put an end to him. You know there is always a place for you here. It's never too late to realize you're on the wrong side."

"Enough," said Fern, who looked like all the blood had been drained from his body. "You've taken too many of my people away from me, Constance. This will end and it will end soon."

"Yes," said Mr. White, "you can surrender anytime in person or via handwritten note." Mr. White touched his chin thoughtfully. "I believe we have some things you may want. I'd be careful how you go about 'ending' things. Infants, you know, they can be so delicate."

"The child," said Fern in resignation.

"You know we do give thanks to your trustworthy crew. It's just too easy with you," said Mr. White. "You care about everyone and everything. Your weaknesses are everywhere."

"Take me," said Fern.

"Take you?"

"Give them the kid and take me."

Mr. White was quiet for the first time. "Take you, the leader of Curiosity, or keep the Jotun child. What's to stop me from calling the rest of the regulators here and capturing you all right now?"

"You have principles, Constance. Even I know that."

Mr. White considered the captain's words.

"Tristan," he said, "bring us the child."

Fern stepped forward slowly and many long, silent seconds stretched between the time Tristan left until he reappeared with the child. Slowly, and with a strangled smile like a grimace on his face, he passed the Jotun baby across the space toward Juniper. She stood with tears in her eyes. Zee and Salem stood next to her. It was wrapped in the furs from its home. He winked as he handed it to her. It was a small action, but it made Salem angry.

On the other side of the room, Fern's hands were bound behind his back.

"Well," said Mr. White, "what an evening. I feel absolutely delighted." Then, with Captain Fern's hands tied, Mr. White raised his hand, chuckling and looking back and forth between Fern and the others. "Principles. You really thought I would just let them walk out of here, Tierney?" Mr. White's face was maniacal, a twisted sort of pleasure that Salem had never seen on a person before.

Then, from through the door at the back of the room, more regulators came streaming in. In a matter of seconds, the half of the room facing Salem and the others was filled with bodies, all silent, all waiting on the command from Mr. White, who, smiling ear to ear, was clearly enjoying the looks of alarm on the faces opposite him.

Salem looked at Tristan. The boy still maintained his air of confidence but something in his eyes said he was not totally okay with what he was witnessing. As if he knew Mr. White was about to go too far. In the same moment, Salem heard a familiar voice come into his head, though he could not believe he was hearing it outside of the Fringe.

Salem!, said the voice of Ichara. *You are in danger. You all must run.*

Ichara! I know, Salem answered. *But there is nowhere to run!*

Out the window, Ichara said, her voice hurried, *there is an open window. I am in the river below. Jump and I'll catch you.* Salem looked to his right and there, just as Ichara described, was a large glass window that Roach had opened only minutes before. The opening was small but could be just big enough for them to jump through.

Mr. White was starting to speak again but all Salem could think about was getting the attention of Juniper and Zee. The regulators in front of them were inching closer and he was sure any minute they would be prisoners like Ulysses and the captain.

Like a ventriloquist, Salem kept his jaw locked, and said as softly as possible to Juniper and Zee, "Rescue outside. Jump out of window. Count of three."

From his peripheries Salem saw the eyes of Juniper and Zee widen.

"One," he whispered. "Two."

Mr. White's voice had risen, which in the short time he had known him had already taught Salem that a grand declaration was about to be made. Salem was sure the command to attack would come next.

"Three!" he yelled and grabbing both Juniper and Zee to make sure they followed pulled them toward the window. "Go, Zee! Go," Salem yelled, and to his enormous relief Zee plunged through the open window, with Juniper and Salem close behind. The Jotun baby screamed in Juniper's arms and Salem did not allow himself to even glance back to see whether the regulators were pursuing them. He was in freefall with his arms wrapped around Juniper and the Jotun baby.

Ichara! Salem cried out to her hoping their special connection had not failed.

I'm here, she said, and then he felt a familiar weightlessness as he fell into her same air pocket he had experienced in the Fringe. Juniper and the child floated down through the warm air safely onto her back next to him, while Zee zoomed into the pocket in his firefly form, popping back into his humanoid self with a massive look of relief on his face. *We need to go!* Salem told Ichara, and gently, but with great speed, the creature of the water dove into the river that was otherwise silent next to the old church.

CHAPTER 40 | WHERE TO GO

"Well, Roach," said Mr. White, "you have taken a large step in earning my respect back once again. And also, you have earned the respect back of your peers. Something I think should be valuable to you."

Roach smiled weakly and nodded. It was valuable to him. He had in fact achieved all that he had hoped to achieve and more. So why, he wondered to himself while Mr. White paced around the room, why did he not feel happier?

"We are going to give you what you want, Roach," said Mr. White.

Roach looked into Mr. White's eyes. He did not enjoy looking into those eyes, but certain moments like this demanded it.

"You're going to be a regulator again, Roach. Now the question is, have you thought about which place will grant you your new title?"

Roach nodded. He had thought about it. Since the day Michael died, he had vowed to return to his home city and cleanse it.

• • •

A floor below, Tierney Fern was tied to a chair in a small room. Maybe it was an old closet. Fern thought it was small enough. The chair was a wooden antique, uncomfortable and outdated, like the organization who held him captive. The room looked not unlike an interrogation room. Fern knew he was not the first one to experience it. He knew he was not the first one to wonder, here, what was coming next.

He was no stranger to imprisonment. He often joked with Ulysses that it was a second hobby. There was something, he had to admit, about being held captive. It brought about a change in perspective.

The door to the room opened and closed. Mr. White entered with a chair, a twin of the one Tierney was tied to.

"Tierney Fern, is there anything I can get you?"

"Constance White," Fern replied. "Do I get to make a phone call?"

"I'm afraid the lines are down, Captain. You can leave your message with me. I will make sure it gets delivered."

"You don't need to keep me here, Constance," said Fern. "You can let me go. Ulysses too."

"Neither of you are going anywhere," corrected Mr. White, "I don't expect you'll be seeing Ulysses again and as for you, well, it was only right that I take away Curiosity's leader."

"Who says that I am really the leader? I've always considered my role to be more decorative than anything. A placeholder."

"Oh please, Tierney. I would hope that as your equal you would give me the courtesy of expecting me to know the goings-on of that floating piece of ancient wood. The crew is leaderless. I'd be surprised if Artichoke knows what he'll make for dinner without you there."

"We're not equals, Constance."

"Well, that is disappointing. And here I thought we were going to have another one of our discussions."

Fern smiled. "Do you own a mirror, Constance?"

"Quite a few, and they get regular use, I can assure you." Mr. White picked something out from between his teeth and smiled toothily.

"Maybe you should spend a little more time in front of one this evening and ask yourself why you're doing what you're doing."

"Ah," said Mr. White, leaning in a little closer so that Fern could smell his cologne and see the wrinkles in his suit. "A short piece of advice from one player to another: Never look too long in the mirror. It will distract you from winning."

"This is not a game, Constance," said Fern. "That is the difference between you and me."

"It is a game, Tierney. And we are the masters. I move, you move. Pieces taken, pieces lost."

Fern only shook his head. "You meddle in things so much bigger than any of us, and you don't even know why you do it."

"I do it to maintain the purity of our planet, Tierney."

"You and I have different definitions of purity."

"Perhaps." Mr. White adjusted his collar. "I just wonder what your people are going to do. They will be so helpless."

"That is where you are wrong, Constance. I do not put my crew on my back; they put me on theirs. I do not raise them; they raise me." Fern smiled, thinking about the heroic way Salem, Juniper, and Zee had rescued the Jotun child. He had never been prouder of his daughter, and he would need to tell her that as soon as he could. "Where is Ulysses?" he demanded.

Mr. White smiled in a way that made Fern's stomach drop. "I'm afraid MAN has him now."

• • •

Salem felt a sincere sense of relief wash over him like a pristine rain as the docks and the floating ship came into view. Ichara had navigated a series of underwater tunnels and without a doubt rescued them from certain imprisonment, or worse.

I am so thankful to you, Salem told her, rubbing her neck with his hand. He had noticed almost upon retrieving the Jotun child that the burning and pressure from the tattoo in his palm had subsided. *We owe you everything.*

Ichara shuddered underneath him, much the way a cat might purr. *We all need to help each other now more than ever,* she said. *Many more difficulties are ahead of you.*

I don't know what I can do, Salem told her, feeling in that moment worthless. *I am not the champion Yggdrasil thought I was. We only survived thanks to you and Captain Fern and Ulysses are still captive.*

I only came because you are the champion who's needed, said Ichara. *Something told me you needed me.*

But how did you come through the disruption to Easterly without the ship?

There are other ways to go between the realms, said Ichara. *I am very old and know the water very well.*

Salem looked up to find they were floating at the base of Curiosity. Dorianna had seen them first and was already sending down a ladder to pull them up, a look of worry uncommon for her written across her face.

Salem helped Juniper and then Zee find the rope and climbed off Ichara's back. Then he took the rope, feeling sad, like he was leaving one of the few beings who provided him with a serene sense of calm.

I will see you sooner than later, Salem Swan. Be well. With that, Ichara spun in the water and dove, leaving nothing but traveling ripples behind.

• • •

Bringing the child back was a triumph, of that there was no doubt. Aurora broke through the line of crew members when she saw Zee carrying the bundle. She had not even asked what it was. She just knew. It made Salem happy to see her, with tears rolling down from her eyes, take the baby from Zee.

"What about Ulysses and Captain?" Dorianna asked.

"They were," said Juniper, "taken."

"What do you mean," said Dorianna, "taken?"

"She means that," said Salem, anger rising in him once again. "Ulysses…was hurt, and Fern was taken prisoner so that we could get the baby back. And it's our fault."

"Salem," said Juniper, "calm down, it's going to be okay."

"How, Juniper? How is it going to be okay?"

"I don't know, but it will."

Salem felt confused, and everyone staring at him did not help.

"Let's go inside," said Dorianna, taking Salem by the arm and motioning to Juniper and Zee, "and you can tell us what happened. It's better to talk about these things in close quarters first."

They entered all together into the mess hall. Three steaming bowls of soup were put down in front of them. It smelled delicious and Salem was sure it would be too, but he had no appetite. All that was reeling through his head were words. Loss, guilt, faults. All the horrible things he was feeling and the realization that much of it would be different if he had only changed his actions. The soup's smell was overpowering, and he looked down into the broth to see what it was.

What he saw startled him into silence. It was the face of his mother, written into the plants and vegetables, looking back at him. He felt his chest twist into a knot as the tears welled in his eyes. She was smiling, or at least he thought so; but what next was certain was that the face shifted to that of a man, and then Ulysses was looking at him. The knot in Salem's chest tightened and the tears burst forth. He had lost them both.

"Salem."

He would have to fix it. He did not know how yet, but he would have to, that much he knew. There was still a chance Ulysses lived.

"Salem."

He refused to believe it was over. He would fight back this time and go back into the fire like he should have done with his mother.

"Salem!"

Juniper was standing above him.

"Wha—"

Salem lay back on a bench in the mess hall.

"You kind of passed out or something," said Zee, coming up behind Juniper. "You were staring at your soup like you saw a ghost or something, and then you face-planted into the bowl."

"Really?" asked Salem. Zee nodded.

"I'm fine," said Salem, sitting up. And he was—only a little dizzy.

"Is he back?" Salem heard Dorianna ask.

"I think so," said Juniper, smiling.

"Good, now, can we get on with what happened?"

"How long was I out?" Salem asked.

"About thirty seconds," said Zee.

"It was a shock reaction," said Dorianna in an unsurprised voice. "You're fine. Now," she said, addressing all of them, "what happened?"

Dorianna and the rest of the crew were silent as the three told the story of their night, recounting in vivid detail the hideout of the Regulat, the automaton called MAN, the capture of Ulysses and the captain, and the heroic rescue by Ichara.

"And then we brought the child straight here," said Juniper at last.

"They'll move," said Artichoke. "Try to conceal themselves using their fringer prisoners."

"They can't keep themselves hidden forever," said Dorianna. "The question is what to do now."

"There is one person," Ena intoned from beside her, "we could go see."

"I know," said Dorianna, "but do you think she will help?"

"What are our other options?" asked Artichoke. "If we try to take them now, we will be outnumbered and overpowered."

"Who is this person?" asked Aurora, beating Salem to the question.

"She was the captain before Fern," said Dorianna. "She was the one who led the fight against the Regulat all those years ago at Crawford."

"A right piece of work she was too," said Artichoke. "One of our best, I'd say." Voices around Artichoke resonated words of agreement.

"Let's say she will help us," said Dorianna. "How do we find her?"

"Last I heard," said Kane from behind a plume of smoke coming up from his pipe, "she was chasing the sun."

EPILOGUE | WE'VE ONLY JUST BEGUN

"What are you in for?"

The voice came from a body covered in something, possibly scales, like a giant reptile that had honed its dictation over millennia but could never lose its forked tongue.

Fern opened what little of his swollen eyes he could. "Living," he answered. He heard a small chortle from the dark.

"You too?"

Fern groaned as he pulled himself up. The regulators had not gone easy during the beating. "World isn't what it used to be," he said, tasting blood and salt.

"Sure isn't," the voice answered back.

A small man of Middle Eastern descent had appeared next to Fern and tended to his wounds.

"Hi," said the man, though he was not the one whose voice Fern had heard in the dark. "I'm Gandha. Let me help you, sir." Fern nodded.

"You know," said the shrouded voice again. "If they keep adding more of us, we're going to talk to them about expanding."

With each word came a growing familiarity. Fern recognized something.

"Feeling a little claustrophobic?" he asked the voice.

There was a dragging sound and the frame of something massive and rotund came into sight.

"I just need space to run around," it said, thick with irony.

"Gilgamesh?" asked Fern. "Is that you?"

"Do we know each other?" the voice asked.

"Gilgamesh!" said Fern, seeing the giant head of a tortoise come into sight. "You're still alive?"

"That's an interesting thing to hear," said the large creature, "from the guy they just threw into your cell."

"Maybe if the guy didn't know you," said Fern.

"You don't know me."

"I do," the captain replied.

"I suppose that makes this awkward," said Gilgamesh. "As I do not have the faintest idea of who you are."

Fern gently pushed Gandha's hand away from his forehead. He lacked the strength to stand but pushed his back up against the wall.

"I recall a small oasis in a big desert," he said, looking into the tortoise's bulbous eyes. The reptile called Gilgamesh was looking fuzzily into the near distance, letting the captain's words materialize from memories. "I recall a family there and the giant nobody wanted around."

Gilgamesh smirked. "The oasis…"

"Do you remember what you said to me?" asked Fern.

"What the shell are you doing here?"

Fern laughed. "That might have been it. No, I think you told me that one day you were going to leave that little oasis behind for all the wonderful things life had waiting for you."

"Oh boy, did I do that," said Gilgamesh.

"We all did," said Fern.

"Sometimes I think about it," said Gilgamesh.

"The oasis?" asked Fern.

Gilgamesh shook his head. "Not that. About the horizon beyond it and the shrinking dot that it became as I left."

• • •

Reynard was halfway up the Cathedral Mountains. It was important that he move fast because time was of the essence. He could hear Iris' wingbeats above him.

"I know flying is faster," he said. "If I could, I would." She called down with her soft coo.

"Listen," said Reynard, "you know as well as I do that he's the only one they might listen to." There was a pause as Reynard listened. "I know they may not love him, but they don't need to love him to respect what he says."

More waiting and listening.

"You're asking me that? Of course, it's not my preference, but what choice do we have? Who's going to go if we don't?"

The air whipped Reynard's face. "I forgot how much colder it is up here," he said, shivering.

The Cathedral Mountains were a part of the Fringe where few residents ever ventured. Barren and beautiful, the peaks that poked into the clouds inspired fear as well as awe. Reynard knew that the unrest escalating in the Fringe would not just go away. For some time, anger had been developing among the residents. It was not that the Fringe was a bad place. Reynard knew as well as anyone that the wild country, caught somewhere between meridians, had become the home no one, himself included, had ever expected. Still, he thought, there was something about the place that made it hard to accept as home.

As he thought about these things, Reynard saw in his mind's eye the woodland grove he had once called home across the meridian. From the hideaway he could visit the villages, talk to the people, play tricks on them to help them see the right, and the wrong. Those days had been simpler, he remembered. People back then could listen. People back then could communicate.

He thought about the kids on the Curiosity. They were so young and already so close to forgetting. There was hope in them, he knew, however small. How had it come down to him to take care of all of this?

Rounding a bend in the path, he stopped. Iris called him from above.

"You see, the tower?" he asked.

She called again.

"Thank you, my love," he told her. "And you're right, his tower is never as close as it looks."

• • •

Back in the old abbey, Tristan stood at the edge of the graveyard. In the church and the buildings behind him, Regulators were deconstructing what was only to be reconstructed back at Crawford now that it was almost ready.

Tristan walked around a headstone. He did not have any special connection with the place or with the morbidity it emphasized, though he had always thought it was a pretty place. Some gravestones were newer and very white. The majority were faded. A few had deteriorated to where they became indistinguishable from the surrounding nature. Small trees or plants grew out of them and their writing was no longer legible, only a mess of drooping indentations. Tristan often came to the graveyard to read and study. Others might say they found the space unsettling or creepy. He found the quiet somehow relaxing and could better think.

"This is what will make you such a good regulator."

Tristan had not heard Mr. White approach.

"Sir?"

"A respect for those who have come before you. It is important."

Tristan could not tell the leader that he only appreciated the stillness the graveyard offered.

"Sir, I feel as though I should have done more during the break-in. I could have taken out that Salem boy and the others, but I hesitated and that cost us."

"Tristan, you stalled long enough to get their orchestrator involved, and now we have taken the head of their snake."

"Let me attack them now, sir," Tristan offered. "They are weak, and we are strong. Let us end this once and for all."

Mr. White placed a hand on Tristan's shoulder.

"The pursuit of a pure world is ongoing, rising regulator. There are still more mythos out there and as long as they survive, we are at risk. Things are far from over."

Leaves were falling on New England, and the cemetery was taking on the golden-red hue of autumn.

"I'm impatient, sir," Tristan admitted.

"I know you are, and that's not a bad thing."

"I can't just sit and keep thinking. It drives me crazy."

"Then let's not do that, hm? Let's talk about you earning your regulatorship."

Tristan looked at Mr. White who was, as usual, beaming.

"This assignment will be one of the most difficult I've ever delegated. It will require cunning and commitment if you are to eliminate the mythos and win a great battle for the Regulat. Many have failed trying."

"Please," said Tristan, feeling that the graveyard was buzzing with energy. "I'm ready."

"Good," said Mr. White, "then let's talk about the World Beneath."

• • •

Easterly was shrinking once again behind them. It had been almost four months since Salem ascended the gangway for the first time with Mr. Gingam.

"If you would have asked a few months ago where I'd be and what I'd be doing…"

"Don't even say it," said Zee. "I thought we were past all the 'I just don't get it' nonsense."

"But it's true! None of it makes any sense!"

"Does it have to?" asked Juniper.

"Sometimes that'd be nice."

"Is it though?" she asked again.

Salem thought about it and smiled. "No, I guess not."

"It's boring," she said, trying to smile.

The smile on Salem's face was short-lived and disappeared as soon as he thought about everything that was happening.

"Don't worry," said Juniper, "they will both be fine."

"How do you know?" asked Salem. "It just feels wrong to be sailing in the opposite direction."

"Where we're going, we're going for them," said Zee.

"Yeah…" Salem shrugged in uncertainty.

"I've heard stories about Captain Laza," said Zee. "Apparently she's a witch and can read minds."

"Nobody can read minds," said Juniper.

"How can you be so sure?"

"Maybe some things can see your thoughts, know what you're going to do next, but no one can read your mind. Your mind is yours and no one else's."

"Oh, just because Reynard taught you about mind-readers, you think you know everything now?" said Zee.

"What was that kid Tristan saying about your sister?" asked Juniper, changing the subject.

"No idea," said Zee. "My sister died with the rest of my family."

"You sure about that?" asked Salem.

Zee looked at him in a mixture of hurt, confusion, and curiosity. "It's hard for me to imagine anything else," said Zee. "I've believed they were gone my entire life. I don't know what I would do if…" Zee stopped short. "It's a terrifying thought, and I'd rather believe it's not true. It would hurt too much if it weren't."

"It's alright," said Juniper, casting her eyes out to the horizon. "That's a bridge we can cross when and if we come to it."

Zee looked unconvinced, but smiled.

"Hey," said Salem, putting his hand on Zee's shoulder, "we're here for you, whatever happens. Just like you both were for me. Thanks again."

Zee's smile widened. "Like you had a choice. You need us. And even if Juniper doesn't want to admit it, we need you."

"I don't know about that," said Juniper. Salem was glad that Juniper was speaking so openly with him again. He knew there were more conversations for them to have in the future about what, if anything, had happened between them. He still did not understand it himself. He thought about what Ulysses had said, about trying to understand the perspectives of others and as he did, any bitterness toward Juniper melted away. He hoped over time it would be the same for her. "Do you miss it, Salem?" she asked then.

"Miss what?"

"Your old life."

"Parts of it," he answered. "I just miss my mom."

"I get that," said Juniper.

"We both do," said Zee.

"What about friends?" asked Juniper. "Do you have any you miss?"

Salem thought about the question. There had been other kids around that he had considered friends but being homeschooled had had its disadvantages in that he never really got the chance to make many friends. He had spent so much time on his own that his thoughts were his friends more than anything. Looking from the face of Zee to that of Juniper and back, he realized how wonderful it was to have people instead of just his own thoughts.

"Not really," he said. "Never got the chance."

"And what about now?" asked Zee.

"What do you mean?"

"If you leave," asked Zee, "would you miss us?"

The words hit Salem like a hammer. "Leave?" he said, shocked. As he looked from Zee to Juniper, it struck him with a feeling he had not had before, or at least not for a long time. "Leaving here is the last thing I want to do," he said. "Sure, my life here doesn't make sense to me a lot of the time, but I'm okay with that. I'd rather be with this crew, with you two, than anywhere else."

It surprised Salem to feel so strongly about what he was saying. He could feel tears forming in his eyes, but he urged himself to keep them in.

"I've learned a lot these past few months," he continued, "a lot of things I never expected to learn, but then again, I guess that's why it feels this way."

"What way?" asked Juniper.

"So strange," said Salem. He laughed.

"Life's better a little strange, though, isn't it?" said Zee.

"I guess so," Salem answered, and then, "no, you're right, it is."

"Come on," Juniper said then. "Artichoke said we need to get to instructions with Raiju and Ena."

"How are we supposed to focus on instructions while Ulysses and the captain are, you know, captives?" Salem had to ask.

"What else are we going to do?"

"Good point," said Salem and then added, "Go ahead, I'll be right there. Just want a minute alone."

He watched Juniper and Zee make their way down to the back of the ship where Ena and Raiju would be waiting for them. He looked back one last time at the shoreline that was reduced now to a single strip, a squiggly line that could have been drawn across the bottom of the sky with a thick pencil. Reaching into his back pocket, Salem pulled out his father's journal. He had not looked at it for many days, and it brought him a sense of immense comfort to hold it now. Yes, the journal had belonged to his parent, but he still did not know much of anything more about the man named Rigel Swan. Even with the bits and pieces from the stories he had heard since arriving on the ship, nothing conclusive had come together which could form a picture of the man he never really knew. He turned open to a page in the middle and to his surprise, he found it was one he had not seen before. Like many of the other pages, it contained lines of his father's scribbled handwriting, as well as sketches of what looked like the entrance to a cave. A rough schematic of what Salem guessed were either tunnels or rivers was drawn out onto the withered page in what looked like a tangled assortment of vines. Normally, Salem would spend many minutes attempting to decipher his father's handwriting, but one section, just below the mixture of pictures and scribbled words, was legible. He read the words out loud to himself.

"Rumors of a World Beneath. Could it exist?" Salem found it strange that his father's thought would end in a question. So far much of what his father had written in the journal was ascertained knowledge—facts and experiences from Rigel's research or travels which he had known to be true. This question, however, broke the mold. Salem made a mental note to ask Ulysses or the captain about the World Beneath, and in the same moment felt a ball of disgust at himself emerge in his stomach. How could he have already forgotten that Ulysses and the captain were missing? As Salem let the fact of Ulysses' and Fern's capture sink in, the boat around him felt less like the home it had become, and more like the wood and steel and fabric he had seen on the first day. *I'm not even mad at you anymore. I don't care if you were in the Regulat*, Salem thought, wishing he could say the words to Ulysses. Salem balled his fists and wished Yggdrasil had given him some ability other than mythlingualism. Why could he not fly or teleport or something useful that would help him bring his uncle and the captain back?

An idea struck him, and he reached down and pulled the obsidian bracelet off his wrist, tying to let his mind wander out and touch the minds of any others. He gasped, feeling the immediate flood of noise rush into his head so he could make no sense of it. It was like the thoughts of the complete town of Easterly were being channeled through to him. Salem slipped the bracelet back on to his wrist and let out a sigh of relief as the storm of noise calmed.

The ocean in front of him looked the same as it always did, vast and unending, like it was the edge of the world and, once reached, everything would just topple over the edge into space. The thought scared Salem, but so too did the thought of a losing more people, more family from his life. He would need to brave whatever was coming at the edge of the world if he wanted to see Ulysses again. Luckily, he knew he would not have to do it alone.

"Don't worry," he said, taking one last look at Easterly. "We're coming back for you."

• • •

Rose Manitou ran along the dock as fast as her legs would carry her, which was, for a lady of her age, fast. Still, the object she chased eluded her. It was now only a shrinking dot in the distance, so that each step Rose took felt less hopeful and more pitiful. She slowed her run to a jog, then to a walk, stopping at the edge of the pier. Her face was covered in small beads of sweat and her hair was no doubt a mess. She had come all the long way to learn that Salem was on that ship and now, as she watched it depart out to sea, she felt a great hopelessness well within her.

"You're looking for someone on that boat?" Rose jumped, shocked to find a woman sitting behind her on a bench. It was clear that the woman had been stunningly beautiful at one time, though Rose could tell that life had taken a toll on her. She was still an exceptional beauty, but there was something in the space above and below her rich brown eyes—a strain across her face that gave her an unrelenting expression of intensity—that Rose found discomforting. The woman's hair, much longer than most women her age, was pulled back into a tight bun. Stuck through the bun was an elegantly formed silver twig pin, holding it all in place. At the twig's tip, Rose saw what looked to be one of the largest jewels she had ever seen. It was bright green and caught the late-day light in a miraculous color. Rose took in the rest of the woman, noticing her trim build which looked light and athletic so that when she sat cross-legged on the bench, she looked more like a perched bird than a person of normal weight and gravity.

"I was," said Rose, collapsing on the bench next to her. "A boy. I was going to offer to adopt him. My husband…he died, saving that boy in a fire, and now that boy is the only thing I have that's familiar anymore. And I think that maybe I am the same for him. I know he didn't want to go to his uncle, and I shouldn't have let it happen." Rose was over-explaining, she knew, but didn't care. She told the stranger everything and not once did the person stop her. When Rose finished, she sat, unsure of what to do or say next. Lucky for her, the stranger picked up the thread.

"Well, Rose Manitou," said the woman. Rose was too fascinated with the woman's question that it did not occur to her that the woman already knew her name. "We may be able to help each other." Rose met the stranger's eyes, shocked, and yet intrigued by the words she heard. "You see," began the woman, imitating Rose's style, "my son-in-law is the captain on that same ship. And I do not think he is fit to be captain any longer." Rose was not sure where the woman was going with this, but the thought of returning to the empty house full of memories without having even spoken with Salem felt like too much to bear. "So what do you say, Rose Manitou," asked the woman. "Are you a woman of action?"

Rose considered the question. She recalled the night of the fire months earlier, when she had let Wayne go alone into the unbearable heat. She had already told herself a thousand times that her help could have made the difference. She had been a woman of inaction then, and it had cost her everything. No, as long as she had air in her lungs and a heart that beat, she would forever more be a woman of action. One day she would be with Wayne again, but until that day, she would honor him by refusing to give up. She balled her fists, looked into the imposing brown eyes opposite her, and nodded.

ACKNOWLEDGEMENTS

As with most big undertakings, many people contributed to the final realization of this book. The team at Black Rose Writing believed in early versions of this story enough to help me bring it to life, and for that I am forever grateful.

A few of the first beta readers provided invaluable feedback to me including Leslie Siron, Sophie Breunig, Bridget Schaller, Lucy Bonacci, Karen Myers, Ben DeMora, Tara Sellers, Sara Zatek, Max Weynand, and Swechhya KC.

The editorial wisdom of Ben Davidoff was instrumental in shaping the final version of this text and will no doubt lead to much more rewarding character development, plot twists, and overall quality of story in this and the successive books of this series.

While a book is much more than its cover, a cover worthy of the story it holds is not always easy to create. Jeff Brown Graphics spun up true magic through the hours spent crafting a gorgeous cover for *Hidden Meridians*. And I cannot wait to see how the rest of this series will look.

Finally, and this thanks goes back a long way, thank you to my family, especially my grandparents who, through hours and hours of selflessness, let me imagine with them the possible worlds, lurking just behind hidden meridians, waiting to be found.

ABOUT THE AUTHOR

J.P. Hostetler is an award-winning author born and raised in Lancaster, Pennsylvania. He writes fiction and non-fiction focused around leaving the comfort zone, preserving cultural diversity, and embracing the uncertainty of adventure. His first book, an illustrated fable called *The Sky Belongs to the Dreamers*, was published by *Atmosphere Press* in 2019 and received the Mom's Choice Gold Award.

J.P. currently lives in Los Angeles, California. You can visit him at: www.jphostetler.com.

NOTE FROM THE AUTHOR

Word-of-mouth is crucial for any author to succeed. If you enjoyed *Around Curiosity's Edge: Hidden Meridians*, please leave a review online—anywhere you are able. Even if it's just a sentence or two. It would make all the difference and would be very much appreciated.

Thanks!
J.P. Hostetler

www.ingramcontent.com/pod-product-compliance
Lightning Source LLC
Chambersburg PA
CBHW011145100726
47899CB00010B/3179
* 9 7 8 1 6 8 4 3 3 6 9 5 1 *